After the news breaks about Cashiel Michaud's involvement in research to undermine the Demoted system, he and Sascha find themselves detained as a legal case develops. Separated, they work from both sides to get released, making sacrifices and arrangements along the way. If they do reunite, will they be the same? Sascha and Cash face a number of threats from the outside world, and some from the people closest to them. When they don't know who to trust, their plans and their relationship are put to the test. And the results of this test could affect the world. (M/M)

I'm given a scratchy jumpsuit, which I pull on quickly, trying to look casual.

"Not as nice as your silk shirts," Bulldog comments. "Ever wondered how the rest of the world lives?"

"No, sir," I answer, just to have something to say. He knows nothing about me, nothing about what I suffered before my master bought me.

"Be grateful," he mutters. "You're getting food and clothes and a place to sleep. Better than what you deserve."

"Yes, sir." I walk behind him.

We reach a big, locked door, and he types in a series of numbers on the keypad. A few seconds later, we hear a click, and we walk through the door. It closes behind us before the next one opens, and once it does, I see the collection of intimidating men with whom I am to spend an indeterminate amount of time.

Bulldog gives me a shove, pushing me away from him. "Boys, meet your new playtoy. Officer Lanza and I will be busy until the dinnertime check, so make sure to show him a warm welcome!"

Also recommended...

You may also enjoy these other ForbiddenFiction works:

Love Is for the Living by Nicholas Kinsley
The zombies have arrived, and Blaine needs to escape. He'd always thought of his London neighborhood as a place of safety, but then his infected neighbors tried to eat him. Blaine packed a bag and fled through growing numbers of shambling, voracious monsters — people, he had to remind himself, they're people — toward his family in Bristol. He would surely have died without the turn of luck that brought him Commander Andrew Peterson. Together, they face the horrors and adversities of the apocalypse, trying to protect their loved ones, and — if they're lucky — find love for themselves. (M/M)
http://forbiddenfiction.com/story/NK1-1.000217

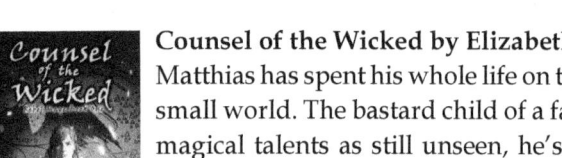

Counsel of the Wicked by Elizabeth Schechter
Matthias has spent his whole life on the edge of a very small world. The bastard child of a fallen woman, his magical talents as still unseen, he's known nothing but judgment and hatred from the harsh, religious people of his enclave — except for Balthazar, the son and heir of the High Elder, Balthazar shows Matthias kindness, love... and desire. When the High Elder discovers what his son has been doing, Matthias is arrested and sent to an isolated prison known simply as "The School". There, and in the wastelands beyond, Matthias learns the secrets behind the hypocrisies of the Council of Elders, and discovers his true heritage, true power, and true love. (M/M, F/M)
http://forbiddenfiction.com/story/ES1-1.000222

Succession

Demoted
Book Three

Alicia Cameron

ForbiddenFiction
www.forbiddenfiction.com

an imprint of

Fantastic Fiction Publishing
www.fantasticfictionpublishing.com

SUCCESSION
A Forbidden Fiction book

Fantastic Fiction Publishing
Hayward, California

© Alicia Cameron, 2015

CREDITS
Editor: James L. Wolf
Cover Design: D.M. Atkins
Cover Art: Natalya Nesterova
Production Editor: Erika L Firanc
Proofreading: JhP323

SKU: AC2-000250-02 FFP
ISBN: 978-1-62234-263-1

Published in the United States of America

DISCLAIMER

This book is a work of fiction which contains explicit erotic content; it is intended for mature readers. Do not read this if it's not legal for you.

All the characters, locations and events herein are fictional. While elements of existing locations or historical characters or events may be used fictitiously, any resemblance to actual people, places or events is coincidental.

This story depicts fictional BDSM; it is not intended to be used as an instruction manual. It contains descriptions of erotic acts that may be immoral, illegal, or unsafe. The characters are not models for the Safe, Sane and Consensual forms embraced by most current practitioners of BDSM. The author takes license with the use of BDSM for dramatic effect. Do not take the events in this story as proof of the plausibility or safety of any particular practice.

To the friends and family I ignored while writing this: I bet you thought living with a writer would be glamorous, didn't you? Always happy to crush your dreams!

Contents

Chapter 1

Detained

"We should get out of here soon. You're not safe here."

The wailing screech of police hov-cars nearly drowns out the bodyguard's orders to Cash and me. We duck as pieces of the interview set fly past our heads, crashing to the ground as the crowd comes closer and closer, fighting their way through the security team's boundaries and evading the tasers that are supposed to hold them back. The smell of smoke is starting to filter in; whether it's from arson or from smoke bombs isn't clear yet.

When I'm given the order to move, I do so without question, rushing alongside our bodyguard as we make our way behind the stage into a utility closet. Cash follows closely, keeping himself between the crowd and me, knowing they are far more likely to hurt a slave than a free man, even with what they're accusing him of. Objects are being thrown at us, but we make it up the narrow set of stairs that bring us to the roof.

The fresh air is a relief, as is the door that we close tightly and lock behind us. We have no other option but to wait for the police force to come and retrieve us.

Despite Cash's protests, I make my way to the edge of the roof. I have to see how far the riot has spread.

Armed guards, dressed head to toe in government-issued teal uniforms, spew from a military vehicle and begin to disperse the crowd. The guards wear facemasks; they are protected from the smoke bombs they throw. Those in the crowd who are strong enough to try and tolerate the noxious fumes are tased or arrested; those who are brave enough to fight back or resist are shot at. There are Demoted people

1

in the crowd, it's easy to pick them out by their lack of high-tech wristbands and the fact that they are being used as human shields.

We did this. Cash and me. We made this happen. We never meant for it to happen like this.

Six Weeks Earlier

I awaken in the backseat of a moving vehicle. For a minute, I have no idea what happened.

Then I sit up, and I feel the burst of pain in my head.

"Nice to see you awake, Sascha," an unfamiliar voice greets me.

I glance around, realizing that I'm in a police hov-car; not the transport vans that usually transport Demoted people, but the kind that would be used for a free person. I stare at the officer, who is looking back at me through the rearview mirror. He's acting like he knows who I am, but I don't remember him. Then again, I don't remember much of what happened to get me here. I don't remember where Cash is.

"You took a good blow to the head back there. Wasn't sure if you'd come around before we arrived."

I struggle to piece the memories together. Cash and I had just finished putting the final results of our research together, just gotten confirmation of the evidence that would damn the Miller System and everyone involved with it. We had gone to bed, set on celebrating our victory and each other, and then....

"Where are you taking me?"

"Leadview Slave Detention Facility," the officer tells me. "Special transport, due to the unique circumstances. Someone thought Kristine Miller might not give you up."

I nod, unable to speak as the memories suddenly come flooding back. My master's mother kidnapped me, using her business as a cover, and I have no doubt she would have killed me. She was set on stopping Cash from releasing his research—a goal I destroyed by releasing in advance. Of course, it didn't stop him from being taken into custody, and me as well. Her blow must have been what knocked me out. I'm surprised she didn't just kill me, but that would have made her and her system look even more corrupt than it already is.

My master's fate rests in the state, now, as does mine. I didn't even get to say goodbye to him.

The officer hasn't cuffed me and he looks sympathetic. I debate the value of staying quiet, but my need for knowledge outweighs it. "Did I do something wrong, sir?"

I try to sound stupid and scared, like a spoiled pet should. My master and I have spent months working on a research project that will overthrow the Miller System, the system that dictates how Demoted slaves are trained. Contrary to the current system, which focuses on intense subjugation and psychological manipulation in order to transform young adults into slaves, our research has shown that slaves can be more productive in less harsh environments. In fact, the Miller System is producing subpar slaves, wasting resources, putting our country, the Democratic Republic of Nitorra at risk of falling behind other countries. Worse, since the Miller System has been exported across the world, our nation can be blamed for sabotaging the international environment.

As I was being kidnapped by the creator of the Miller System, I released the data that proves these accusations to the media.

The Miller System's deficiencies have been hidden for decades by its creator, a fact that few people are aware of, and a fact that the rest of our research can show. Since Kristine Miller is my master's mother, everything is so much more personal. She's powerful, motivated, and since we anticipated a negative response to the results, we didn't release the evidence that showed the failings of Kristine Miller and the Miller System. For the same reasons, we didn't let on that our Demoted test subjects often outperformed non-Demoted test subjects on measures of intelligence, critical thinking and problem-solving.

I don't know why I'm being taken to a detention facility, and I don't know what Kristine has told anyone else about the project that my master and I are working on. Helping Cashiel conduct research to dismantle the existing slave training system is exciting when he's around to protect me; it's a liability when he's not. Last I saw, he was being arrested, presumably taken to jail for his treasonous acts. He can't protect me anymore, and his absence is painful and threatening.

"You haven't done anything wrong," the officer tells me. "Leadview is for slaves whose masters have been incarcerated."

I nod, silent, staring out the window. Cash had a simple goal when he started researching. He wanted to make money, to outshine his mother, to find the best system possible. Somewhere along the way, those noble goals turned into treason, but he was naïve to think that anything else would happen in a totalitarian country. Nitorra pretends to represent the best interests of its citizens, but even those who aren't officially enslaved are subject to near total control. My master should have known, having been arrested for the same "crime" years ago, but sometimes he's more persistent than subtle. He is determined to advance his theory and research until nobody can deny the benefits it can bring.

As we leave the confines of the city, the effects of the data release are noticeable. Military vehicles are out in greater numbers than usual, but there are no riots here, and the smoke from distant fires, probably in the cities, seem to fade into the clouds. I listen idly to the police scanner, unsurprised to hear that there have been curfews instituted across the nation.

I wish the drive to the detention facility was longer, because I see the dark grey concrete and iron fence and I'm filled with dread. It reminds me too much of a prison, too much of the re-education centers, and neither of those are places I ever wanted to willingly go again. When the officer comes to collect me from the backseat, I hesitate for a moment, looking up at him desperately, wishing he would save me.

"You'll be all right," he says, forcing his voice to be a little gruffer than it has been so far. "Let's start by not having to be dragged inside."

I nod and he leads me forward, restrained only by a surprisingly light grip on my upper arm. He shows his wristband for identification in the entranceway, then takes me through to a small, bare room with a table and chairs.

"You'll wait here," he says, releasing my arm. "Someone will be with you shortly. It's tight protocol around here. Think back to your training."

"Thank you, sir." He's given me a valuable piece of information.

He leaves, and a few minutes later, the door opens and two men step in. Judging by the uniforms, I assume they're guards. Both look about my master's age, one is a little taller and thinner, the other one slightly shorter but stocky. Intimidating.

"Get your clothes off, slave," the short, stocky one barks, like I've already disobeyed. His aggressive tone and stance prompts me to dub him "Bulldog."

I comply, starting with the buttons on my shirt. I move quickly enough not to seem defiant, but I try to retain a little dignity. I wonder if they know who I am, to whom I belong.

"You want me to rip them off?" Bulldog threatens.

"His clothes are worth more than a month's pay," the other guard intervenes. "You might not have anything better to do than get your pay docked, but I have a family to take care of, and they like to eat. Besides, his master's making waves. There will be a lot of attention on this one."

"I don't care who his master is. It's stupid spending that much on clothes for a slave."

Nobody responds, especially not me. I marvel at the reputation that I've already developed as I set my shirt aside and remove my pants seconds later. Bulldog would have approved of the clothes I wore a few years ago. As a washed-up brothel whore, there would have been nothing for him to envy, barely anything to be removed. I thought it would be that way forever, but since Cashiel Michaud bought me on a whim, I've enjoyed the finer things in life. Not just clothes, but food, safety... and the respect and affection of a man who's just as pleased as I am to meet an intellectual equal, no matter what our stations in life.

The taller guard takes my clothes and places them in a bag, where I assume they'll be kept until I'm released.

"Time for the fun part," Bulldog says, smirking at me like he really will enjoy whatever horrors they're going to inflict on me.

The other guard frowns at him and takes a step toward me.

"I'm going to search you for contraband," he informs me. "This will be a visual and manual inspection. If you don't cooperate, Officer Reynolds will restrain you, and there may be additional consequences later."

Bulldog Reynolds. It has a ring to it. When I was first Demoted, I might have commented on it out loud, but I've since learned the value of silence. "I'll cooperate, sir."

"Good." The officer nods at me. "Spread your legs and hold your arms out."

I do as he asks and he looks me over while putting a pair of gloves on. The sight of gloves makes me shudder, as does the feeling of them on my skin. He's clinical about it, feeling through my hair, behind my ears, and around my dick and balls. As thorough as he is, he doesn't hurt me, and I appreciate that enough to want to comply.

"Open your mouth," he orders, and when I do, he sticks one finger from each hand in there quickly, checking under my tongue and around my cheeks with startling efficiency. "Good."

He takes a step back, catching my eye before issuing the next order. "Lean over, place your hands flat on the table, and spread your legs."

I feel all my muscles tense, but I know I can't fight it. I do as he asks. I'm mildly comforted to hear lube squirt from a tube, and a second later, I feel a hand on my hip. He holds me in place firmly and I feel his other hand going between my asscheeks.

"Breathe out," he says quietly. As I do, he presses his fingers into me.

I grunt at the unexpected pain. It's not like I don't get fucked all the time, but I'm turned on when I'm fucked. I try to make myself relax as I feel his fingers probing insistently, checking for contraband. It's barely started before it's over, and I feel him withdrawing, more carefully than I would have expected. I stay positioned over the table, breathing shallowly as I listen to the sound of the gloves being removed.

A light touch on my shoulder brings me back to the present, and I stand again.

"Good," the guard says, nodding at me. "You may kneel for the rest."

I drop to my knees silently. I'm going to stay silent for as long as possible; I can't get into as much trouble that way. They might let something slip, something that can help me or Cash.

Bulldog eyes me up. "Listen up, boy, here's the situation: You are being detained as evidence at Leadview Slave Detention Facility until further notice. Your master has committed or is being held for questioning for a crime worthy of incarceration, and you will remain at Leadview until such time as he is released, unless a third party has been arranged for your safekeeping. Do you know of any such third party?"

I wrack my brain, hoping to come up with anyone who would vouch for me. My master doesn't really keep close friends or associates, especially with our need for secrecy for the project. My mind briefly flickers to Abriel, but I realize I would rather stay in a detention facility than suffer through his wife ever again. My master's business partner, Oliver Torenze would take me. He probably has the legal right to do so, and I don't doubt that he would be eager to have me in his home again. It might even make his partnership with Cash look more legitimate, assuming he would take me, and assuming I could survive it. Last time I spent the day with him, he savored every minute of my torture, raping, beating, and humiliating me until I thought I would break. Just thinking about him brings the memories back, rushing in, almost too much to handle. Suddenly, the grey concrete of the detention facility looks appealing.

"No, sir," I mumble, shaking my head.

Bulldog grins at that. "Well, then you're ours for a while," he announces, triumphant, like he's just made a great discovery. "You will obey any and all guards immediately. Obstinacy, insolence, and defiance will be punished immediately. Physical violence or fighting will be punished immediately. Any attempt to start or participate in a riot will be punished. Punishments will consist primarily of lashes, but may include other physical correction, and difficulty interacting with others may result in solitary confinement. That clear, boy?"

He's still looking triumphant, and I can't help but feel appalled at the thought that this strange brute might lay hands on me, might actually whip me. Cash has gotten me too used to good treatment, to protection. Reality crashes back down as I'm reminded that I'm still a slave, no matter how well I'm treated at home. I stare at him, slack-jawed.

"I guess I'll familiarize you with the punishment for insolence now," he says, smiling as he takes a step toward me.

The other guard grabs him by his arm and jerks him back. "Reynolds, don't be a hard-ass. You saw what he was wearing when he came in, and you saw the news report. We have to be careful with this one. The whole country's got eyes on his master and the Demoted system—what do you think happens to us if we leave so much as one unnecessary mark on his spoiled little pet? Don't ask for trouble. There are plenty of throwaways here."

"Christ, Lanza, look at the boy!" Bulldog counters, pulling his arm away, "He's scarred up all over. Think his master would notice a few more to add to the mix?"

I start to tremble, the reality of my situation becoming quickly clear. I forget what I look like, sometimes, with Cash, but in the rest of the world, the scars are a liability. They mark me as worthless, and they mark me as difficult.

"Yes, I see him, and I see the scars," Lanza says. "But since I'm not nearly as keen on torturing the boy as you, I can also see that this one hasn't been seriously harmed in months, if not years. A few from rough play, maybe, but the deep ones are old. New ones will be noticeable. His master will have your job or more."

Bulldog grunts, and I can't decide whether it's at me or at his partner.

Lanza looks at me sternly. "Please respond when you are asked a direct question," he orders. "Do you understand the rules that Officer Reynolds read to you?"

"Yes, sir," I manage, relieved to be spoken to like a human being.

"You'll be taken to shower and then given a jumpsuit," Lanza informs me. "After that you'll be released into the common room with the rest of the slaves. A word of advice—we are not babysitters. We exist to maintain a calm, safe environment, but we will not attend to the petty squabbles of slaves. It is recommended that you do not cause trouble—especially not a slave as delicate as you are."

"Yes, sir." I can't tell if he wants an answer or not.

I'm nervous when Bulldog is the one who takes me to the showers, but he's surprisingly professional. He sprays too hard and scrubs too vigorously, but he doesn't molest me, and he doesn't threaten me with anything but his looks. Cash would have his job if he heard him so much as threatening me, but that would depend on Cash coming for me sometime soon.

I can't bring myself to consider the alternative.

I'm given a scratchy jumpsuit, which I pull on quickly, trying to look casual.

"Not as nice as your silk shirts," Bulldog comments. "Ever wondered how the rest of the world lives?"

"No, sir," I answer, just to have something to say. He knows nothing about me, nothing about what I suffered before my master bought me.

"Be grateful," he mutters. "You're getting food and clothes and a place to sleep. Better than what you deserve."

"Yes, sir." I walk behind him.

We reach a big, locked door, and he types in a series of numbers on the keypad. A few seconds later, we hear a click, and we walk through the door. It closes behind us before the next one opens, and once it does, I see the collection of intimidating men with whom I am to spend an indeterminate amount of time.

Bulldog gives me a shove, pushing me away from him. "Boys, meet your new playtoy. Officer Lanza and I will be busy until the dinnertime check, so make sure to show him a warm welcome!"

The bastard laughs as he walks off, and I try to swallow my dread as I hear the electronic locks on the doors activate as he walks back through them.

Chapter 2
Claimed

I recognize the boy the moment Reynolds brings him through the doors, but it takes me a few more moments to believe my good fortune.

It's been months since I've seen the pretty boy, before I was brought to Leadview almost eight months ago. I hadn't gotten a good look at him, then, just a few glances at an event my master took me to. He's just another pretty slave boy. It's the way he acts that makes me realize it's him, the way he looks around the room like he's committing every detail to memory, the way he studies and analyzes things. The way he looks down at the rest of us.

He should, probably. We are criminals, at least our masters are. I recall little about the pretty boy's master, other than his partnership with Oliver Torenze, which made him somewhat relevant. The boy is here for some white-collar crime of his master's, probably. If that crime is of interest to the 27th Street Gang, the organization my master belongs to, he might be of use to me. If the boy is of interest to the Argova family, the organized crime syndicate the 27th Street Gang answers to, he might be my saving grace.

One of the other men approaches the pretty boy and he stiffens. I can see him trying not to show fear, but it's written all over his face. The others are drawn to it. The first time I was in a place like this, I probably looked the same. It's intimidating; the detention facilities are housed in old prisons, metal bars and everything. The slaves in here take full advantage of the setting, trading favors with the guards and abusing those less powerful than themselves. Marvin is one of the more powerful. He's the one whispering in the boy's ear, even as he tries to pull away.

Two of Marvin's associates join, and I can hear the boy's voice changing to a whimper. He's giving them exactly what they want. He'll lose if he tries to fight them. The room goes quiet as we wait to see what happens, if the boy will cave and submit willingly, or if Marvin and his crew will force him. The guards won't care either way, but I doubt I'll be able to do anything with the boy once Marvin's finished with him.

I watch as they force him to his knees. He's silent, fighting back tears. I sigh. Time to cash in on the single favor I have left in Leadview.

"Leave him alone."

The room was quiet before, just the low din of conversations competing with the buzzing of the lights. It goes silent when I speak. I walk toward Marvin and the boy.

"I want him," I announce, keeping my voice just loud enough to be heard.

"Sy," Marvin starts, not releasing his grip on the boy yet.

"You owe me," I remind him calmly. For months, I've waited for the best opportunity to use the favor I earned when I first got here, the one that ended with me being locked in the tiny solitary confinement cell for weeks. Killing another slave for Marvin had not only secured my protection then, but would be my ticket to claiming this bargaining tool for myself. "I want him, and I don't share. Give him to me."

"Marvin, come on!" One of the others protests, his jumpsuit already unzipped and his dick out. "We haven't had one this good looking in ages!"

"Leave it, or you can take his place!" Marvin snaps. He pulls the boy to his feet and gives him a shove, glaring at me. "Take him, then. And you better enjoy him, because we're even after this."

"Done."

I catch the pretty boy as he stumbles toward me, glancing up at me in grateful terror. I'm repulsed by what I see in his eyes, what he expects from me. He sizes me up without even trying to hide it. I'm a giant compared to him, built and trained as professional muscle, with enough scars to illustrate my rough history. He's attractive, but I'm far more interested in finding out what he can do for me. I have bigger ambitions than a cheap fuck.

"What's your name?" I ask.

"Sascha." His eyes lock on mine like nothing else matters. It's unnerving, especially since we have an audience. He doesn't seem to realize that.

"Syrus. Most people call me Sy."

"Okay."

"Come with me."

I start walking immediately, certain he'll follow. I lead him to a cell, and a small crowd follows a few steps behind. I don't need to look to know that Marvin will be at the front, making sure I really do just want the pretty boy to fuck. If anyone knows he might have other value, I risk losing him. A fuck isn't worth getting into a fight; the chance to please a master or provide useful information is worth fighting or even killing for. I'd rather not put myself or Sascha in that position.

"Face the wall and unzip," I say. The crowd that followed us voices their displeasure. They want to see the boy, but I can tell he's starting to panic. It's best that I keep him facing away from the others. All they need is proof that I'm fucking him.

"If you don't like it, go look at one of the boys on display," I growl, placing a possessive hand on Sascha's hip. "This one's mine. I'll do exactly what I want with him."

I feel Sascha shudder, but he unzips and waits for the next order. I need him scared, not frozen.

"Put your arms back," I tell him, barely loud enough to hear. I'm trying to be gentle with him, but he doesn't seem to notice.

He obeys, tense, and I reach around him, taking the edges of his jumpsuit and stripping of off easily. I slide it down, letting it pool around his ankles, and I grip his waist firmly and lift him as I kick the jumpsuit aside. It's the best I can do to make him comfortable.

"Get to fucking him already!" a voice calls out.

"Give it to him hard!"

We're entertainment. I'm glad they can't see Sascha's face, or mine, because he is terrified beyond belief and I'm growing irritated. For a pretty pet, the boy can't act to save his goddamned life.

"Get against that wall and spread those little legs of yours," I order, indicating the one area in the room that's not taken up by a bed, toilet, or sink.

He complies, trembling. I wonder what's been done to him to make him this afraid. The scars that cover his back point me in the logical direction, but I'm certain there's more. I just hope he gets through this without spoiling it for both of us.

I unzip and press against his back, clamping a hand over his shoulder to make sure he stays in place. I don't trust him not to do something stupid like fight back or try to beg, but when I place my cock against his ass, I feel him brace himself. I start to thrust, careful, riding between his asscheeks but not penetrating him. Sascha tenses and I wait for him to catch on.

"Oh yeah," I moan, loud enough that our crowd can hear it. "Yeah, this pretty boy has such a tight little ass!"

Sascha is awfully stiff for someone whose ass I'm supposed to be pounding. I lean forward, pressing my face into his neck, frustrated when he tenses and pulls away like he's expecting me to bite him.

"Make some noise, Sascha," I whisper in his ear. "I can't do all the work, here."

He makes a half-assed attempt, a few grunts and gasps, but he seems more confused than anything. He's still tense, waiting. I don't know how much more obvious I have to make it.

"Stop holding back, Sy!" someone from the crowd calls. "Fuck him harder!"

"Oh, I'll fuck this little bitch hard all right!" I reply, thrusting more vigorously. I ride up and down the crack of his ass, pretending to love it.

"Scream for me, pretty boy!" I order, pounding against him hard enough that he struggles to keep his head from banging against the wall. "Let everyone know how much my cock is tearing up your ass!"

Instead, he stays quiet, keeping up with the moans and whimpers like we're engaging in a rather dull session of foreplay. I nibble at his earlobe, hoping to pull him out of whatever trance he's in.

"Scream, Sascha," I whisper, my words taking on a desperate edge.

Something must click for him, because he lets out a believable, pained scream as I thrust at him again. "Please," he whimpers. "You're too big! It hurts!"

The crowd starts clapping. I'm relieved that we're convincing enough, and I hope the boy doesn't disappear on me again.

"You'll take it, pretty boy!" I demand, adding to the mood. "You'll take it and you'll thank me for it later! You're mine!"

Sascha makes some more whimpering pleas and begs for mercy. I lean in, close enough that I can see the slight smile on his face. He's finally figured out that we're acting.

"Come on his face!" The cheers and roars of approval indicate that this would be the preferred method of discharge.

"You'd like that, wouldn't you, pretty boy?" I taunt, loud enough for everyone to hear. "You'd like to wear my come on your face all day?"

"I'd rather have it down my throat," he replies, just barely sarcastic enough to be believable.

I keep rutting against him for a few more minutes, trying not to laugh, then I twist Sascha around to face me.

"Get on your knees," I order, hoping my face conveys my apologies. When the laughter and taunting from the crowd brings that haunted look back to Sascha's face, I decide to finish up quickly. I grab my cock, jerking it like it's my sole priority.

"Better close your eyes, pretty boy!" I taunt. "And open that pretty mouth of yours, while you're at it!"

Sascha obeys, resigned to what he thinks is his fate, and I try not think about how it actually would feel to have his lips around my cock. I have to finish our show, though, and I moan as I bring myself closer. When I'm almost there, I grab Sascha by the hair, pulling him close, and almost out of the path of my come. The onlookers make a noise of disappointment.

"Come on, how the hell could you miss!" a disappointed voice calls out. "I had better aim when I was twelve!"

Sascha opens his eyes and closes his mouth, looking shocked. I grin at him before looking back over my shoulder.

"I guess I was a little off-balance from squeezing into that tight ass," I call back, cocky and sated. "Too bad you won't ever know how good it is!"

There are a couple of grumbles after this, but the crowd quickly disperses. Sascha and I are left alone. I brush the come off of his face with my finger, wiping it on my leg before offering him my hand. It's the best I can offer.

He stands warily.

"Stay close to me, Sascha," I say quietly, once we're face-to-face. "My reputation only goes so far. Follow my lead and you'll do all right."

He nods.

"We can talk more tonight. If I tell you to do anything, anything at all, you need to do it. Promise me you'll do it?"

"I promise," he answers without a thought. Someone has beaten obedience into him.

"I'm sorry," I add on, almost a whisper. "It was the best I could do."

"I appreciate it," he replies. At least this time, I can tell he's being honest.

I stay close to Sy, as ordered. He keeps me close, even taking me to use the toilet. It's humiliating, but I'm pretty certain he's working in my best interest. Once I figured out what he was doing in the cell, it made sense. Once I stopped having flashbacks of what Torenze and Cash's mother did to me, it was even sort of fun to join Sy in his game. I'm still nervous, because I still don't know why he's so set on protecting me.

After dinner, we filter back into the common room. Two guards come in, different ones than were here this morning.

"We hear there's a new boy! Which one of you is it?"

I raise my hand, looking for Sy for approval. He nods at me, barely.

The guard whistles. "Bet you've been claimed already, haven't you, sweetcheeks?"

I nod. "Yes, sir."

The guards leer at me. "And who might you belong to?"

"Sy wanted him," Marvin volunteers, sounding apologetic. "Boring little fuck, anyway."

"Syrus," the first guard muses, glaring.

Sy steps up, seemingly unfazed. "Yes, sir."

"Look at you, always keeping your nose clean. Is this what you were waiting for, the perfect boy? It's a pity with your reluctance to share. Didn't your mother teach you any manners?" The guard is trying to get a rise.

"I guess not, sir," Sy answers, still impassive. "I don't take part in other people's enjoyment; I expect to keep mine to myself."

"Isn't that grand," the second guard rolls his eyes. "A felon's slave with a heart of gold."

"Well, we'd still like to watch that enjoyment," the first guard decides. "Now."

"Yes, sir," Sy answers. "On your knees, pretty boy."

The words are there, the domineering, cutting tone is there, but his heart isn't behind it. His lips are pressed too tightly together and he won't look me in the eye. He's faking disinterest about as poorly as Cash fakes it. I take a step closer to him, hesitating in case he changes his mind.

Bad idea.

He grabs me by the hair and kicks my legs out from under me; the pressure on my scalp the only thing keeping me from eating the concrete with my teeth. While he holds me in place, his free hand jerks his zipper down and yanks his cock out, shoving it toward my face.

"Show them who you belong to, pretty boy."

I feel tears spring to my eyes from pain and humiliation. I'm smarter than this; I shouldn't let my stupid feelings fuck up whatever plans Sy has for me. His plans are keeping me safe.

I go to my task immediately, and it takes a few moments before I can bring myself to look up at him, expecting disappointment. Instead, he mouths "sorry" at me between grunts and thrusts.

It's not long before I feel Sy's hands fisting in my hair, pretending to pull me down. As soon as I move, he stops pulling, allowing me to stay there on my own. The guards are appreciating our show.

He finishes in my mouth. I don't need to be told to swallow. When I finish, I stay on my knees since I haven't been told otherwise. Sy zips up his jumpsuit as if this were an everyday occurrence. Maybe it is.

"Someone else will benefit from how worked up you just got me," one of the guards comments, casting a lustful eye over the rest of the population. "We want two of you. If you feel so gracious as to share one of your pets, we might share favors in return!"

"What's up for grabs tonight?" Marvin asks, like a businessman.

"We have one leftover dinner and a cigarette," the second guard declares. "Been a long time since we've had one of those. Trade restrictions outside are getting awfully tight, especially with the riots that have been happening out there. Hard enough to get cigarettes for myself."

A few voices murmur through the slaves, and I wonder if anyone but me knows the cause of the riots. After a few moments, two slaves "volunteer" to go with the guards, with considerable pressure. Once again, I'm thankful to be with Sy.

I feel his fingers brushing through my hair and I look up, wishing I could ask him the thousands of questions that are swirling through my head. I stand, relieved when he keeps a possessive hand on my shoulder.

"You okay?"

I nod quickly.

"Sascha," he looks at me desperately. "Please do as I say from now on."

I'm not the only one at risk. He is, too. "I will. I'm sorry."

He nods. "It will be time for bed soon. We can talk then."

I follow him around as he makes his way around the common room. Sy has quite a few people who seem fond of him. I wonder just how long he's been here, how many other "boys" he's had before me. I wonder what he ended up doing with them. Our arrangement can't be very rewarding for him. Everyone else is getting real sex, real energetic blowjobs, favors from the guards — all this arrangement seems to gain him is a lot of trouble and some dirty looks.

Finally, we are directed to our cells for bed. Sy pulls me along, making it clear to everyone that I will sleep with him. The other beds in the cell are empty.

I stand there, uncertain, the faint lights from the exit sign at the end of the row barely illuminating anything.

"Take your jumpsuit off," Sy orders, loud.

I fail to hold back the shaky breath that I'm trying not to let out. I don't understand him. Was the show earlier just because he wanted to wait until we were alone? I feel around for the zipper and start to strip.

"We get clean jumpsuits every other day," Sy explains quietly. "They smell better if you don't sleep in them."

I breathe a little more easily. Trusting Cash is hard enough. I know what he wants from me. Trusting Sy is nearly impossible.

"Besides, if you shift around too much, your dick rubs against the zipper and it hurts like a son of a bitch."

I laugh, in part because of the sheer ridiculousness of the advice, and in part because this is the first thing I've heard Sy say that's not completely serious. He's trying to joke, to lighten the mood. I appreciate it.

Still, I flinch when I feel him come up next to me.

"Easy," he says, barely loud enough for me to hear. "My bed is over here. Get in, under the sheets."

I'm still skeptical, but I obey. I slip between the cold, scratchy sheets, and I shiver. I feel the thin mattress depress next to me, and wait for the unwelcome sensation of a strange body next to me, someone else's unfamiliar skin touching mine, someone who's not my master, someone who has no reason to care about me.

I'm surprised when I realize that Sy has placed himself on top of the sheet, keeping us from touching.

"I'm not out to hurt you, Sascha," he whispers, settling in. "I'm sorry if I made you think that."

"I don't understand." I hate that I don't know his motivations.

"I just wanted to help you out. It's not every day that we get someone in here who looks like he's about to cry. I felt bad for you."

"I could have handled it!" I retort, offended. I realize how ungrateful I sound. "I mean, thank you. I know I probably seem like some rich guy's pet, but it hasn't always been like that. I can handle myself."

"Never thought you couldn't. The marks on you confirmed that. I'm guessing your current master treats you better?"

I smile, thinking of Cash. "Yeah. He's good to me. He'll get me out of here soon."

Sy is quiet for a moment, long enough that I wonder if he's fallen asleep.

"So it's like that," he says, finally.

I wait, wondering what "like that" means.

"The pretty slave boy, in love with his master, waiting for him to swoop in and rescue him," Sy muses, clarifying his earlier statement. "And here I am, a poor substitution."

"It's not like that," I protest. Actually, it kind of is exactly like that, every goddamn word, and I feel ungrateful just thinking that about this man who's trying to help me.

Sy lets it go. "So, what's your darling master in for, then?"

I'm happy for the change in topic. "Conspiracy to commit treason," I tell him, aware of exactly how pretentious it sounds. "Yours?"

"Murder."

I can feel Sy shrug, and I hope it prevents him from feeling me shudder.

"A white-collar criminal. Fitting. You're confident he'll get off?"

"Completely." I'm amazed by how much faith I really do have in Cash. "He's been through it before. It's political. He's trying to redesign the whole re-education center system, which doesn't make him very popular. But his information is solid, it's released already. I know he'll get out. And he'll come and get me."

"You don't have to convince me. I just hope he comes for you soon. This isn't the type of place you want to spend a lot of time in."

"No," I answer, wondering how my master retrieving me fits into Sy's plans. Nobody is that generous. "How long have you been here?"

"About eight months. My master won't be coming for me anytime soon. I watched him kill the man he's on trial for killing. They can't make me testify against him, but they can make me testify against others in our organization. If he gets out before the detention fees become too much and they sell me, he'll beat me to death to stop that from happening. Hell, if he doesn't, one of his associates will probably buy me and do the same."

I'm quiet for a moment, processing this. Am I some sort of guilt thing, a last salvation before he gets killed?

"You probably don't want to hear sob stories from some criminal's slave. Hopefully you'll be on your way to your penthouse pretty soon."

"Yeah," I agree, entirely unsatisfied. "I appreciate your help."

"Don't mention it," he says, tightening the blankets around both of us. "I'm just sorry about what I have to do to keep up appearances." It hasn't been all bad. "Did you at least enjoy the blowjob?"

He laughs, making the whole bed rumble. "I didn't like forcing you, but yes. God damn, you are good with your tongue."

I smile, feeling strangely proud of my talents. "I'm glad I could put it to good use."

"Go to sleep, pretty boy," he says, the nickname taking on an entirely different tone than it has all the other times he's said it to me today. "They like to wake us up early. Tired is compliant, after all."

He hasn't answered all my questions, but maybe he doesn't need to. Cash will come for me soon enough. I try to get comfortable, missing the pillow-top mattress that Cash and I share, the soft sheets, the nice pillows, the way his body feels pressed against mine. I've tried to hold it together today, disappearing into my own thoughts and fantasies enough that I feel like a zombie, but lying here in the dark, I can't escape. I press my fist against my teeth to keep from crying out or making too much noise, but I can't help the sobs that wrack my body, making the bed frame start to squeal. I can't help the sinking feeling of aloneness that threatens to consume me.

I feel an arm wrap around my waist, and I fight it for half a second before clinging to it. I don't know this man or what he wants, but he's kind and safe. With Sy's arm wrapped tightly around me and his unfamiliar, undemanding body pressed against my back, I finally cry myself to sleep.

Chapter 3

Imprisoned

By the time I'm booked into the state prison, I've earned a few bruises. They stick to the places where they won't be seen, jabbing me in the ribs and pulling too hard on the handcuffs, but I don't bother to complain. I resisted arrest, too concerned about Sascha's safety, the safety of our project to worry. I should know better; in today's world, something as simple as arguing with an arresting officer is grounds for getting killed or at least tased. Actually fighting back should have gotten me killed. Someone wanted me alive, but I was too distracted to notice.

From the moment they came to take Sascha, his safety was all I was concerned about. My mother's plan had worked perfectly; so distracted by my need to go to him, to save him, I left the house without a second thought. The last time I left her alone with him, she had tortured him, brought in his rapist to help her get answers from him, humiliated and terrified him. The next time we engaged with her, she had me whip him, betraying him when he had worked to defend me, to save our project. When she seized him from my house, I was blind with rage. The bitch took a move directly from a cliché spy story and I fell into it, clueless.

I struggle to memorize the way he felt in my arms, holding him close, right before they took him.

It didn't dawn on me that I had been taken advantage of until I was at the courthouse, demanding that my slave be returned. While no state process is speedy, the level of runaround I was given trying to straighten things out was excessive. By the time it hit me, there were officers everywhere, armed and unarmed, and I wondered if it was only my notoriety that saved me from being shot and disposed of when I resisted.

Last time I was arrested for this very thing, I was far, far calmer. Scared for myself, I could manage to behave accordingly; scared for Sascha, I lost my mind. I have to find him.

The booking process is similar to last time. They read my rights, collect my fingerprints, take a series of photos. My identity flashes across a processing screen, the name "Cashiel Michaud" appearing as though it was given to me at birth. I watch with disdain as my belongings are stripped from me, replaced by a bright orange jumpsuit. I say as little as possible, eager to avoid incriminating myself or doing something else utterly stupid.

"I want my lawyer," I mutter, furious that it has come to this.

"I'll bet," one of the officers comments, shuffling me along a gloomy hallway.

"I get a phone call. I'm a goddamned citizen. I have the right to speak to my lawyer."

The officer doesn't reply, just keeps walking. We arrive at a small cell, well-secured with laser bars that can burn through flesh and bone if they're set right. I don't protest when I'm shoved inside, uncuffed, and left behind the buzzing technology.

They leave me alone in my cell for two days. An armed guard brings me food three times a day, and when I ask why I'm being secluded, he shrugs and mentions something about uprisings and riots and danger. He won't elaborate, and I am left frustrated, trying to figure out what is happening, both in this prison, and wherever Sascha is at. A part of me isn't even sure if he's alive.

On the third day, I'm informed that I have a visitor. I'm hoping that my lawyer will be waiting for me in the private room that I am taken to.

When I see my mother, I'm glad that I've been handcuffed again. I would strangle her with my bare hands if I could.

"Mr. Michaud," she starts, giving me a fake, professional smile.

The guard pushes me to sit in the chair across from her, cuffs me to it, and leaves without a word.

"I have nothing to say to you."

"Now, Cashi, is that really the way you want to talk to the one person who wants to visit you?"

I seethe. "I want my lawyer. Or my business partner." Or anybody except my mother. Not only is she the cause of my problems at the moment, she'll have nothing to do with solving them. I need someone who can get me out of here, someone I can use. Kristine Miller is an impediment.

She shakes her head. "Your lawyer made a statement this morning that he knows nothing about your project and wants nothing to do with it. Oliver is refusing to comment on anything, even whether he's truly in business with you or not. And I thought you might want news about your pretty little pet."

I pause. I do want news about Sascha, but every time my mother gets involved with him, it goes badly.

"How did your evaluation go, Ms. Miller?" I ask, pretending we're just business rivals. If she wants to ignore our history, I can only assume it's because she's meeting her own needs or protecting her image in the event that our conversation is being recorded. I want to expose her history with me, let the world know what she's done to me in the past, but it would damage my case as well. I've had plenty of time to think in the past few days and I know I need to be cautious, especially where my mother is involved.

"It got interrupted," my mother admits, a frown deepening on her face. "It seems that someone made the decision to release a vast amount of incriminating research. That same someone was taken into state custody just as you were being arrested."

I smile. We hadn't planned the release, but it makes sense. Sascha has always been a step ahead of my mother, often a step ahead of me as well. His action contributed to my arrest, but it was inevitable, and worth it. Obviously, my mother's plans were interrupted by this action as well. Sascha is smart, sometimes too smart for his own good, but today I'm just pleased that he was smart enough to come up with this. I know he did it at considerable risk to himself, and I'm sure he's miserable wherever he's being held. But I also know that he can survive, especially if he's out of my mother's reach. She wouldn't be here, taunting me about him, if she had the authority to actually do anything to him.

"Have they told you anything about what's been happening out there?" my mother asks.

"No. Nobody's talked to me at all. I assume I'm being held under some sort of terrorism charges."

"Terrorism, treason, something of that sort. You've been naughty; they're trying to make an example out of you. You'll get a trial eventually, but for now, the state is far more interested in shutting down any and all information about you. You've created quite a stir with your little research project."

"Where did he release the research to?" I ask. I hate engaging with her, but she's sharing information. I know it's a ploy to get me to talk, to try to trust her, but I don't have any other options.

"Everywhere he could," Kristine replies, looking extremely irritated by the fact. "And the few places he didn't reach, someone else passed the message along. Congratulations, Cash, you're the most notorious man in the country right now."

I smile widely at that, only to have the smile slapped off my face. My face burns, and I taste copper where the inside of my cheek grazed my teeth. For a moment, I feel like I'm ten years old again.

"Do you realize you could spend the rest of your life in here for this?" she demands.

I just shrug. It's unlikely, but if it happens, it's done already. "I thought you'd be happy about that."

My mother gives me a confused look, like she actually cares about me. "Cashi, I never wanted you to suffer. I just wanted you to behave. To fall in line. To uphold your responsibility to this country... and to our family."

So it seems we do have a private room.

"Besides, you aren't the only one at risk of going down as a result of this idiocy. It's bad enough that the Miller System will likely be destroyed, but your research makes some particularly incriminating accusations about me. Some of the statements you prepared—that your pretty little pet released—they point to me, personally. They say I covered it up, that I was hindering our nation's progress all along! You say that I tried to foil international development just to promote my own image."

"You did," I remind her of the truth. For more years than I can remember, my mother has been hiding results, paying off key players, and doing things like getting me put in jail. It wouldn't surprise me if she's done it to others as well. "Did you really think it would never come back to haunt you?"

My mother purses her lips, looking like she's just eaten something sour. "When they ask what happened, you need to tell them that you released the data. Don't let on that it was the boy."

I give her a curious look. "Are you that set on pinning this on me?"

My mother shakes her head. "It's nothing to do with that. If they think Sascha acted alone, he could be euthanized, permanently seized as evidence, accused of behaving above his status. They'll discredit your research, say it was interfered with by one of the Demoted."

I consider it. What she's saying makes sense; from anyone else, I would consider it good advice. But it's not anyone else. It's Kristine Miller, the head of the Miller System, the woman who let slaves raise me and then tried to destroy me from the moment I had independent thoughts.

"You brought a man who raped my slave to torture him," I remind her. "You coerced me into beating him. You kidnapped him and did god knows what to him. Why in the hell would you want to help him now?"

She laughs, a tinny, evil sound that makes me shudder. "Oh, Cash, I don't care about the slave. I care about what I always have— my legacy."

I can't tell if she's talking about me, or the Miller System.

"My business is going down," she admits. "You've finally done it. I pushed you to it, and I'll feel that guilt forever. But you... your new system, it just might work. And as much as I hate to fail, I'd like the comfort of knowing that I created something bigger, better, grander."

I just stare at her in disbelief. She has some sort of angle she's playing, I just can't figure out which one it is. She doesn't care about me and she doesn't care about Sascha. This is either another scheme, or she needs something from me.

"Besides," she says, giving me a nervous look. "You've made a lot of awful accusations in the information you released. A rephrasing, a reinterpretation of the data... it might help my case."

The truth, it seems, is that she's saving her own ass. "And what case might that be?" I ask, surprised that the state would take any sort of action against the beloved director of the Miller System.

My mother smiles, and for the first time, I see her looking worn out, exhausted. I see a glimmer of fear. "The only reason I'm on this side of the table is because the state's publicity department needs someone to make it look like they've been doing the right thing for all these years. I'm the public face of conformity, of tradition. When this tradition gets exposed as inadequate, our roles might be reversed. If you come out of this alive and free, they'll place the blame somewhere else. Right now I'm the most likely candidate."

I sit there, silent. It's a game, manipulation, but the look on her face makes me wonder. I wouldn't put it past her to lie about this; she's lied about everything for as long as I can remember. But the state doesn't do forgiveness well. If she isn't lying, she could be in considerable danger if the state chooses my side over hers. Even if they don't, she might go down alongside of me. I struggle, trying to figure out what she's gaining from her advice concerning Sascha, but other than me putting the blame somewhere else, she's getting nothing. A part of me wants to watch her go down.

"Thanks for the tip. I'll think about how I present your involvement to anyone who cares."

She nods, standing up. "That's fair of you." She turns and walks to the door, pausing before pressing the button that will call for the guards to let her out. "I still have some friends in the judicial department. When I arranged to visit with you, I spoke to someone about the conditions you're being kept in. You won't be secluded any longer."

I stare at her, surprised, and trying not to be pleased. I don't trust her, especially when it seems like she's doing something nice. "Why?"

"Because I taught you not to give favors freely, and I came here to ask you a favor."

Because she taught me strategy, in addition to cruelty, and she knows I learned it well. It's what she would want in this situation.

"I do love you, Cashi," she says softly. "I've just done what I thought was best."

Before I have a chance to reply, she pushes the button, and a guard immediately opens the door, letting her out before freeing me.

True to her word, I'm returned to my cell only briefly, where I contemplate her words, her visit, her motives. There's nothing that I can see her gaining from it, unless what she really said was true. But I know my mother, have known for years how manipulative she can be. I can't trust her, but I have no one else to trust.

An opportunity to correct that problem presents itself sooner than I expect.

I'm given the option to attend activities in the common room, and I take it, if only to break the monotony. More than anything, I'm eager to find out more about the outside world, to see what connections I can make, to use what little I have at my disposal while I'm stuck in here.

The first thing I do is find a vidscreen; fortunately, the major prisons are equipped with them, as enough studies have shown that they do a remarkably good job of keeping the population calm and compliant. I'm not surprised to see the thinly veiled propaganda—coverage of national unity events, historical productions detailing and glorifying the Peace Declaration occurred after the fourth World War so many decades ago, educational videos about slave ownership and the value of the Demoted system. There is always some sort of media available for these events, but the amount skyrockets any time there is political upset. The news won't show the riots that I'm certain are happening, that will be hidden in favor of "positive" news—that which benefits the system. Some of the other inmates are complaining about the lack of entertaining shows, and I try not to smile, certain that Sascha and I are responsible for the interruption of their regular programming.

I sit on an empty chair, welded to a metal table along with a few others. Harder to throw, hard to sit on. I wonder what sorts of accommodations Sascha is enjoying.

Only a few minutes pass before another inmate joins me. I keep staring at the vidscreen, wondering if he's just in need of a place to sit.

"Mr. Michaud?"

When he says my name, I look at him. I don't recognize him, not even a little. Why would I?

"Yes."

The man smiles a little. He's found what he's looking for. "It's good to see you out of your cell. I've been waiting for you."

I wait, silent. He seems to know who I am; I won't give him any other information until I find out who he is, what he wants. Why he's been waiting for me.

"My name is Emile Argova. I've been interested in your work for quite some time. We have a common interest in the Demoted."

I can't tell if he's bluffing, so I wait, keeping my face blank.

"We also share a partner in business," he continues, like we're in a board room instead of a prison. "Mr. Torenze has worked with my organization for many years. He mentioned a new partnership, hinted that there might be some changes in the future. I have to admit, I expected something less dramatic. The information reveal you staged makes a lot of important people look very stupid."

"What's your interest in my business?" I ask, still unsure of who he is.

Argova smiles at me. "I like to make sure that my industry ties stay relevant. It looks like the Miller System is about to take some hard hits. You, however... you're a good candidate for succession. I'd like to build a relationship with you."

It's unnerving that he knows this much about me. I wonder if he's working with my mother, but the fact that he's working with Oliver makes me doubt it. They're rivals; more importantly, they don't usually run in the same circles. My mother's circles are legitimate, political, governmental. Oliver's tend to be more underground, bordering on criminal. "I'm not sure how criminal ties would improve my chances for success," I remind him, hoping to dismiss him.

He just shakes his head. "It's all the same in the end, Mr. Michaud. The government, my organization, your business, the Miller System. We're all working toward the same goal. We can just help you get there faster. Set you up with a competent legal advisor, support your future negotiations. It's good to have friends in the industry. You've been alone for far too long."

I try not to frown, because what he's saying is correct. "And what would I have to do to earn your help?"

Argova smiles at me like a kindly grandfather. "Nothing. Promoting your development is in line with our interests. The Argova family would be grateful if you would consider a relationship with us in the future, but we're offering our support now with no strings attached. Consider it a welcome gift."

"Welcome to what?" I ask.

"To the new future of the Demoted system."

Chapter 4

Defense

While I become accustomed to the routine of the detention facility, I try to figure out my new protector. Sy doesn't usually answer my questions directly, brushing me off or shaking his head, like he's bound to some code of silence. I try to draw him out in other ways, exploring how he thinks, trying to understand him.

He's still. He almost always is, and I envy him for his calm and ability to tolerate anything that comes his way. I'm bored, fidgety, unnerved by my utter inability to do more than think about what I will do when Cash gets me out. I'm grateful that we aren't being forced to do hard labor or menial tasks like we did at the re-education center, but I'd rather have something to fill my time. I spend probably an hour one day debating the cost of hiring labor when there are perfectly good slaves who could be doing it. I explain in great detail to Sy how it would provide us with a sense of purpose and ownership and responsibility, and all sorts of things, and his response is simple and elegant.

"Work is a liability, Sascha. I hear some detention facilities lock the slaves up in small rooms where they can't possibly hurt themselves. All they want is to make sure they keep you unharmed and alive to generate fines."

He's right, of course.

As I get to know him better, I realize that a lot of people mistake him as simple, a misconception he doesn't bother to correct. He's quiet, observant, and when he does talk, he doesn't like it to be about him. I've pried a few pieces of information out of him, though, and they only confuse me more. He's told me that he grew up poor, never had many hopes of succeeding, and now he's Demoted. He says it like that's all there is to him. He's a bodyguard, or he was, and after displeasing his first master, he was sold to a low-level street thug who used him as an intimidating guard dog and human shield. He describes the tiny pieces of his history with as much detachment and factual accuracy as possible, and he never seems bothered, not even when I ask about the knife wounds on his stomach.

I have some knife wounds, too, but mine were from purposeful torture. They're light cuts and grazes and slices; deep enough that they hurt and bled a lot, but not quite deep enough that I really needed stitches.

His were punishment for flinching, and from what he tells me, his went deep enough require stitches inside and outside of the wound. They were done by one of his master's friends, with a sewing needle and some dental floss, and the closest thing to anesthesia he received was a punch in the face when he struggled. The rough dots surrounding the scars back his story up, and the thick, ridged edge makes me believe him. I am horrified when I hear the story, but he just shrugs.

"I don't flinch anymore," he remarks, staring off into space.

Most of the guards ignore him, as do most of the other slaves. We move around the common areas together, keeping an eye out for drama or disputes. Sy is distant from it, but not immune.

Marvin, the slave who first tried to claim me as his own, is at the center of most of the excitement that occurs. He toys with slaves and guards alike for his own amusement, and he does it with finesse. Sy tells me that Marvin is the only slave who has been here longer than he has. One of Marvin's favorite tricks is inciting fights between slaves that have offended him, ensuring that they are whipped or sent to solitary for their actions. Somehow, he always manages to come out looking clean and innocent no matter how deep his involvement runs.

He maintains his interest in me. With the power that Marvin throws around, he could have half the men in here if he wanted them, but maybe that's what makes me special.

We've been outside for maybe twenty minutes, and Marvin refuses to leave us alone, making snide comments, feigning innocence as he keeps coming closer and closer, catching the barest touch of my ass. Sy glares and moves away, but Marvin doesn't let up. When he doesn't get the response he wants from me, he moves on to Sy.

Unsurprisingly, Sy doesn't respond.

"What's the matter, big man?" Marvin teases, his face just inches from Sy's. "Too afraid to fight back?"

Sy sets his jaw and stares ahead.

"Worn out from fucking that tight little ass all night?" Marvin continues, gesturing lewdly toward me. "I couldn't imagine he puts up that much of a fight. Are you sure it's not the other way around? Maybe I should start calling the pretty boy the big man, huh?"

He's close enough that Sy must feel his breath. It angers me. If I didn't know better, I'd say Sy wasn't irritated, except I can feel him tense at my side.

Marvin continues his taunts, and out of the corner of my eye I catch a glimpse of him bringing his leg up to knee Sy in the groin. My eyes widen in shock.

Sy pulls away, but shows no other response.

"Didn't feel anything?" Marvin continues. "Maybe you don't have anything down there!"

Sy tries to steer us away, but Marvin is a step ahead, keeping himself face-to-face with Sy and kneeing him again. The guards are either enjoying the show or Marvin is standing too close for them to notice. When I was at the re-education center, that was how my fellow slaves tormented me. A familiar sense of fury and indignation creeps through my body.

"I claimed him fairly," Sy remind him. "You owed me. Let it go."

"Like you let anything go!" Marvin hisses, pressing against Sy, his hand darting between the two of them. From the sharp intake of breath, whatever he's doing is painful instead of sexual. "How many months did you hold on to that favor for? And you waste it on this fucking little pansy? Do you hold him at night while he cries? Do you like the thought of redeeming yourself before they put you down?"

It happens before I know it. I've never been a violent person. I've always used my biting sarcasm and wit to exact my revenge, but something about me has changed, something about seeing Sy hurting in place like this triggers something inside of me. Maybe it's just finally time for me to break.

My fist moves faster than my brain, and Martin is stumbling backwards a moment later, a drop of blood showing on his lip. A look of shock crosses his face, but it is instantly replaced by a satisfied grin.

Shit. I've given him exactly what he wanted.

"Officer Reynolds!" he cries out, sounding pathetic and entirely too hurt. "Officer Reynolds, sir, the new slave — he just hit me!"

I look to Sy with wide eyes, terrified now that I've actually done something to warrant punishment. Will they whip me? Worse? I start to tremble.

"Dammit," Sy mutters. He presses his fist to his mouth. He seems to be thinking very hard, but I can't imagine any way he could help me.

Bulldog and Lanza come over, and Bulldog has the most gleeful look on his face.

"Officer Lanza, remind everyone what the punishment is for fighting?" Bulldog asks, smiling into my face.

"Twenty lashes," Lanza replies dutifully. At least he doesn't look happy about it. "Come on, Sascha."

"That's not necessary, sir," Sy says quietly. His body is turned squarely to face the two guards, and his head is inclined toward them, but his eyes are downcast. Perfectly submissive. "It wasn't him who did it. Marvin was mistaken, sirs."

"Bullshit! That little fuck hit me!" Marvin protests. "Split my lip open!"

"Stop trying to cover for your toy," Bulldog snaps. "Or I'll make sure he stays far away from you."

This threat alone is enough to get me to shut up, and when Bulldog grabs at me, I go toward him immediately, eager to avoid the threat of being separated from my protection.

Sy turns to Lanza, nodding deferentially before speaking. "Look at my hand, sir. I split my knuckle on his teeth."

He holds his hand out, and the officer takes it carefully, observing the gash and the blood.

That's why he was pressing his fist to his teeth. Sy split his own knuckle so he could take the punishment for me.

"Sy —" I start, desperate to avoid letting him take my punishment.

"Shut your mouth, Sascha," he warns. "This was between me and

Marvin, and this wouldn't have happened if you would have stayed out of it."

His words are true, even if his version of the events isn't.

Marvin keeps protesting from the sidelines until Bulldog threatens to whip him for insolence, and then he stalks out, pouting and touching his lip. Only the fact that I left a mark on him eases the injustice I feel.

"Punishment remains the same," Lanza provides. "Twenty lashes—you got the whip?"

"Let's make it twenty-five," Bulldog bargains, flashing a smile at me and Sy. "After all, he is a repeat offender."

Lanza just shrugs and taps at his tablet, entering the date and offense and number of lashes.

Sy doesn't need to be ordered to strip, he does so automatically. His hands are still and confident as he grabs the zipper and pulls it down, slips his arms out of the sleeves, and drops the jumpsuit to the ground. As if this were the most normal thing in the world, he steps out of it, picks it up, folds the fucking thing, and hands it to me.

"Would you like me on the perimeter or the ground, sir?" he asks, his tone just as even as it was before. I shudder at the image of him lying on the ground, waiting to be beaten.

"Perimeter," Bulldog grunts.

Bulldog follows Sy to the edge of the yard, where the chain link fence provides stability for Sy to lean against and grip with his hands. Afraid and alone, I stand close to Officer Lanza, who allows me to follow him.

I'm horrified to realize how good a view I'm getting. Some of the other slaves have gathered, keeping a respectful distance. Sy's face is pressed into the fence, but I can still see his blank expression.

"Begin," Lanza announces.

Bulldog lets the first lash fly.

He's not as fast as he is when he's whipped the other slaves. It's like he's drawing it out, savoring it, and the half-smile on his face confirms that. I hate him. He also seems to be hitting harder, or maybe it's just my guilt. Welts spring up almost instantly, and he's managed to cross the lashes and draw blood by the eighth lash.

Sy stands there like a stone, his face and posture and expression exactly as they were when they began. Even as the whip falls, cracking as the leather connects with his skin, he doesn't respond, doesn't flinch, doesn't let out so much as a whimper. I think he blinks, once, but I realize it's just a coincidence. For all anyone can tell, he's just looking at the clouds.

Bulldog isn't doing as well; as every lash fails to draw a response from Sy, he hits harder, his face going from satisfied to frustrated as he reaches twenty. He loses control of the whip and manages to wrap it around Sy's ribs. From where I'm standing, I can see the tip wrapping around his chest, the tip striking his neck. This draws only the slightest jerk from Sy, but Officer Lanza gasps and snaps at his partner.

"Dammit, Reynolds, have you been drinking again?" he strides over and grabs Bulldog's hand, jerking the whip out of it. "You blind him or something and we'll both get written up! I can't afford to lose this job!"

Bulldog mutters something I can't quite make out, but he doesn't sound happy.

"We're calling it," Lanza decides, tapping something into the tablet. "Punishment finished at twenty-one lashes."

Sy stays frozen on the fence, not so much as dropping his hands. The red marks seem to glow against his skin. Here and there, blood is pooling just at the edge of the lash marks, smeared where the whip struck repeatedly, but not yet dripping. The single line of dripping blood comes from Sy's ribs. I can see that his muscles are tense, but every other part of him is calm, controlled.

"Give it up, Syrus, you're off the hook!" Bulldog snaps, storming away. His pride has clearly been hurt and he's furious. I only hope that Sy isn't the one to feel that wrath later.

Lanza nods at me and I rush toward Sy, who's already turning around.

"Sy, I'm so sorry," I babble, fighting back tears. It isn't fair, none of this is fair, I shouldn't have gotten him into trouble, and I shouldn't have stood there and let him get whipped because of me. "I'm sorry, I'll never do it again, Sy, please—"

"Sascha, I warned you once today to shut your mouth, do you need a more physical warning?"

As kind as he's been to me, it occurs to me that he could hurt me, and his demeaning tone and casual threat of violence has me cowering.

"I'm sorry," I mumble, looking down. I want to crawl into the concrete, burrow under the ground and hide like a worm.

"Give me my jumpsuit."

I hand it over wordlessly, feeling my guilt mounting as he steps into it and pulls it on. The faded orange fabric is animated by the spots of blood that show on his back.

I become vaguely aware of the crowd watching us, some commenting on Sy's decision to step up and protect me. Marvin is pouting in the corner, one of his boys sucking his dick to soothe his pride. Sy doesn't speak to me for a while; he doesn't speak to anyone. He gets a few approving nods from the other slaves, presumably for his unflappable attitude during the whipping. In typical Sy fashion, he doesn't respond, just stares off into space.

I stay close to him, out of habit and self-preservation, but I don't touch him like I usually do, because I'm afraid he'll disapprove. I don't speak, either. I've seen other slaves punish their pets, and it can be anything from an extra rough fucking to pinching to taking away meals. I hadn't thought Sy would do that, but then, I hadn't thought I'd be responsible for him getting whipped either.

When we're allowed back inside, Sy takes me by the arm and drags me down the hallway. A few lecherous slaves follow until Sy turns, glaring at them.

"No audience," he orders, his eyes cold. "This won't be entertaining."

He drags me into his cell and starts stripping off his jumpsuit, face stone solid again as he pulls the fabric out of the cuts on his back.

"Take your fucking jumpsuit off and get in the bed!" he yells at me, his voice booming through the cells.

I tremble, wondering what he's going to do to me, but I follow his orders. I deserve it.

Sy goes to the sink and fills a flimsy plastic cup with water, grabbing a washcloth as well.

I wonder if he's planning to gag me.

He crawls in bed next to me, slower and stiffer than usual, and he proceeds to lie on his stomach, his head turned toward me. It's not what I'm expecting, but I'm still afraid, and I'm still trembling. I wait for his orders.

He hands me the cup and the washcloth.

"Calm down," he whispers. "I'm not really going to hurt you. After that stupid little stunt you pulled earlier, we need to keep up appearances. Help me clean up."

"Oh." I take a few minutes to understand what he said. Another act.

I wet the washcloth and dab at his back, as gentle as possible.

"You won't break me," he comments, prompting me to press a little harder. "You do something like that again and I'll bring you back here and knock you around, got it?"

"Yes," I have to fight to keep from adding "sir" to the end of the sentence.

"It was between me and Marvin, you didn't need to get involved," he mutters, clenching his teeth as I wipe a stubborn piece of lint out of one of the deeper cuts on his back.

"You didn't have to do that for me," I hiss at him.

"That's not up to you."

I can't argue with that. I bite my tongue against all my comebacks and focus on what I'm doing. I don't understand why he's so hell-bent on helping me, but I'm not so rude as to be ungrateful.

Finally, I feel a hand on my leg.

"Sorry if I scared you," Sy whispers. "But plenty of people saw what you did, and they saw that I took your place. There needed to be some sort of consequence. I'd never really be that cruel."

"But you'll knock me around next time?" I tease, only half-kidding.

"Probably not," Sy admits. "But don't think that a part of me doesn't want to."

I smile, thinking of Cash. Something as stupid as what I did would have earned me at least a meeting with his belt, back in the day. He always has been able to keep me in line, but he hasn't really had to, not since he let me in on his plans. I work so much better when I know what I'm facing.

"Why are you helping me?" I ask again. "This is more than just winning me over, more than just looking tough. What are you working toward?"

"You can just thank me and move on," Sy evades my question, letting his head rest on his arms.

I think back to Marvin's last taunt, about being put down like a dog. I wonder if it's true, and more importantly, if Sy will tell me. "Are you really at risk of being killed? What did you do?"

He sighs. "It's better if you don't know about it."

I wait, frowning, resisting the urge to poke at his wounds until he talks, but I know better. I've seen the scars; even if he wouldn't smack me across the cell, he wouldn't talk, either. I take another angle, one I doubt he's been trained to resist.

"If you're going to use me, you could at least tell me how. I owe you. I won't get in your way."

I can see from the slight redness that graces his face that shame cuts far deeper than the whip did. He glances over at me, shaking his head.

"You're too smart for your own safety," he says. "Look, I know who you are. More accurately, I know who your master is, who his associates are. I know I might be able to use your safety as a bargaining tool. My master is a member of the 27th Street Gang—it's small, but the gang has ties with the Argova crime family. They have interest in the slave industry."

It's not that I thought he had fallen instantly in love with me or anything, but it still stings to hear someone else's plans laid out so carefully.

"It should have been me killing the man my master murdered. I fucked it up, so he did it instead... and he got caught," Sy confesses. "He wants me dead for that mistake, but his superiors aren't so vengeful. I have it on good authority that the Argova family is interested in your master. They have a part to play in everything, they keep the lower level gangs in line. If I'm useful enough to them, they might cut the 27th Street Gang out of the equation entirely. You're the first useful thing that has come in these doors since I got here."

I raise an eyebrow, curious. I know I'm useful to Cash, but I fail to see how an organized crime unit would have any use for me.

"The people who own me, they have business dealings with Oliver Torenze. Your master's partner. That's how I recognized you, I saw you at a social event probably a year ago."

Always observant.

"Sascha, I'm dead when I leave here. My master will be imprisoned or executed; when the trial is over, his associates will likely do the same to me. Keeping you safe is a stretch, but it might win me some favor."

I frown. Torenze's corruption has followed me into a detention facility. I wonder when Sy first saw me. Was it at one of the parties that I attended so faithfully with my master? The one where he beat me for Toreneze's amusement? I hadn't noticed Sy, but I rarely notice other slaves. My job is to focus on people who matter. Bodyguards, servants, slaves, we blend in.

"How are they connected?" I ask.

Sy smiles. "Torenze has a lucrative side business connecting medical supplies with organizations that need them. Officially it's research, but mostly they sell organs to the highest bidder. The Argova family facilitates the business end. They hired my master and the 27th Street Gang to move the products and clean up the mess. We're bottom feeders, but I've been around long enough to recognize the important players. It's kept me alive."

I shudder. Cash has mentioned Torenze's connections into the medical industry, his role in experimentation on the Demoted, but I never realized that something as grisly as a black market organ trade was part of it. At one time, I was almost part of that population.

"Torenze seemed fond of you," Sy recalled. "Your master certainly was. You're a bargaining chip. From what you've told me over the past few weeks, this research thing, the way your master is challenging the Miller System, you might be even more valuable."

I nod, trying to remember everything I've told him. I underestimated him; I thought I could speak freely about the project since he's just another slave. Just the big dumb bodyguard of a street thug.

"The stuff with the Miller System is a government program," I remind him. "I'm not sure how useful I'll be."

"You're too smart to miss the levels of corruption in the Demoted system," Sy chastises. "The government, the Argova family... they're all working toward the same goals. The only difference is whose name shows up in the media. Besides, you'll be more of a personal favor.

Please your master, please his partner. It positions us for better deals in the future."

I nod, seeing his point. It's a stretch, but he sounds like he'll take whatever he can get. Then again, so will I.

Chapter 5

Making Deals

The longer I stay in the detention facility, the more worried I become about my master.

I don't get news about him; I don't get news at all. Time seems to stop in here, at least for slaves. Knowing why Sy is helping me makes me a little less confused, and I pay him back how I can, sharing extra food with him at mealtimes and staying out of trouble. It's the least I can do for him.

We're in the common room, playing a game of cards with some of the other slaves, when Officer Lanza comes over, eyeing me and Sy up skeptically. He glances at me. "You've got a visitor," he informs me. "He's requested a private room. Think your master would allow that?"

I look nervously at Sy, who just nods his approval. "Who is it, sir?"

"Some guy by the name of Torenze," Lanza replies, shrugging. "Says he's a friend of your master. You're not required to go, but you are allowed."

A part of me wants to hide, to stay here with Sy and wait for Cash, but if Torenze is here, he wants something. I can only hope that it's something that will help my master. If nothing else, he can give me information.

"All right," I agree, rising and following the guard. He doesn't say much, just leads me back out through the series of locked doors and into a small room.

"The room is sound proofed. A guard will be watching the camera; raise your left hand if you want to end the visit," Lanza advises before leaving me.

Moments later, Oliver Torenze walks in, his face a mask.

"You should have called me to come get you, Sascha," he chides. "There's plenty of room in my house for another slave."

I feel my skin crawl. My last memory of visiting his house had left me miserable for weeks; the marks are barely healed. "My master would prefer that I stay safe."

Torenze sits. "Like he preferred not to tell me that he was going to release the results of his little research project?"

"He didn't," I mutter. "I did."

Torenze shakes his head at me. "Yes, well, your actions don't happen without consequence, boy. Do you have any idea how much trouble you've caused?"

I don't back down. "His mother was trying to expose him. She kidnapped me, said it was part of a slave evaluation, and then she raided the house. You're his business partner — you knew the research would come out eventually."

Torenze scowls at me. "I expected it to be fully developed, fully documented, and released in a reasonable manner. You have no idea what your stupid plan has caused, do you?"

I shrug, thinking of the riots I saw the day I was brought here. I can only assume it has gotten worse. "You don't look like you're suffering from it."

"This has become an international problem, and the only reason I'm not sharing a cell with your master is because they haven't found the data I'm hiding, yet," he informs me, furious. "I haven't decided whether to tell them I'm more than just a business partner, or to say I had nothing to do with it. They want a villain. I'd rather it not be me. I might do better to cooperate, but then, Cashiel might come out of this in one piece if he gets the right help. Doesn't seem like he'll be getting that anytime soon. His lawyer dropped him the moment this hit the news, and they're not allowing him visitors."

"Then how do you even know?" I ask, wondering if he's just bluffing.

"Unlike Cashiel, I have a lot of connections," Torenze reminds me, looking smug.

I sigh. Torenze does have connections, and plenty that Cash and I know nothing about. I need to take help where I can get it, at least until there's another option. "I'm sure you didn't just come here to visit."

"I want a show of good faith," he tells me, smiling. "I'm going to put a lot at risk here just by being involved. Cash has nothing left that I want. You do."

It suddenly hits me that he's not talking to me as a worthless slave. He's negotiating with me. Not with Cash, not with Sy, just with me. I don't smile back. "Let's talk business, then."

Torenze stands, slowly, and comes behind me. He places his hands on my shoulders and leans down to whisper in my ear. "I'm not interested in any more business. I want things that you can give me."

I shudder, knowing exactly what he means. "You'll help Cash if I do?"

"Yes," Torenze agrees, pulling me out of the chair and turning me to face him.

I nod. "What do you want?"

Torenze smiles at me again, making my stomach turn. "You. Today. Right here. And again once your dear master is out."

I unzip the jumpsuit, ready to meet his demands. "You can't hurt me in here," I inform him. "It's against the visitation policy."

"I doubt that's true. But there will be time for that, later. I'd rather take my time with you again. Today, I just want to know you want me. Bad."

"Okay." Cash will be furious when he hears I've brokered this deal, but I can deal with him once we're free. I toss the jumpsuit aside, eyes wide and ready to go.

"You'll visit me at least every other month," Torenze demands. "Once you're out. I'll even be nice and give you a few weeks to readjust."

He sickens me, but if things go well, we can back out of the agreement. It's not like it's a legal contract. Once our project gains popularity, we won't even need his fucking money anymore.

"Fine," I agree, shrugging. "Let's get to it."

Torenze grabs me roughly, squeezing my cock until it hurts. "I'll need something else from you," he hisses. "Something that will guarantee your promises will be kept."

"I don't have anything," I insist.

For a few seconds, Torenze squeezes hard, bringing tears to my eyes, and then he lets go and turns away. "I guess our deal is off."

I panic. "Wait, no, hold on! I don't have anything else about the business, but I do have... there's something about me. Something personal. Leverage."

Torenze raises an eyebrow at me, waiting.

I battle with myself for a few seconds before realizing it might be my only chance at getting out of here, my only chance at helping Cash and our project. "I... I wasn't supposed to be Demoted. I switched Assessments with someone. I took their place."

Torenze shakes his head. "Nice try, but that can't be done. And anyway, that doesn't tell me anything. What are they going to do, Demote you again?"

I grit my teeth. "It can be done, and when I get out of here, I'll tell you how." When Torenze is obviously not satisfied, I continue. "It was my brother. I switched Assessments with my brother and it worked."

Torenze looks surprised, giving me a moment of victory even as I realize how much danger I've put my brother and his family in. But my real family, my master, the man I care about more than anyone else in the world is more important than that.

"What an interesting story that makes," Torenze agrees.

I wait, nervous, hoping for his approval.

"Beg me to fuck you," he orders. "Down on your knees."

"Do we have a deal?" I demand. I need to hear it first.

"Oh, yes," he agrees. "After all, I don't want my business partner to suffer. Poor publicity. Puts me at risk."

I wonder if he's been playing me this whole time, if he would have helped anyway. I can't think about it, so I drop to my knees instead. "Please fuck me," I start. "I want it so bad."

Torenze laughs. "If you could swap Assessments, I think you can act better than that. Show me. Show me just how desperate you are. Make it good."

I nod, realizing I hadn't tried very hard to begin with. I also realize that he's flashing a smile up at the camera, and I'm not sure if he's made a deal with the guards, or if he just likes taunting them.

Regardless, I put on the show he wants. I get down on my knees, I beg him, I wrap my arms around his legs and run my lips over his cock, through his pants. I touch myself, and when it makes him smile, I do it more, stripping off my jumpsuit so he can get a good view. I rut against his leg, the desperation turning real as it occurs to me that my failure spells my and Cash's demise. I unfasten his pants with my teeth and take his cock into my mouth greedily, touching myself as I do.

When I've convinced him and brought him to hardness, the show is suddenly over. Without a word, he hauls me up, throws me over the table, and drives into me, hard and ruthless. I press my face into the table, wrapping my hands around my head, and bite back the screams that threaten to emerge every time he thrusts into me, dry and unprepared. When I try to relax, he winds one hand down to grab at my balls, squeezing tightly enough to make me yelp and tense up.

He finishes quickly, but not before turning me around, pressing my aching ass against the table, and jerking violently on my cock.

"Show the camera how much you love it."

I wish I could think of Cash as I come, but I can't spoil my memories of him. I think of my days at the re-education centers, at the brothel, and I force my body to comply with Torenze's wishes. I come across his hand and he wipes it on my chest before pushing me away.

"I have a meeting with your master at ten tomorrow morning," he tells me, triumphant. "I'll make sure to give him your regards."

I say nothing, just collapse to the floor and watch him dress. Without another word, he leaves the room.

Officer Lanza comes in a few minutes later and hands me a box of tissues. I mumble "thank you," as I clean up and dress myself, and he escorts me back to the locked area.

"If he comes again, do you want to see him?" Lanza asks.

I nod immediately. "Yes, sir. Thank you."

He nods, giving me a concerned look, and takes me directly back to Sy. I don't know what to say to my new friend, so I just stand there. He must know. Tissues don't remove the smell of semen, and they certainly don't remove the smell of sweat. He motions for me to come closer and I wait for him to hurt me, even if only to satisfy some strange detention facility custom.

He puts his arm around me.

"Everything taken care of?" he asks.

I just nod, unable to speak.

"You can tell me about it later if you want," Sy offers. "And don't worry. What free people do... it doesn't count in here."

When the guards come back to torment us that evening, I'm ordered to my knees again by Sy. This time, I don't fight it. I go to my knees immediately, strangely comforted as I feel his fingers slipping through my hair, holding my head. He doesn't pull me onto his cock, but our audience can't tell the difference. We move in time, my head, his hand, and I take him into my mouth without a second thought.

He's soft at first, but it only takes a few flicks of my tongue to get him hard. I wrap my arms around his legs, supporting myself, and I make sure to bob my head up and down. As his cock works deep into my throat and back out, almost past my lips, I curl my head around, working it from other angles. In different circumstances, it might be fun to explore Sy's body, noting the way he responds to the tip of my tongue tracing around the head of his cock, or the way he gasps when I suddenly take him deep, flicking my tongue up and down across the underside. I don't mind that he's enjoying it; it makes the whole ordeal go more quickly and makes me feel like I'm doing something worthwhile.

Even if I hate the audience, I do like putting my skills to good use. For a moment, I can even zone out, pretending I'm somewhere else. I close my eyes, focusing only on the task in front of me, and I feel him tensing, responding both to my touch and the threat of displeasing the guards.

This time, Sy's hand stays soft and comforting in my hair as I bring him off as quickly as possible. He holds my head in place, probably making sure I don't pull off and embarrass us both, but he doesn't need to. As his come fills my mouth, I swallow quickly, keeping my lips wrapped tightly around his cock until he's finished. I feel him soften under my tongue, and I wait until he moves my hand and takes my arm to pull me to my feet.

Chapter 6
Protection

A part of me is thrilled when I hear that Oliver Torenze is visiting Sascha. It makes me nervous that my new friend is being taken to a private room with the man; I am fully aware of Torenze's penchant for torture. While I wasn't often around in his meetings with my master, I knew that they both dealt in slave organs, and it was common knowledge that Torenze liked to conduct his own "experiments" at home. I saw it myself in the slaves he brought along with him. His pretty pets, most of whom changed with every meeting, tended to sport bruises, cuts, and burns. And those were just the injuries I could see. The way that they cringed, limped or struggled to breathe hinted at even worse tortures occurring behind closed doors. I would rather not see Sascha going home with him, not only because I want to use Sascha for my own purposes, but because I've come to like the pretty boy. But the visit gives me hope.

Slaves don't typically get visitors in detention facilities, especially from private interests. I've been ignored for almost my entire stay here—I assume that any visitor I will get will tell me that I'm being sold. Worse, a visit might result in my immediate or impending death. For Torenze to lower himself to visiting a place like this, there must be a reason. I doubt he would have come just to retrieve his business partner's slave. Sascha must have something he wants. If Sascha is valuable to Torenze, he might be valuable to my master and the Argova family. It gives me hope. Maybe he can be useful. Maybe I can as well.

I can't help feeling guilty for exploiting Sascha, though. I'm not just forcing him to suck my cock, I'm using him as a pawn for my master's games and to save my own ass. Torenze obviously took his turn terrifying the boy and fucking him against his will; I don't want to be in that same category.

"Sorry about earlier," I tell him, once we're alone for the night. "I swear, the guards will lose interest in a couple of days, and then you won't have to do it anymore."

"It's okay," Sascha insists, smiling at me. "I don't mind. I think I'd rather if you enjoyed it."

I laugh. "I'm not going to say that I don't enjoy it, but I don't like taking advantage of you. It's wrong."

"Well, then, can we stick with 'thank you' instead of 'sorry'?" Sascha presses. "I don't think you have to apologize for it. You're doing a lot for me; don't think I'm not aware of it."

"Sascha, I think you're aware of everything," I point out. He's aware that I'm already using him, just in other ways. He shouldn't have to do this, too. "I see you all day. Watching. Observing. You act like you're just aching to get back to some higher purpose, like you're distracted from saving the world or something."

"We're taking on the Miller System," Sascha reminds me. "We are trying to fix the Demoted system, or at least a part of it. I don't mind making a few sacrifices."

I feel uncomfortable, realizing that I am one of those sacrifices. I've killed for my masters before, but taking advantage of Sascha seems wrong. Doing it just to save my own ass seems very wrong.

"Are you all right?" I ask. "Your visitor didn't seem to make you very happy. I thought maybe he'd take you home, keep you out of here until your master comes back."

Sascha shakes his head. "I'd never go with that bastard. He's a sadistic asshole. You know what he does for business. In private, he tends more toward humiliation and suffering. He's shown me his preferences before. But we need him. He has connections, and he has the rest of our data. He can try to get my master out of prison."

"And you pay the price for his help." I understand. I've been there before. I'm there right now, trying to commit every detail of what Sascha tells me to memory so I can pay off my own debts. "I'm sorry."

"It's not your fault," Sascha says. "You're doing enough for me in here. I appreciate it. I really don't mind giving you head. You're nice about it. And I know that you're not abusing it or anything, so, please, enjoy me."

I sigh. Sascha's trying to make me feel better, but I feel guilty instead. Sascha might be keeping me alive, and he appreciates being forced to play the part of my whore? I've made my peace with killing as ordered, but I've never been the one to manipulate someone on my own time. I feel like as much of a monster as those pulling the strings from the outside.

"Sascha, I know it's not the same..." I start, uncertain of how he'll react. "But would you like me to return the favor?"

Sascha is quiet for a moment, probably confused. I wonder if I've made a mistake, if he'll be offended, if he'll think that I'm playing him or just trying to get more action.

"Oh, I..." he stammers. "I mean, I'm flattered, and I'm sure I would enjoy it, but...."

"Sorry," I say, once Sascha goes too long without speaking. I want to pull away, to hide from my own shame and inadequacy. Stick to mission. "I didn't mean to presume. I just figured, even if you aren't attracted to me, it's dark, and I have been used for that quite a bit—"

"No!" Sascha cuts me off. "Sy, it's not that. I just don't want you to do something you don't want to do, and besides, my master doesn't really like to share me, either. I guess that's something the two of you have in common."

"Yeah," I say, quiet. He's nice enough not to reject me outright, but I realize what I must seem like to him. I'm a criminal, a lowlife. It's been the same ever since I could remember, even before I was Demoted. Even if we weren't separated by more than a decade, Sascha and I would never have been friends growing up. We wouldn't even have lived in the same neighborhood. If he saw someone like me walking along his street at night, he would probably report me to the officials—even before I was Demoted. I'm using him. He's confiding in me because I'm all he has, but he'd rather not associate with my type. I probably wouldn't either, if I was in his position.

"Look, if circumstances were different, I'd love to fool around with you, but right now... let's just keep it at this, okay? You don't owe me anything. You're giving me so much already."

"All right," I agree. I don't believe him, but I don't contradict him, either. We don't talk after that, and he still presses tight against me as we sleep.

I've learned to do what I have to do to survive, but something about Sascha makes me wonder if I could do it better.

Lanza comes for me a few days later, his face a little sad. He's always been a decent man, unlike many of the others. "Syrus, come with me. You have a visitor."

I stand to follow him, and Sascha does as well. I realize the dilemma I'm causing by leaving him; he's at risk of harassment. I give Lanza a pleading look, something I'd never do for myself, but I'll do for Sascha.

Lanza frowns. "Sascha, you can spend a few hours in solitary to work on that attitude."

Sascha understands, looking grateful even as he's taken to the small, dark cell. I've been in there for weeks, after earning my favor from Marvin, and I feel a chill at the sight of it. The utter darkness and isolation make you hallucinate and panic after long enough, and you can barely sit, let alone lie down. He won't be comfortable, but he'll be safe.

I'm taken to one of the visiting rooms, where I'm greeted by one of my master's associates. Conrad never liked me much, said I was too quiet and serious for his tastes. Alongside my master, he's one of the leaders of the 27th Street Gang. I doubt I'm about to hear good news.

"Your master has forfeited his rights to you," he informs me. "You won't be in here long, boy. Anything useful?"

I nod. "Yes, sir."

"Well, what is it?" he demands.

If I had told him immediately, he would have slapped me for speaking out of turn. "A slave, sir. He belongs to Oliver Torenze's business partner. I've been protecting him."

Conrad looks surprised. "Cashiel Michaud's boy?" he confirms. When I nod, he continues. "Not bad, Syrus. Looks like we might keep you around, after all. Mr. Argova will be pleased. Michaud has pissed off the whole world. Someone must be looking for information about what he's doing. This could give the 27s a chance to move up. What do you have?"

I consider it. Sascha has told me quite a bit about the research he and his master have been doing, Torenze's role, their eventual goal. I could buy myself some time with this, win favor, resume my old role with the organization.

But how long will it be before I'm right back where I am now, the same threat of death facing me? It seemed so worth it when I first saw Sascha, but it's tiring. I've been doing this for too long. I don't know how much longer I'll last.

"Nothing, sir," I lie, my face blank. "He's just a pretty pet. Doesn't even understand what his master was arrested for."

Conrad's face drops, and he glares at me.

"I'll try to get closer, sir," I mention, still not entirely sure whether I want to lie down and die, or destroy Sascha's life and die in a few years, anyway. "I'll keep working."

Conrad scowls. "We don't have money to waste on your detention fees. Find out something useful about Michaud or his associates, and we'll contact you once you've been auctioned."

"Yes, sir."

He doesn't bother to say anything as he leaves, nor does he bother to explain the consequences should I fail at my task. He'll find me and he'll kill me. With my master still in prison, Conrad is next in line for disposal duties — the term they use to refer to killing slaves. Murder is too harsh of a word for something similar to taking out the garbage. A criminal's slave isn't a good loose end to leave running around in the world.

I'm quiet when I'm brought back, glad to have a few moments to think before Sascha joins me. He's thrilled to see me, but he respects my mood, waiting until we're in bed to talk to me. I tell him what happened, about the forfeit, about the auction, about the threats.

"Sy, I'm sorry." He sounds like he truly means it. But he sounds scared when he asks the next question. "What does this mean for me and Cash? What sort of deal did you make?"

I shake my head. Just the fact that he assumes it about me hurts. "I didn't tell them anything, Sascha."

He's quiet for a moment. "Why not?"

51

"I like you," I admit. "I think that what you're doing, what your master is doing... it's a good thing. It's nice to be a part of something like that."

"I thought you said you needed me as a bargaining chip to stay alive?" Sascha protests. "We can figure something out, you know, something to tell them, a deal—"

"If they wanted me dead, they would have done it today." It's only half a lie. They're waiting to see if I come up with something better now that the stakes are raised. They're hoping I can come up with something to please the Argova family. "They're letting me get auctioned off. They probably don't want to risk drawing attention to themselves by killing me yet. Too risky."

"So you'll just get sold?" Sascha asks, sounding horrified.

I laugh, bitter. "Maybe I'll get lucky this time around. What do you think, is there a market for an oversized, thirty-something man with a history of violence and martial-arts training?"

Sascha cuddles close, clearly upset. "You're not telling me everything."

No, I'm not. But I like the fact that this is my decision. A final "fuck you" to the people who've had me doing their dirty work for so long. "Lanza said it could take up to three weeks to get clearance to sell me. I'm going to find someone to give you to before I go. I'll find someone who won't go out of their way to hurt you."

Chapter 7

Assistance

My mother doesn't return. I assume she wasn't pleased with the results of our last visit, and I'm not particularly inclined to care. I assume she was bluffing, anyway.

Some government official comes by to notify me of the exact charges that I'm facing. There are a number of them, all adding up to treason against the government. Together, they carry execution penalties. They confirm what my mother said about my lawyer, and they offer me a public defendant like I'm some common criminal, too poor to pay for my own legal defense.

I seek out Argova again. I need someone to get me out of here, to get me back to Sascha, and if he's telling the truth, he has someone better than a public defender for me.

"I'd like to take you up on your offer." I'm not entirely sure what I'm getting myself into, but I need to take some sort of action. I can deal with the consequences later. What's important now is to get out of here, get Sascha back, and then I can deal with everything else.

Argova smiles at me, like he knew all along that I would accept. "I have someone arranged by the end of the day. We're very pleased that you've considered our offer."

I wait for the demands, for the other shoe to drop. It's what my mother always taught me to expect.

"I hear you have a pet in Leadview."

I tense, waiting for the threat.

"We have an associate keeping him safe," Argova informs me. "A courtesy, if you will."

I don't bother to hide my relief, because I know how obvious it is.

He notices instantly.

"Is he important to your project, Mr. Michaud?"

How do I answer that? If Argova is interested in my project, admitting Sascha's role in it could make him valuable enough to protect. But if his motives are darker, if anyone else finds out how big a role Sascha plays in my life, I could be setting us both up for danger.

"No," I bluff. "It's personal. He's very loyal."

Argova nods, but doesn't comment on it. "All the same, he's being kept safe."

He leaves me then, startling me. I assume he's going to make arrangements with the lawyer he mentioned, or with another "associate," and I can't help recalling the years of training my mother subjected me to. The person in power can leave whenever they want, with no need for niceties. I've been trained for so long to attend to these petty power plays that I can't help wondering if his abrupt departure was intentional.

My thoughts are interrupted by another visitor. I'm surprised when I enter the interview room to find Oliver sitting across the table.

"Cashiel," he says, a smile spreading across his face. "Nice to see you getting along so well in your new home."

I glare at him. "Where have you been?" I demand. It's not all I want to ask him, but it's a start. He was supposed to have been here from the start. From the moment he heard what my mother was planning to do, he's left me and Sascha out in the cold.

"I had some loose ends to tie up," he says, giving me a sarcastic smile. "Besides, I was a little shocked by your reveal. Seems like something you would tell your partner in advance."

I frown, about to point out that Sascha was the one to release it, and then I consider my mother's advice. "I had to make a quick decision," I mention instead.

Oliver laughs. "Cash, I know it was the boy. Just like I know a few other things about him. I went and saw him yesterday."

I wait, trying not to seem too eager. Oliver is a master of torture; if he knows I want this, he'll exploit it as best he can.

"He's at the Leadview Detention Facility," he informs me. I realize he doesn't know that I've been updated about Sascha's status already. "I had a good look at him while I was there, talked to him for a while. He seems to be doing just fine. A pretty face like that, I'd think he found himself a big, tough boyfriend to protect him... but then again, he did seem a little out of practice."

If I'm interpreting Oliver's taunts correctly, he fucked my slave. It's not the first time, but after the first time, I told Sascha it would be the last. What bothers me the most is that Sascha probably thought he had to agree to it.

"Sharing is the foundation of strong friendships," Oliver reminds me, as if we're talking about a vacation house or a luxury hov-car. "Anyway, he was very, very interested in getting me to come here and help you out. Such a caring boy, that one. I was going to back out at first, say I had no idea what you were doing, wash my hands of the whole mess. But I don't want to abandon such a good friend in a time of need. After all, you don't have anyone left."

I nod, pretending it's true. He seems to have no idea that my mother has contacted me, or Argova. I've grown popular in prison.

"I heard your lawyer bailed on you," Oliver mentions, a look of superiority on his face. "Seems you pick slaves better than lawyers. But I found you another one. She'll be a perfect addition to our team."

I frown at the thought of being on a "team" with Oliver. He is my business partner out of necessity, but he's talking like we're about to take on the world. Like he hasn't abandoned me here while exploiting my slave.

"I've already made legal arrangements. I'm just in prison. I'm not dead."

The look on his face reveals his surprise and annoyance. It doesn't make me trust him any less than I already do. Argova is a relative stranger, but that still puts him in a more trustworthy position than Oliver. Argova has never tortured me or mine.

"Well, if you think that's wise," Oliver says, clearly disapproving. "I assumed you needed my support."

I can't burn bridges with him just yet. He has our data, and he knows far too much about our project. "I do. I appreciate it, I just moved on this as quickly as possible. Your public support will be vital to making this work out, and I'll need someone to post bail."

Oliver shakes his head. "Try not to look like you hate me when you say it," he advises, standing up. "Sascha played his part far better.

I do look forward to seeing him again."

Always, Oliver has to get the last dig in, but I can see he's still in my corner. He can stay there until I'm finished with him.

I don't even have a chance to leave the visiting room before the guard announces that my lawyer has arrived. I just told Oliver I have arranged for my own lawyer; if this is one he hired, I won't risk speaking to her. An older woman comes in, eyeing me up as I sit there, cuffed.

"Hello Mr. Michaud," she says, sitting across from me and pulling out a tablet. "My name is Adele Edson."

"Hello."

She studies me for a moment. "Mr. Argova said you needed assistance. I rearranged my schedule to consult with you. Have I been misinformed?"

"No. I apologize. It's nice to meet you." I watch her, trying to figure out what she's doing, why she's interested. It's been so long that I've trusted anyone, and she's as much of a stranger as Argova.

"I've been in the industry since I started my career; I know all the players. Some, like Ms. Miller, are well-known. Others are a bit more behind the scenes. And then there's you. You took us all by surprise."

I nod, welcoming her introduction. I don't know her well enough to trust her, but in her line of work, I would imagine that trust is hard to come by.

"The data you released set off quite a movement. When this first broke, you were just a villain. But things have changed. You've become a household name, a popular topic. You're being set up as a victim of a corrupt system, the perfect symbol of change, of meeting the demands of the new generation. You're a martyr, a whistleblower."

"And what does that do for me?" I ask. I assume it's what's kept me alive so far, but I'm not sure whether I'm being kept alive for good, or for the right time to arise to execute me.

"Hopefully, it gets you out of prison and keeps you out," Edson suggests. "For now, the state wants you out of the way. You caught them by surprise; right as your story was moving from tabloids to reputable news venues, you were having your house raided, getting arrested. You couldn't have staged it more perfectly if you and Ms.

Miller had actually coordinated it in advance, except you've exposed her errors. I've run up against her before. She would never have approved of something so detrimental to her business."

I nod in agreement. It seems she does know my mother, or at least knows of her. "I'm assuming I've caused a national commotion."

"International," Edson corrects. "The Miller System's foreign supporters aren't too pleased."

As twisted as it is, it makes me smile. Sascha was smart to release the information like he did, when he did. It makes it look like Kristine tried to frame me for exposing her system. Of course, Sascha would have made it work perfectly. He makes everything work perfectly.

"So they want me out of the spotlight."

"Yes," Edson confirms. "Dampen your effect a little bit. Make everyone forget you. Not to mention give them time to gather any additional evidence against you. Which leaves me plenty of time to gather information about your case."

"They won't forget, though," I theorize. "This is big. As much as they're trying to keep it out of the media, it creeps in. I've heard the inmates here talking about it. Everyone has to know."

"Yes, and we'll make sure that they don't forget," Edson says, a smile spreading across her face.

"Publicity? That really requires me to be out of prison."

"It will happen," Edson promises. "Your bail hearing has been set for a few weeks from now. They'll set bail; the public won't stand for it if they don't. With what you've done already, there are riots, protests, unrest. The attention of the nation is focused on you—if your imprisonment continues, it will add fuel to that fire. With the data you released, you're being viewed as a hero, a revolutionary. With the raid and all, you responded like you did as an act of desperation. It fits, all of it, and it fits perfectly. I was quite happy when our mutual friend sent me your case."

I nod. This would be a career making case. But I know that's not enough for most professionals to take the risk that Edson is taking. Fighting the Miller System is stupid. Fighting the government that supports the Miller System is worse. It's why my own lawyer bailed. "I assume you want more than fame?"

Edson smiles. "You'll pay me a significant amount of money," she says. "And, if things go well, we'll be in a position to make other arrangements in the future."

She's talking about Argova. His cut, his demands that I consider working with him. She's not threatening, she's just moving forward as if it's assumed.

"And if I'm not interested in future arrangements?"

Edson lets out a slight laugh. "I'm certain you will be. You're a slaveowner, a businessman, a compliant citizen, perfectly attuned to the way our world works. You can't just dump a bunch of research and then retreat. Do you really think the state would let you do that?"

Honestly, I haven't known what to think. She's making it sound political, like the state might have a vested interest in my involvement. It makes sense; I know my mother's connections run deep, and they run high.

"I'm not really into politics," I start, trying to exit before this even gets off the ground.

"You are, now," Edson says. "Or at least, you're connected. Are you going to fight it, or are you going to make the best of it?"

I think of Argova's advice, his statement that we are all working toward the same goal. I think of my mother's backroom meetings with politicians, judges, sponsors. When she still wanted me to be her prodigal son, she let me attend some of those meetings, just a taste. I was too self-centered at the time to pay much attention back then, but I always knew she was in deep. The Miller System was a private company, so it was acceptable for outside interests to support it. Our proud nation, Nitorra, adopted the Miller System, which didn't interfere with that at all.

"I suppose I made that choice when I released the data." More accurately, when Sascha released the data. I never intended to get political with this.

The lawyer nods. "You put the truth above your own safety. Without that, they might have just locked you away without a thought, but this will be a trial heavily influenced by public opinion."

No matter what my intentions were when I set out with this research, it is political now. And it isn't about money, or research, or even changing the face of the Demoted system. It's about keeping myself and Sascha safe. The only way we can even try to come out of this unscathed is to go with it, full force, to play our roles like wanted this all along. And we have to pretend that we're doing it for the sake of the Demoted system, for the sake of the nation.

"We can use that," It's what I've been doing already, building my image, buying Sascha, attending the right events. I just need to make it a lot more public.

"Yes we can. And we'll need to. We need to make you more of an asset than a threat."

Chapter 8

Retrieved

A week after his visitor arrived, Sy has interviewed a few men to take care of me, and I feel the impending threat of his absence looming. I try not to pout, because he is helping me, but I can't stand the thought of being here without him. I can't even think of what his penalties will be for keeping my secrets, but I know. When I ask him about it, he just shakes his head, changing the subject. He is determined to protect me, even from that.

Bulldog interrupts my sadness, and he doesn't sound too pleased. "Pretty boy, get your ass over here!" he snaps. "Make it quick."

I glance at Sy before getting up, and we walk over to our least favorite guard together.

Bulldog gives Sy a shove. "Fuck off, mountain man, the kid can come with me."

Lanza joins us. "Syrus, you come with me. I have something to talk to you about."

Lanza takes Sy in one direction, and I am taken by Bulldog in the other. He leads me out of the locked area, a door that I haven't gone through since I was brought here, just over five weeks ago. Five weeks and two days, to be exact. I grow increasingly nervous as we walk.

"Sascha."

Everything in my world collides and collapses. The hopes and dreams and fantasies that my master would come and rescue me—all of a sudden, it all comes true, and Cash is standing there, looking almost exactly as he did when I last saw him on Kristine Miller's tablet being arrested. He's wearing the same outfit, even. His hair is longer, and he looks exhausted, but it's my master.

I go to run toward him, but am held back by Bulldog's death grip. I struggle, desperate to get back to Cash.

"If you so much as scratch him I will have your job and ruin any hopes of happiness you've ever entertained."

Cash doesn't even raise his voice to make the threat, and somehow that makes him even more threatening. I shiver, forgetting how intimidating the man can be. I stare at him in awe.

He strides toward us, his somewhat disheveled appearance still managing to look sort of regal, especially in comparison to my jumpsuit or Bulldog's uniform. His outfit is wrinkled, courtesy of a few months in storage, and the unruly, overgrown hairstyle gives him a playful edge. I hope I get the chance to play with it before he cuts it back to his typical orderly style.

He glares at the officer's arm as if it's a separate tool, not part of a human, and certainly not something that should be touching his slave.

"Remove your hand from my property this instant," Cash growls, and the minute Bulldog complies, I run to him, pressing close.

I don't care if I look like a lost child in a shopping center, or a weak, pathetic slave who can't stand not touching his master. All I want to do is feel Cash wrap his arms around me and promise me that everything will be okay.

I may have spent a little too much time fantasizing about this moment in the past few weeks, because that is something that Cash would pretty much never do in public.

I'm surprised when he caresses my head for a few seconds, pulling me close before grabbing me firmly by both shoulders and pushing me away.

"Sascha, are you all right?" he asks, his expression intense.

God, I missed looking into those deep, dark eyes. The way they bore into me, demanding every part of me. The way his hands feel, his fingers, every part of his body that I know so well.

The way his face quickly goes from concerned to impatient when I become too lost in his eyes and hands and body to respond.

"Yes, master," I mumble.

"Did they hurt you?" he demands, severe. "Any of them?"

How do I answer that? They didn't, really. If Sy hadn't been there,

I would have been hurt, many times, by numerous people. He was using me — probably still is — but he's kept me as safe as possible. I've been terrified and cold and hungry and lonely, but that's not what Cash is asking.

Cash doesn't take his hands off me, but he glares in Bulldog's direction.

"I will need a private room to inspect my slave before signing any sort of release forms to bring him home," he demands, his tone as cold and condescending as if he were talking to a slave.

"We don't usually give private rooms like that," Bulldog complains.

"Did I ask what you usually do?" Cash snaps. "I told you, I will need a private room. Or should I assume there is a reason you would rather not let me look over my slave?"

Bulldog grumbles something, but he waves us toward one of the offices, similar to the ones that he and Lanza first terrified me in. He stands in the doorway, like he's going to watch.

"By 'private,' I mean without an audience," Cash snaps, glaring until the door closes and we are alone.

The relief makes me start to tremble. It always happens like this, all the fear and terror and anxiety just builds up until I'm safe. I try to fight it, because maybe I'm not safe, I'm still not home, maybe Cash just came to visit—

"Sascha, it's okay." Cash does have his arms around me now, just like I imagined it so many times. "It's okay. I'm sorry it took so long for me to come for you. I never thought it would have taken this long. Five goddamned weeks. I'm so sorry you had to go through this."

I lean into his arms, feeling his lips brush against my neck. I don't care that I'm wearing a jumpsuit that's on its second day of wear, I don't care that the soap here smells like chemicals, all I care about is that he's here with me, and he's not letting me go.

After a few moments, I feel my heart rate stabilize again, and Cash must notice that I've calmed down, because he turns me gently so I can look at him.

"Did they hurt you?" he demands again, softer this time.

"Not really," I manage to answer like a human being instead of a scared animal. "I was scared a lot, and I had to do things, but no.

Nobody hurt me."

Cash nods, even though he looks unhappy about it. "Sascha, didn't they feed you?"

I flush, aware of how much thinner I've grown. "I don't like the food here." I don't mention that I regularly passed half of my meals to Sy. I don't even know how to start telling Cash about him; he was my protector, but he's also a threat. I'm not sure how my master will react, and I'm even less sure if this room is secure enough to discuss such things.

"You damn well better put weight on when we go back home. That threat I made when I first bought you and you weren't eating still stands!"

I smile. It's a threat, and it's disgustingly smothering, but in a way I like being smothered. I like the fact that he's so worried about me that he feels the need to threaten me. "Yes, master," I reply, smiling at him. "I missed you, too."

Cash nods, then goes to the door and summons Bulldog back. "Bring me the paperwork and his belongings, please," he requests, slightly more civil now that he knows I haven't been harmed.

A few minutes later, some papers and a bag with my clothes in it are brought in. As he fills out the paperwork, I strip the jumpsuit off and change back into my clothes, shocked by how loose they really have become on me. I don't pay much attention to my body; when it's bared, I expect something unpleasant, or it's at night in the dark, or we're in the showers. Hell, the only time I've even gotten off since I've been here is the two or three times when Sy has jerked me off to appease some voyeuristic request. I barely recognize myself.

And then I realize that I might never see Sy again.

It's something I haven't considered, up until this point, because Sy was part of the detention facility. Not seeing Sy would mean that I had gone home, and every time I thought about going home, I was so happy that nothing else mattered. In my fantasies, Cash would come, swoop me away, and nothing else bad would ever happen again, ever.

But those were fantasies. This is real life, and suddenly, reality is hitting hard.

"Cash, there's something I have to ask you," I spit out, impulsive.

"What's that?" he asks, not bothering to look up from the paper-work.

"There's a slave here, another one who was detained..." How do I even describe what Sy is to me, what he's done for me? "He helped me out, Cash. He protected me, from the first day I got here."

"That was kind of him," Cash dismisses me, focusing on finishing the last page of paperwork. "Finish getting dressed, I'm not taking you home half-naked."

I struggle into my clothes, irritated by his attitude. "Can we take him with us?" I burst out.

Cash finally looks up at me. "Sascha, don't be ridiculous. I'm sure his master will come and claim him eventually."

"No he won't! He told me; his master forfeited rights, and he'll be sold, and he doesn't have the best background, and if he hadn't helped me I would have been raped and beaten and hurt every day! He helped me and he protected me and I can't just leave him here!"

My voice is rising and I don't care. I won't be ignored. This is important, and now that I know what I want, I'm going to go for it, consequences be damned.

"What, you want me to buy him?" Cash clarifies, looking less than happy about the situation.

I consider it for a moment. My master isn't easily swayed by emo-tional appeals, not even from me. "He knows more about the project than he probably should."

Cash narrows his eyes at me. He looks like he's putting something together, and he lowers his voice before speaking. "Is this slave con-nected to something bigger?"

I'm surprised that Cash has already made the connection; then again, if the Argova family is closely connected with Sy's master and his gang, it makes sense that they might have contacted Cash as well. Still, I don't want to say too much in here. I nod, confirming his sus-picions.

Cash gives me a suspicious look. I resent it, but then again, I've been talking about things that we don't generally talk about with oth-er people.

"I had to talk to someone! What I've been through in here, and Torenze came to visit me... he took care of me, Cash. When you weren't here, he was. We should keep him close. He can be useful to us, I promise."

Cash sighs. "All right. We don't need any more risks. I guess this is how I make the past month up to you."

"Thank you," I whisper, staying close as we walk out. Cash hands the papers over to where Bulldog and Lanza are standing.

"The other slave that Sascha was with when you were bringing him out—the bigger one?" Cash adds, casually. "I'd like to purchase him."

Just like that. So typical of Cash.

Lanza looks surprised for half a second, then he glances at me and a look of understanding crosses his face. "The courts haven't quite figured out what to do with him to settle the account his master built up. It could be another week or two before he's ready for sale."

I feel my heart drop, and I try to remind myself that it's okay, that Sy will be out soon, that Lanza will probably update him. I try to convince myself that the "associates" he mentioned won't really come in here and kill him once his bargaining chip is gone.

"Look into bypassing that, please," Cash requests. "Get it taken care of quickly and I'll pay any fees on the account as well as a finder's fee to you for arranging it. I'd like to bring him home with me tonight."

Lanza's eyes widen at the bribe. "Of course, sir, right away."

Cash and I are left standing there, and I look at him in awe. I missed his power, his ability to throw his funds around like they mean nothing. He smirks at me, leaning over to whisper in my ear.

"Miss me?"

I smile, leaning against him. "You have no idea." It's not just his money, or his power. When he's around, everything seems to go right. I feel like I have my other half back at my side again.

Chapter 9

Homecoming

We don't wait long. Lanza puts a rush on the process, and in less than thirty minutes, his com calls have revealed plenty of loopholes to close any open accounts and free Sy for purchase. I am elated. Lanza informs us that he is going to get Sy, and leaves Bulldog to fill out paperwork.

"What the hell do you want him for?" he asks, laughing. "I would have guessed you to be the type to stick with the pretty boys!"

"I saw him with my slave," Cash answers, much more friendly than I'd be. "I thought they looked quite nice together. I'd like to replicate that in other settings."

For as friendly as Cash is being, he comes off as rather creepy. He's eyeing me up, head to toe, and he has a lustful look on his face. "There are just so many more options with another prop."

Bulldog shuts his mouth as he prepares the rest of the sale quickly.

"He's got a history of violence," Bulldog points out. "Want cuffs to keep him in line?"

Cash hesitates for a fraction of a second, and I can tell that he wants to say no. Finally, he smiles. "You know, that would be much appreciated," he agrees. "I'll purchase a set of ankle and wrist cuffs, the connecting kind, please."

I want to protest, badly, but I can tell that Cash has some sort of motivation, so I shut my mouth. I've followed Sy's lead without arguing for weeks, following Cash comes back to me easily. I wait, silent, as Cash goes over the paperwork to facilitate the transfer of ownership. Suddenly, Sy is his. I can only hope Cash and Sy take it the right way.

Lanza leads Sy through the door, naked except for the cuffs. If he's shocked or embarrassed, he doesn't let on. He just stands there, naked and still.

"Does he not have clothing?" Cash asks, the picture of an offended aristocrat.

"Sorry, Mr. Michaud, his clothes were taken as evidence. I doubt we'll ever see them, the trial is still in progress."

Cash frowns, and then takes off his own jacket, striding over and placing it around Sy's shoulders. It's far too small for him, especially with his arms restrained.

"Well, at least he's not completely naked," Cash mutters. "Are we finished?"

"Yes, sir," Lanza replies, smiling more at me and Sy than at Cash. "Best of luck to you."

Cash barely grunts; apparently, he has decided to hate everyone here. Without another word, he heads out the door, leading us to the hov-car garage that connects to the building.

"I have a rental," Cash mutters, his tone sour. "It was the fastest way to get here. I can only imagine what the house looks like."

My eyes widen at the realization. "You haven't been home?"

Cash finds the rental, opening the back door for Sy. I get into the passenger seat, happy when Cash climbs into the driver's side next to me.

"Of course I haven't been home, Sascha, the first thing on my mind was getting you home."

I smile at him. It's nice to know he cares. I guess I do, in general, but he's not particularly good at showing it most days. It's this sort of thing where he really shines.

"Is everything taken care of?" I ask, suddenly realizing that I haven't bothered to inquire about his life at all. The fact that he's here tells me that everything is fine, at least until I'm settled enough to hear the details. I'll want all of them, but he knows that.

"For now, yes. There was a lot of interest in postponing any sort of legal actions so that I could be locked up for a while, regardless of innocence or guilt. They're still watching me closely. And the media has gone wild with this! Did you know that I have plans to bomb the national peace centers? Or that I've arranged an army of super-slaves to do my bidding?"

I can't help but laugh. It's ridiculous, and a part of me is looking forward to going home and looking through my tablet to see the tabloids. "Please tell me they've got some sort of satire cartoon of you?"

Cash glares at me, teasing for once. "They have plenty of satire cartoons of me. I hear one company is looking to license my image for a tablet cover and wristband."

I grin at the image of people sporting a little cartoon Cash on their tablets. "Did you think it would get this big?"

"Not at all." He shakes his head. "You really set things off, Sascha. I appreciate it—it probably saved both our asses—but there are repercussions to deal with. I have a lawyer, now. We have plans for how to make this work. There's so much I need to fill you in on. I've hired a security company to guard the house, and maybe it's good that I bought your friend—I could really use a bodyguard at this point."

Suddenly, I become aware that Sy is in the backseat, silent and still. How quickly I can forget the man who has made my life tolerable for the past few weeks.

Cash rummages in his pockets until he finds something, which he tosses at me carelessly. "Get those cuffs off him, would you? With the attention I've been getting, being spotted with an unrestrained monster like that would certainly draw criticism. I'm being criticized enough for being a revolutionary. I need to maintain an image that fits with and works with the existing system. Maybe I'll look into a shock collars for when we're out in public."

I sit there, keys in hand, mouth open. "What the hell?" I manage, appalled that he would even consider using one of those things on Sy. Has prison really changed my master that much?

He takes his eyes off the road for a minute to frown at me. "I'd deactivate it, Sascha. It would just be for appearances. They didn't lobotomize me, you know."

I breathe a sigh of relief.

"Get moving; the ugly one put the cuffs on far too tight."

I grin at his description of Bulldog and I crawl between the front seats, unable to stop myself from giggling as a light smack lands on my ass. God, I missed Cash.

I drop into the seat next to Sy and smile at him. He looks... exactly how he always looks. Calm, wary. I uncuff him quickly, frowning at the red marks where they pressed too tightly. I'd be whining and rubbing at them to ease the burn, but Sy just sits there, silent, waiting.

Cash hits the auto-drive button and adjusts the mirror so he can look back at us. "What's your name?" he asks, much more cordial than he was when he first bought me.

"Syrus, master." Sy is formal and stiff. It's strange to hear.

"Hello, Syrus," Cash says, nodding. "I hear you were responsible for protecting Sascha?"

"I did the best I could, master," Sy answers.

"Well, you must have done something right," Cash comments. "I read through your history—you've served as a bodyguard before?"

"Yes, master."

"Good," Cash nods. "Sascha can use some guarding."

I recognize the statement as one of Cash's terrible jokes; his humor is always off and a little offensive, but I grin anyway.

Sy just nods. "Yes, master."

"We need to stop for food, and I suppose you'll need some clothes, too," Cash observes. He makes a sudden turn into a parking lot, sending his auto-drive into a screeching fit as he overrides it carelessly. "Wait in the car. I might take Sascha in like that, but not you."

"As you wish, master." It's hard to tell, but I think I see the beginnings of a smile on the edge of Sy's lips.

We enter a superstore, the kind that Cash typically wouldn't be caught dead in, and we collect a variety of food, clothes, and even some personal care items. Cash looks at it all distastefully, but it's the fastest solution. Even his elitist tendencies seem to have some flexibility when necessary. He tosses the clothes to Sy the moment we reach the car, and Sy dresses himself quickly.

The security team is in place at the house, and it's chilling to see. They try not to be too obvious, but they aren't hiding. Uniformed guards stand at every corner of the house, and I'm certain there are some we haven't seen yet. The grass is overgrown and some debris litters our door—handwritten letters, bottles that must have been thrown from passing vehicles. It looks abandoned, save for the security.

"My maintenance crew quit once this hit the news," Cash comments. "It seems there was a bit of harassment going on."

Sy carries the bags without question. I am thrilled to be back home, looking around with surprise. Since the first time Cash brought me here, it has been immaculate, nearly unsettling in how empty and clean it is. Cash doesn't like a mess, and the house is big enough that all the expensive furniture and artwork barely begins to fill the space. Now, though, it's messy, torn apart by Kristine Miller's little raid. They've left the furniture unturned, cushions tossed around the room, drawer contents and emptied trash can mess littering the floor. On top of it all is a layer of dust; so unusual, it gives the whole house an eerie feel.

Cash nods at Sy to follow him, and Sy complies like the perfectly trained slave that he probably is. We make our way down the hallway, slightly cleaner than the rest of the house, and we arrive at one of the guest bedrooms. It's been looked through, obviously, but there was so little in it to begin with. I used to keep my bedroom messier when I was a kid, just some sheets on the floor and an overturned end table.

"This can be your room," Cash explains, depositing him in one of the spare rooms. "Bathroom's attached, you're free to shower, sleep, eat whatever's in the kitchen."

Sy nods. "Yes, master."

It's infuriating to see him so subdued.

"Now, I'm going to take Sascha and show him how much I missed him," Cash says, a smile spreading across his face. "I'm sure you understand—after all, you got to have him all to yourself for all this time."

Sy doesn't say anything, he just grins as Cash pulls me out the door.

Sascha and I don't even make it to the bedroom before I pin him against a wall, kissing him hard and deep and leaving him standing there with his eyes glazed and mouth hanging open. I've missed him so much; touching him is like coming back to a home I didn't realize I had.

"You have no idea how much I missed you," I whisper, my voice low as I grip his shoulders tightly, holding him in place.

He doesn't respond, he just clings to me.

"They wouldn't let me send letters or anything—they said detention facilities aren't 'equipped' to deal with such things," I tell him, repulsed. It still angers me that Sascha was forced to stay there so long. "My lawyer convinced me that it was too risky to try to bribe anyone. We set this whole plan in motion, and I couldn't be caught going outside the law to talk to you."

Sascha's face clearly shows his relief, and I wonder what he really thought. Did he think I actually left him there like a discarded piece of trash? Like his friend's master did?

I kiss him again, shoving us both through the door to our bedroom. I close it with a little more force than necessary, the slam echoing through the house. I hate that he ever thought I had abandoned him.

"I'm sorry, Sascha," I whisper, stripping his shirt off. "I'm so sorry I didn't have something arranged to take better care of you. It won't happen again."

"Thank you."

I've apologized to Sascha on only a few occasions but he has deserved it every time. I am ashamed of the way I've treated him in the past; even more, I'm horrified that I let him be detained. He goes above and beyond to protect me, to protect our project. As a slave, that shouldn't be his responsibility, but it is my responsibility to protect him. I should have had a backup plan in place before any of this ever started.

I start to make amends by stripping him naked and touching him all over. From the way he melts into my hands, I'm certain I'm on the right track.

Sascha takes a few steps back toward the bed, but I stop him, grabbing his hips roughly and smiling when he lets out a desperate gasp.

"Sascha, I've missed you, but there is no way I am letting you into my bed smelling like cheap soap and a detention facility," I caution, making him blush. As it is, the bed has been torn apart, sheets half-attached at the corners, the mattress and box spring thrown to the floor. I pull him close to bite at his neck before continuing. "And there is no way I want to figure out how to get the smell of prison out of my bed. It's bad enough I'm going to burn this suit—let's not take the bed down with it."

"I like your bed," Sascha mumbles, his eyes fixated on me with a huge smile plastered on his face. He stares into my eyes as he tugs at the buttons of my pants, jerking them down forcefully. I respond in kind, pulling him with me into the bathroom.

He makes quick work of my shirt while I start the shower; he's tearing it off, but I did say I was going to throw it out. We're naked and under the faucet in seconds.

Sascha makes a soft moaning noise as the water hits him. I'm startled for a minute, and then I pause, watching him as he luxuriates under the stream. I've been looking forward to my shower as well; the prison shower was lukewarm at best, but Sascha's enjoyment is enough to convince me to wait my turn. He presses the button that turns on the massager jets and arches his back as the water washes over him, closing his eyes and running his hands over his own body.

I give him a few moments before running my hands firmly over his body. He's mine. I want to reclaim him.

He pulls away, pressing his back against the wall of the shower. He gives me a guarded look and I retreat, letting my hands drop to my sides. This wasn't what I had expected.

He must notice how strongly his reaction affects me, because he rushes toward me, pressing himself into me, clinging tightly.

"Cash," he whimpers. "Please... I'm sorry."

I stay still for a minute, trying not to scare him further, but I can feel him growing tenser. Slowly, I run my hands over his head, down his back. I'm angry, but not at him.

"Please," he begs. "I want you to touch me!"

I want to believe him, but I know he'll lie to me if he thinks it's what I want. I also know that he'll be crushed if he thinks I'm rejecting him, even if it is for his own good.

I move carefully, trying to keep my face calm. I'm furious at the thought of someone hurting him, terrified that he doesn't want this anymore. More than anything, I don't want to push him too hard. I place a light hand on his chin and turn his head up to face me.

"What did they do to you that you pull away when I touch you?"

I ask, keeping my voice calm, but still unable to stop the murderous undertones. I had been told that Sascha was being kept safe. Had it been a relative term? "Who was it? Was it the guards? Was it that man you brought home? Tell me."

"Nobody did anything, Cash. The guards were professional when they touched me. The other slaves left me alone because Sy was protecting me. And Sy... he never enjoyed it. He touched me, yes, because it was expected, but he didn't enjoy it. It was clinical. An act. I just... I haven't been touched for real in so long, I didn't know what to do."

Some of the tension goes out of my body, and I allow my touch to become more firm again. When Sascha doesn't seem opposed, I pull him close, and he wraps his arms around me.

"Don't let me go," he begs. For the first time since I picked him up, he really seems afraid. "I didn't know when I'd ever see you again, ever feel your hands on me."

"Okay," I agree, still stroking my hands down his back. "You still want this, then? You still want me to touch you?"

"I want to feel you everywhere," he says, quietly, like he's embarrassed by it. "It's all I've wanted since the moment we were separated. I just... I need to take it slowly."

"Okay." I lean in, placing a kiss on his neck, and then I let him have some space. "Whatever you want."

He looks nervous, as if the three inches between us is a mile. We both get to washing ourselves, enjoying the comforts and privacy of our home. I was fortunate enough to enjoy private showers, but I doubt Sascha has been as lucky. I finish before him and lean against the back wall of the shower, admiring his body. He doesn't realize it at first, but once he does, he blushes.

"You're beautiful," I tell him, not moving an inch.

He looks torn between coming closer and staying where he is. I appreciate the view; the cascade of water highlights all his best features, and blush remaining on his face makes him look even more attractive. I stand, taking my weight off the wall, and raise an eyebrow at him. "Can I touch you, now?"

I'm careful of my tone. If he says "no," I really will back down, give him the space he needs, but I want him. He needs to know this, needs to know that he is still the one person I desire most in this world.

"Please," he whimpers, gazing at me.

I take a step closer, my arms coming up to grip his shoulders lightly, pinning him there with only the force of my will. "Please what?" I ask, smiling. I've asked him this question so many times, because he's so damned hard to read when he's scared.

"Please touch me," he whispers, leaning into me. "Fuck me. Do whatever you want with me, just do it now and don't hold back. I've missed you so much. I didn't know if you were really coming back for me. I thought you might have been charged with something, and maybe it would stick, and I'd be stuck there forever and if Sy left I would have been alone, and —"

I cut off his words with a harsh kiss, the kind that I know will leave his lips bruised and his cock aching. He struggles against me, fighting the very thing he wants, and I don't stop kissing him. When I first bought him, he spent months convincing me that he didn't want this; once I found out it was untrue, I discovered that it was far easier to just push through the fear with him. I grab a handful of his hair, holding him tight and kissing him until he stops struggling.

"I will always come for you, Sascha," I whisper, finally breaking the kiss but still holding him by his hair. "You're mine. That doesn't change."

He leans into my grip, moving his head just enough that I pull on his hair. I drop one hand down between us to grab at his cock, finding it hard. He gasps and rocks.

"Get back against that wall," I growl, pushing him playfully. "You'll need something to steady yourself."

He grins and starts to turn around. I grab him by the shoulders and slam his back against the wall instead.

"I didn't tell you to turn around," I tease, smiling at him to let him know I'm not angry.

Before Sascha figures out what's happening, I'm on my knees, gripping his legs roughly and taking his cock into my mouth. I feel his legs shake and I increase my efforts, working his cock fast and hard. Above me, Sascha is letting out a series of pleas and moans. I'm thrilled that I've taken him to this point so quickly. His hands rest on my head, playing with my hair. I'm so thrilled to have him back.

I bring him to orgasm quickly, and I can tell from the way he struggles and whimpers that he's not ready for it to end. I let an appreciative hum pass through my lips as he comes, increasing the sensation even further. Sascha slides down the wall, panting, and I rise to pull him under the showerhead again.

"Cash." He looks at me in amazement.

"You're welcome," I tease, shutting the water off and grabbing towels for us. Sascha stands there, shocked, and I dry him off before dragging him into the bedroom. I pause just long enough to yank the box spring and mattress back onto the frame before pushing him face down on the bed. He waits patiently, only the slightest bit of tension noticeable in his body.

Chapter 10

Reacquainted

Sascha yelps when I drip oil across his back, turning his head to look at me.

I grin, holding the bottle up, making him laugh. It's been so long since either of us has felt something as nice as the expensive oils and lotions that I have, and I want to treat him. I drip some more oil over him and start working it into his skin, tracing over the familiar body that I've missed so much. He is still for a moment, and then I see him clutching at the rumpled sheets, running his fingers over the expensive fabric.

I slide my way up his body, pressing down on him insistently. "Did you really miss me, Sascha, or did you just miss my bed?"

He laughs, a playful sound that I've longed to hear over the past few weeks.

"I missed everything about you," he confesses.

"Good." I assumed, but I'm pleased to hear him say it. I continue to rub oil over him, every part of me touching him. I kiss and bite around his neck, harder and harder, until he squirms underneath of me.

"I want to mark you," I tell him, unable to hide the desire I feel for him. "I want to see my marks on you for days."

"I'm yours," he says, too turned on by the idea to say anything more.

I start slowly, biting down where his neck meets his shoulder, increasing the pressure until he cries out underneath me. I know I'm hurting him, but I know it's the kind of pain he likes.

I add a matching bite on the other side, and somehow this one seems to hurt him more, maybe because he knows it's coming. Sascha writhes underneath me and whimpers. I don't stop, and when I've had my fill of marking up his neck, I trail my tongue down his back, tracing a line to his ass. He trembles, but the way he's breathing lets me know he's not scared, he's just excited.

I knead his ass with my hands, slowly spreading his cheeks and dipping my tongue inside. Sascha clutches at the sheets some more and moans for me. I hadn't made him come earlier, I'm certain he would be coming now.

I pull back after a few moments, and I caress his ass with my hands again. Sascha rocks back, seeking more contact, trying to press himself against me as much as possible.

"Can I mark you here?" I ask, my voice neutral. I'm careful not to be too demanding, giving him the space that he can't bring himself to ask for.

"Yes." He braces himself.

I slap his ass lightly with my hand.

"Like this," I whisper. "I want to see my handprints on your ass."

"Yes," he moans, rocking desperately against the mattress. "Please. Please, and then fuck me!"

A sharp slap makes him jerk and gasp. Sascha's head turns, his eyes fly open, and he whimpers a little. A bright, red handprint glows on the right side of his ass.

The look on his face is utter bliss.

"I'll fuck you when I'm good and ready, Sascha," I tell him calmly. After so long fantasizing about this, I feel like we have all the time in the world.

Another slap, this time to the left side. Sascha makes a high whining sound. He stills, and I can tell he's trying to be good, holding back from thrusting against the mattress.

I draw another whine from him as I place my hands on the burning handprints I just left on his ass. I squeeze them, hard, pleased when he whimpers and starts to struggle. I can't tell if he's struggling to get away or to get closer, but I'm certain he's enjoying it.

"I love leaving marks on you," I whisper, squeezing hard before letting go.

I leave Sascha gasping, and I pour some more oil onto my fingers, rubbing around his ass, demanding entrance. I can tell he's trying to relax, but the harder he tries, the worse it gets. I feel him tensing underneath of me. I prod more insistently; hoping his body will respond, but he tenses even more.

"Cash, please, I—"

"Sascha, I am going to fuck you," I hiss, keeping the pressure at his ass consistent. "Because neither one of us just waited five weeks to be stopped by a case of nerves. I am going to fuck you, and it is going to feel wonderful, and you're going to wonder why you were ever nervous to begin with."

I present the statements as facts, because I know that logic works better than anything to cut through his fear. I'll stop if he really wants me to, but I doubt that's what he wants. He enjoys it when I'm possessive, demanding, and I want to make him feel good. He doesn't reply, but he doesn't ask me to stop, either. He's nervous, but backing out now will only postpone the nerves. Slowly, I slip one finger inside, thrilled when I feel him clench down around it. Being even a tiny bit inside of him makes my cock throb.

"Good," I say, working my finger in and out while caressing his hip with my other hand. "I've thought about doing this so many times. How tight you'd be. How much I want you."

I'm turning him on, but I'm calming him as well. We have too much history to come apart from a few weeks of separation; we've both worked too hard to build this trust between us. I keep talking to him as I work my fingers inside of him, stretching him carefully, reacquainting his body with mine. I'm demanding, but I take my time. Any pain I cause him tonight is going to be intentional. I tell him how much I missed him, how worried I was, how tight he is, the fantasies I had about him in prison. I doubt he hears most of it; he's more attuned to the sound of my voice than the words that accompany it. His body finally cooperates, relaxing to the point that I can fuck his ass hard and fast with my fingers, rubbing up and down his body with the other hand.

"Turn over," I insist, tugging on his arm until he moves. "I want to see your face when I fuck you."

He shudders as I flip him, rotating him around on my fingers. He reacts even more desperately as I position myself, slide my fingers out of his body, and replace them with the head of my cock. I wait, letting him adjust.

"Fuck me," he begs, staring into my eyes.

I enter him slowly, savoring each moment as his tightness surrounds me. I feel his muscles tense, squeezing down on my cock as he grows more excited. I watch as he struggles not to twist or jerk and pull away like he does sometimes. He still scares easily, and he pulls away from what feels good, like it will overwhelm him.

But I am set on overwhelming Sascha. As I slide into him, I grab his cock, stroking and jerking it in the ways I knows he loves, making him cry out and clutch at my arms. I could come immediately from his reaction but I want to keep fucking him for hours, to make up for all the lost time. I need to pace myself, and from the looks of it, Sascha could use a little help with the pacing as well.

Once I'm completely inside of him, I pause, let go of his cock, let him calm down for a moment. He whines, but I can tell he needs it. I wait until he relaxes before I start to move, pumping in and out of him slowly. Sascha tries to move underneath of me, and I pin him forcefully by the shoulders, looking at him with a dangerous expression.

"Don't move," I order, staring into his eyes as I fuck him hard and slowly. "All you're going to do right now is lie there and feel it."

Sascha whimpers. With no pressure or ability to move, he's left with nothing to do but feel it. I thrust deep, feeling his muscles clench tight around me. I go slowly for a while, letting him catch his breath, then fast, hard, hard enough to bring tears to his eyes. I'm still holding him down, but he brings his hands up to clutch at my arms.

I go slow again, working in and out of him more carefully. He cries out, tries to squirm, but I push him tighter to the bed. If he really wanted to come, he could have when I was pounding him; now that I'm going slowly, he's left begging. I love taking him to this place.

After a while, I speed up again, my thrusts rocking Sascha and the bed underneath us. I feel him break out in a sweat and he starts to squirm. I meet his efforts by pinning him harder, leaning over him, and kissing him brutally. With everything I'm doing to him, he still struggles to kiss me back, but I won't have it. I bring one arm down across his collarbone, not quite choking him, but holding him exactly where I want him. He complies, letting me take him with his tongue just like I'm taking him with my cock. Exactly how I want him.

My arms start to shake from the pressure and I slow down again, leaning back. I can see the outlines of bruises forming on his shoulders and around his neck. They highlight his beauty.

Still inside of Sascha, I lean back, pulling him with me. Holding him close, I roll onto my back, pulling him on top of me. Sascha gasps as I slide deeper inside of him.

"Ride me," I order, taking his cock into my hand. "Ride me hard, and don't stop until I tell you to."

"Fuck," he breathes, rocking slowly on my cock. It feels so good, and I know he's got to be getting sore. He keeps moving slowly until I become impatient, thrusting my hips up at him, jabbing into him and making him cry out.

"I said ride me, Sascha, not shiver on top of me," I challenge. Sascha takes the bait.

He rides me, harder and harder. I can see his legs shaking as he does. He clenches his teeth, trying to focus as he works himself on top of me. I tighten my grip on his cock and start working it with renewed vigor, pleased when he cries out again.

"Jesus, Cash," he moans, bouncing up and down on top of me. "Please, I want to come."

I agree, smiling at him. "Another minute, and then you can come."

Sascha moans. I love making him wait, making him beg. Every second that I make him hold off, his ecstasy seems to multiply. I don't watch a clock, but I do watch his body, and when he's started to plead and beg incoherently, I smile at him and give my order.

"Come for me, but keep going." I try to keep my voice quiet, but the demand comes through and the way he shudders lets me know Sascha is perfectly aware of it. "Come, then ride me until I finish."

Sascha whimpers. He knows this game very well. I overstimulate him, then keep fucking him, enjoying the way he suffers for me. It turns him on as well, and he comes a moment later, gripping tight around my cock and thrusting into my hands. He slows for a moment and I know he's desperate to wind down and relax, but that's not part of our game. I thrust into his ass, sharply, roughly, reminding him that we're not finished.

He gasps, and I reluctantly let go of his cock, trailing the line of come between us. I love touching him, but it's too much right now. I give him this reprieve, and he works my cock with his ass, tightening his muscles with precision. I reach my hands around, clutching at the spots where I left handprints on his ass earlier. He tenses with the pain and I jerk him down on my cock, holding him there.

Sascha stops moving, but I feel myself coming inside of him just seconds later. I've claimed him again, and I dig my fingers into his skin, reveling in the feeling. After a few seconds, I lift Sascha by his hips, pulling him off my cock, smiling as he lets out a deep breath. I pull him forward to lie on my chest, shaking and panting.

God, I missed him.

Chapter 11
Introductions

Cash and I stay like wrapped up in each other for what seems like forever, pressed together, damp and dirty and so blissfully happy. I close my eyes and listen to his heartbeat, strong and familiar. I missed that sound, just like I missed the pattern of his breath, the way he trails his hand across my back and over my head in just that way that reminds me again how deeply I belong to him.

There are other matters to attend to, though, and I smile at Cash, getting up out of bed and shocking myself when I catch sight of the bruises on my chest and shoulders. I can only imagine that my neck looks the same, and a quick peek back at my ass indicates that his handprints are going to stay a while as well.

"I may have gotten a bit carried away," Cash admits, standing next to me and kissing lightly along the bruises on my chest.

"I loved it and so did you," I point out, shuddering as he touches me. Every inch of my body seems intent on responding to him.

"We should go see how your friend is doing." He pauses, giving me a curious look. "What is your relationship with him?"

I blush. "Sy kind of claimed me as his own... kept me safe, kept the others away from me, provided me some protection against the guards. We kept it as simple as possible, but there was a sort of sexual thing to it."

Cash just waits. I start to grow nervous, wondering what his response will be when he hears everything I've done.

"It was what I had to do to stay safe," I remind him.

"I know."

Cash goes quiet for a few more minutes while he cleans up and puts some clothes on. I busy myself with dressing myself and putting the sheets and blankets back on the bed properly, unable to look at him. After what seems like forever, he comes to me and turns me to face him.

"Did he tell you he was working with a crime organization?"

I'm startled, but not really surprised. "Yes. He told me. He protected me for a reason. His master is part of a street gang, the 27th Street Gang, and they're trying to impress a larger group. This group, they're interested in you. I would have told you sooner, but I didn't know if we were safe at the detention facility."

"The Argova family," Cash supplies. "I met with one of them. The set me up with the lawyer who facilitated my release. They've made it very clear that they want to start a 'relationship' with me."

I nod. It matches what Sy told me. "Sy didn't tell them anything," I insist. I can tell Cash doesn't believe me, but he's not saying I'm lying, either. It's Sy that he doubts, the unknown slave who has ties to multiple criminal organizations. I understand his suspicions.

"Did he fuck you?"

It's not an accusation. He's asking honestly, and his face is blank. He may as well be asking whether they let us play table tennis. But it's the calm that worries me.

"No," I assure him, keeping as much conviction in my voice as humanly possible. "Never. He could have, but he didn't."

Do I tell him more? Do I tell him what we did do, how he pretended to fuck me, how he denied himself over and over again? Do I tell him how he got me off when he needed to, how I gave him head when I needed to, but only to put on a show? Do I tell him how Sy offered to get me off, to let me fuck him to get even?

Do I tell my master how I felt like I would be betraying him by taking Sy up on his offer?

"Good," Cash answers, kissing me lightly.

The questions and answers are avoided for a little longer.

"Let's go eat," he suggests, playfully poking at my stomach. "You're far too thin. I'll order food. The kitchen will need to be thoroughly cleaned, but go get us some drinks while we wait."

"Yes, master," I answer playfully. We get dressed and I head to the kitchen, leaving Cash to find a working tablet to order food from.

I survey the damage; the kitchen has been as worked over as thoroughly as the rest of the house, food tossed from the pantry without care. Even the frozen food has been searched through, although most of the cold content seems to have been tossed back inside, however carelessly.

I pull a few sodas from the fridge, covering my nose at the smell of whatever is fermenting in there. A quiet cough catches my attention and I turn, expecting to see Cash.

Sy is standing there, looking stiff and uncomfortable, wearing the clothes Cash and I bought while we were out.

"The master asked me to help with whatever you needed," he says, quiet.

I realize I've never seen him in anything other than the detention facility jumpsuit. He's shaved more closely, trimmed his hair, even. I wonder if he heard the ruckus Cash and I made with our fucking, and what he thought of it, or if he thought of it at all.

"He ordered food for me," Sy mentions, surprised. "I saw the order screen—I think he spent more money on dinner for me than my last master spent feeding me the whole time he owned me."

I smile, because I'm pretty sure it's supposed to be a joke. "He'll do that," I agree. "He has plenty of funds to cover it. He's generous, and he's nice. Well, for the most part. I mean, he's nice to me. I think he'll probably be nice to you. He can be strict, but not mean about it, and once you get to know him... he comes off kind of cold, but you'll see, when he warms up, he's really a good guy. I think you'll be happy here, at least, you'll be all right...."

I'm babbling and I can't stop. Bringing him home seemed to be the best idea, but now that he's here, I wonder if I assumed too much, if I interfered where I wasn't welcome. "Sy, I'm sorry if I went too far, but I didn't want to leave you there."

He smiles at me. "It's okay, Sascha," he says, ever calm. "I was surprised. Thank you."

I relax, glad that he doesn't hate me.

"I never thought that when I helped a pretty boy, he'd be my ticket to the good life," he muses. "I just wanted to see you safe."

"I did too." At the detention facility, he protected me. Now that the tables are turned, I want to do my part.

"He hurts you," Sy says quietly, looking at the bruises that I realize are visible around the collar of my shirt. He looks distressed, and I can tell that he's itching to protect me, to intervene, but he can't, not here.

"It's not like that," I rush to correct him. Before he gets the wrong idea, before he gives me that look when Cash is watching. "It's just love bites. I told him he could."

"I heard him hitting you and I heard you screaming," he points out.

Damn it. I was hoping to postpone this conversation indefinitely, but who knew the walls were so thin? "Look, Sy, I..." I struggle with the phrasing. "I like it, all right? I like him to hurt me in bed. I kind of need the pain to get off. He's never... not for a really long time has he ever hurt me in ways that I didn't want. And he'll stop if I ask him to. Please, just trust me on this."

Sy nods, looking doubtful but slightly relieved. He glances back, a little anxious. "We should probably get back, don't want to keep him waiting."

"Cash is good at waiting," I assure him.

Sy says nothing, he just takes the items I give him and heads through the door.

Cash sits in the dining room with his tablet. The table has been righted and the chairs replaced, but debris surrounds him. I assume he had Sy deal with the furniture while he ordered, putting his strength to use. I can only imagine all the other things Cash has to take care of, but his first priority is feeding us. I drop down in my usual seat next to him, feeling as natural as ever until I realize that Sy is standing off to one edge of the room, looking out of place again.

I want to tell him to sit down, but should I? Would that really be my place? I don't think it would be, in fact, I think it would most definitely not be my place. I nudge Cash under the table instead.

Absently, he takes my hand, finishing whatever business he's attending to, and only then glancing up at me. I look at Sy, rather pointedly, until he gets my point.

"Ah," Cash sighs. "Syrus, come here. Have a seat."

Sy approaches slowly, sitting to my right, across from Cash. He doesn't look any less out of place.

"You may sit when we're alone," Cash says. "I'll expect you to be standing most of the time in public, since you're there as a bodyguard, not a pet. You won't need to kneel unless the circumstances are very unusual, and I'll tell you to do so then."

"Yes, master," Sy agrees, settling back into his chair.

There's a momentary pause, and I hope my master plans to use it to do something nice, maybe to reassure Sy that he's not going to be an absolute bastard.

No such luck.

"Did you fuck my boy?" he asks, glaring.

"Jesus Christ, Cash!" I protest, at the same time as Sy is calmly answering "No, master."

"You claimed him as your own? Kept everyone else away from him? And you never fucked him?"

"Stop it! I told you earlier—"

"Hush, Sascha." Cash raises an eyebrow at me, warning me.

I fume.

"No, master."

"What did you do with him?" Cash asks, his face cold.

Sy takes a breath before answering. "I simulated having sex with him, master. I rubbed against him and gave the impression that I was raping him. I used his mouth, and I brought him to orgasm with my hand. It was what I thought was best to keep him safe, and keep the others away from him."

Cash is still glaring, but he remains silent. He glances at me, both in search of verification, and with a possessive look in his eyes. He looks like he might grab me and throw me down on the table, prove that I'm his.

"Please, master," Sy interrupts, bowing his head deferentially in acknowledgement. "Sascha complied with what I did to him, but if he hadn't, I would have forced him. If you are displeased with the actions that occurred between us, I ask that you punish me. Don't punish Sascha; he didn't have a choice in the matter."

"You'd take punishment for him?" Cash asks, intrigued.

"He already has," I mutter, not sure whether to be more pissed off at Cash for being such a monster, or more pissed off at Sy for offering himself up in my place again. "He didn't do anything wrong!"

"Most masters would object more strongly to some random slave using their pet," Cash muses.

"This is bullshit!"

"Sascha, stop!" This time the warning and the hard look comes from Sy, and I stop for a moment.

"My god, you're loyal," my master observes.

"Yes, master," Sy answers, seemingly unruffled by the statement.

"And your ties to the Argova family?" Cash demands.

If Sy's surprised by the question, he doesn't show it. "The 27th Street Gang is a low-level associate of the Argova family. They've owned me for many years, and I know the 27s are interested in impressing Mr. Argova. I took an interest in Sascha because I wanted a bargaining chip. They were pleased that I was protecting him, but angry when I told them I had no information about him or you. There might be an order out to kill me, since I didn't comply with their request for information, or they might think I arranged for you to purchase me so I could continue my mission."

"Was that your plan?"

"I wasn't trying to plan my own death, but I didn't see a way to prevent it. If they wanted to kill me, they could have done it easily, either in Leadview or once I was sold. I didn't see an alternative. I had no idea Sascha would ask you to purchase me."

Cash glances from Sy to me, seemingly satisfied that I'm not manipulating him into anything.

"I can trust you to protect him."

"Yes, master." Sy hesitates before asking another question. "You've said that you want me to protect him—does that mean from you as well, master?"

Cash's face darkens. "Sascha does not need protection from me."

"I apologize, master, but on the off chance that he does, is that what you want from me?"

The glare progresses into a scowl. "It won't."

Sy keeps looking back, undeterred. "My loyalty stays with Sascha, master."

They are both so ridiculously possessive. In another context, it could be hot, but right now I'm just getting anxious. I know that Cash will lash out if he's pushed too far, and what's more, I know he's perfectly well within his rights to do so. I worry that Sy will end up hurt.

"Sascha belongs to me, Syrus," Cash reminds him, his voice cold and smooth and sharp. He places a hand on my leg: obvious, intentional. "He is invaluable in my business, very dear to me, and my companion in bed. You will not interfere with that in any way."

"No, master," Sy agrees. "I won't."

Cash nods, his face softening a little. His hand relaxes on my thigh. "Thank you. For protecting Sascha, and for your respect."

The doorbell rings, and Cash is already on his feet, leaving me and Sy both rather shocked. He couldn't have timed that more perfectly if he had tried.

"I'm sorry," I whisper, looking nervously at Sy and feeling terrible for bringing him into this. "He's not usually like this. I swear."

"I can tell," Sy smiles at me, filling me with a sense of relief that I had almost forgotten. "He's proving a point, showing me my place. There's worse ways he could do it. Don't you think I've been involved in enough power plays to know what's going on?"

I nod, still feeling awful. I feel responsible for them, for both of them, and yet I doubt I can make either of them act any differently.

Cash returns with our takeout orders and places them on the table, reaching into the bag to start dividing them up as if nothing is out of the ordinary.

Chapter 12
Loyalty

I know it's unfair to take out my frustrations on Sascha's friend, but his presence reminds me of my own inadequacy, and the fact that he admitted to using Sascha as a bargaining chip grates on me. I should have been the one protecting Sascha. I try to watch my tone, but I still need to figure what his larger motivations are, what role he plays in this.

"Do you go by Sy or Syrus?" I ask as we start to eat.

"Whichever you prefer, master," the big slave answers automatically.

I'm trying to be nicer, so I don't speak. I just set my fork down and glare at him. I eye him up, taking in the way he sits low in his chair, as if he can downplay his height and muscles, noticing the meticulous way he's trimmed his hair with only the most basic of grooming tools.

"Sy, master, that's what people usually call me," he corrects himself quickly. "But I don't mind Syrus."

I nod, pleased that he can at least answer when ordered. Sascha is stabbing at his food, looking nervously from me to Sy, like he's waiting to step between us if we get out of line. I hope he didn't expect me to warm to this stranger the same way I've warmed to him; Sascha is my exception. Sy holds a sort of rugged appeal, far more substantial and masculine than Sascha, but his looks are not enough to win my favor. The fact that he could probably pick me up like a child adds nothing to this assessment. Perhaps I could share Sascha's attraction once I stop viewing him as a threat.

"When were you Demoted?" I ask, breaking the silence. I could have found out from the slave records that the detention facility provided, but that would involve reading through them.

"Nearly twenty years, master."

"Were you always a part of organized crime?"

"No, master. Just the past twelve years. I became the property of the 27s after other more legitimate work. They've been associated with the Argova family for just a few years, moving their less legitimate merchandise. Before that, it was street drugs."

It's a long time to belong to criminals. It makes me nervous, especially when I don't know what he's told Sascha, or what Sascha's told him.

"Sascha is rather familiar with me," I point out. "He knows enough to refer to me properly in public, but at home, he's free to use my name. I suppose it's only fair that I extend the courtesy to you."

"As you wish, master," Sy answers, still formal.

"I assume you know who I am. You may call me Cashiel or Cash. You've been a slave long enough to judge the level of formality in public."

"Yes, sir." Sy nods, not missing a beat.

I'm starting to get frustrated with his instantaneous responses, but I realize he needs the rules laid out. "You don't need to respond to every statement. For someone as closed-mouth as you seem, you are certainly attentive to that; I can only imagine what was done to you to make it such an ingrained habit."

Sy doesn't respond this time, he just sets his jaw. I wonder what was done to him.

"I don't like being overly formal, but my public image is very important; more so now than ever. What has Sascha told you about our project?"

For the first time, he hesitates, glancing over at Sascha like he's trying to verify their story. His loyalty does stay with Sascha.

"I told him about all of it," Sascha confirms.

He tells me the details, all the things he's confessed to his new protector, the connection that Sy has with the street gang and the Argova family and how it kept him safe. I listen, trying not to let my irritation show. After all, I was spilling secrets to the same people. I return the favor, detailing my interactions with Emile Argova, the arrangement I made with my lawyer, and the visits from my mother and Oliver. Sascha is furious when he realizes that Oliver played him, but neither of us had the information we needed at the time.

I glance back at Sy. "I didn't just buy you to appease Sascha; I needed a bodyguard. I had no idea that you were the one protecting him. The Argova family is supposed to contact me; I'll see what I can arrange for you, then."

"Thank you, sir," Sy says.

"My views, my research puts me in a rather awkward position. A bodyguard is perfect. You provide real physical protection as well as appearance. Owning more slaves improves my image. If you step out of line in public, even the slightest bit, I will not hesitate to beat you until you bleed. Is that perfectly clear?"

"Yes, master," Sy nods.

I see Sascha flinch, but Sy sits calmly, eating his food with no sign of intimidation. I'm starting to gain a little respect for the man. "I encourage you to talk to Sascha about the way things are around here. You probably deserve better explanations, but I'm exhausted and starting to realize how much work I'll need to do to recover from the past few weeks. It doesn't put me in the best of moods."

Sy nods, as if it's a good enough excuse. Sascha is looking at me like I've just committed a crime.

"And Sascha, if you don't quit scowling at me I'm going to reach over there and shake you!" I snap.

He cowers away, still scowling. I'm frustrated, but I know this can't be easy for him. I reach toward him, startled when he flinches. The look of relief on his face when I merely take his hand lets me know how on edge he is, how much I'm scaring him.

"Sorry," I tell him, looking into his eyes. "I'm sure we'll all settle down in a few days."

Sascha nods, relaxing a little, but he doesn't speak. I give his hand a gentle squeeze and we both pick at our food. Put us in threatening situations and we respond like we always do—Sascha withdraws and becomes terrified, I become a phenomenal asshole. What a pair. Sy is quietly observing us, eating quickly and efficiently. I almost envy him.

"Perhaps you should be protecting Sascha from me," I admit,

hoping to lighten the mood. Sy looks up at me, assessing my face before responding.

"You didn't hurt him," he says, but the implications are there. I didn't hurt him this time. If Sascha's told him about our project, he's likely told him about our relationship's rough start. A part of me wonders if Sy would really defend Sascha against me, against all his training. It's more than his organized crime connections would ever demand.

"Did you enjoy it?" I ask Sy. "What you did with Sascha. Touching him. Using him. Did you enjoy it?"

Sy considers it a moment before answering. "Sascha is very attractive, and I am very fond of him. But I would never actually enjoy doing something like that to another person against their will."

It's only a partial answer, but it tells me more about him than I even asked. He's smart enough to evade. I still don't trust him.

"Do you want to fuck him?" I ask, ignoring the outraged look on Sascha's face.

"That would be up to Sascha," Sy defers.

"That's not what I asked. Do you want to fuck to my slave?"

"I wouldn't do anything to Sascha if he didn't want me to," Sy insists, looking up now. There it is, a hint of defiance. It's nice to see him not so perfect for a minute.

"It doesn't matter what he wants!" I snap. "I asked you a very simple question, and I intend to hear you answer. Do you want to fuck Sascha or not?"

"You can threaten me and hurt me all you want, master, but you will not get me to do anything to Sascha against his will," Sy replies, his tone as hard and unmoving as his face. "And I would hope that you wouldn't want that either."

For all I know, this man is in my home to spy on me, to use me as a bargaining chip like he used Sascha. That, or he's genuinely interested in helping Sascha, and I'm harassing him for no other reason than a power play.

"You will answer my question or you will be replaced." The words tumble out of my mouth like an echo of bad history. I sound like my mother; worse, I know I lost the argument by stooping so low.

Sy glares at me, the challenge in his eye more evident now than ever. "Fine," he concedes. "Yes. I want to fuck him. I've thought about it more times than I'm proud to admit, and few things would make my day better than being inside of him. Happy? But know that you will never force me to rape him. I'd rather you beat me or sell me first."

"Thank you," I reply stiffly. I am ashamed of my behavior. "I just needed to know."

Sy doesn't reply, putting his newfound privilege of silence to use effectively.

"Do you guys want to piss on my leg?" Sascha snaps, giving us both a disgusted look. "Mark your territory a little further?"

I stare at Sascha in shock. The part of me that just channeled my mother is tempted to slap him, and I'm as repulsed by the urge as I was by the threat I made to Syrus. I look away, noticing that Sy looks chastised as well.

"I would never force Sascha to do something he didn't want to," I say quietly. "Perhaps I didn't make that clear enough. Despite the image I might give off, I really do care about him."

"I do too, sir," Sy agrees. "I apologize if I was out of line."

I shake my head. "I baited you. I'm not used to someone responding to that bait."

Sy nods. He doesn't properly accept, but I didn't properly apologize. It seems fair.

"I'm going to go get some sleep, now," I decide, giving up on my food. I glance at Sascha. "Join me when you're ready; I think you and Syrus probably need to talk without me for a while."

Sascha nods. A part of me wonders if he'll really join me tonight or not. I start to walk out of the room before glancing back at Sy. "Thank you for protecting him when I couldn't. I won't forget that."

"Yes, sir." Sy nods at me.

I feel some of the tension leaving my body when Cash leaves Sascha and me alone to talk.

"I'm sorry, Sascha," I begin. I've gotten so used to protecting the boy, I forgot how many consequences there could be for my actions now that we're back with his master. Our master.

He looks at me, confused.

"I didn't mean to cause trouble between the two of you," I say quietly. "Or... mark my territory. I know that I have no claim to you anymore."

"It's okay. I appreciate it, I just get nervous. I don't think it would end well if you challenged him."

"No, probably not."

"He would beat you, I think," Sascha says, like it's a death sentence. If he wasn't so worried about me, I'd laugh. "I doubt he'd sell you unless you really fucked up."

"It comes with the territory," I remind him. "Show me a slave who hasn't been beaten."

Sascha frowns, like he's offended. I think of his delicate pet status, the fact that Cashiel is clearly in love with him. "He's actually followed through with it with you, then?"

Sascha shrugs. "Yeah. Not like what he threatened to do to you, but he does come through on his threats."

I do laugh at that. "What, did he put you over his knee and spank you?"

Sascha blushes, and I think he tries to glare. He relationship with his master is obvious and Sascha's emotions are transparent; it's easy to see that he's embarrassed. "Something like that," he mumbles.

"Nothing wrong with that," I remind him, grinning. "I'd take that over the whipping he promised any day."

Sascha looks surprised, like I'd place pride over safety. He's clearly overrating me. "Survival, Sascha. Something you seem pretty terrible at understanding. I'd take humiliation over being made to bleed; I'd take submission over rebellion. I know when I won't win."

"That's why you backed down to Cash."

I nod. I understood Cash's point; he was testing me. Relenting, letting him win, it was his way of reestablishing his power over me, and over Sascha in a way. Sascha panicked, like he did that first day in the detention facility, but he and his master were the only ones out of control. I knew the whole time how it would end. I've learned to judge situations like that quickly and effectively, since my life more often than not depended on it. I don't begrudge either of them for lacking the same skills, but I'm glad I have them.

"I'd just feel guilty if you were in trouble because of me," Sascha says. "I mean, I brought you here. I thought I could trust Cash to be different. He's being cruel."

I smile, reassuring him. "He's doing what he feels is necessary. I wouldn't do much different if I was in his situation. I think he and I will come to an agreement more quickly than you think. We have the same goals, and he's offered to secure my protection. I'm not worried about being killed or sold for now. But tell me the slave stuff. The real insider perspective, now that you're not all starry-eyed at the very thought of him being near you."

Sascha smiles, the self-aware look he always gets when I call him out on his eccentricities. "He's irritable, but he's not likely to take it out on you too hard. He's a lot harsher with threats than follow-through, but don't challenge him. He'll win, and it will end badly for you. He hates it when you take the moral high ground, but he won't hurt you for doing so. He gets kind of taken down by that."

"He's ashamed of himself when he acts like a monster," I clarify. "Good to know."

"Seriously, don't fuck up in public," he emphasizes. "With the project, the case, it's a death sentence."

"No worries about that. I've played the big dumb bodyguard enough to know how to keep my mouth shut. I'm assuming he'll have the paperwork in order for me to lay hands on free people?"

Sascha looks surprised, and he shudders a little. He must realize the consequences that would occur if those protections aren't in place. "I'll make sure he does."

"I've been a bodyguard for almost twenty years, Sascha, I know how it works," I remind him lightly. "And I've had some pretty irritable masters before, too. I have a feeling I can handle myself with this one."

"That's a long time. Do you enjoy it?"

"It's an all right job for a slave." I can pretend that I'm doing something worthwhile, at least. "It wasn't what I wanted to be, but I guess it worked out. I sure lived a hell of a lot longer."

"What you wanted to be?" Sascha asks.

"I always thought I'd go military," I admit. It's not something I tell most people; it doesn't fit with my current status as a criminal. "Since I was a kid, I figured it would be the most noble thing to do. I could use my life to keep peace, follow orders, be a part of something bigger. And I hear that the Demoted in the military don't get treated too badly, none of the intimidation and brainwashing and stuff that happens outside. You die honorably, your family even gets special commendations. One of my brothers did, a few years before me. I always thought that's how I'd go."

"You planned to be Demoted?" Sascha's eyes are wide with shock.

I smile ruefully. "You were one of the bright ones. You know what percent is Demoted annually, right?"

"Approximately sixteen percent," he answers instantly. "It always stays the same, because anyone who's more than one standard deviation away from the year's — "

"Don't bother with the math," I cut him off. "One in six, they told us. Like if you held up six fingers and someone shot one of them off, that one was Demoted."

Sascha stares at me. I doubt he's ever heard it explained that way. When he nods, I continue. "Where I grew up, it was ninety percent."

Sascha still looks stunned. He thinks about it for a minute, then it dawns on him.

"My school boasted an eight percent Demoted rate," he admits. "Some of the best ones in the country claim to have less than one percent. The differences had to have been made up somewhere, the numbers can't lie."

"It's not that big a deal." Where I grew up, it wasn't the exception. It was inevitable. We thought of the best Demoted future instead of worrying about how many of our friends and family were being Demoted. "Where I come from, people have bigger families. They figure, you have a better shot at your one in ten. So, I hoped I would go military, but someone at the re-education center got a look at me and decided I would be much better off as a bodyguard. I have a 'look,' I guess. Scary and not unattractive, or so they say. I was never a pretty boy like you are, but when I was your age, I wasn't so bad, either."

"You're not unattractive now," Sascha says, trying not to blush. "Don't talk about yourself like you are."

"I wish I was," I reply. "Hell, I wish I had six eyes and a beak and scales. Although, that wouldn't have stopped most of them anyway, it wasn't about what I looked like. It never is, not really."

Sascha nods. He knows exactly what I'm talking about.

"And you went to a nice school and had a good chance and threw it all away for what? Drugs? Rebellion?" I ask. He's never told me that part of his story. "I hope you've gotten a little brighter since then."

"I swapped Assessments with my brother," Sascha admits. "I couldn't take the thought of him being Demoted. I thought I was helping him."

I'm surprised. I underestimated Sascha's compassion. I try not to let it show, but I'm certain I do. I consider his statement, that he thought he was helping. "Didn't work out?"

Sascha shakes his head. "He's got a wife, a kid, a lot of self-worth issues. He knows he shouldn't be there, and he knows what it cost me. And his wife is the devil. He tried to rescue me from Cash a couple months ago. It didn't go well. There's no place for me in his world; hell, there's no place for him in his world."

"I doubt you needed rescuing from Cashiel."

Sascha smiles. "Not usually."

"Your master really cares about you." It's obvious, from the worry to the possessiveness. It's a liability, but it's also their main advantage. Cashiel is the only one who doesn't underestimate Sascha.

"You should go to him," I tell him. "I could use some sleep as well."

"Isn't there anything else you want to know, anything else I can tell you?" Sascha says, hesitant. He looks guilty, like he owes me something.

"I'm sure we'll have plenty of opportunity to talk," I remind him. "Besides. I'm looking forward to trying out that bed again. It's been too long since I've been in a comfortable bed, and honestly, I like sleeping alone. Skinny little boys like you are all elbows, everywhere."

Sascha smiles. I said it to make him feel better, and he catches on, but that doesn't change the sentiment. When I stand, he follows, falling easily into the patterns we have established. We walk down the hall, coming to my bedroom quickly. Sascha is torn, and I turn away, hoping to let him go. He throws himself at me, wrapping his arms around my waist, and I turn to pull him in close. He's scared, but he needs to go back to his master. I doubt he's really afraid of Cashiel; from what I've seen, the two of them are hopelessly devoted to each other. But time away from someone can be a challenge, especially for a slave. Knowing Sascha, he's not thinking about how much Cash cares for him, he's probably too busy worrying about everything that might be. I hold him like that until he's ready to let go, and when he does, he looks up at me nervously.

"I'll be right here," I promise. "Thank you for bringing me home. I really do appreciate it."

"Thank you for everything you've done," he whispers. "I'll see you tomorrow."

"Good night, pretty boy," I tell him, stepping into the room and closing the door.

Chapter 13
Close Ties

I'm alone for the first time in weeks.

I take a few minutes to collect myself. Everything is happening so fast, and I've never really done well with change. I want to go back to Cash, but a part of me wants to rush in and stay with Sy, because he has grown familiar. While Cash and I fucked like crazy earlier, we didn't talk so much. A part of me is scared about what he'll say. I don't think he'd be upset at me for doing what I had to do with Sy, but his attitude tonight frightened me. I'm still a little angry with him, because of how he's treating Sy, and I don't know how we're going to deal with the threats in front of us. Cash is out of prison, that's a good thing, but the rest? I don't know if we can trust Torenze, or this new lawyer I have yet to meet, or even this Argova family, whoever they are. I don't want to be in the public eye more than I have to, and I certainly don't want ties to some criminal organization.

The detention facility was terrible, but was comforting in a way; there weren't important problems to deal with. Now, it seems like there are so many of them, and all I want to do is curl up and hide until they go away.

I consider going back to my old room and sleeping there. I'm sure it's as destroyed as the rest of the house. I haven't even looked at it yet, too busy with everything else, but I'm certain that my room would have been scrutinized as much as Cash's. It would probably be for the best to sleep there; I'm exhausted, confused. I need time to sleep, and I really need time by myself to process everything that's happened.

It's not that I don't want to talk to him. I just don't know where to start. I need a few hours to relax, to stop wondering whether I'm really home or whether I'm dreaming again. I need time to reconcile my feelings for Cash and Sy. But I know Cash would be worried, hurt. Sy was right, I do care about him, and I care about hurting him. Resigned, I make my way to the bedroom, half hoping that he's asleep when I get there.

My wishes never come true.

The light is off when I go in, but the street lights streaming in the window make my master's face instantly visible. I can see him staring up at the ceiling, pensive. I step into the room tentatively, almost waiting for something. After only a few seconds, Cash turns to me.

"Come to bed, Sascha." His voice is quiet, and despite the fact that the words indicate an order, I hear something that's almost a request. A hopeful one, at that.

I slip off my clothes and slide into bed next to him, trembling at the size of the bed, the high quality sheets, the pillows that are actually sturdy enough to accomplish something, the sensation of someone other than Sy bedding down with me for the night. I feel a hand on my hip and I freeze.

"Everything okay?" Cash asks. I can tell he's trying to keep the irritation out of his voice. "You know, if you're uncomfortable sleeping with me—"

"Please don't make me go!" I beg, clutching at his hand. It would be too much, I couldn't take that. Not tonight. I wasn't sure what I wanted, but now that I'm in bed with Cash, I know I don't want to be away from him again. I don't want to be alone. I do want to sleep with Cash, I just need time to adjust. I bite back tears as I cling to his hand, willing him not to send me away.

Cash sighs, reaching around with his other arm and pulling me close before I have a chance to fight him.

"Sascha, I won't make you go anywhere," he growls into my ear, holding me until I'm still before pushing me back just a little, just enough so he can look at me. "I just wanted to give you the option. If you want to sleep with me, I'd love it more than anything; but if you want to sleep alone, you may. Even if you want to get out of my bed and sleep with that hulking monster down the hall, I wouldn't stop you."

I breathe a little more easily with the reassurance and wriggle closer to him. "I want to stay here."

"Good, then it's not a problem," Cash says, exasperated. "Is Sy all settled in?"

Suddenly, I remember the other reason I was reluctant to come to bed, the shitty way that he treated Sy. "Yeah, no thanks to you."

I try to pretend that my words are threatening and forceful, even though I'm cuddled up with my master and loving the feeling of his skin touching mine.

Cash snorts. "And exactly what did I do that was so terrible?" He asks, mostly rhetorically. "Getting him out the detention facility? Feeding and clothing him? Offering to arrange for his continued existence and safety?"

"You intimidated him!" I protest, feeling the burn of righteous anger that I had earlier. I'd pull away to emphasize my point, but I'd rather stay cuddled up.

"Was he really intimidated? I didn't think anything could faze the man."

I'm about to say yes, but then I stop and think about it, I was the only one upset by their exchange. "You were being intimidating," I amend.

Cash shrugs. "I'm his master."

I'm quiet, trying to put my thoughts into words. Sy dismissed me when I apologized for Cash, now Cash is dismissing me when I try to confront him. "He's not the only slave you own."

"I probably should have had most of that discussion with him in private," Cash relents. "There was no need to put you in the middle of it, and there was no need to have you witness it, either. It was petty of me, but I was tired, and I didn't want to send you away. Besides, you would have thrown a goddamned fit if I had asked you to leave me alone with him."

I would have. "So you wouldn't, like..." I can't finish, because I don't want to ask anything specific.

"I won't mistreat him, if that's what you're asking." Cash shifts me into a better position. "I wouldn't hesitate to punish him if I thought it was necessary, but I highly doubt that it will ever be necessary. Unlike you, he has quite a bit of restraint. And I wouldn't sell him over a petty moment of obstinacy, although I think it didn't hurt to remind him of that possibility. I know you, Sascha, I trust you, I can depend on you. He's a complete stranger. He's aligned with a criminal organization. I need to make it clear that it is my will that will be obeyed."

"I trust him," I mumble, pulling away a little.

Cash lets me go without a fight. "I know you do, and I don't doubt that I will come to share your faith in him, but it's a little much all at once."

"I just want everything back to normal," I manage.

"I'm working on it," Cash assures me. "And if it will really make you feel better, I'll apologize to Sy in the morning. I may have carried things a little too far, despite my best intentions. I've been rather defensive with the man since I met him."

I smile, cuddling up against him again. "Thank you, Cash."

We lie silently for a few minutes. "Why did you ask him if he wanted to fuck me?" I blurt out. I assumed it was just to shame Sy, to put him in a vulnerable position, but it doesn't make sense. It's so petty; even at his worst, Cash has never relied on outright humiliation.

Cash shrugs, cool as ever. "I'm trying to understand his motivation. I get that you're grateful that he helped you — I am, too — but he used you, and he's a marked man. I need to know that he isn't a threat. If he didn't know he was going home with you, and he didn't really fuck you, I don't understand why he was helping you."

"Maybe because he's a decent human being?" I wonder why Cash is trying so hard to find an ulterior motive.

"Perhaps," Cash says, doubtful. "Or, he's infatuated with you. Makes more sense in my mind."

I just nod. Let Cash assign his motives as he will. I trust Sy; that's good enough for me.

"Besides, I wasn't lying when I said you two made an attractive pair," Cash mentions. "Sy isn't really my type, but he has a certain appeal. It's not like I missed the way you look at him. I was exploring the possibility."

"You didn't ask me if I wanted to," I mention, not entirely sure of what that means.

"I knew you would tell me if you weren't interested," Cash dismisses me. "Syrus would see it as a power play; humiliation, perhaps, to make him admit that he desired you. If you didn't return the feelings, it would become a non-issue."

I'm glad he doesn't make me admit that I've thought about it. The thought turns me on, sending a shiver through my body. "Would you want to be there?"

Cash smiles. "I would love to watch someone else fucking you, perhaps while my cock is in your mouth. I've never suggested it, because I would never let another free person fuck you like that, and it's not like I'm about to borrow a slave. Besides, I would want to be in complete control. I know you're safe when I own both of you; someone who I don't own might be able to do things to you that I wouldn't approve of, and that wouldn't end well."

Cash is always so possessive.

"But the main thing is, I've never seen you so attracted to another person," Cash says. "I am a little jealous. There seems to be attraction there, and it seems to go both ways."

I grin, breathy with excitement. I've never had a threesome before, not with two other people I actually wanted to have sex with. Gang rapes don't count.

"It's up to him, mostly," Cash shrugs. "I know this will be a lot of adjustment, and I think he feels guilty about what he's done to you, he feels, without your permission."

Sy has told me about as much, and no matter how much I disagree with him or correct him, he still insists on acting like he forced me to do things.

"I didn't let him do anything, but I wanted to," I admit to Cash. "I wanted to take him up on his offers to give me head, to jerk me off... so many things."

Cash smiles. "Nothing wrong with that," he muses. "You're young. Healthy. Sexual appetite is something you don't need to worry about."

I blush at the strangely paternal comment, especially from a man not quite ten years my senior, a man I like to fuck as often as possible. It is nice to know, that he doesn't automatically assume it's because I'm a whore, some sort of sex-crazed fiend. No, he just says it's normal, and he says it so nonchalantly that I have to believe him.

"You really do like the idea," he comments, reaching down to stroke my cock, noticing it's grown hard during our conversation.

I arch into his touch, needing more. It wasn't how I planned to end the night, but I welcome it.

He doesn't have sex with me so much as drag an orgasm from my body, working my cock with one hand while using the other to pull me on top of him by my hair, only to pull me down to kiss him. It's a position I like, and I know he likes it, and I feel myself getting close quickly, thrusting harder into his hand, jerking my head so that he pulls harder at my hair. I work myself into his fist, trying to finish.

"Stop." Cash sits up and pushes me down on my back.

I whine at him with need and impatience, and get rewarded with a light smack to the inside of my leg, pushing me even closer to the edge.

Leaning forward, he puts his head between my legs and takes my cock into his throat, sucking hard and intensely. Within seconds, I feel myself come, and I whimper as I clutch the bedspread. He finishes me off with his tongue, licking a slow trail back up to my lips to kiss me again.

I lie there exhausted. A part of me feels like I should reciprocate, half from desire, half from courtesy.

"I can... if you want." I don't even know what to suggest.

"You're tired," he shakes his head at me. "You can wake me up like that if you really want to, but right now, I just want to sleep with you. Don't feel pressured."

I cuddle into his arms, and even though I do feel his cock poking hard into my leg, he doesn't move to do anything about it, and neither do I. Eventually, I feel myself drifting off to sleep, thinking of just how fucking lucky I am.

Chapter 14
Rekindling Relationships

I awaken the next morning with Sascha curled tight around me, his arms and legs intertwined with mine and his face pressed firmly against my chest. I wonder if Sy has been subject to this sort of affection over the past few weeks, or if Sascha has saved it all for me. I run my hand down his back, stroking over the soft skin, and I think of how glad I am to have him back. I need to start making arrangements immediately; ensure that he is never subject to that again.

As I plan, I hear the insistent beeping of a com call, and the display lets me know that Oliver is calling. As much as I am reluctant to talk to him, I can't very well ignore my business partner.

"Good morning," I answer, trying to stay neutral. I don't know what sort of deal he made with Sascha; with everything else going on, we didn't get a chance to talk about that yesterday.

"Cashiel," he replies, sounding pleased. "I trust you're safe at home?"

"Yes. Thank you for posting bail. I'll arrange to pay you back as soon as I can," I answer, giving him the credit he deserves. "I appreciate it, Oliver."

"Never a problem. I thought I might stop by and visit. I can bring some food by—you know what, I'll even bring my new toy along. I know, you never want to play, but he cleans well, and I saw what was done to your home. Kristine and her little raid. Looks like it's backfiring against her, now! Fluffy can get your place back in order while we talk business."

I cringe at the name he's assigned his newest slave. It's bad enough that he tortures them in private; I wish he'd at least have the courtesy to spare me the details. "That would be great, Oliver," I lie. I don't want him around. I know he's going to place demands on me in exchange for his help. "I just woke up, I'll need a little time —"

"See you in an hour," Oliver cuts me off. "And make sure Sascha's there. We can discuss the arrangement I made with him as well."

He hangs up, leaving me frustrated. I don't want him anywhere near Sascha. I glance down, wishing I could just let him sleep peacefully, but I need him awake. I give his shoulder a gentle shake, prompting him to open his eyes and look at me hopefully.

"Just a little longer?" He slides his legs up and down against mine. "I miss waking up with you."

I lean over and kiss him, pulling him up to sit. I want to linger, but I'd rather have time to prepare. I break off the kiss and go to my feet. "Oliver's coming over," I tell him, watching as his face falls. "He's bringing one of his slaves to clean the place up, breakfast for us to eat, and he's going to fill us in on what's been happening."

Sascha nods, getting out of bed.

"He also wants to discuss the deal you made with him."

When I mention it, Sascha goes still, pale. He's scared, and I hate that I ever brought him around Oliver Torenze.

"Sascha, what did you agree to?"

He doesn't look at me, he just goes to his space in my closet and starts digging through clothes.

"It's not a big deal," he says, his words muffled. "I saw him in the detention facility. I said I'd visit him again. He said he'd give me some time to readjust."

"Visit him... as in what?"

Sascha is quiet again, picking out clothes before turning around. "Like last time," he says, quiet. "I'm sure he wants to fuck me, torture me, humiliate me. It's fine, Cash, I can handle it. I've done it before."

I beckon him close, putting my arms around him. "You don't have to do this, Sascha. We can find another way."

He starts shaking. "I do. And I agreed to do it every other month."

"What?" I demand, furious. "Absolutely not. I'll cut ties with him. Fuck his support, fuck his money, we don't need —"

"I told him about Abriel," Sascha says, stopping me mid-sentence.

"He needed some sort of leverage; he knew we'd back out. I gave him what he wanted."

I sigh. "Christ, Sascha. You didn't need to do that."

"I thought I did," he reminds me. "I didn't know you had spoken to anyone else; from the way he made it sound, you were in there alone, cut off from everyone. I needed you. I wanted you out. It was my decision. I chose your safety over Abriel's."

He chose my safety over his own, too, and he's acting like I won't notice it. I run my hand through his hair. "You are the most amazing person I've ever met," I tell him. "Thank you."

He looks up at me, nervous. "You're not mad?"

I shake my head. "Not at you. I appreciate you so much. And I'll do whatever I can to keep you as safe as possible."

We get dressed quickly, collecting Syrus from his room as we pass. He's awake, neatly dressed, and looking ready to take on anything.

"Oliver Torenze is coming over in a few minutes," I inform him. "He's the one who bailed me out of prison, and he's one of the few people I hate anywhere near as much as I hate my mother. I assume you're familiar with him, with his history with me and Sascha and my mother?"

"Yes, sir," Sy replies. "I know his role in the industry as well. His association with the Argova family and with you. That was what drew me to Sascha."

At least Oliver has been good for one thing. I fill Sy in quickly, giving him a little more on the long history behind me and Oliver, the part that his industry ties probably don't cover, the part where he borrowed and tortured Sascha a few months ago. I don't give him all the details about that; I'll let Sascha discuss it if he wants to. To his credit, Sy listens attentively, and if it really is a look of rage that I see in his eyes when I describe the condition he left Sascha in last time, he hides it before I can really tell. I'm uncomfortable telling someone else this much about my life and my business arrangements, but if Sascha has already told him almost everything, the best plan is to fill him in completely.

"What would you like me to do when he visits today, master?" he asks, once I'm finished.

"Official business. You're there as my bodyguard. Act the part."

Sy nods, and we make our way to the dining room. Sascha and I sit while Sy stands, ever attentive. He really does play his role well.

Oliver arrives shortly, trailed by a young male slave with a round baby face and a slight limp. The rate at which he goes through slaves is appalling.

He sets the boy to cleaning my house as if he owns it, ordering him to pick up and stack anything neatly, to dust, to clean toilets and bathrooms, and to finish in the kitchen. The slave seems grateful for the task, and Oliver seems jovial as he joins Sascha and me at the table. Syrus stands a few feet away, even more quiet and professional than usual. It's a nice touch.

"Where'd you get that one?" Oliver asks, eyeing up Syrus. "Doesn't match your set."

"Souvenir from the detention facility," I answer, not bothering to explain. I'm pleased when he doesn't seem to recognize my newest acquisition. "With the state of things, I thought a bodyguard might be necessary."

Oliver nods, then addresses Sy directly. "All your paperwork in order, big boy? A bodyguard needs to protect its master. Something like you even looks at a free man without the proper documentation and you'll be put down."

"You'll need to ask my master about that, sir," Sy replies, a bored look on his face. But I can see him watching everything, positioning himself between me and Sascha.

"I haven't gotten it taken care of yet, no," I answer. "Before we're out in public I will."

"No point having a guard dog that can't bite," Oliver says before turning his attention to Sascha. "Nice to see you made it out of that detention facility in one piece."

Sascha nods and waits. I'm surprised that he's joined us at the table; he comes looking like a free man prepared to do business. Then again, he and Oliver already did business behind my back. I'm certain he and Oliver both know what messages they're sending to one another.

"Where are we with business?" I ask, hoping to direct the conversation away from my slaves. "Have you heard anything new? I spoke to my lawyer at the bail hearing, she said things were about the same."

Oliver huffs. "I haven't heard a word from the woman. Not sure where you found her, anyway. I don't appreciate casting my support for you and getting nothing in return."

"I'm sorry, she was quite busy getting me out of prison," I remind him. Actually, I asked her to avoid speaking with Oliver more than necessary. He wavered when he should have been supporting me. "Besides, she came highly recommended."

"What would you know about that?" Oliver challenges. "For all anyone else is supposed to know you're an overpaid financial advisor. It's not like you have any contacts. That's what you needed me for."

"I do still need you, Oliver," I pacify him. "But prison is a great way to meet people with experience in legal matters. The lawyer knows about the progress of my research, the start of our partnership, but she's not directly involved. Trust me, I'm in good hands."

I like the idea of keeping Oliver out of this process, and Edson had agreed when I suggested it to her. Oliver might have been my connection to the Argova family, but it's not him they want to build a relationship with.

"I've taken over while you were gone," Oliver informs me. "I've been coordinating with the data analyzer you hired. He was a little spooked at first, but I convinced him that he was a valuable part of Michaud & Torenze. We need to get these results out before the state does whatever they're going to do with the data. The preliminary results that Sascha released are strong, but too obviously biased. And if it gets out that you had a slave do it? You'll lose all credibility."

I nod. It wasn't a risk we had anticipated; the results were supposed to be in well before the information became public. My mother ruined that. "Do you know if they're moving on it? I don't think they even got all of the data. There was so little of it stored here, they probably didn't find much when they raided the place."

Oliver smiles. "Nobody thought to investigate what I'm holding for you. Your information is safe with me, my boy. As soon as it's analyzed, we can release it to investors. Get the right sorts of people behind this project."

In spite of everything Oliver has done to me and Sascha, I'm relieved to have him on our side. My new friends might have connections, but I know Oliver. In a strange way, I trust him, at least with business.

"And Kristine Miller?" Sascha asks, surprising both me and Oliver. "How does she play into all of this? Has she been a problem?"

"She's always a problem," Oliver reminds us. "She's doing everything she can to interfere. For every news venue that tries to release the information, she's finding some way to shut them down, to accuse them of spreading lies. She's got people watching us—you, me, anyone we're associated with. I doubt she'll try anything as direct as what she did last time, but she's playing her game well. The Miller System won't go down without a fight. We need to destroy her. Take her down. Find anything we can to discredit her. Sascha, I know you're skilled with research. Do you know about her history, what she's done, anything she's tried to hide or blatantly disregarded? The Miller System has to have some flaws. We have to expose them."

"I'm certain I could find some things," Sascha agrees. I see the excited look in his eye; clearly, he's eager to have another project to work on.

"Do that." Oliver considers me for a moment. "You're probably best letting Sascha handle that part of the research, the business part. You should consider more personal history. I know you've been estranged for a number of years, but you should be able to find something on her. The state wants this mess to be blamed on someone—if it isn't you, it will be her."

I nod, fully approving of the idea. I hadn't meant to make it personal, but it has become that way. My mother would do the same.

We discuss the details further, brainstorming a list of likely sponsors, a tentative timeline, and ways to defend ourselves against my mother. I'm glad to have help with this, and the fact that he's including Sascha is surprising, but pleasant.

Of course, the pleasantries end the moment we're finished discussing the project.

"Has Sascha informed you about the other terms of our agreement?" Oliver asks, a smile on his face that would be friendly coming from anyone else.

"Yes," I mutter, trying not to look too angry. Sascha reaches over and places his hand on my leg under the table, reminding me to stay civil. We need Oliver, at least for now. "I'll give my consent, but you can't bring him back like you did last time. I need him functioning. That shit you pulled, the water, the injuries... no."

Oliver gives me an amused look. "Well, then, by all means. What would your limits be?"

I haven't had the time to think about it, or the desire. "Nothing that could cause actual medical harm," I stipulate. "No forcing him to drink. No hitting him in soft spots. No broken skin. Nothing on the face."

Oliver sighs. "You just don't like to have fun, do you?"

I wait, hoping he doesn't reject the offer.

He looks at Sascha instead. "Pity that you hadn't negotiated better the first time around," he teases, but he's not saying no, yet. "Seems your master doesn't want his pretty little pet to get hurt."

"You can hurt me," Sascha points out. "Just not like you did last time. I'm certain a man with your talents can come up with something."

I see Oliver's arm pull back to strike, but before I can do anything, Syrus is there, placing himself in front of Sascha. Oliver stops, laughing at the spectacle he's caused.

"How about this? Send the big one over and I'll meet your terms."

Sascha is saying "no" as I'm saying "yes."

"This was between you and me!" Sascha reminds Oliver, a furious look on his face. Somehow, his words seem less offensive since he's hiding behind another slave.

"Oh, it will stay between you and me, darling," Oliver says, a smile spreading across his face. "I just want him to watch. You have my word; I won't put a hand on him. Or an object. I'll even let him wear his suit and tie. After all, he is guarding that body of yours. I want him to see exactly what I do to it."

I wait, letting Sascha decide. As I watch, Sy takes a step back, giving Sascha a stern look and a nod. I expect him to protest, but he defers to Sy with only a defeated look.

"Done," he agrees.

"I like working with you, Sascha," Oliver comments. "You're smart, but you're an easy little whore."

We set a date a few weeks from now, and while Sascha doesn't look pleased, he is the one promoting this arrangement. I go along, but I can't feel comfortable until Oliver finally leaves, taking his slave along with him.

I glance at Sascha and Syrus, who look as relieved as I do.

"You shouldn't have to do this," Sascha mumbles, looking at Sy with guilt in his eyes. "This was my deal, my problem. I told him about my brother; I'm the one who should suffer."

Sy sits next to Sascha and puts a hand on his shoulder. "You will be. I just hope it's not worse because I'm there."

Sascha shakes his head. "I don't mind the extra support. I mean... I don't really like to talk about it, but you can probably imagine the things he's done. You've told me the things you've been made to do. It was nothing permanent, just humiliating. Survival, right?"

"I'd like it if you kept an eye on him," I ask Sy. "Make sure Oliver doesn't go too far."

"Of course," Sy agrees. "I'll make sure nothing happens to him. I've been doing that for a while now."

I try not to be bothered by the comment, but I am. Being reminded of my failures, no matter how well-intentioned, never sits well.

But I can't exactly lash out at Syrus for something I'm grateful for. Instead, I fix Sascha with a hard look. "No more making deals without consulting me," I order.

Sascha pulls back, closer to Sy, and he frowns at me. "I needed to do something," he points out. "Torenze was our only option. Again."

"I appreciate it," I admit. "But I found another way that didn't involve risking you. I know you weren't aware of that; I wasn't able to communicate with you. But you did it in the detention facility, and you and Syrus just did it here, again. It can't become a habit."

I'm waiting for him to apologize, to concede, to defer to me like he did to Sy, but he doesn't.

"Fine, next time you're stuck in prison, I'll let you handle it on your own," he replies, flippant.

"Sascha, I appreciated your help!" I snap at him, because I do want him to back down. "But if you keep doing shit like this, it will come out in public."

"Because I'm not capable of playing the part when I need to? Why don't you ask your mother how well I can play up your image? Maybe she can invite one of my rapists, or maybe she can have you beat me again. I guess I could use some practice."

I'm silent. I have no way of responding that won't make everything worse, and I'm not sure if I'm being irrational or if Sascha is. All I want is to make sure he's safe. Letting him take the consequences for my actions isn't something I plan on allowing ever again.

He stands. "I'm going to go get started on some research or something. See how well Torenze's slave cleaned up the house."

I don't protest, I just sit there fuming. Sascha stalks out, and I'm left sitting with Syrus.

"He's upset about what he's going to have to do, sir," Sy points out. "He was snappy all day after that man visited him in the detention facility."

"Wait until he spends a whole day with him. You'll get to watch it all."

"Yes," Sy agrees.

I was hoping to anger him with the statement, but he's still calm.

"Do you enjoy having sex with men?" I challenge him. I need to think about something other than the fate I've allowed Sascha to submit to.

Sy gives me a questioning look, but he responds quickly. "Yes, sir."

"Would you rather top, or bottom?" I egg him on. I'm looking for a fight.

"As it pleases you, master."

The change is noticeable, even though I don't know him well. It's the first time Sy has avoided a direct answer.

I harden my tone. "Do you like getting fucked?"

"As it pleases—"

"Do you enjoy being penetrated by another man?" Suddenly, all I want is his answer. I want him to submit to me, to answer my question, to act like the good slave that Sascha will never be because I love him too much to demand it. "Do not make me ask again."

Sy glares back at me, defiance finally starting to show in his eyes. "No, master. I do not. But I won't fight you."

"Of course you won't. I won't force you. I'm not interesting in doing anything sexual with someone who hates it." Once I get what I want, I don't want it anymore. I'm ashamed again, appalled that I would make this man who has been nothing but helpful suffer through such humiliation.

"I won't come between you and Sascha, sir," Syrus tells me, his voice quiet. "But you'll push him away. He needs you. You were all he wanted, the whole time we were in the detention facility. If you want to hurt someone, to feel powerful, you can use me. I can handle it. He can't. He doesn't even need to know it happened."

"I'm not an animal," I mutter, although it's exactly how I've been behaving. "I'm sorry. For this, and for yesterday. You've been so helpful to me and Sascha, you deserve better."

Syrus just nods. It would be easier to handle him if he were combative.

"Perhaps, sometime, if everyone is in agreement, you would like to join us," I offer quietly. "That's what I was going to ask before I turned our conversation into a pissing match. I do find you attractive, and while I wouldn't do anything to you that you didn't like, the idea of watching you and Sascha together holds its appeal."

"I'll take that into consideration, sir," Sy answers. "What would you like me to do while we're at home? Is there work, anything I should know about?"

I shake my head. "I'll get you set up with a tablet," I decide. "You can do whatever you'd like. Relax, enjoy yourself, try to excuse my rude behavior."

Sy smiles at me. "That should keep me busy."

It takes me a moment to realize he's joking, but I appreciate it. For his sake, and for Sascha's, I vow to try harder with him.

Chapter 15

Public Eye

Edson has advised me to take "any publicity, good or bad," in order to seem more relatable to the public. While the state attorney's office has forbidden me from discussing the actual details of the legal case against me, they haven't ordered me not to discuss anything else, and my lawyer reminds me repeatedly how important it is to have the support of the public in this very media-saturated issue.

I arrange my first public event as an interview with an internet reporter who calls himself "Veracity." He's not the biggest name in the business, but he was the first one to offer me and opportunity to meet with him, in front of a live audience, and answer his questions and ask my own without being held to a script. He's thrilled to have me, hoping my appearance will push his small-time feature into a household name, and within a few days of my release, his team has rented an event venue and sold out thousands of tickets.

It's strangely unnerving to see my face on advertisements for days before the event.

He has also graciously allowed me to bring both Sascha and Syrus, completing my image as a friendly, neighborhood slave owner. I've completed all the paperwork needed to legitimize Syrus as my bodyguard, and Sascha and I have reviewed a variety of publicity statements, making sure I am prepared to answer any questions in the most beneficial manner possible. The three of us arrive hours early, and we are still hounded by media reporters as we push our way out of the hov-car and into the back of the venue. Hearing that the public is incited about something and being in the midst of that excitement are two entirely different things. Sy blocks me as much as he blocks

Sascha, and with the help of the venue's security team, we make it inside unscathed.

Looking out at the crowd that has assembled for us is daunting. Social events and parties are one thing; to be the center of attention for an entire room is entirely something else. Veracity has introduced me to his audience already, at the same time as he showed them clips of me being arrested. They actually boo me as I take my seat. Veracity smiles, because bad reactions draw so many more viewers.

"Cashiel—can I call you that? I hope you don't mind—it seems like you don't have too many friends here!" Veracity observes, still looking pleased about the fact.

"I guess not," I admit. "But exposing a broken system doesn't make many friends. I wish I had discovered something different, but it's time for change."

Veracity nods. "You're taking on the Miller System! That's a lot of change. What do you hope to accomplish with this move?"

I can hear the crowd growing more agitated, and Sascha shifts, moving closer to me. "I want the best," I answer. "I want the most efficient system, one that works better than any other. The Miller System worked for years, but some of my research shows that it might not be that great anymore. We can do more with our Demoted population. They are an underutilized resource."

"I see you have a few of your resources with you," Veracity motions at Sascha. "Come on over, let the audience get a good look at you!"

Sascha pretends to be shy, hiding next to me for a moment until I shoo him away. We planned it in advance; he needs to continue strengthening my image. He slinks over to our host, the thin fabric he's chosen clinging to his body and emphasizing all of his best features. He stands in front of the host, his head bowed deferentially, and he waits.

"What is it that you do for your master?" Veracity asks, giving the audience a knowing smile.

Sascha turns to me, waiting until I nod my permission for him to answer. He turns his body so he can face both the audience and the host, and he gives a sweet smile. "Well, there's the obvious, sir," he begins, drawing a few laughs. Once the crowd quiets, he becomes more serious. "I help my master to cook and clean, entertain business guests, to relax. And I help him with his research. I check his figures, help him figure out problems, research things for him so he has more time to focus on what's important. I like to work with numbers, and he's given me the training to do what he needs. Nobody wants a product that only serves one purpose."

Before Veracity can ask another question, Sascha recoils as a soda bottle hits him in the head.

"I've got a purpose for you right here!" the person who threw the bottle calls out, gesturing to his crotch.

The bottle is nearly empty, and the venue's security rushes over quickly, but not before I catch our host signaling for the camera crew to zoom in the conflict. They miss the shaken look that Sascha gives me, focusing instead on the commotion starting in the audience. As the man is dragged out between two security guards, the audience takes it upon themselves to air their opinions, yelling and booing.

"I'm the only one putting on a show today," Veracity reminds our audience, trying to make light of it. "Our guest is just trying to make the system better, right?"

The crowd erupts in protests again; they refrain from throwing things this time, but it's clear that our host's inflammatory statement hit its mark.

"Leave the Miller System alone!" someone yells.

"We don't need any more changes!"

"Go do your research in a nation that cares! The Miller System works!"

It's not like I don't understand why they're angry. The state of the Demoted system was so bad before the Miller System that nobody wants to risk going back to anything of the sort. The Miller System worked for decades and people have come to love it. Worse, the history of the nation before the fourth World War was so miserable that any perceived challenge to the structures that were put into place, including the Demoted system, brings threats of a return to those conditions. Some are afraid that the Demoted system will be destroyed, others are afraid that its reach will enslave more people. Change is a threat, and my research brings that threat to life. The audience members glare at me, hating the possibilities that my data has created.

Lewd gestures and unfriendly faces litter the audience.

Sy takes it upon himself to step out from behind my shoulder, placing himself next to Sascha instead. I'm glad I have him with me.

"Cashiel, your public records indicate that you went years without owning a slave," Veracity changes course. "You bought the little one not long ago, and it seems that your bodyguard is a very new addition. Care to share with the audience why you've suddenly become interested in the more personal side of the industry?"

I nod, pleased with the question. "I bought Sascha to do exactly what he described. As a younger man, I didn't have much responsibility—work, friends, nothing that required much of my time. But once I became interested in improving the Demoted system, I reconsidered it. Not only that, but my own research was showing me just how great a resource they could be, when trained properly."

Veracity adjusts his microphone and leans in, pretending to be intimate. "I heard you found him at a brothel?"

"Demoted whore!" someone yells from the audience.

The catcalls from the audience grow louder and more critical, but I'm prepared. Sascha has researched our interviewer and shared the details with me. "The two of you have a common start," I reply. "I heard you got your start filming Demoted fetish videos."

The interviewer turns bright red, making some sort of hand signal to turn the cameras away from him. The camera crew focuses on Sy and Sascha, instead.

"Your newest acquisition is your bodyguard," Veracity continues, ignoring our last topic. "Tell me how he fits into your plans. Many of your abolitionist supporters were shocked when they saw the footage of you with another slave. Is this a strategic move?"

The noise from the crowd makes it difficult to hear, and the venue's security has their hands full containing the agitated group. I speak loudly, hoping they aren't drowning me out.

"Sometimes people throw things, sometimes they might do more," I explain, casual. "I thought a bodyguard might be necessary. I'm no abolitionist, and I have better things to do than strategize my purchases. I bought the bodyguard because I needed a bodyguard. It is exactly what my research focuses on, though—we need to use our resources, not waste time with them. They are productivity tools, something the Miller System seems to have overlooked in the past few years."

"I take it you didn't pick him up at a brothel?" Veracity asks, flashing a challenging look at me.

"No, I did not." I'm not here to talk about Syrus. I'm supposed to be here to talk about the project.

"So, where did he come from?" Veracity persists. "There doesn't seem to be much public record for him. Just your purchase a few days ago. Isn't that unusual?"

The crowd titters like I've committed some sort of crime. I hear more people shouting at me, at us, accusing me of sabotaging the entire Demoted system, of being a traitor to my country, to being in love with my slaves. This is the first I've heard about Sy's lack of record; the last I knew, he had a full, accessible record, one that I have a copy of. I wonder who exactly is hiding it.

"I guess there are other things that our system has overlooked," I answer, shrugging. It's flippant, but I'm hoping to take the focus away from my personal life. Instead, the criticisms get louder, stronger.

"Like letting scum like you out of prison!" someone calls, making me wonder if I'm really helping my case here. If I didn't know better, I would guess that the audience had been hand-picked from those who oppose me.

The crowd has risen to its feet, and fistfights have broken out between the attendees and the guards, some between the attendees themselves. Veracity is quiet for a moment, likely listening to the event staff on the small device clipped to his ear, but after a moment, he continues.

"Why target the Miller System?" he asks. "Why not the whole Demoted industry?"

"Traitor!" a chorus of voices shouts.

"Take your terrorist ass and kill yourself!" another adds. "Take your slaves with you!"

This time it's a shoe that comes flying, and this time it's at my head. Sy bats it away easily now that he's watching for it. I continue to answer, pretending nothing is wrong.

"I have no problem with the Demoted industry," I state, making my voice loud and firm. "The Demoted system has revolutionized the developed world, just like the international hov-car lanes did decades ago. But that doesn't mean that we don't keep updating the roadways. At its core, the Demoted system works. It's the foundation of our country's peace and prosperity. I would never want to change that. I just want to make it better. The Miller System is the weakest point of the industry."

My words incite the crowd further, and even those who had been listening attentively at first have devolved into screaming. Some are holding up signs with slurs against me, most are holding up signs supporting the Miller System. Many have started using the signs as weapons. Veracity covers his microphone and snaps at the security team to get their shit together, but the sheer number of people who are angry far outweighs the available staff. In a move of bravery or ignorance, our host continues the interview at a yell.

"Cashiel, we may have to take a break—what is one thing you would like our viewers to remember about this interview?"

Before I have a chance to answer, a blur of light whizzes through the air, and when it lands, fire spreads across the stage. Someone has thrown some sort of Molotov cocktail, and others contribute by throwing whatever they have handy.

I choose my response quickly. Years of training and experience guarding my masters has prepared me for this situation far better than the guards who are failing, perhaps on purpose, to control the situation.

My first concern should be my master, but it's really Sascha. I compromise and grab one of them with each hand, shoving them behind one of the lighting panels where they are surrounded by thrown objects and flames. The event security is trying and failing to handle the crowd, and I realize that nobody will put out the flames. I grab the fire extinguisher from where I took note of it earlier, spraying it out. I hope it looks like an accident when I spray the few audience members who rush the stage, but it's not. I'm protecting my interests.

Our idiot host is standing there with wide eyes, torn between smiling and cringing away from the debris. I catch his attention and motion for him to follow me off-stage, guarding him carefully until he joins Cashiel and Sascha.

He looks exhilarated, and I wonder whether knocking him down could be excused in the level of chaos we're experiencing.

"This is going to get so many views!" he exclaims, the fact that he's bleeding slightly from a cut on his face not dampening his excitement at all. He yells at his camera crew "don't stop recording!"

"Is that why you failed to control the crowd?" Cash snaps at him. I've never seen him so angry, and I'm glad I'm not the only one who realizes we've been set up.

One of the crowd members makes his way onto the stage and rushes to where Cash and Sascha are hiding. I handle him with ease and precision, snatching the knife from his hand and pinning him to the ground. He struggles, but I don't back off; Cashiel has arranged my paperwork, and I am perfectly within my rights to restrain this assailant.

Through the smoke, I see another figure approaching, and I glance around, hoping for the event security to start doing their job. I don't see them, but the face of this person becomes familiar. With my ex-master out of the picture, Conrad is the new "executioner" for the 27th Street Gang.

"You seemed awfully cozy with your new master," Conrad accuses me. My ex-master's associate has a dark look on his face, the look he had right before the state department had intervened and stopped him from killing me so they could take me to Leadview.

I don't respond. For all I know, they're still filming, and my past ownership could cause problems. Besides, speaking has never been my strong point.

Conrad doesn't say much, either, he just grabs a metal bar from the half-destroyed set and comes toward me with it, his intentions clear. The man I'm restraining stops struggling for a moment, looking pleased. I wonder whether this was all a diversion, and whether that diversion was meant to kill me, my master, or both of us.

A slave, even a bodyguard can't defend himself against a free man, not when that free man isn't putting his master's safety at risk. Conrad knows this, it's evident on his face as he swings the bar, striking me hard. I move so he misses my head, but he gets my back hard enough to knock the wind out of me, and I feel the pain deeply. He raises it again and I make my move, darting away at the last second, watching in relief as he strikes the knife-wielding diversion, instead. A startled look crosses Conrad's face, but I've always been a better fighter than he is. The security team finally catches up, handcuffing the man who had the knife, the one who's just taken the hit I was supposed to receive. Conrad darts away, taking his improvised weapon with him. He's smart enough not to leave fingerprints, at least.

I hurry back to my master, relieved to see him and Sascha still safe.

"Master, we should get out of here soon," I advise, giving him a warning look. "You're not safe here."

I'm not, either, but that's not something I can discuss in public.

Cash nods his agreement, and I hear the wailing screech of police hov-cars approaching. They should have been here ten, fifteen minutes ago. They're working on their own public image, I'm sure.

"Get the police to send a unit to retrieve us!" Cash snaps at Veracity. "Before someone gets hurt or this place burns down!"

"There's people outside protesting, too," our host informs us, an apologetic look on his face. "It might be a while."

The crowd's noises are becoming louder, and we hear crashing noises as they begin to destroy what parts of the set they can reach before the event security holds them back. Pieces of the set are flying everywhere, and the security team is having an increasingly difficult time keeping them all back. We won't last until a police unit retrieves us.

"We'll go out another way, master," I suggest. While Sascha was researching our host's sordid history, I was memorizing the layout of the venue. Large appliances and exhaust fans are accessible from the roof, and a utility closet behind the stage should contain the stairs to make it out there.

Sascha follows me without question; only after he moves does Cash join him, then Veracity. I barrel my way through the few audience members who have made their way back here, guarding Cash and Sascha as well as I can. I slap at the people and the objects they throw, but only when they're at risk of harming Sascha or Cash. The rest I let hit me. It allows me to focus.

On the roof, at least, we are safe. Trapped, but safe. We don't wait long before Veracity is screaming to the security staff to rescue him, to send a parachute or a helicopter, but nobody else is that dramatic. The police force has started doing their job in earnest, breaking up the crowd and arresting those who resist. From the distance, I can see armed vehicles, likely full of reinforcements and weapons. They should already have been here; either the event host wanted the drama and neglected to inform the authorities of a possible incident, or the rest of the riots throughout the city are tapping the vast resources. The local officers are doing their best on the ground, but there are simply too many people to contain easily. The electrical buzz of tasers can be heard every few seconds, and the unmistakable smell of a smoke bomb reaches my nose. I keep my eye on the door to the building, prepared to slam it down on anyone who shouldn't be coming through there.

Once the building is cleared adequately, a team of officers retrieves us, casting a suspicious look in my direction when they see me tense and ready. I retreat immediately, bowing my head and stepping back, making myself look as small and unintimidating as possible. They could beat me just for looking at them wrong, and Sascha and Cash need me around. They seem placated, and escort us down a metal ladder on the side of the building.

The presence of the officers doesn't deter the most aggressive rioters; the few feet we have to walk before reaching the hov-car are filled with rocks—and worse—being thrown at us. I guard my charges carefully until we reach the car, making sure they are safely inside before relaxing. Cashiel takes off with a screech. Protesters are blocking our way, but since the officers seem happy to shoot rubber bullets at them, my master makes his way through quickly, joining the team of state police officers that surround us on all sides, escorting us to safety.

The drive home is tense; Sascha informs me that there has been an emergency curfew imposed on entire area for the rest of the night. He scans his tablet for information, discovering that similar protests have erupted in a few major cities. The police have responded by authorizing the use of deadly force, and the estimated number of dead citizens is approaching double digits already. Our hunt for information is quickly ended, as the signal jams up. Later, I'm sure the officials will cite the increased number of people accessing information as the cause of the data disruption, but it's more likely that they've released a low-wave magnetic pulse to quiet everything down. The fact that the next few streetlights we come to have mysteriously stopped working adds to my theory.

The officers direct us to take an alternative route home; while a savvy protestor could find the home address, most are just following the crowd. After a few hours, we lose the parties who are following us. The police officers stay, adding to my master's private security team, and we arrive home relatively unharmed.

I notice a hov-car parked outside of the house. It's not an officer, and it's not a member of the private security team.

"Cash," I caution him as we pull up. "On your left."

I expect him to keep driving, to notify our police escort, but he just scowls.

"Fucking bitch," he mumbles. He gives the officers and security team a thumbs-up and pulls up alongside of the vehicle.

A woman is sitting inside of the car, a wide-brimmed hat and sunglasses hiding her identity.

"What in the hell do you want?" my master spits out. I wonder who he hates so much.

"I need a word with you, Cashiel," the woman demands.

"It's not really a good time," Cash tells her, sarcastic. I can hear the hatred in his voice.

"Make it a good time or I'll find it in my records that it was your little whore who released that data!" the woman snarls. "You do not get to do this to me and then ignore me!"

I glance at my master, slowly putting the puzzle together. I see the way his lips curl back, the way he doesn't even try to hide his rage. A moment later, he composes himself, setting his jaw and nodding deferentially. Something about this woman has made him admit defeat.

"I'll clear you with the security team."

They roll up their windows and Cash drives into his garage, slamming the vehicle into park like it did something wrong. Sascha gives me an apologetic look.

"You get to meet the creator of the Miller System."

Chapter 16

Suspicions

Without making my business too public, there is no good way to tell my security team to send Kristine Miller on her way back home, or to hell, so I let her in. The threat she levied against Sascha played a part in that as well. The fact that she's coming alone, without her guards and officials, gives me hope.

Syrus stays standing, attentive, his eyes never leaving my mother. He's identified his threat, and he stays with her. He's taken to his bodyguard duties quite well.

My mother gives him an appraising look, like she's examining a rare dog breed.

"Good move, Cash. The muscle really shows you taking this thing seriously. I always thought you should have more slaves. Something legitimate, not just the whore."

I shake my head. My mother was never a fan of slaves that didn't serve a purpose. Our house was staffed by Demoted of all types; there were those who cooked, those who cleaned, and those who raised me so my mother didn't have to dirty her hands with a child. I know my father visited brothels on occasion, and I'm sure my mother made use of slaves in some way while at work, but they were never a household item.

"Did you threaten your way into my house just to critique my slaves?" I'm tired, worn out from the drama. I want to tell her to leave, but that doesn't work. Going along with her intimidation tactics has always resulted in a less painful ending to whatever plot she's concocted.

"I came to see if you've thought about my request," she replies, handing her coat to Sy like he's a butler. He takes it, an amused expression on his face. "Judging by your performance on that trashy talk show today, you're still committed to bringing me down."

"I kept it civil," I remind her. "I didn't tell them everything you've done. The lies. The cover ups. The research you ignore because it doesn't fit in your financial plan. It's not the right time for that."

"Who told you that?" Kristine snarls. "Your fancy lawyer? She's represented plenty of criminals in the past, Cash. Are you sure you really want her on your case?"

That's exactly why I want her on my case. "What does it matter to you?"

"What matters to me is that your goddamned research project is going to bring me down with you!"

I pause. My mother doesn't curse often; she considers it a sign of low breeding and unintelligence. If she's losing her composure this much, she must really be threatened by something.

"What changed?" I ask. "Since the last time we spoke. You weren't so anxious, then."

Kristine glares at me for a moment before responding. "Your lawyer? Edson? I contacted her before you did. She turned me down. So has everyone else I've spoken to since then."

I resist the urge to smile, to mock her. It's nice to see her getting what she deserves. "Maybe they recognize the likelihood of success with your case."

"That isn't the only thing, Cash. Your data analyst? The one who was supposed to be verifying your research and confirming all the crimes you've been accusing me of? He's accepted a lucrative relocation and witness protection deal in exchange for that research."

I stare at my mother in shock, not quite sure whether I want to believe her. I should be hearing this from Torenze, from my lawyer, on the news—I should be arrested by now. "How do you know this?"

Kristine shrugs. "I heard it from an old friend at the state attorney's office. Someone whom I had a more personal relationship with."

She guides us into my living room. Syrus stays standing, guarding, while Sascha takes his place on the couch next to me. My mother frowns at him, like she would if she saw an animal on the furniture, but she stays quiet about it, seating herself in another chair and continuing on as if Sascha doesn't matter. Or, as if she knows just how involved he is in this, but won't acknowledge it.

"The state attorney's office is keeping it quiet for now, no doubt planning the best time to release it," she continues.

It doesn't make sense. "The best time to release it is immediately. They could get me back in prison, out of the way, they could destroy you whenever they chose—"

"That's obviously not what they want, you stupid child!"

I stop, thinking it over. If the state's agents really needed me out of the way, they could have arranged a thousand ways for me to die already. The arrest, prison... hell, they could have had someone murder me at the talk show today. I wouldn't be the first political dissenter to meet an untimely end. They want me alive to set an example, to use me, to do something that I can't do while dead.

"Cash, all the data that was turned over with that deal directly places the failings of the Miller System on me! Personally! There was nothing left that makes you guilty of anything, nothing that even hints at you or Oliver doing a thing wrong! Everything incriminating... it all points to me!"

"Isn't that true?" I ask. Unless I've misinterpreted our results, this seems to be an accurate assessment.

Sascha sits up. I know he's been attending to the conversation, pretending like he hasn't been, but this is his passion, too. He gives Kristine a curious look.

"Where did the rest of it go?" he asks.

My mother gives him a dirty look, but she engages with him.

"I don't know," she admits, speaking more to me than to Sascha. "But there are things missing. Things you released last time, things that connect to the research in the past. Anything that could paint Cashiel as a repeat offender—as someone committing treason—it's all gone. What's left is a bunch of evidence against me and my system."

"And you're telling us this why?" Sascha asks. "You can't be here officially. You don't have your team with you. You're driving a rental. I saw it on the security cameras. What do you get out of this?"

I've been wondering the same thing; Sascha has just said it out loud. He's bold, and the fact that he's so freely insulting my mother makes me wonder what he knows, or what he suspects. He thinks on her level.

"Because I don't know who's protecting you, and I wanted to see if you did," Kristine says, shaking her head. "Clearly, you know even less than I do."

"Could Torenze have set this up?" I suggest. "He was the one dealing with the data analyst while I was in prison. He has just as much motivation to destroy you as I do."

"If he did, he planned it well," Kristine decides. "Arranged it in advance. He would have made sure that Michaud & Torenze didn't go down in the deal. That analyst is probably rolling in money in a luxury condo right now. He never had anything to worry about."

Not from Torenze, but it occurs to me that one of our new Argova associates might have taken it upon themselves to help us again. But that still doesn't explain why the state hasn't moved on the evidence. And it doesn't explain why my mother is here, asking for our help.

"So why come to us?" I challenge. "Why not bring it to the news, try to find an unbiased party at the state level?"

"Cashi, there are no unbiased parties at the state level," my mother reminds me, giving me the same look she always has when I dared to ask a stupid question. "I have nowhere else to turn. My fall from grace has left me with few friends. I know I've burned bridges. I don't regret doing it. It's business. If things had gone my way, you and Torenze would both be out of the picture. But that didn't happen. Oliver Torenze has tried to destroy me since I kicked him off of my professional team. Do you know why that happened?"

I sigh. She'll paint my business partner to look like some sort of malicious evildoer, but he's told me enough about their relationship that I can fill in the blanks. "You were upset because he tried to outperform and steal your spotlight."

My mother laughs. "He was never that successful. He put my information at risk, and he did anything for a price. I made a considerable amount of money off of the Miller System, but he wanted more. He still wants more. Keep an eye on him, Cash. You can't trust him."

She's told me this about Oliver on multiple occasions. As always, it seems to serve her purposes more than fulfilling any sort of truth.

"It seems like he's working in my best interest," I remind her.

"For now," she counters. "What's to stop him from getting you out of the way after he gets me out of the way? First he releases the data that incriminates me, don't you think you'll be next?"

"My involvement is tied to him," I remind her.

"For now," Kristine repeats, shaking her head. "Records can be edited. You know all about that."

"I learned it from the best," I remind her. "You've given me your message. Did you have anything else of importance? Or did you just want a way to sneak in here and bug my house again?"

"I know you have a lot of information that you could release about me. Suspicions, facts, research. Evidence that isn't even included in what that data analyst turned over. You haven't released a lot of it. I appreciate that. I'm sure you're just waiting for the right time, but I didn't raise you any other way. Please just consider what Torenze is getting out of this. You can take over the re-education centers without taking me down. It makes your case more clear; you can look like a martyr instead of a scorned rival. And... even though I'm sure you wouldn't want me around, it's better to have me as a supporter."

I glare at her. She's begging for my sympathy like I should care. After all she's done to me and Sascha, I'd rather us both go down than act like I'm helping her.

"Get out of my house and don't contact me again," I demand, my voice low. I can't look at her. I pretend I'm not afraid, but a part of me is. This sort of tone would never have been allowed, not when I was a child, not when I was an adult. But I'm sick of her hold over me.

To my surprise, she stands, straightening her clothes for a moment, and then makes her way to the door without another word.

I should be pleased to see Kristine Miller give up without a fight, but it alarms me. Normally, she would threaten, terrorize, remind me of how much power she has over me. If she's giving in so easily, she must have no other option than to try and win my favor. And for a woman of her status to be left without options, there must be something major happening.

I turn to Sascha the moment she leaves. "Find out everything you can about that data analyst. Who he was, who his family is, where he is now. See if there's security footage on his building, if anyone visited him. Find out when he last talked to Oliver. Legal or illegal means, I don't care. Just make sure to stay away from the state investigation."

"What about the Argova family?" Sascha asks, thinking along the same lines as I was. He glances at Sy. "Would this be something they're interested in?"

Sy nods. "They have a vested interest in the Demoted system, and in your research. But I wouldn't bother looking into them. If they're involved, you won't find anything. They have people who are skilled enough to make themselves invisible if they so choose."

Sascha looks back at me. "Do you want me to start looking into Torenze?"

I pause for a moment, startled by his blatant accusation. "Do you really think he was involved?"

Sascha shrugs. "We shouldn't immediately rule him out. We only partnered with him because we thought he'd keep us safe from Kristine. What has he even done to help us?"

"He safeguarded our data," I remind him, frowning. "He bailed me out of prison... he's my partner in this business, Sascha. If we go down, so does he."

Sascha goes quiet, nodding. "Right. Sorry."

It's rare to see him shut down so quickly, especially about our research. I go to him, placing a hand on his shoulder. "You don't need to apologize," I remind him. "I know you're just checking bases. I appreciate it. You see a lot of things that I don't. I'm just a little jumpy, and my mother has messed things up for us so much in the past. If you think Oliver is worth the time, you are welcome to check him out in any way possible. I don't think it will lead anywhere, but I won't stand in your way."

Sascha looks up at me, a grateful smile on his face. "Thanks," he says, reaching up to cover my hand with his. "I'm probably just being paranoid."

"This business is officially Michaud & Torenze," I remind him. "But you're the one I want to share everything with, not Oliver. You're the only one I trust completely. That doesn't change."

Sascha pulls my hand to his lips, placing a light kiss on it before letting it go. "You should call him," he advises. "Let me see what I can find."

I smile, lingering a moment before moving away. As Sascha gets to work, I place a call to Oliver.

"Did you know that our data analyst has given our data to the state?" I ask, not bothering with formalities.

Oliver is silent for a moment. "No. I was unaware. How did you find this out?"

"I have my sources," I try to be vague.

"Kristine?" Oliver suggests.

I don't try to deny it; he guessed it too quickly. "How soon until the police start asking questions?"

"I have no idea. This is the first I've heard," Oliver says. He sounds worried. "Did he turn it all over, then? Should I start making arrangements?"

If he's acting, he's acting well. "There were plenty of data in there that would have cast Michaud & Torenze in a very negative light. Apparently, that didn't get included. Nothing in there makes us look bad."

"And your mother told you this?" Oliver asks, skeptical. "I wouldn't trust that. Either there is no data breach, or it includes data about us as well. She's lying, Cash. Like she has been this whole time."

Except that my mother's extortion plans almost always include something in her benefit. She's the victim here, and she would never willingly choose that role.

"What can I say, Cash? I thought we could trust the analyst, so did you. See what your mother is up to. Hasn't it always been her calling the shots?"

I pause. This isn't adding up, but I can't tell that to Oliver. I don't trust him or my mother, and I don't trust the connection with the Argova family, either. Instead, I try my best to be subtle. "Let me handle hiring a new analyst. No need for you to deal with that on top of everything else."

"If you think that's the best plan, I won't stand in the way of it," Oliver agrees. "Is everything else going all right? You sound a little distressed."

I scowl, glad that he can't see me. He knows that I have plenty of reasons to be distressed; he's making me aware of how obvious it is. "I'm fine," I lie. "Just surprised to hear about our data analyst. It will push back the results. I'm hoping to have a definitive, unbiased report by the time my court date comes around."

"Yes, that would help your case considerably. If you need a back-up copy of any of your data, it's all still housed on my servers. Just tell me what you need, or have Sascha get in touch with me. I always welcome his voice."

"All right," I agree, trying not to be annoyed that he even dares to talk about Sascha. "Let me know if you hear anything else."

"Of course," Oliver agrees. "Anything to help business."

I can't help but wonder whose business he's really interested in promoting: ours or his.

Chapter 17
Teasing

When Cash coms his lawyer to question her about the supposed deal between the analyst and the state attorney's office, she is unavailable. She remains unavailable throughout the day, and sends him a message later, directing him to go along with the plan.

If the Argova family is involved, they are keeping it under wraps. So is the state attorney's office; despite the anxiety I feel as I wait for my master to be arrested, my fears are unfounded for now. Cash makes arrangements for me and Sy in the event that something of that nature should happen, but there is no indication that we are at risk for now. We are left to wait.

While we do, we work on our research and our image. Over and over, I check the numbers, looking for any indication that there are problems, anything that would weaken our case. At the same time, Cash answers reporters' questions, prepares press releases. Our message must be clear: we are reporting the facts for the betterment of the nation. That we stand to profit and show up Kristine is simply an added benefit.

We watch the news and scour the media furiously. In order to stay ahead, we have to know about the questions, the suspicions, and another other developments as soon as they occur. We watch the riot coverage in a mix of fascination and horror. The last time there were this many riots, I was a little boy; I barely remember the bloodshed, the tighter control over citizens' lives, the constant wail of police sirens.

I stand in front of the sliding glass doors in our bedroom, staring at the city below. Normally we can see the sparkling lights, far enough away to give us some privacy. Cash likes to watch me strip against the city background; otherwise, we take it for granted. Now, smoke twists up from various sectors. There is a remarkable lack of hov-cars after curfew.

I hear Cash coming into the room, finishing whatever he's been working on.

"Shut the blinds?" he says, making it a request. "I'm tired of looking at destruction all day."

I comply. As interesting as it is, it kills the mood. When we aren't working, we both prefer ignore the threats that loom in favor of exploring each other. I turn, walking slowly toward the bed and joining him. He gets a smile on his face, the kind he gets right before he tells me to do something that makes me highly uncomfortable, but that I usually end up loving.

"I was thinking about Sy," Cash says, neglecting to provide me with any other details, any clues as to what he was thinking about my friend.

A smiling Cash is dangerous. I crawl over to him, draping my body over his in hopes that my thinly veiled attempt at seduction will encourage him to open up a little bit more.

Cash grabs my hips and holds me in place, pressing my body tighter against his. "He was quite helpful the other day. I'm really starting to like him."

I'm glad. Sy has started to mean so much to me in such a short period of time; I had no idea how it would work once we got back home. At first he was so stiff and awkward, I was afraid that he would never really feel at home here. The vicious competition between him and Cash didn't help, but it has died down recently. As I had hoped, their annoying mutual interest in taking care of me seems to have superseded any other feelings between them.

"I see the way you look at him, Sascha," Cash teases, the hard-on he's sporting indicating that he isn't at all bothered by it.

"I like him," I admit, slightly embarrassed. "It's weird. At the detention facility, we had a different relationship. Close."

"Yes, you did," Cash agrees. "You miss him. I can tell."

I blush. It's not that I never see him; I see him every day. But I miss the constant connection that we had in the detention facility, the closeness. I miss the thought of touching him, feeling him touch me, because we don't anymore. Sy is exceedingly professional, especially when Cash is around, and it leaves me confused and longing.

"Go get him," Cash says suddenly, pushing me off the side of the bed. "Tell him to come here, that I have a question for him."

I look at my master nervously, wondering what sort of scheme he has planned now.

"That's an order." The fact that he's grinning makes me a little more calm.

Still, I trust that when he gives me an order, he expects it to be followed, so I hurry out, walking down to Sy's room where I find him lounging casually, watching a video on his tablet.

"Hey," I say, taking in the nearly empty room. Cash has offered him whatever he would need or like to decorate with, but as usual, Sy seems ridiculously content with what was provided.

"Hey there, pretty boy," he says, stopping the video to smile at me. "Looking for trouble?"

"Cash wants you," I explain. "He said he has a question for you."

Sy is on his feet instantly, despite our master's frequent reassurance he can be casual. Sy seems to reject anything casual. If the rioters came to our door right now, he'd be ready for them. I think the formality makes him more comfortable. He even stops to straighten his collar and flatten the creases on his pants before following me out. Still, as he walks past me, he touches my shoulder, reassuring me.

I follow him back to the bedroom, where Cash is still sprawled out on the bed, lazy and comfortable. I suppose he should be; everything here is his. The house, the bed, the two other people standing in his bedroom. He beckons me over with his finger, and I come like an obedient pet.

"Sascha said you had a question for me, sir?" Sy asks, somehow managing to sound proper and respectful despite the fact that he's prodding Cash to speak.

Cash waits for a moment, irking me, because I know he's making Sy uncomfortable. I'm just about to jab at his chest to get him moving when he pops the question.

"Syrus, would you like to watch Sascha strip?" Cash offers, calm, like he's inviting Sy to watch a movie.

Sy thinks about it for a moment without letting the shock show like I would have. I would kill to be as cool as he is.

"It would be enjoyable, sir," he replies, but he glances at me.

I recall their previous fight over me and my consent, and I decide to contribute before it can escalate again. "I don't mind." I'm embarrassed to say it out loud. "Actually, I'd enjoy it. I'd like it."

I can't help but feel a little bit like a whore again. It comes and goes, but this triggers it. I feel Cash rest his hand on my lower back, and I know he understands. It helps, because I know he doesn't think that way about me.

"All right," Sy says, looking as out of place as I feel.

Cash sits up, easing me onto my feet. He summons Sy closer, pointing at the bed. "Sit," he orders, then glances at me. "And you — put on some music. Pick something you can move to. Something to drown out those sirens. You know what I like."

Low beats, dance music, electronic noise created in labs. We both like it, and no matter how terrible it is as actual music, it's a great background for stripping, and an even better precursor to sex. I go to where both of our tablets have been dropped on top of each other, as careless as Cash and I fall into bed together, and I connect mine to the speaker system that is integrated into the walls. The music fills the room, and I turn to look back at the two men in my life.

I'm a little dismayed to see how stiff and uncomfortable Sy looks, sitting on the very edge of the bed. I glance at Cash, prompting him with a glare to make things better. I know he's not exactly the best candidate, but this is his job. He's our master.

"You don't have to stay if you don't want to," Cash says. "Sascha's going to strip for me either way. I just thought you might like to watch. I know for a fact that he doesn't mind. Unlike you, he has no problem telling me when he doesn't want to do something."

I laugh because it's true. It wasn't at first, but it became that way quickly, and now I wouldn't hesitate to tell him no if I didn't want to do something in bed. "I've only told you I didn't want to do something a few times," I remind him, taking my place in front of the window where I know he likes to watch me strip.

"That's because you've only ever not wanted to do something a few times," Cash smirks. "You like it as much as I do."

Sy seems to relax, just a little, and actually rests his weight on the bed instead of hovering over it. I suppose that a chair might have been preferable; the assumptions that are made when being invited into a bed probably aren't the best, but the way the bedroom is set up makes sitting in the chairs awkward, and he definitely wouldn't have a very good view. Besides, I think this is Cash's strange attempt to ease tension between them.

I start by moving to the music, gently swaying and twisting my hips. I enjoy it, dancing, moving like this, knowing I'm turning them on. I liked dancing when I was younger, the few times I snuck out and went to illegal underage clubs, but after the brothel the thought of performing for someone made my stomach churn. It was debasing, then; I knew I looked awful, and it was just a precursor to sex I didn't want. But I want it, now, and Cash doesn't debase me, he values me. I can only guess that Sy feels the same, because it doesn't seem like anything could make him feel that way about me.

I remove my shirt, carefully playing with the hem, teasing with little bits of skin here and there. I've been facing away from them until now, looking at the closed blinds and missing the skyline that usually serves as a background. Now I turn, looking first at Cash, taking in his sly smile. He always looks so content while he's watching me.

I play with my shirt a little more, slipping it over my head and tossing it aside before turning to Sy. He doesn't look as uncomfortable as he did a minute ago, but I can't tell if he's enjoying it or not. His face has that stone expression that he gets when he doesn't want to reveal more about himself, like he might be hurt if he actually reveals that he likes something. I take a few more steps toward him, swaying my body back and forth and smiling, hoping to get some response out of him.

I don't fail. He smiles and leans back a little, looking embarrassed in a way I've never seen from him. It's not a bad thing; at least, I don't think it is. I think he likes it, which encourages me.

I move my hands to the waistband of my pants, trailing my thumbs around the inside. I pause at the button, then take a few steps closer to Sy, thrusting my hips out at him, glancing at him with a questioning look on my face. I toy with the button again, glancing at him, prompting him as I nearly straddle his legs.

Finally, he gets it, reaching out and unbuttoning my pants. I keep eye contact with him, trying to encourage him. He eases the zipper down, almost chaste, like he's hesitant to touch me. I'd push farther, if I knew he liked it, but I'm not sure. I keep rolling my hips just inches away from his legs as I slide my pants down, leaving me wearing only a tight, black pair of underwear.

I try to keep things balanced, making my way over to Cash, smiling when he sits up and slides over to the edge of the bed to meet me. We've done this before, plenty of times, and he knows the game. He reaches out, capturing my hips in a firm grasp, and pulls me close, forcing me to straddle his knee. I let out a small sound as I feel him making contact with my cock, and it's all I can do not to throw myself on top of him and beg him to fuck me.

I don't, though, because I am still putting on a show.

Instead, I grind against him, keeping it slow and smooth and not as stimulating as a certain part of me would like. He reaches back to cup my ass possessively, lifting me up onto my toes and tipping me back, keeping me off balance. I know he won't let me fall.

After a few moments, he lets me sit up again, and I slide off his leg, dipping my hand down into my underwear, touching myself. It feels good, but I don't let it feel too good. After all, we're just beginning.

I glance over at Sy, who's watching with wide eyes. He's never really seen me touch myself, and I can tell it's affecting him nicely. I slowly strip the underwear off, toying with my cock as I do, swaying to the music. I'm naked, finally, and I make my way over to Sy, curious to how he'll respond.

Again, he leans back like he's afraid to touch me. I come up between his legs, pressing my body against his, and I lean over, nuzzling up against his neck.

I whisper in his ear, "Is this okay?" I doubt Cash can hear, although I'm sure he would be fine with the question if he could.

"I think so..." Sy says, but he seems uncertain.

Cash does pick up on that part, and he looks at both of us with a worried expression. "Syrus, is there something making you uncomfortable?"

Leave it to Cash to be disgustingly transparent.

Sy gulps a little; the question has made him less comfortable, instead of more. "I don't want to do anything that you would disapprove of, sir."

"I invited you in here," Cash reminds him. "If you or Sascha do anything I don't like, I'll tell you. Right now, I just want you to enjoy yourself. Sascha's having fun. Follow his lead. You have my permission to touch him. He'll tell you if he doesn't like something."

Sy turns red at the clear instructions, but he nods, turning back to face me. I smile at him, hoping I can encourage him. I can feel his cock growing hard where I'm pressed up close to him, so I know he's interested. I'm surprised to realize that he's nervous, because he is so rarely nervous. His hands come up, lightly touching my sides, running up and down over my hips like he's afraid he'll break me. I sigh, enjoying the touch, the way his hands seem to cover so much of my body. I catch his eye and he smiles, looking shy for a minute. I pretend this is our first time ever touching each other, and it isn't very hard to pretend, because this is the first time we've touched each other for real, not for someone else's enjoyment or to prove a point.

Well, Cash is enjoying it, but that's different.

I grind against him, his clothes rough against my bare skin, but I don't mind. I want him to be a bit more assertive with me; maybe not as rough as Cash is, but he's barely touching me, and I want more. I take his hand in mine and press it firmly to my chest, pulling it down, giving him the idea of what I want before letting his hand go. He takes the hint, touching me firmly, trailing his hand down to almost touch my cock, then backing off.

I whine, because I really did want that.

Cash laughs and I remind myself to tease him more on his next turn. I keep moving against Sy, slithering my body over his, wishing he were naked so I could feel his skin. I'm not sure whether I should ask him or not.

The song changes and I take it as my cue to disentangle myself from Sy, pleased when I see that he is flushed and excited. I make my way over to Cash, and I'm barely within arm's reach before he grabs me by the arm and pulls me down on top of him, kissing me roughly as he holds me in place by my hair. I probably should be embarrassed to enjoy this so much while Sy is watching, but I really can't feel anything other than turned on.

After Cash breaks off the kiss, leaving me panting and dizzy, he pushes me to my feet again.

"Undress me," he orders, his voice deceptively soft. I take my time, pleased by the knowledge that he gets frustrated when I take too long. Unbuttoning his shirt is an agonizing process, and I slide it over his shoulders, down his arms, teasing him. I wonder if Sy enjoys the show as much as Cash enjoyed watching him and me. I hope he does.

As usual, Cash loses patience by the time I reach his pants, and he bats my hands away and strips them off in seconds. Now that he's naked, his cock seems so demanding, pointing up at me. I take it in my hand and just hold it, not stroking him, just teasing as he tries to maintain his composure.

"You're a fucking tease, Sascha," he mutters, making no move to correct that.

I smile, squeezing a little, resisting the urge to make him moan by jerking his cock like I usually do. The sharp intake of breath lets me know I'm on the right track.

"Syrus, come here," Cash says, his voice still breathy. He's looking at me when he says it, which is perhaps why he misses the nervous look on Sy's face.

Ever obedient, Sy moves across the bed, closer to the head of the bed where Cash and I are situated. If it were me, I would have crawled, but Sy somehow manages to just slide over, his sturdy body somehow so graceful. He stops a few inches from Cash, a solid, emotionless expression hiding the apprehension that his body shows.

"Is there something you would like me to do, master?"

It's a simple question, but I've long realized that few things are simple with Sy, and Cash knows it as well. Sy addresses Cash as "master" much more frequently than I do, which fits with how proper he is all the time. Right now, it signals something else, and Cash notices it instantly. He extracts himself from the haze of sex we are lost in and looks seriously at Sy.

"I wanted you closer so I didn't have to yell over the music," Cash explains, his voice calm, yet a little apologetic. "As you can see, we've moved past stripping, and I wanted to make it completely clear to you that you don't have to stay if you don't want to. You don't have to join if you don't want to. I do hope you enjoyed yourself, enjoyed Sascha. I would personally appreciate it if you decided to stay, but I hope you don't feel pressured. That was never my intention."

Sy nods, considering it. "If I stay, would you like me to take off my clothes?"

I can't detect an emotion from him; his question seems routine.

"It's up to you," Cash shrugs. "It might be more enjoyable if you do, but you choose to do what you'd like."

Sy nods again, not making a movement either way.

"I think you should," I say playfully, leaving Cash for a moment to crawl over to Sy. I reach him, and I place my hands on his legs, marveling at the strong muscles I can feel even through his clothes. "Come on, the atmosphere here is way better than the detention facility!"

This gets a laugh out of Sy, breaking the uncomfortably serious mood.

"Trust me," I say, looking at him sincerely. "This will be fun. Cash won't make you do anything you don't want to do. And I want to see what it's like."

"All right," Sy agrees. "But only because you're so cute when you ask nicely."

"You should see him when he begs," Cash comments.

I can tell that the thought turns Sy on, and it turns me on even more. I make quick work of Sy's shirt. It's like the fabric is getting in the way; now that he's made up his mind, he's determined to get naked as quickly as possible. Once his shirt is off, I pause, because I've never really had much of a chance to study his body. I've seen the scars, the big one from the knife, the smaller ones from past whippings. There are others I don't know the story of; something that might be a gunshot wound, maybe other knife wounds. A dark bruise stretches across his back, leftover from the talk show the other day. His arms look like they have a few burn marks, cigarettes, maybe. He has a few tattoos that I've never really noticed before. When we showered together at the detention facility, I was too terrified to notice much of anything. I'll ask him about them, one day.

I take in his broad chest, the clearly defined muscles. While Cash doesn't sport the waif-thin appearance that I do, he is all lean muscle, the kind that comes from working out at a gym twice a week and eating healthy. Sy has the look of work about him, the look of hard labor and solid strength. I know he can pick me up, and I bet he can pick Cash up as well, although I doubt either of them would allow that to happen. Sy's hands come up to touch me again, and I'm struck by how gentle this man is with me when I'm sure he could crush me if he wanted to.

"Kiss him," Cash suggests, and I can't really tell if he's talking to me or to Sy.

Sy takes it as an order, and his hand comes up to cup my head. He pulls me close, pressing his lips against mine.

It's strange. We've done a lot of things, but never this, and I get that blushing virgin feeling. He's gentle, moving our mouths together carefully and stroking my hair as he does. I relax in his arms, loving the way it feels, and after a while, I part my lips, wondering if he'll return the favor.

He does, and I get to experience the pleasure of his tongue on mine, soft and yielding, so unlike the rest of him. He takes his time with me, and I can't help but feel like I'm melting into his touch. I wrap my arms around him to hold on. It feels nice, like I belong there.

After what seems like a pleasant forever, he pulls back, smiling at me. I decide that I want his pants off, and when I move to unfasten them, he doesn't protest, he just leans back and lifts his hips obligingly.

I'm naked in bed with two men I like very much, and I can feel both their eyes boring into me.

Chapter 18

Exploration

I run my hands down Sy's legs, so familiar, yet still so new. I like the exploration, and if his cock is any indication, he likes it too. I touch it carefully, unsure of what he likes. It's strange, because I know exactly how to get him off as quickly as possible with my mouth, but I don't know what he actually likes, whether he likes it slow or fast, whether he really does prefer to get off as quickly as possible or whether he likes to draw it out like Cash does. It has always been about efficiency and show with us before. We've never had the chance to interact on our own.

Of course, we're not on our own, and I'm reminded of that just moments later.

"Go down on him, Sascha," Cash suggests, still playful. He glances at Sy. "He's pretty amazing with his mouth."

"I'd rather—" Sy starts, then clamps his mouth shut, looking down at the floor.

I work my way up, pausing with my hands pressed flat against his chest. "You'd rather what?" I press, eager to find out what he was about to say before he stopped himself.

He shakes his head.

"Sy..." I'm torn. Cash deserves to be here, he is our master, and he's made it rather clear that he doesn't want me and Sy hooking up alone. At the same time, I can't help but think that Sy would be more comfortable if it was just the two of us. I don't think it's an option. "Sy, tell me what you want to do. I'm okay with it. Cash will be okay with it."

Cash doesn't agree, but he doesn't correct me.

"You've done it enough times, Sascha," Sy mumbles. "I'd rather return the favor."

"Oh," I say, surprised. He's made the offer before, but I always thought it was a guilt thing. I'm still not entirely sure that it's not a guilt thing, but I'm also not entirely sure that I care that much. I wait for him or Cash to make a move.

"Well, neither I or Sascha would be opposed to that, as far as I know," Cash suggests.

"Do you want me to?" Sy asks me, looking nervous.

"Yeah," I nod, wondering how it will feel. Cash is amazing at sucking cock, I wonder how Sy is. I want to find out.

Instead, we both sit there, awkwardly touching each other, neither one of us sure of what to do, or how to do it. The detention facility was easier in a way. I was on my knees, Sy was grabbing my hair and jerking me onto his cock. We had a script to follow. Now that we have choices and free will, it's like we're both unable to move.

"Sascha, come around here and lie on your back," Cash orders, throwing a pillow at me.

Obediently, I move to where he points, positioning the pillow behind me so that I'm comfortable. It's easier to not have a choice, even if I really do.

"Spread your legs, Sascha, unless you plan on having him suck on your knees instead," Cash reaches over, giving my thigh a light slap that makes me jump and makes my cock harder.

He smirks at me before turning to Sy. "Now, Syrus, it's time for you to see what it looks like when the boy begs."

Sy looks uncertain for half a second, glancing back and forth between me and Cash. Finally, he seems satisfied that this is all in good fun. He moves over, positioning himself between my legs.

Once again, I'm surprised by how graceful he is, fitting between my legs smoothly and placing his hands lightly on my inner thighs. I tremble as I feel the warmth from his breath on my cock. His tongue touches the tip, tentative, and I make a little whimpering sound.

He takes it as a cue to wrap his lips around my cock, sucking slowly and sensually. It fits, for him, everything he does seems so deliberate, intentional and skillful. In the span of just a few minutes I'm panting, looking down at his head bobbing up and down on my cock.

He trails one hand along the inside of my leg, stopping to caress my balls and rub my ass, never demanding, just exciting, tempting.

I respond by arching my back, curving my ass up so he has better access. He's making my cock feel so good, I simply can't wait to feel him inside of me, whether it's his tongue, his fingers, or his cock.

With Sy I feel safe, comfortable. I know I can trust him, because I've really always been able to trust him; this won't be anything different. I look down and see him peering up at me, a half-smile penetrated with my cock. I squirm, seeking more contact.

He's skilled, using the tricks and tips that you rarely encounter outside of sex slaves; the artful twisting of the tongue, the use of the muscles deep in the throat to squeeze. For the first time, I can appreciate those skills instead of resenting them, and I can understand exactly why these skills were so important to train into us.

His hand replaces his mouth, and I thrust harder into it, knowing I won't risk gagging him, and the moment I do, I cry out in absolute ecstasy as I feel his tongue sliding in, probing deep and opening me up, turning me on more. A finger joins his tongue, alternating as he slides in and out, and I press down hard, wanting more. It goes on forever, and I can feel myself growing more and more worked up. I want more; I want to feel him inside of me.

"Please," I whimper, rutting up and down. "Please, Sy!"

He looks up at me, his face almost guilty with pleasure. He holds eye contact with me while he wriggles his finger inside of me, slides it out, then presses two fingers against my entrance.

A bottle of lube rolls over, as if created by my sheer desire, and I realize that Cash is there, silently watching.

Sy must realize it, too, because he freezes, looking uncertain again.

Cash sighs. "Don't stop on my account. Do you think I gave you lube to stop you from fucking him?"

At the mention of being fucked, I moan, shuddering at how much I want this.

"Please, Sy," I whimper again. "Please don't stop!"

Sy hesitates for just a moment, glancing between me and our master, and then he continues, working his fingers inside of me carefully. His hands are bigger than Cash's, and the feeling of being spread open by them makes me shudder. He keeps sucking my cock as he does, keeping me worked up, excited. I'm squirming and desperate, making pleas I can barely understand. All I want is to feel this way forever and to be fucked.

"Please, fuck me," I beg, finally shameless enough to beg for it. "Please, god, please fuck me!"

Sy laughs, working me harder with his fingers, and Cash reaches over to touch my face. I struggle to increase skin contact with both of them.

"Who do you want to fuck you?" Cash asks, teasing my lips with his finger.

"Both of you," I answer. It's good that I don't have time to think about it or feel ashamed.

Now it's Cash's turn to laugh, and as he does, he lets his finger dip into my mouth. I suck at it greedily. It's not as good as someone fucking me, but I like the way it feels, like feeling him in my mouth while Sy is working my ass and cock.

"What do you think, Syrus?" Cash asks, the conversational tone getting me even hotter. "How should we take care of him?"

Sy pulls off my cock, resting his head on my thigh. I feel him tense. "As you think best, sir," he says, so formal in contrast to the mood I thought we had established.

Cash frowns. "If it wasn't in such poor taste, I'd smack you for that," he muses, making no move to do so. I wonder if he's this graceful with free people or if he just saves his social ineptness for slaves.

Sy doesn't seem to take it as a threat, but he doesn't respond.

"Sascha's too worked up to make clear decisions, so I thought I'd let you choose," Cash explains, working his fingers in and out of my mouth just as demandingly as he was before, almost making me choke when I get distracted. "I want to know what you're comfortable with."

Sy is quiet, unable to respond for the first time I can recall. His hand stills on my cock, and I worry that he'll back out. I make a little whine of displeasure, twisting my hips at him.

"Sascha is enjoying you," Cash states the obvious. "And I'm enjoying both of you. What about you? Is this good for you? I'm asking because I don't know you that well. I want to make sure you have a good time."

Sy is still quiet, looking more and more bothered.

"I won't fuck you, if that's what you're worried about," Cash says calmly. "We've established that you don't like that, and that's fine. I was thinking perhaps you'd like to fuck Sascha while I use his mouth, or maybe the other way around. Or maybe you'd like to leave all together. That is an option, of course, although Sascha would whine and pout about it for days."

I realize he's making a joke, one in poor taste, and I bite down playfully on the three fingers he has in my mouth. He responds by gripping at my jaw with his thumb and pinky finger, nearly choking me as he pins my head in place. Sy notices, and he looks confused. It's clear that my cock gives me away, because I feel it growing harder in Sy's hand.

"So what will it be?" Cash asks, his voice low with danger and sexuality.

"I would like to fuck him," Sy admits, for once lacking his armor of indifference and formality. Of course, he regains it a half-second later. "But is there anything I should do for you, master?"

Cash makes a noise of thinly veiled disgust. "You should refrain from calling me master while we're in bed, and you should stop pretending that you wouldn't resent the idea of servicing me," he spits out, his tone sharp and reprimanding. "If you're ever truly interested, you can say so, but I'm not so desperate as to force you to do something you don't want."

Sy blushes, and for a minute, I think he really might get up and leave. I struggle against Cash's grip, bringing a hand up to detach his fingers from my mouth and throat. He complies, placing a possessive hand on my chest instead.

"Please stay," I ask Sy, looking at him in desperation. "Please, I want to feel you fuck me. I've wanted to for weeks, since we were at the detention facility. I spent so many nights thinking of how it would feel, and I still wonder, and I want you. Don't worry about Cash, if he says he doesn't mind, he won't. Sy, I want to feel you inside of me!"

Sy seems to think about it for a moment, lazily caressing my cock, keeping me hard. The son of a bitch seems to be as interested in tormenting me as Cash is, and I can't seem to do anything to stop either one of them.

"Would it help if I left?" Cash offers, sounding regretful.

"You would do that?" Sy asks, surprised.

"Well, I wouldn't want to," Cash reminds him, sounding a little bitter. "But, yes, if I am really that much in the way, I'll let you and Sascha be alone."

I whine from underneath of them, too eager to feel them both touching me at once.

Cash smacks my chest lightly, making me all the more excited.

"Hush," he warns, smiling at little. "If you're still so needy after he finishes with you, I'll come in and fuck you again after he's done."

I think of how it would feel, to already be spent and tired, and having Cash come and fuck me again. I know he wouldn't take any mercy on me, just like he doesn't take any mercy when he makes me come and continues to fuck me for a while. The thought of being taken twice in a row like that is exciting, but not nearly as exciting as having them both at the same time.

"I don't mind if you're here," Sy says, finally. "Sascha seems to love it."

"Yes," Cash agrees. He pauses, waiting for a while before continuing to speak. "Why don't you fuck him while I use his mouth?"

Sy nods. "All right."

"Don't sound so excited," Cash mutters, rolling his eyes. "Sascha, turn over and come here. I've got something else for your mouth."

I obey as quickly as possible, moved along by Sy's fingers retracting from my ass. I crawl over to Cash, who is waiting on his back, his cock hard and ready for me. I get on my knees, my ass up and ready for Sy. My whole body quivers with anticipation. I go to take Cash's cock into my mouth, but he holds me back.

"I want to hear you when he enters you," Cash explains, holding me by my hair.

He doesn't wait long. I feel Sy coming up behind me, spreading me open with his hands, positioning his cock at my entrance. I try to thrust back against him, but he grips my ass more firmly. It's clear that I'll be waiting until he's ready. I make a high whining sound, eager to feel him, and suddenly, my wish is granted, and I feel his thick cock filling me a second later.

I moan, too caught up to decide whether it feels good or painful, because he did enter me quickly. I can't even adjust before he pulls out and slides in again, relentless, making me cry out. As I do, Cash pulls my head down, not quite forcing me onto his cock, but clearly giving me the idea that this is what he wants. I struggle to accommodate him, trying to take his cock as deep into my throat as Sy's cock is in my ass.

Sy fucks me with sheer determination, like he does everything, never seeming to get too caught up in his own passion to stop him from slamming into me, hitting every spot that feels good. I wait for him to lose control, but he doesn't. I try my best to keep up with my mouth on Cash's cock, but I doubt I'm giving the best head ever. Still, every time Sy pounds into me and I whimper, I can feel Cash responding.

I can't tell if they plan it, but Sy grips my hips tightly, and at the same time, Cash takes hold of my shoulders, digging his fingernails into my skin, bruising. It feels so good, I want to come. I want someone to touch my cock as well. I whimper, and I even pull off of Cash's cock for a moment, looking up at him desperately.

"Please," I whimper, unable to say more.

He pushes my head back down before responding.

"Don't even think of coming yet, Sascha," he warns as I take his cock deep into my throat again. "We will both be fucking you for a while longer."

It makes me more excited, and I push back harder on Sy's cock, wishing he would grant me the release that I so desperately desire. He responds by fucking me faster, but it's still not enough.

I struggle to accommodate both rhythms, both Sy pounding in and out of my ass, and Cash thrusting into my throat. Their hands start to roam, Sy touching my hips, my legs, my back, Cash gripping my arms and touching my hair. It's too much stimulation, and I feel tears forming at the corners of my eyes. I try to bring my leg up to rub against my cock, anything to get some stimulation there. I almost succeed, and I feel my own pleasure mounting.

"Try picking his legs up," Cash suggests, smiling at Sy.

I moan and squirm, frustrated that he's figured out my game.

Sy complies, wrapping his arms around my legs and pulling them up, resting them on his hips. It allows him to drive deeper into me, and I'm stuck, helpless, unable to do anything but squirm and whimper and feel them fucking me. After a while, Sy takes pity on me, pinning my leg in place with his elbow while he reaches around and grabs my cock. I freeze for a moment, too turned on to respond. I struggle to breathe, a task which is made even more difficult by the fact that Cash's cock is wedged deep in my throat. He pulls me up by my hair so I can get some air before thrusting in again.

Sy's hand is strong and sure on my cock, and I feel myself getting close. I'm only dimly aware that Cash has started thrusting harder into my mouth, working in time with Sy's thrusts from behind. I swallow instinctively as I feel Cash come, his hands tightening in my hair. I glance up at him, thrilled to see the look of excitement on his face, and I continue to work his cock gently as it softens, leaving him satisfied. If Sy notices, it doesn't have any effect on how he fucks me. He keeps going, rocking his cock in and out of me, one hand working up and down on my cock while the other keeps a firm grip on my legs.

I'm startled, to feel another hand on my cock, and Sy must be as well, because he breaks his rhythm for a second. I look up, my vision sort of blurry, and I see Cash smiling at him.

"Is this all right?" he asks, his voice sounding far away.

Sy might respond; I'm too far gone to notice. Both of them have their hands wrapped around my cock, fingers almost intertwined, and it feels better than pretty much anything in the world. Sy fucks me harder and harder until I can't keep up, can't match his rhythm. I relax all of my muscles, letting the feeling of Sy pounding into me wash over me, combining with the hands on my cock. A sharp scratch graces my back, and I moan helplessly, knowing it's Cash.

"Are you ready, Sascha?" he whispers.

I moan, unable to make words happen. I feel a hand grabbing at my balls, pulling them, twisting them, and I try to squirm, but Sy holds my legs more tightly and fucks me harder.

"Please," I manage, pressing my head into Cash's leg, wanting to come but still wanting this to last forever. "Please, yes."

I hear Sy saying "yes" above me, and I'm too far gone to realize or care what he's agreeing to. I feel him going faster, harder than I thought was possible. At the same time, I feel him and Cash working my cock. Cash digs his nails into my back, drawing four sharp lines of fire, and I know it's my cue to come. I don't really have a choice; between Sy and Cash, I am reduced to little more than gasps and shaking muscles. As I feel myself coming, I feel Sy thrusting inside of me and staying there, coming as well. I let out a scream of enjoyment.

The three of us lie there for a while, spent and exhausted. I don't want it to stop. Cash has started to gently stroke my hair, and Sy is relaxed against my ass and legs. After a few moments, he eases me down to lie on the bed, taking the pressure off of my knees. He slides out of me, pulls his hand from Cash's where it rests around my cock. I want him to come back.

"I should probably go," Sy says quietly, although I can tell he doesn't really want to. But I guess he doesn't really want to cuddle with me and Cash, either. I want to protest, but I won't subject him to that sort of humiliation.

Cash doesn't seem to have a problem with it, though, and the fact that Sy seems to be asking permission probably encourages him.

"Come here, first," he says, soft, his hand still carding through my hair.

Sy obeys, moving a few inches closer to the head of the bed where Cash rests, arrogant and sated. I try to protest, but I'm tired and comfortable, and all that comes out is a sort of half-whimper. I manage to lift my head at least, and I look at Sy, inching closer to our master, a stoic and determined look on his face.

I think Cash is going to touch him, but he doesn't.

"Thank you for joining us tonight," he tells Sy quietly. "I enjoyed it, and so did Sascha, and I do hope that you did."

Sy nods, oddly quiet, even for him.

"I think I've made a mistake, though," Cash muses.

I feel myself starting to tense, wondering if the "mistake" was letting Sy fuck me at all, or if it was deciding not to have his way with Sy as well. As much as I trust Cash to take care of me, I don't really trust him with Sy. I wish this wasn't getting spoiled so quickly.

"Insisting that I be around to partake in the activities between you and Sascha was selfish," Cash admits, surprising me. "He can take care of himself, and I trust him with you. If you want, in the future, you're welcome to play with him."

"Thank you, sir," Sy manages, barely concealing his surprise.

I glance up, staring at Cash in shock. I wasn't expecting this, and it's almost too good to seem true.

"That goes for you, too, Sascha," Cash reminds me, giving my hair a teasing tug. "Feel free to have fun. I won't deny the two of you that."

I grin up at him, feeling my face go red with excitement. I press my head into his leg again.

Sy gets up, taking everything that's been said as his cue to leave, and he smiles back at me and Cash as he does.

"Oh, and Syrus?" Cash adds, right as he reaches the door.

Sy turns back, somehow managing to look dignified despite the fact that he is naked, clutching his clothes in one hand.

"Sir?" he asks.

"Don't hesitate to join us again in the future," Cash suggests, his smile predatory and full of lust.

"I won't," Sy agrees, smiling back.

I let out a breath, relieved that they finally seem to be on the same page about something.

Chapter 19

Arrangements

Something shifts after I join Sascha and our master in bed. I've never been involved with any of my masters in that capacity. Certainly they've fucked me. Whether it was out of convenience, or boredom, or to assert their power over me, most of my masters have taken that opportunity and invited their associates to do the same.

With Cashiel, it's different. He doesn't love me the way he loves Sascha; he barely even knows me, and he's far above pretending. But it's not about power or humiliation with him. He enjoyed it, enjoyed seeing Sascha explore, enjoyed seeing me relax a little. In a strange way, it makes me more comfortable around him.

When I overhear him setting up a meeting with his lawyer a few days later, I push aside the reluctance I've had since the talk show. I find him in his office, Sascha busy working in another room.

"Master, there's something I need to tell you."

He glances up at me, like he wants to spend as little time speaking to me as possible. Sascha explained that he gets too intense with his work. As usual, Sascha knows him best.

I push through the hesitation, the years of training that scream at me to shut my mouth. "At the talk show, it wasn't just people out to hurt you. One of the men who rushed the stage, the one who left that bruise... I knew him."

Cash nods. "Go on."

I calm myself by remembering that he's not the type to just kill me and dump the body somewhere. If anything, Sascha would never forgive him. "He's a member of the 27th Street Gang, one of my former master's associates. The one who threatened to kill me if I didn't give

153

him information for the Argova family."

My master frowns, a look of unrestrained annoyance crossing his face. "You should have told me immediately."

"Yes, sir." I'm usually good at judging my masters' moods, how severely they'll punish me, but I get nothing from Cash. It's almost worse.

"Well?" he asks. "What do we do about it? I'm certain there's a reason you've told me about it now."

I nod, hiding my relief out of habit. Relief shows you are afraid of something; fear makes you weak. "I know you're meeting with Ms. Edson later today. With her ties to the Argova family, I thought she might be able to set up a meeting, to put something in place. The 27th Street Gang wouldn't go against the wishes of the Argova family."

"All right."

I wait for the threats, the conditions, the expected payment. I wait to be reminded of my failures.

"Go get Sascha for me. I'd like to see how he's coming with what he's got planned. Make sure we have everything ready for the lawyer when she comes."

"Yes, sir," I reply. I know I shouldn't feel so relieved, but I do.

I compose myself by the time I retrieve Sascha, and he doesn't notice a thing.

While he and Cash talk, I am quiet, relaxing and not paying much attention. They review details that I am already aware of, consider new angles, make plans to tell the lawyer. I've spent years trying not to listen too closely to my masters' conversations; it's listening that would be the hard part.

When Edson arrives, the security team outside informs Cash, but I go to open the door anyway. It's my responsibility, and I enjoy the opportunity to be useful. My continued presence, not to mention existence, has always hinged on usefulness. Just because I doubt Cash would discard me so easily doesn't mean I'm willing to let that go.

Cash guides us to the dining room. He doesn't tell me to sit, so I remain standing. The three of them settle in, and Edson gives me a curious look. She's seen me before, but she's not sure where. Just another bodyguard. I remember all the times I've seen her. She's not the lawyer who dealt with most of my old master's legal issues, but she has been around. Many of the interactions that my old master's associates had with the Argova family had taken place on their territory. I've seen Edson coming and going, and I've heard her give significant advice to my old master about the shipment of the "products" that the 27s handled. Edson never referred to the drugs or slave organs by name.

"There's been some development on the case," Edson begins, a knowing smile on her face. "It seems that someone has been kind enough to encourage your data analyst to turn in some evidence that looks quite bad for the Miller System."

"I've heard," Cash replies.

Edson just nods, like she expected it. "This places you in a good position. From what I've heard from an inside source, it doesn't harm your case. It actually strengthens it, and gets your mother out of the way, potentially."

"But what about the rest of the data?" Sascha cuts in. "There was a lot more that didn't get released. Whoever was behind this has to have access to that data."

Edson smiles. "I believe it's in our best interest to focus on the rest of the case. I have a feeling that whoever arranged for this information to come out has the same interests as we do."

She doesn't come right out and say it, but she may as well. She knows who pressured the data analyst, and they're working with us. Sascha smiles, and Cash moves on quickly to the next point.

"Kristine Miller. She was upset about the information, she came by here the other day."

"So let her hang herself," Edson advises. "You're not out to get her. You're just presenting facts. How those facts get interpreted in court, or by the state... well, that's nothing you can control."

"She knows it was me who released the first set of data," Sascha mentions. "She says she can prove it, she has official records, the bug she planted in our house. She might actually be able to prove that it wasn't Cash who did it."

"So you did it on his orders," Edson dismisses.

"But what happens when he can't explain the data as well as I can?" Sascha continues.

Edson frowns at Cash. "If you can't wrap your head around the data analysis that your Demoted slave conducted, I made quite a mistake in letting you hire me, and someone made an even bigger mistake in recommending I consider your case."

"I'll learn it all," Cash says quickly. "In detail, in plenty of time before the trial."

Satisfied, Edson continues. "I wouldn't be so worried about Ms. Miller. She might just be losing some of her special privileges once this data goes public."

"She'll take the blame for this," Sascha realizes.

"She deserves to," Cash reminds him.

"Don't let your feelings get in the way of this case," Edson says. "The world is ready for a new system. You can start that system with your work in the re-education centers. It's nothing personal, at least as far as anyone else is ever going to know. You sympathize with Ms. Miller, respect the foundation she has established in the field, and you wish her the best. For all you know, you might work with her in the future. She is everything that our current system values."

Cash and Sascha both nod. I wonder what this lawyer isn't telling us. She's the trusted advisor and legal representative of the Argova family. She's very well-connected, and from the few interactions I've witnessed, she knows how to put these connections to use. If the Argova family trusts her, she represents their interests. She seems quite certain that Cash is going to come out of this clean and happy. In that past, I've found that to mean that whoever is doing the talking knows far more than they're willing to admit. The question is whether she's being kept in the dark by the Argova family, or whether she's keeping Cash in the dark for the Argova family.

"Your performance at the talk show went well," Edson tells them. "I'm not so sure I like the way it ended, but more groups have taken interest in your case as a result. That can be good or bad, so you need to keep building up your image. More appearances, more interviews. You have to be a real person for this work. Talk about how scared you were, how much more you have to contribute — all that sort of thing. Ms. Miller has a number of supporters, but she's reached celebrity status. You're the everyday citizen. Buy your own groceries, pet your slave in public and look embarrassed. You've spent a long time looking perfect and staying out of the spotlight; now you need to do the exact opposite. You want people to like you."

I resist laughing. Since I've gotten to know Cash, it isn't that he's unlikeable, he's just distant. For anyone else, the data, formal social interaction, and the danger would be the challenges. For my master, it's the informal parts he struggles with. He and Sascha both listen carefully, like they can study how to casually interact.

"You'll be attending more events, and closer to your trial date, you'll be holding a sponsorship rally," Edson explains. "You can strengthen relationships and locate funders for your project."

"Would anyone actually want to put their funds into a project where the lead person might be imprisoned for starting it?" Cash asks.

Edson sighs. "You're not going to prison. Not if I have anything to say about it. Besides, it doesn't matter to most of them whether your project gets off the ground, anyway. They'll gain exposure simply by being associated with you. You're a novelty, Mr. Michaud. We don't have many new faces in business or in politics these days. You've managed to be both. With some luck, you might win the government's support as the new Demoted system creator—if you do it well enough, you might not even need a highly politicized role. You can have your business and be a government sponsored contractor."

Cash nods, like he's not sure he wants either. From what Sascha's told me, he doesn't, but now that he's in it, he has to play it out. There's no way he can walk away from this with the rest of his life intact.

"Where does your business partner stand on this issue?" Edson asks.

Cash shrugs. "He's supporting me."

"He's using us to support his own needs," Sascha clarifies. "He's in it for the money, for his cut in the medical research department. He bailed Cash out so the project could continue, and because he likes to play savior."

Cash shrugs a little, not denying it, and Edson shakes her head at both of them.

"Let me know if the man becomes a problem. Although it sounds like a personal issue between the three of you. Keep it personal."

"He's got the rest of our data," Sascha informs the lawyer. "The old stuff, the part that Cash has kept out of the media. And he knows who released the research."

Edson considers it for a moment. "He'd be doing his own interests a significant disservice at this point, and he can't prove anything about you, Sascha. Keep him uninformed about new developments, but keep him close. You can't seem wary of your own partner. You have to proceed as if nothing is wrong, as if you are completely innocent."

Cash nods. "One more thing. I have a more personal favor."

Edson gives him a questioning look.

"Syrus," Cash says, gesturing toward me. "My new bodyguard. It seems he has a bit of a problem with some connections from his previous master."

Edson glances from Cash to me and back again. "Why is this my problem?"

"They tried to kill him at that talk show the other day," Cash says. "Some old debt, and they're angry at him for not sharing information about my project."

"That's unfortunate," Edson says.

"Syrus's previous master was closely connected to the Argova family," Cash mentions, casual. "I believe that facilitating my relationship with the Argova family is one of your goals."

"Yes. But my instructions include establishing strong business connections, not whatever you think I can do for your slave," Edson tries to dismiss him.

"Tell whoever it matters to that Syrus is very valuable to me," Cash continues, ignoring her. It's a bluff, but he does it well. "If someone were to convince his previous associates that he is no longer of interest to them, I'd be interested in meeting with that person to discuss our future business ties. Say, at the sponsorship event we discussed."

Edson smiles, the first I've seen that doesn't look contrived. "I don't think that will be any problem at all. To those who matter, something that small will be a welcome gift."

"Sy's master was the head of a low-level street gang," Sascha informs her. "They run drugs and organs. They were in business with the Argova family, as well as my master's business partner, Oliver Torenze. Now that Sy's master is in prison, they're under new leadership. Someone named Conrad has been sent to kill him."

The lawyer's smile widens. I know she's met Conrad. She must be figuring out which low-level street gang she is discussing, but in the same way as she never mentioned the products that the 27th Street Gang moved, she isn't mentioning the name of the gang now. "This will not be a problem. I believe I know exactly who you're talking about. I'll have someone let them know that Syrus has moved on to more important things. If they don't like it, they can end up where his former master did."

"Let's hope I don't end up in prison," Cash mutters. "Sounds like I won't have friends there."

Edson laughs. "He's no longer in prison. He was executed a few days ago. Habitual offender, resisted attempts to rehabilitate, poor legal defense. Someone who mattered decided that he would be a risk to society. They eliminated that risk."

From the way she speaks, she may as well have given the lethal injection herself. Was that what it was all about, then? Had someone wanted my former master dead all along? They should have just asked me to kill him, but then, that wouldn't have sent the same message. Having him legally executed demonstrates the reach of the Argova family; having me kill him would have just brought a smile to my face. No wonder he forfeited his rights to me.

They spend the rest of their time together discussing the finer details, the dates, the events, and I let myself tune out again. For the first time in decades, I feel like I might live to have a future.

Chapter 20

Permission

Over the next few days, Cash does his part to set in place the events and plans that we discussed with Edson. As much as I want to be with him, I'm glad he doesn't bring me out to run errands. I'm tired of playing slave in public, and the very fact that I even consider it to be "playing" reminds me that I need to get my shit together. For Sy, it seems effortless.

With my work completed for the day and nothing else pressing, I stand at Sy's doorway, wondering if I should go in. Sy's in there, I can hear him breathing through the door, and I figure it's probably creepy of me to just stand here listening. It's the first time we've really been alone since we got back from the detention facility, and it's the first time I've ever seriously thought about being with him alone. Cash said he wouldn't mind, but it still seems strange.

I ponder that for a moment, because why should it feel strange? It doesn't feel strange that Cash and I fuck pretty much every night, and during the day, sometimes. Since that first time the three of us had sex, we've fooled around a few more times, and it has been amazing every time. I don't think I'd feel left out if Cash and Sy were to do anything alone, even though I doubt they ever would. The truth is, I miss spending time with Sy, time when I can let my guard down and not have to worry about his Cash's ego or trying to balance my attention between the two of them. And a part of me is curious, every time he and Cash are sharing me, how it would be to be alone with him. Finally, I knock at the door, lightly at first, then loudly enough to hear. I wait, anxious as I hear footsteps approaching the door.

"Sascha," he says, smiling at me.

"Hey," I say, suddenly unable to speak.

He smiles at me, and for a moment, I think he might just make me wait forever until I can find words.

"Did you need something?" he asks, exceedingly polite.

I push my way into his room, deciding to go ahead and try to do this thing. I sit on the edge of his bed, determined, but still not sure how to start things. After a minute, he sits next to me, tentative. I glance at him nervously, feeling like an awkward schoolboy trying to make a move. I'm a sex slave, I have been for years, but somehow the idea of making a move on Sy is making me blush.

I reach over, placing my hand on his leg, hoping he gets it. Maybe this will be easier than speaking.

"Oh." He smiles at me. "So that's what you want, pretty boy?"

I jerk my hand away, feeling the blush deepen. I don't know how to initiate this. Usually, it's Cash; he's the one who starts everything, the one who invites Sy in and woos him and gets him to want to have amazing sex with us. Well, Cash gets Sy to want to have amazing sex with me, but Cash is involved. They don't do more than share the occasional glance or touch, even though a part of me is curious about how that would go.

A hand on my shoulder pulls me back to the present and out of my thoughts, and I look at Sy nervously, waiting.

"Did I misjudge?" Sy asks, raising an eyebrow.

I shake my head.

"You sure the master will be okay with this?" Sy asks, and I get the sense that he's not trying to find excuses, he's just checking bases. Thorough, always.

"I'm sure," I answer easily, surprised by how much faith I put in Cash. "He'll just be a little jealous that he missed out on the fun."

Sy is quiet for a moment, smiling at me. Finally, when I'm starting to wonder whether this really was a good idea or not, he places his hand on my shoulder and turns me to face him. I wait, frozen, until he pulls me close and kisses me until I whimper.

He pauses, breaking our lips apart, caressing the back of my head. "Is that a good sound?"

I nod, slightly, caught up in the excitement of the moment. When nothing happens, I force myself to speak. "Yeah."

Sy leans back against the pillows that are perfectly aligned against the headboard, pulling me along. I rest on top of him, his firm body somehow contouring to mine, comforting and familiar. I nuzzle up against his neck, seeking out the familiar smell of him and brushing my lips against his skin.

"What would you like?" he asks, running his hands over my body and making me squirm.

"I just..." I pause, considering it. "I just want to have fun with you. Whatever you want to do. We've never really... you know... alone."

"Are you looking to fool around a little bit, or are you looking to fuck?" Sy asks, running his hands over my ass, massaging, but not demanding.

It feels good, it feels really good, and it takes me a minute to realize that he probably wants me to answer.

"I want you to fuck me," I hear the words come out. I think I was going to say that we should just start out with fooling around, maybe I could give him head or something, but I really do want him to fuck me. I want to feel what it's like to have him fuck me when it's just the two of us.

Sy smiles, kisses me again. "All right," he says, his hands coming up to strip my shirt off. "I can't say I haven't thought about this."

He has me naked in seconds, and it's just so efficient and sexy. Cash strips me slowly sometimes, rips my clothes off sometimes, and has me strip myself sometimes, but he never does it quite this efficiently. In the same way, Sy begins removing his own clothes, but I stop him, covering his hands with mine.

"Can I?" I ask, looking up at him hopefully. He might like the efficiency, but I kind of want to play with him a little.

He looks startled, but he relaxes, letting his hands drop back to give me free access. "All right," he says, smiling. "I guess I'm not really used to that."

I don't think too much about what he is used to; I know enough from what he's told me that he was never a pampered toy like I am; he was used harshly and without care. I don't want it to be like that between us. I've seen how caring he can be with me, and I want to show him the same consideration in return. I want to appreciate him, especially now that I have him all to myself.

I go slowly, sliding my hands under his shirt to feel his skin, and I glance up at him as I do, smiling. I can't tell if he likes it or if he's just tolerating it, but I'm determined to make him enjoy it. I feel his chest and I smile as I place myself on top of him again. I straddle his hips, resting my ass just barely against his cock. I'm satisfied when I feel that he's hard.

I slip his shirt over his head slowly, sensually, and the second it leaves his body I begin working over his chest and neck with my lips and teeth. I pay attention to the spots that make his cock hard and his breath quicken. He brings his arms up to touch me as well, and I begin to slide my body up and down his, feeling the friction between our skin. He pulls my head closer, demanding, but not too forceful, and he kisses me again, our mouths moving in time with our bodies.

It's nice, relaxing even, and I'm glad I can share this with him. I snake my hand down his pants and find his cock, claiming it, holding back a laugh when I feel him jerk in surprise.

We continue for a while until we stop to breathe, and I look at Sy with a satisfied smile. "Do you like this?" I check.

"I do," he answers, cupping my ass in his hands and kneading my skin. He knows exactly what I like by now.

Satisfied, I slither down his body, trailing my tongue across his stomach until I reach the top of his pants. I unfasten the button and pull the zipper down with my teeth, pleased when I hear him give a strangled sort of groan. His hands have trailed up my body as I slid down, and now they leave my back and go to his pants.

"Is this okay?" He pauses before pushing his own pants off.

It's strangely hot to hear him asking permission; while I've grown used being asked permission before things are done to me, it's rare that someone ask me permission to do something to their own body. I like it more than I thought I would.

"Yes," I nod, a strange thrill going through me as I realize he's waiting for my approval.

He slips his pants over his hips, and I take over and pull them off of his legs. Once he's naked, I stroke and caress my way back up, teasing. I take my time, nibbling at his thighs, coming closer and closer to his cock as he gently pets my head. I touch him with my hands, caressing his balls, feeling around his ass, pleased when he rocks against my touch. I lean in and breathe warm air over his cock, feeling his hands form into fists against my neck. He isn't pulling my hair, although I wouldn't mind. I can tell he's holding back.

"Sascha, you feel amazing."

"So do you." I like taking my time with him, teasing him. I continue until he starts to let desperate moans slip out, and then I take his cock into my mouth, swallowing him deep all at once as he gasps in surprise.

"Fuck, Sascha," he mutters, rocking his hips gently.

I stay focused on my task, but his pleasure is contagious. I feel my body warming alongside his, my cock growing hard in anticipation.

I keep going for a while, and I'm getting really into it when I feel his hand pressing on my forehead, almost too gently to feel it. I pull off, looking up at him and appreciating the way his face is flushed.

"Can I..." he starts, pausing to catch a breath. "Sascha, I want to be inside of you."

I smirk, because he's always so polite about it, so gentle and careful. I want him to lose that control, to be rough and demanding and vulgar. I slide up his body, making sure that we have as much contact as possible. "Oh, do you?" I tease, grinding against him.

He sighs, lustful. "Yes," he says, looking at me firmly, but still with a touch of restraint.

"Do you really?" I continue to torment him, thrusting my hips against his.

Sy goes quiet, looking away and stilling a little. I turn his face toward mine, feeling guilty when I notice the embarrassed expression. I lean in and kiss him, reigniting the friction between us, and hopefully apologizing.

But in case it didn't work as an apology, I pull back and look at him sincerely. "Sorry," I say softly. "I'm just playing. I really didn't mean to make you..." I don't even know what made him, but I didn't want to.

Sy smiles, the trace of humiliation erased as though it was never there. "I'll tell you about that another day," he says softly, the faintest trace of bitterness in his voice at the memory I know nothing about. "But yes, right now I really do want to be inside of you. I want to feel you tight around me. I want to feel my cock deep inside of you, ramming you hard until you beg me for more. I do. But I don't usually want to talk about it. I'd rather just do it."

I kiss at his neck again. "I want to feel you inside of me. Please. I like to beg."

"I won't even make you beg," Sy grins at me. "But I do plan to make you scream."

The promise provokes a little whimper, the likes of which Sy would never make. I feel his hands on my waist, and I don't fight as he lifts me off of him and sets me to the side. He flips me to my back and holds me down with one arm as he sits up and grabs at my cock with his other hand.

I make a strangled noise of pleasure as he jerks my cock, getting me even more turned on than I already was. Seconds later, he takes my cock into his mouth, sucking hard and firm and fast, bringing me almost to the point of coming before he stops. I lie panting, wanting more, and he doesn't let me down. He slides two fingers into me easily. When and where he got lube, I'm not sure, but right now, everything seems to be moving too quickly to keep up. I thrust back against his fingers, riding them with my ass, wishing there was more.

"Sy," I whimper, unable to make words happen.

His response is to add another finger inside, rocking and thrusting and stretching me efficiently. I can't keep up, but I try, relaxing at the expert way he's working my body, one hand working my ass, the other jerking my cock.

His fingers slip out one more time, and I don't even have time to realize what's happening before feeling his cock replace it, driving deep into me until I reach up and claw at his shoulders. I love the feeling of him over top of me. He's still quiet, but he he's smiling slightly. Every time he draws a sound from me his smile seems to grow wider in response. He grabs me firmly by the hips, holding me in place while he fucks me harder and harder.

His promise comes true, and I scream for him.

I want his hands back on my cock, because I want to come. He doesn't grant me that, he just keeps fucking me, holding me still as he does. The torment is wonderful.

"Please let me come," I finally give in and beg, half because I like begging, and half because I really do want to come.

Looking pleased, Sy releases the grip his has on my hip with one hand and grabs my cock again, jerking quick and hard as I squirm underneath of him.

I thrust, I squirm, I squeeze with my ass, but I realize with a bit of dismay that it's not going to do it for me. While I can get off on being terrified, nothing about Sy terrifies me anymore, and he's not really fucking me hard enough to hurt me. I try to struggle against his hand, hoping to hurt myself somehow. He loosens his grip, probably thinking that I'm uncomfortable, but it just frustrates me more.

"Please hurt me," I mumble, feeling the fresh shame of having to ask for it. It never really occurred to me, but when we're with Cash, he always makes sure that this is taken care of. Sy knows it, I think, logically, but I don't think he really gets it. The surprise on his face shows that. "Please, Sy, just a little? I can't get off without it. Please!"

Sy doesn't slow down fucking me, and he doesn't let up on my cock. The sensation is so much that it's frustrating, almost painful, but not the right kind of pain. He takes the hand that's gripping my hip and trails it up over my chest, resting it there.

"What would you like me to do?" he asks softly. I can tell he's not just teasing, he really does want direction.

I am almost too far gone to give any sort of direction. "I don't care!" I blurt out. "Bite me. Hit me. Scratch me. Do what you want; just make me feel it!"

Looking troubled, Sy swats at my chest lightly, almost playfully. I moan, because it's not enough, although I do appreciate him trying. At one point, it might have been enough, but Cash has spoiled me. Cash takes me rougher and rougher each time, and I've grown to love it.

"Please," I beg, "harder."

Sy swats at me again, and if he does it harder, I don't notice it. I have the horrible fear that maybe we won't be able to do this, maybe it won't work, maybe he won't really be able to make me come like I want him to.

I moan, debating whether to just dig my own nails into my skin instead.

"Not enough?" Sy asks, picking up on my frustration.

I whimper, because I can't bear admitting it.

"All right," Sy says, groping across my chest again. His fingers press harder, digging his nails into my skin, and I feel my cock respond immediately. "You like that?" he asks, sounding surprised.

"Yes, please, more," I mumble, letting the pain wash over me.

He continues, raking his nails across my chest, leaving red lines that cross and burn. He captures my nipples in between his fingers, squeezing softly at first. As I squirm harder underneath of him, he squeezes harder, making me cry out.

"Fuck, Sy, that's good. That's amazing." I'm desperate to let him know how much I'm enjoying it.

"Good," he says, sounding pleased. "I can't wait to feel you come, pretty boy."

I moan in response, the nickname somehow sounding sexy in this context. He thrusts into me again and again, increasing the pressure and pain on my nipples, and I come, reaching up to clutch at his arms. It doesn't matter that he's stopped jerking my cock, I come anyway, and I feel him come just a few seconds later, while I'm still trying to catch my breath. I'm left a shaking mess.

Sy runs his hands across my chest again, soothing the irritated skin, then leans down to kiss me. He waits for a moment, letting me relax before easing out. As I lie there, staring at the ceiling and waiting for my vision to clear, he gets up and returns with a towel, meticulously cleaning us both off before slipping back into bed next to me, lying on his back. I wiggle closer, a little demanding, and he doesn't hesitate to pull me close. I rest against the curve of his body, shuddering at the memory of the sex we just had.

"That was amazing," I can still feel his hands on me, still feel the lingering burn from his cock inside of me. "Thank you."

"Thank you," Sy asserts, running his hand down my side softly. "You're sure I didn't hurt you too much?"

I shake my head, pressing closer to him. "No," I reassure him. "I really do like it. I promise. And I really can't get off without it most of the time."

Sy is quiet for a moment, considering it. "I always kind of thought Cash was exaggerating," he admits. "I thought he was the one who liked it."

"He does like it. But I do, too. He wouldn't hurt me if I didn't."

Sy nods. "I'm starting to get that. He's a bit hard for me to figure out at times. I suppose I can take him at his word."

I smile. I'm glad they're not competing anymore. "He's good for his word. Always has been."

Sy nods. "Better hope that's true," he muses, gesturing to our post-sex condition. He doesn't seem overly concerned.

"I wouldn't let him do anything to you!" I protest, feeling oddly protective over this man who can so clearly take care of himself. "It was my idea in the first place."

Sy ruffles my hair, and while I think it should probably make me feel like a child, it's actually pretty nice.

"Listen, pretty boy, if he gets upset about it, you'll let me handle it, just like you let me handle things at the detention facility," he says, the slight order in his voice crushing any resistance I might have felt. "I doubt he'll kill me or sell me. I can handle him."

I consider it. I worried in the past that Cash would sell me; at one point, I even considered that he might kill me. The thought had terrified me. For Sy, it's an everyday occurrence. The threat of being slapped has me more worked up than that, which makes me give him a curious look. I'm not sure if I want to know how he's become so immune to fear.

"Another day, pretty boy.

But that's always what he says when I ask about his past. I guess it's nicer than just telling me to leave him alone.

Chapter 21
Bodyguard

When Torenze first told me about what was happening with Cash's case, he told me that they wanted a villain. For Cash to prove that he's not one, he needs to appeal to the public. Sometimes he can get away with making solo appearances, but more often, he wants me and Sy in attendance.

Today's event is exactly that. The conservative rally is filled with supporters of the Demoted system, particularly those who are most likely to support harsh treatment, things like the Miller System. It's a risk for us to be here, but Edson and even Cash are convinced that this is exactly the crowd we need to appeal to. They chose the location for the rally carefully, in front of the well-manicured lawn of one of the Miller System's government research facilities. As a public space, it is available to anyone who can manage to obtain a permit; Edson acquired one for us easily. We make a strong show, answering questions, challenging assumptions, making it clear that we belong with these people. We are on their side.

I almost believed it during Cash's speech; now that we're trying to navigate our way through the crowd to go home, I can't help but wonder if we are siding with the enemy.

The crowd is closing in on us, demanding more answers, more information, more contact. It's some sort of goddamned pandemonium and I hate it. I want to go home, where I'm safe, and I really start to lose it when they start to touch me, reaching out like I'm some sort of exotic animal at a petting zoo.

Sy does his best to place himself between me and the crowd, but he's also doing his best to place himself between Cash and the crowd.

He's a big man, but there are two of us, and Cash has practically peeled me off of his legs more than once today. I don't want to look clingy and risk making him look weak.

"What makes you qualified to change the Demoted system?" One of the supporters yells, giving Cash a dirty look.

Cash announced thirty minutes ago that he had answered his last question, but when he sticks to his word, the crowd gets more aggressive, grabbing at Cash's clothes and my skin in an attempt to slow us down.

"Who else is your master meeting with? Is he an abolitionist? Are you really even a slave?"

"Do you stupid Demoted whores think you can change anything?"

I pull away from the hands that reach out toward me, poking and grabbing, never long enough to hold on, but long enough to make me uncomfortable. Cash swats them away, and Sy struggles to block their access. He's better at evading their touch—as a bodyguard, he was taught those skills.

"Where do you think you're going? Off to play with your spoiled pets? Let's see how well-behaved they really are!"

Maybe they're not trying to separate Sy and me from our master, but they do.

The last order I hear Cash bark at Sy is "Take care of Sascha." He speaks loudly enough for the cameras to pick it up, and I know it's intentional.

Sy responds with military precision, shifting away from Cash and focusing on protecting just me. He places his hands around my waist, pulling me close in front of him so he can guide me through the crowd without losing me. Cash falls behind, cursing the press and calling for more security; paid security, free people who can brandish crowd control weapons. Sy might be a good human shield, but his ability to physically defend either me or Cash is limited by his status.

A microphone is jammed into my face, hitting me, and the overzealous reporter doesn't seem to care.

"Does your master have ties with an abolitionist movement?" the man demands, his microphone jabbing into my lip. "Have you heard him discussing plans with foreign enemies?"

"Stop it!" I snap, forgetting my manners and my place. I backpedal. "Sir, you're hurting me!"

Sy tries to shift me away, but the reporter is determined. He grabs my arm, twisting it until I cry out.

"Answer my question, boy!" he growls, refusing to let go. "I'll beat you like a proper master should!"

The statement incites me. I've heard my master mocked too many times today. I struggle to wrench my arm away, furious when the man grabs me again.

"Let me go!" I yell, pulling away with one hand while striking out with the other.

My fist never connects, because the reporter simply isn't there by the time it gets there. I stumble, startled to have connected with thin air, and I realize what I've just caused. Sy's longer, faster arms were able to knock the man to the ground before I had a chance to even graze him.

Those arms are wrapped tightly around me, now, shielding me from the blows that other free people are directing at us as well as the things that are being thrown. I want to struggle, but he's holding me too tightly. As I start to panic, he tightens his grip.

"Don't fight me, Sascha," Sy whispers. "You'll make it worse for all of us."

I sag in his arms, feeling the weight of that truth a moment later. The crowd calls for officers to take vengeance against the violent slave who dared to lay hands on a free person.

"Get on your knees," Sy whispers, pulling me down with him. "Don't touch me. If they tase me, it will pass to you."

He stays close, kneeling perfectly, head bowed, waiting for commands or punishments. He's still between me and the officers, and I don't doubt that he'll throw himself on top of me to protect me. I want Cash. Where the hell is he?

"That's the one!" I hear the voice of the reporter accusing us. "That beast attacked me!"

"Hit him," an officer orders. A moment later, I hear a popping noise, and I watch as Sy falls to the ground, his muscles twitching as the electricity passes through him. I bite back tears of helplessness.

"Enough!"

The sound of Cash's voice calms me. He'll fix this. He has to.

"The slave is subdued," Cash points out. The crowd parts for him as he strides over to us. The altercation, combined with the sound of tasers, has prompted all but the most unruly of people to give us some space. "Harm him again and I'll have the department for the medical bills."

The threat of financial consequences makes the officers back down quickly.

"Your slave attacked me!" the reporter declares. "Pushed me right to the ground!"

Cash frowns, glancing at me, because Sy is on the ground. "Is this true?"

Sy rises to his knees again, still shaking, and looks at our master calmly. "Yes, master."

The crowd roars, demanding he be killed, beaten, tased some more. A few people cheer him, probably because the reporter was equally as annoying to them as he was to us.

A bitter look crosses Cash's face for a moment before he crushes it. "Come here, boy."

He never calls Sy that, and it's chilling to hear him do it so callously. Sy is on his feet and walking to our master in a second. I rise as well. Cash didn't call me, but I want him. I run to his side, dropping to my knees again. I'm the pretty little pleasure slave; nobody is going to think twice about me hiding behind my master's legs. If I had done so in the first place, none of this would have happened.

Cash glances at the officers. "I'll need to talk to the chief of security."

One nods, turning to fetch the person Cash requested. I look at Sy, kneeling just a few inches from me. He's perfectly positioned, his face calm and serene. I'm not doing as well. Cash reaches down to run his finger through my hair, reassuring me in the only way that is proper in a setting like this. The kindness brings tears to my eyes, and I turn toward him, away from the crowd that will surely mock my affection.

The chief of security arrives in minutes, directing his team to push the crowd further away from where we wait, giving us the space to resolve the incident. "Mr. Michaud, would you care to explain the incident that your slaves have caused?"

"Of course," Cash says smoothly. "First off, I want to make it know that this one is a registered bodyguard who has received appropriate training and documentation in this state. Further, I want to make it completely clear that any and all actions he took today were sanctioned by me and fell under his orders as my personal protection."

"Noted." The chief of security glances at Sy first, then at me. "I assume that you will send a copy of that documentation to the department?"

"Immediately," Cash promises. "I can flash them from my wristband right now, if you need."

The chief of security nods, then glances at me again. "What about that one?"

I cower, hoping it makes me look pathetic. I won't let Sy's protection be in vain.

"A pleasure slave," Cash says. "A toy. He's no more capable of doing harm than a purse dog."

It was me who was about to hit the reporter. The only reason it didn't come to pass was because Sy beat me to it.

"There are plenty of videos of the incident," Cash says, dismissive. "I can guarantee that the only one of my slaves who dared to take action was my bodyguard, who was acting on my orders."

I start to calm a little bit, holding onto hope that we might escape further harm.

"You were nowhere around when this incident occurred, correct?" the chief of security asks.

"Correct," Cash admits. "We were separated by the crowd. The one your department failed to control."

The chief doesn't respond to that last comment, he just frowns at Cash a little. "You are aware that a slave, even a bodyguard, is prohibited from causing harm to a free person in order to defend another slave?"

Silence settles over the crowd as they wait for Cash's response. I think I might throw up. I know the penalty for laying hands on a free person. While I didn't know the laws about Sy protecting me, I assume Cash did, and I'm certain Sy did. It's not worth it for Sy to risk his life for me like this. It wasn't worth it for me to act so spoiled and uppity that I dared to even attempt to push a free person away. How could I put Sy in this position?

"I am quite aware of that," Cash replies, maintaining his calm. "I am also aware that the statutes do not call for execution or re-training in the event that a bodyguard is defending his master's personal property. They allow for mild correction at the master's hand, given both parties involved can come to an agreement."

The chief of security nods, looking surprised that Cash is as well-versed in the legal world as he is. A few crowd members cry out in protest, but they are quickly silenced by the security team or their fellow media. Those with cameras and microphones are subtly moving closer, eager to hear as much as they can of the exchange.

"Sascha, get up," Cash orders.

It takes me far longer than it should to realize he's talking to me, because I'm trying to think of any way to get Sy out of this. I'm failing him after he protected me again. I rise, shaking and scared, and look at Cash for further orders.

"The reporter Sy pushed, did he hurt you?" Cash asks, his eyes meeting mine. For a moment, we are the only people in the world. If this can be fixed, he'll fix it.

"Yes, master," I whisper.

"Show me."

I remove pull back my sleeve, displaying bright red marks that are already darkening into bruises. For once, I'm glad I mark easily. Cash puts a protective arm around me and glares at the reporter hatefully.

"I'll be having the boy checked out by a medical professional later. Would you like me to file a property damage complaint against you, or would you like to settle this?"

The reporter flushes at the threat. "Um, I'll settle," he mumbles.

"I'm sorry, I couldn't hear you." Cash's tone is cold and demeaning, like one would use on a slave. "Speak loudly enough that the security officers can hear your answer."

"I'd like to hear the terms and settle," the reporter says, a little more loudly this time. He's shaking. Cash can terrify a free man as easily as he can terrify me.

Cash nods. "I understand that the bodyguard exemptions do not cover personal property. The slave will be publicly beaten to remind him of his place. In return, I will refrain from pressing charges for destruction of property. I will not send you any bills, and you will be given top priority in reporting this incident."

The reporter looks thrilled at that last statement. This incident could make his career.

"I want to administer the beating," he demands.

Cash clenches his jaw, and I can feel him tense.

"You may assist," he grinds out. "Under my terms. I assure you, I have more than adequate training to administer such a punishment, unlike you."

The reporter looks like he might protest.

"Or we can make a formal case out of this and I can find someone else to give exclusive priority to," Cash threatens. He glances out at the crowd. "I'm sure someone here would love to be the exclusive witness to a private punishment."

The crowd cheers and the reporter quickly reconsiders.

"No, I'll take it, I was just asking!" he rushes to correct himself. "I'll assist."

Cash stares him down for a few moments before answering. "Good," he says, although his tone and his face suggest that he is anything but pleased with the man.

Cash pulls me along with him as he walks to Sy. He touches Sy lightly on the shoulder, indicating for him to rise, and when he does, Cash turns Sy to face us.

"Remove your clothes and lie on the ground," he orders softly. "Face down. Arms above your head."

"Yes, master," Sy responds immediately, kneeling to remove his shoes.

I bite back tears. This isn't right. This shouldn't be happening. It's my fault, I should do something to stop it, Cash should do something to stop it.

"Go help him undress, Sascha," he says quietly, pushing me toward Sy. "Let's get this over with."

I obey silently, going to Sy with tears in my eyes and helping him to undress. As he steps out of his pants, he leans over, as if he's using me for balance. I know the man would have perfect balance standing on one foot on the roof of a moving hov-car.

"Cause a scene and I'll backhand you before Cash has a chance to," Sy warns, his voice barely loud enough to hear. "I didn't do this so you'd end up getting hurt, too."

I look up at him, chastised. "I'm so sorry!"

"It's not your fault," Sy says kindly, his hand brushing over mine as he reaches up to remove his shirt. "Don't make me regret it."

I nod. Cash can order me to do things, and he can threaten with the best, but there is something about being given an order from Sy that makes me comply instantly. Perhaps it's because he gives orders so infrequently; perhaps it's because he's been putting himself in danger for me on a regular basis. I respect him more than anyone I've ever met. I would do anything for him, but he won't let me. Maybe that's what makes me so willing to follow his lead.

Sy removes his clothes and hands them to me, reminding me of the detention facility. He goes to his knees, then lies flat on the ground, on his stomach, raising his arms above his head and resting his face between them. He looks proper, but not humbled. Sy looks proud even when lying in the dirt.

"Spread your legs," Cash speaks, his voice chillingly cold.

As Sy complies, Cash reaches over to the pile of clothes I'm holding, grabbing the belt Sy had been wearing. I'm relieved that he's not going to have someone fetch a whip. Maybe this is just for show.

My relief is killed when I see our master wrapping the leather around his fist, leaving the buckle out at the end. I realize what he's about to do and I feel fresh tears on my cheeks.

"Please, master, no." I'd rather he beat me than Sy.

Cash turns toward me for a moment, a resigned look on his face. "Get on your knees and stay there," he orders. "You don't have to watch."

Cash isn't really just telling me I don't have to watch, he's telling me that it's not going to change. He's giving me a simple order that looks good for the cameras, but he's hidden a message: I can solve the other problems we face, but neither one of us can stop this. I don't know why I thought we could in the first place; maybe I'm thinking too highly of myself. Maybe I'm thinking too highly of Cash.

"Are you ready?" Cash asks the reporter, who looks smug behind his camera and microphone.

"Can I get a statement from you first?" the reporter asks, jabbing his microphone toward Cash.

He smacks it away with a scowl. "Only if you can be civil about it."

The reporter hands it over, flushing. "I'd like to know how this fits in with your overthrow of the Demoted system. Your research has gotten a lot of abolitionist attention, how do you think everyone will respond to this harsh display?"

"I have never been an abolitionist. This correction is perfectly in line with my business. My research focuses on effective training. Most training occurs at the re-education centers; additional training occurs throughout the life of a slave."

He hands the microphone back, and turns. "I'll begin now."

Chapter 22

Consequences

It's more a warning for Sy than anything else. I see Sy tense for half a second, then he relaxes.

Cash brings the buckle end of the belt down, leaving a wide red welt where the leather strikes and a deep purple mark where the buckle connects. I know the damage it can do.

Sy doesn't respond, he just lies there.

Cash is quick about it. In the span of a few minutes, he's covered every inch of Sy's back, ass, and thighs with angry-looking marks. He's methodical, placing one above the other, avoiding organs and not coming too close to his head. I realize why he wanted him lying on the ground; Cash isn't much of one for humiliation, he's making sure that the weapon he uses won't wrap around and do even more damage.

On the first pass, the buckle caused red spots to well up under Sy's skin, but the second pass draws blood, tearing at flesh. I've felt it on my own skin, the bite of flying metal. Cash has beaten me before, but never like this. He gave me the punishment that one would expect for a spoiled pleasure slave, but he's giving Sy the punishment meant for a working slave. Sy won't suffer a reduction in value for having a few more marks on him.

Sy is starting to breathe more heavily, his body moving up and down as he gasps in air. He's silent, except for the air whistling into his lungs and the sharp exhale every time he's hit. He doesn't move or cry out, even when Cash brings the belt between his legs, striking his inner thighs. He spreads his legs further apart, giving our master free access to hurt him.

It's me who cries for him. I have to watch, not because I was ordered to, but because I owe it to Sy. I caused this; I deserve to watch it, no matter how ashamed and helpless it makes me feel.

It seems like an eternity before Cash finishes, and by the time he does, Sy has blood running down his sides. I want to run to him, comfort him, but I've been ordered to stay.

Cash turns to the reporter. "As promised, you may assist."

He presses the buckle end of the belt into the reporter's hand, smearing his palm with Sy's blood. "You use it this way, and you avoid hitting him anywhere that I haven't hit already," he warns, like the reporter is completely stupid.

"How many?" the reporter asks, scowling.

"Until you're tired or I tell you to stop," Cash replies. "I won't have him damaged."

The reporter nods, shrugging himself away from Cash.

He raises the belt and lets it fly. I know it must hurt, burning against the already abraded skin. The spots of blood grow larger with the continued abuse. Cash watches, looking cold and hard as an executioner.

In that moment I hate him because he's not willing to stop any of this. He's not just beating Sy, he's letting someone else do it. I don't understand how he can do it. In spite of all the kind things he's done for me, all the wonderful nights we've spent together, I hate him. At that moment, he is slavery, and everything it represents, and I want to destroy it.

I'm sobbing, and I don't care that at least one of the cameras are pointed at me. Let them see it. Someone should cry for him.

I hear Cash saying "that's enough," above my head, and the sickening thud of lashes stops. The crowd begins to murmur again, discussing the events. A man has been beaten to a bloody pulp in front of them and they are comparing who got the better footage, whose station will air it first. I want to be sick, and the feeling doesn't go away when I feel Cash's hand on my shoulder.

I jerk away, glaring at him. He pulls back in surprise, but quickly masks his expression. We are still in the public eye, after all.

"Help him get dressed," he orders, his voice strained.

I stumble to my feet, blinded by tears and anger, and I only grow more furious when Cash places his hand on my hip, steadying me. I wrench away and lurch toward Sy, who is still lying in the ground, panting.

By the time I reach Sy, he's moved to his knees, gritting his teeth against the pain. He looks all right, a little tired, maybe, like he has been doing heavy lifting. He rises to his feet slowly, a dignified expression on his face in odd contrast to the dirt and blood that covers him. He doesn't bother to brush himself off; he just holds his hand out for his clothes.

I give him his pants, having already tucked his boxers into my pocket. The less he has to put on, the faster everything will be over. I planned it this way, and I hope he understands. Sy nods approvingly at me and steps into them, clenching his jaw as he pulls the fabric over his skin. He doesn't look at me, doesn't look at anything, he just stares off into space.

As he does, I ready his shirt, making sure it is right-side out and holding it out for him to put his arms into. His shoulders took many lashes, and I know it must hurt to move them. I dress him like the servant I am, coming in front of him to help him button it.

My hands are shaking too badly to manage a fine motor task like buttons, and as I fail to match up the second one, Sy's hands cover mine.

"I'll be fine, pretty boy," he whispers, his own fingers strong and sure and steady. "Go get me my boots."

I nod, unable to speak, and I kneel to help him. I manage to tie the laces; at least I can do this. I stay on my knees, hoping to compose myself. I hear Cash arranging for an additional security escort to our hov-car. I should feel grateful for the care he's taking, but I don't. If he had gotten the extra security in the first place, none of this would have happened.

It's Sy that gets me to my feet, touching my shoulder in the signal that masters use for their slaves to get them to rise. The fact that it works says something about him, or about me, but I don't dwell on it. I obey, too confused and angry to do much else, and when he keeps himself close to protect me further, I let him.

Sascha, Syrus, and I walk silently to the hov-car. The security is keeping the crowd away, and the intensity of the scene everyone just witnessed hangs heavily. I can tell that I've pleased the media; it wasn't my intention, but at least we haven't ruined everything.

We reach the hov-car, and I don't look at either of the men I own before giving the orders.

"Sascha, up front. Syrus, I want you in the back seat; lie on your stomach. I won't have blood all over my seats."

The few reporters that have tailed us snicker at that comment, and I feel the rage building inside of me. Their intrusive attitudes have caused this, disrupting my life and harming my slave. I catch Sascha's glare as he gets into the front seat, slamming the door and wrapping his arms around his legs. I shut the door behind Sy as he lies on the back seat, his legs bent back up and curled out of the way of the door. He's silent and obviously in pain. It can't be helped.

I take off from the parking garage with a flourish of speed, zooming past the city shops with boarded-up windows, leftover from the riots. I hate the destruction, the reminders of the damage I have caused, and I hate that half the streets have been shut down to control traffic. I start to feel a little better once I'm outside the boundaries of the city, and I increase my speed for a few miles, despite the limits. I can afford the speeding tickets, I need to vent at least some of the anger I'm feeling. I would rather drive through the crowd of reporters, but I would prefer to avoid prison again.

"Syrus, are you all right?" I ask, dropping my speed to something slightly more reasonable as I glance into the rearview mirror to look at him.

"Yes, master," Sy replies, his voice still strained. "I'll be fine."

"I mean, have I hurt you seriously?" I clarify. "I can take you to a doctor."

"No, master," Sy answers quickly, his tone a little lighter. "I guess your training paid off. It hurts like hell, but it's clean. Nothing broken, no organs were hit. Thank you."

I'm relieved. I didn't think I did any real damage, but I needed to make sure. Sascha pouts for days if I dare to raise my voice to him; Syrus is thanking me for making him bleed. "Glad to hear."

It's quiet for a moment. Sascha is staring out the window; he hasn't looked at me since we left. I can't tell if he's angry or ashamed of himself, or if he just needs time to process what happened. I'm annoyed with him for causing a scene, but I can't really blame him. If he hadn't lost his temper with the reporters, I would have. I was being hounded just as much as my slaves were, and the only thing that kept me from throwing punches on my own was my desire to maintain my image. Besides, I wouldn't have had Syrus to intervene on my behalf. It's unfortunate that the penalty fell on him when he was the only one behaving appropriately.

"Sy, you didn't do anything wrong," I remind him. "You know I had to —"

"I know," Sy cuts me off. "I knew when I did it. You went easier on me than most would. Thank you."

I nod, but I don't say anything. Anything I can think of to say sounds trite.

When we arrive at home, Sascha gets out of the car immediately, slamming the door behind him. He stands to the side, glaring at me like I've done something horrible. I ignore him, going to help Sy out of the car.

Sascha gets there before I do, and the icy look he gives me is enough to make me back off. Sy notices; he gives Sascha a curious expression, but Sascha just scowls and helps him toward the house, looking at me expectantly until I open the door.

He's the one who caused this, and he's acting like I did something wrong.

I wait until we get inside, door shut and safe, to say anything.

"Sascha, for fuck's sake, it's not like I dismembered him!" I snap. I feel guilty enough for doing what I had to do; I can't deal with this attitude on top of it.

I don't think I'm trying to pick a fight, but when Sascha turns his back on me and storms down the hallway, I want one. I can push back against defiance; outright dismissal is something I didn't expect.

"Don't you dare walk away from me!" I command, stomping after him.

I have the dignity not to chase him, but Sascha breaks into a run, darting down the hall and slamming the door to his bedroom before I'm even halfway there. I keep going, idle thoughts of hurting him flashing through my mind. He has no right.

"Let him go," Sy requests, his voice calm but still booming through the house. "Cash. He's upset. Let him go. Please."

I stop. Sascha's pleas would only serve to incite me further, but the request from Sy gives me pause. He's never asked for anything and a part of me feels like I owe him something. If this is his request, I would be a monster to deny it. His goal this whole time was keeping Sascha safe.

I huff, walking back down the hall.

"Fine," I mutter, although I'm not happy about it.

"He knows he messed up," Sy reminds me. "Just give him some time to calm down."

I nod, still not pleased about the situation. "He better goddamned straighten up," I mutter, trying to hold on to at least some of the illusion that I am the master in this house.

Sy doesn't reply, he just waits. It's hard to stay angry when he's so calm. He's the one who deserves to be angry. I failed to arrange for adequate protection. Sascha made an understandable mistake. I let Sy take the fall for it. Sy should be furious at us both, at least annoyed, but he's not. I can't be angry at him, and if the only reward he wants is for me to put up with Sascha's bullshit, I owe it to him to at least try.

"Can I help clean you up?" I offer. It needs to be done, and it will give me something active to take my mind off of the mess.

"I'd appreciate that," Sy replies.

We make our way to his bedroom, where he lays out a towel on the bed before stripping and lying down on it. The wounds have almost all stopped bleeding; just a few spots remain damp where the metal bit in too hard. I gather a few washcloths, some water, and some disinfectant and sit next to him on the bed. He's silent as I clean out the wounds; the only way I can tell that I'm hurting him is the way the muscles in his back tense.

"Thank you for what you did today," I tell him. "I know what you did for Sascha, what he was about to do. You may very well have saved his life."

I see Sy nod.

"I know," he says. "I was happy to do it. He's been through a lot."

"He should be here, now," I mutter, still trying to decide how to deal with Sascha's behavior, both at the rally and once we got home. I never thought I'd be tempted to punish him again, but I never thought I'd be so scared of losing him. "Is there anything I can do to repay you?"

Sy thinks about it for a moment. "Don't come down on Sascha because of it. I didn't take his place so you could punish him later."

I'm glad he has his face turned away from me, because I doubt he'd be pleased with the look of irritation on my face. He must sense it, somehow, because he continues.

"You must know as well as I do that it was harder for him to watch me being hurt than to suffer the same fate himself. I've seen the scars on him, heard some of the stories from his time at that brothel. He would have taken ten times what you did to me without putting up a fuss, but it destroyed him to know that he caused it to happen to me. Let it go. I'll make sure it doesn't happen again."

I sigh, resigned. If this is his request, I'll grant it. I wish he could be bought by things or privileges, but it seems Sascha is his only concern. I can relate to the sentiment.

"All right," I agree, and Sy turns his head, giving me an approving smile.

I'm careful as I attend to the damage I caused, applying antibiotic cream and bandages. It's more than is necessary, but I'm glad to have something to do, something to occupy my time. I let him rest when we're finished, spending a few hours looking up footage of today's event. The beating is as horrible as I thought it would be, but it has been well-received. I have unintentionally strengthened my position as an avid supporter of the Demoted system.

Somehow, it doesn't make me feel any better.

I can't help but notice Sascha's absence. He's silent, hiding away in his room, and the more I think about it, the angrier I become. I've promised Sy I wouldn't punish Sascha for his actions at the event today, but I can't just sit here and be disrespected by my own slave in my own home. It's been a few hours; he should be ready to talk to me by now. I need him.

I get up and make my way down the hallway, telling myself I'm just going to talk to Sascha.

Sy has other plans, because he meets me in the hall. He doesn't say anything, he just places himself in my path.

"Get out of my way, I'm going in there!" The thought of being denied makes me angrier, and the fact that Sascha hasn't even opened his door only makes it worse.

"Just let him be, sir," Sy pleads with me. "You'll regret going in there right now."

"The hell I will!" I snap. I brush past him, pounding on Sascha's door.

"He's upset and scared," Sy points out, his voice still calm. "What happened today was hard for all of us, and you won't make it better by terrifying him. Just give him some time to calm down."

"Give him some time?" I snap back. "He's had time. He's my slave, this is my house, and if I want to talk to him about his attitude, I'm going to do so! Sascha, get out here this instant before I come in there!"

"Cash," Sy's voice cuts through my anger, soft, but still insistent. "Don't. Please. Let me talk to him. You've said I could protect him. I did that today, let me do it again."

I stop pounding and turn to glare at Syrus. I told him that Sascha doesn't need protection from me, and I intended to make that true. But the way he's looking at me tells me he's afraid, not for himself, but for Sascha. I hate that I'm the only one who can't see how harsh I'm being. I am embarrassed by my own actions, but just as desperate to feel some sort of control again, even if it is only over my own slaves.

"Get him to straighten up. He gets a pass for what happened earlier, but this attitude can't continue in my house!"

"Of course, sir," Sy says, conciliatory.

Chapter 23

Resentment

I retreat, humbled by Sy's quiet acceptance. My childish temper tantrum was just as bad as Sascha's. I make myself a drink, go to the dining room, and look on my tablet for a while as I wait for Sy and Sascha to talk. I'm a little surprised when they come out a while later, Sascha almost hiding behind Sy.

I take a moment before addressing them so I don't start yelling at Sascha.

"I take it you've talked some sense into him?" I ask, looking at Sy.

"Yes, sir."

I look at Sascha, noticing the way he cowers, just slightly, as though he's trying very hard not to. It's a little amusing that I intimidate him this much, especially when his loyal bodyguard would probably rip me in half if I really hurt him. "Come here, Sascha."

He hesitates for half a second, probably wanting to stay where Sy can reach him. Eventually he walks over, standing next to me and looking like a child about to be chastised.

"Well, do you have anything to say for yourself?" I ask, adding to the mood.

"I'm sorry, master."

He looks as startled by the sudden formality as I am, and I can't help but laugh a little. He always reverts to formal titles when he panics, but it's been so long since he's panicked with me. Then again, I haven't been doing much better. I respond to guilt with anger, he responds to his with fear. It's good to keep this in mind as I try to deal with him.

"Sascha, do I really intimidate you that much?"

He looks at me, guarded, and then looks at Sy. I can't figure out their communication, but maybe he just likes the reassurance that Sy is there, keeping me from doing whatever horrible things he's imagining. I grab him by the hips and pull him close, holding him tightly when he tries to get away. After a moment, he relaxes against my chest. I can still feel his heart racing.

"I'm not going to hurt you. I was angry because you were acting like a spoiled pet. I might have overreacted. But if you can move past that, then so can I."

"I can." His tone and the look he barely gives me are wary, still resentful. But his arms have crept up to wrap around my waist.

I'm not trying to demean him, but he was acting like a child. I don't need a child, I need a partner who I can trust, who will talk to me. I know he needs the same from me. "I'm sorry I scared you."

He nods, leaning into me a little more. I see him look from me to Sy. Sy is smiling at him, taking a seat now that he's assured that I won't hurt the boy. The slight wince that crosses his face as he sits makes me feel guilty, and Sascha must notice it too. He pulls away from me and shoots me another dirty look.

"Sascha, I hope you know that I wasn't being arbitrarily cruel earlier," I remind him. "I didn't want to have to do that, but I wouldn't have had a leg to stand on if I protested."

"I guess I realized that when Sy explained it to me," Sascha mumbles.

"I know it upsets you," I admit, wishing he would just see my point. "But, as I'm sure Sy explained, we were okay with it. And if he and I are okay with it, you don't get to throw a fit about it later."

"I know, I just wanted—"

"Sascha, it doesn't matter what you wanted!" I snap, banging my fist down and making Sascha cringe away.

Sy casts a glare at me, the likes of which I've never seen from him before, much less directed at me. As his master, it should incite me further, but it makes me feel guilty instead.

"Regardless of what you want, I need to keep you safe, and Sy. I need to try to keep up the image of master for this business."

"Then maybe you should have arranged for more security," Sascha reminds me. "You want to keep us safe? If you had arranged a safe way for us to get out of the rally, this wouldn't have happened!"

I resist the urge to remind him of his role in this. If I start blaming him, we both lose, and this is about so much more than logistics. Sascha wants someone else to blame for what happened to Sy; as the person who beat him without a second thought, I am the perfect target. "I made a mistake. Sy did what he needed to do, and so did I. It was the most expedient means of solving the problem."

I glance at Sy, and he nods, approving of my tone this time. I tell myself I'm not doing it to please him, but I am.

"I didn't mean to upset you," I tell Sascha, conciliatory. "But Sy and I have an agreement. All either one of us asks is that you go along with it and refrain from causing problems."

"All right," Sascha concedes, glancing from me to Sy and back again. He has no chance of winning against both of us.

We have a quick dinner and Sy announces he's going to bed. I don't blame him, today had to be exhausting. I know he's got to be sore from the damage I caused earlier, although he does his best not to show it. I offer him some painkillers, which he rejected earlier, and he accepts this time. I can't tell if he really wants them or if he's just placating me. Sascha promises to check in on him in the morning, change bandages or anything, and I offer as well. Sy's smile tells us both that we're worrying about him too much. Given his choice, Sy would probably rather have dumped a bottle of straight rubbing alcohol over his back to disinfect it and gone about his day.

Once Sy is gone, Sascha and I are left alone. There is more that we need to talk about, and I can tell that Sascha isn't really looking forward to it. He's not terrified like he was earlier, he's just anxious. It's like a difficult conversation with a lover.

"Come here," I order, after he's cleared away the plates and wiped down the table.

He comes to me, rather reluctantly, standing in front of me and trying not to tremble. I don't want him scared.

I catch his hands, pull him over so he's straddling my legs, resting tentatively on the tops of my thighs. I pull him close and kiss him, calming him with my touch. Even when I break the kiss, I keep him close.

"I beat your friend today," I state the facts. "I beat Syrus rather severely, and I didn't say a single word to try to help him, and it angered you. I understand that. Please don't think I missed it somehow, or that I missed how unfair it was to both of you."

Sascha is silent for a moment. He's looking away from me, not in fear this time, but in what I can only imagine is disgust. "You didn't even try. You didn't say a single word to defend him."

I want to get angry again, but I feel guilty about the same thing. Both at the rally and once we get home, I agonized over the decision, reaching the same conclusion each time. "If there had been another solution, I would have tried it, but there wasn't. If I hadn't acted quickly enough, Sy would have been taken to some sort of holding facility. He would have been hurt worse there. It's part of the job description, Sascha, and he knows it."

"You still could have said something," he reminds me. "You acted like it didn't matter."

"It did matter, but no protest I made would have stopped it from happening. You've let yourself get hurt enough times in the line of duty to know what it's like. I regret that it happened, and I'm doing what I can to make it up to him. We all make sacrifices; you and Sy just make more because you're slaves. If the occasion rises again, I will ask him to do it again. Is that clear enough?"

"Yes." Sascha nods. While I can see that he understands my point, I can also tell that he isn't too happy about it.

"The second part I want to address is your bullshit attitude when we got home," I continue, looking at him hard. He tries to shrivel away, but I don't let him. I take his face in my hands and gently turn him to look at me. "You can't do that, Sascha."

"I know," he mumbles. "I know better, and I need to obey you, and even if I'm upset—"

I press a finger against his lips, stopping him. I can't hear him acting like this is about obedience. It's so much more. He looks at me nervously.

"Not as a master, Sascha, but as..." I pause, thinking of how to continue. "As a lover. As a friend. You can't just run away and refuse to talk to me. It doesn't make anything better; not for me, not for you, and certainly not for Syrus."

Sascha looks ashamed at the mention of Sy, but his eyes narrow in anger again. He pulls out of my grasp and glares at me. "What was I supposed to do? I saw what you did, I heard what you said — how was I supposed to know it wasn't going to be me, next?"

"Because I wouldn't do that to you!" I'm appalled at the very thought. Even when I first bought Sascha, I would never have torn him apart like that.

Sascha just stares at me, challenging me. "You acted like I shouldn't have been upset about it. You made it very clear that your public image was far more important than anything else. What the hell else was I supposed to think? You took off from that parking garage like it was on fire, you slammed the door when we came in the house... I've never seen you beat anyone like that. It was too much."

Sascha has never seen me that scared; the last time it happened, my mother had kidnapped him and I was being arrested. He was spared my violent outburst. "I risked losing you. That would have been too much for me. I apologized to Sy for the way I acted, and I owe you an apology, too. I'm sorry that I wasn't more understanding, and I'm sorry that I didn't at least try to explain to you what was happening. Sascha, I realized later that Sy knew the whole time what was going on, and so did I, but you didn't. You were kept in the dark through this whole thing, so I understand why you were so angry. You deserved to be."

"That's not how you made it seem when we got home," he reminds me, a look of distress on his face. "I fucked up at the rally; Sy took care of that, but I was trying to do what you've always asked and save my attitude until we got home. I couldn't talk to you at the event, I didn't even want to risk talking to you in the car. I didn't trust anything I was going to say."

"And then I got home and I terrorized you," I finish. "I'm sorry. I knew you were upset, although I have to say that it took me a while to figure out what you were even angry about. I'm not the best at reading you, and the fact that you hide so well doesn't make it any easier. Sy plays mediator quite well, though."

"I didn't know how to deal with you," Sascha admits, moving close again and allowing me to run my hand across his back. "I didn't think to talk to you. I was just so angry, and it seemed like you had no idea why."

"I realize that, now," I say, smiling at him. "But do you think that in the future you could help me figure it out instead of storming off? You know I need you. It's not a one-way street. I need you as much as you need me, if not more."

He smiles, his face making my heart beat faster. I need him so much.

"I'll try if you do," he promises, looking up at me hopefully.

"I suppose that will do," I agree. I know he's trying not to agree to anything that isn't true. I'd do the same. "Now, if we're finished, can we take this discussion to the bedroom? Perhaps we can give it a little more chance to sink in."

I'm still shaken, but going to bed with Cash has always meant good things. He starts by pulling me into his arms the moment we are in the bedroom, kissing me hard. I melt into his touch.

"What do you want tonight?" he asks, barely pulling his lips away from mine.

"You." It's rare that he asks me. He's usually the one making the plans in bed. "Something different. Something rough to take my mind off of today. You pick the details."

For a moment, I think I see him frown, but maybe he's just thinking it over. In a moment, he's smiling at me, the dangerous look that I've come to associate with exciting sex.

"Get your clothes off, and get on the bed," Cash orders, and I immediately start stripping. "I want you on all fours."

I shudder with the thrill and excitement of the command. He rarely fucks me in this position, but when he does, I like the way he pounds deep into me. I'm naked and waiting for him in the span of a few seconds, shivering as a cool breeze blows through the open window.

"Cold?" Cash asks, stroking a hand over my back like I'm a show dog on display.

"Yes," I answer, somehow made colder by talking about it.

"You'll be warmed up by the time I finish with you."

He stops touching me, and I turn my head, watching him move

through the room while still holding the position he wants me in. I see him disappear into the bathroom, making me wait. He comes out naked, goes to the cabinet where we keep a variety of sex toys, and returns with a black piece of fabric in his hands.

"You're far too curious," he states. He wraps the blindfold around my eyes, tying it tightly so that I am cast into darkness.

I tremble. He's giving me an idea of how the night might play out, dark and dangerous.

He goes silent, increasing my anxiety, and I start to fidget after a few moments.

A light swat on my ass stills me.

"Squirmy tonight, aren't you?" Cash teases, giving my ass and legs a few more gentle swats that I yearn to press back into.

"Mm hmm," I mumble, relaxing into the pattern he's drumming out on my ass and legs. It feels good, like a deep tissue massage, one that also turns me on.

A sharper smack, hard enough to make me yelp. I like the burn that spreads across my ass, and I wait for more. I want to disappear into the sensations, to feel him lighting my ass on fire until he plunges into me.

"Is this what you want?" he asks.

I think I nod, but I must not, because a moment later, he still hasn't hit me again.

"More?" I suggest, trying to look at him through the blindfold. "I want to feel—"

I'm stopped by a hand clamped over my mouth, forcing my head back.

"All that question required was a yes or no answer," Cash warns, dragging his fingers across my lips as I shudder. "You'll answer when you're spoken to. Think you can manage that?"

He releases his hand from my mouth, and I nod rapidly. "Yes, sir!" I reply, onto the game he's playing. He's taking on the same tone as he did at the rally today, but I was the one who asked for him to be rough. His tone set me on edge, but I'm sure I'll settle in a few minutes.

My mouth is covered again, this time by his lips, and I stop feeling nervous for a moment so I can enjoy the sensation. He kisses me roughly, holding me by the hair and directing my movements, but I don't mind. It feels good.

The kiss is broken all too soon as Cash pulls away, leaving me with another stinging smack on my ass that has me wishing for more. I want him to keep touching me, but he just leaves me. He's in an odd mood, and it's unsettling. I try to remind myself that I always like our games, but it seems too soon, now, too close to what I witnessed earlier. I'm starting to get scared, but I don't want to back out. I wonder if he's still angry.

I hear rummaging in the cabinet again, and when Cash comes back, I flinch when I feel his hand on my ass. He strokes my skin, no doubt feeling the heat. It occurs to me that I'm no longer cold, the breeze is actually welcome.

"Perhaps you need a little reminder to behave."

We've played the punishment game before in bed and I usually enjoy it. Usually, I don't feel like he would have any reason to punish me. He's usually more playful, but tonight, all I hear is threat. Everything seems too real. I want to ask him to stop, but I don't. A part of me wants this.

I stay silent, trying not to tremble, trying to remind myself that he won't hurt me too badly. I wonder what he's brought from the cabinet to use on me. We have a lot of toys, but wielded properly, I know they can hurt. I'm suddenly glad for the blindfold, because I can feel tears starting to form in my eyes. I don't want my master to see the effect he's having on me. "Yes, sir. I'll be good for you."

Something presses against my lips and I open my mouth immediately, years of training kicking in.

"Good," Cash comments, stroking my head. "Feel this with your tongue. Try to guess what it is."

It feels stiff and hard, not like a cock, although the similarity isn't lost on me. It's leather, and from the size and shape, I'm guessing it's the stiff, heavy strap that Cash owns. We tried it out once, but I thought it hurt too much and Cash has respected that, since.

It scares me that he wants to use this on me. Even though he's never hurt me in bed, I start to feel the familiar sense of panic threatening to take me over, and my breath starts coming more shallowly. He keeps working it in and out of my mouth, and I keep licking and sucking on it obediently, almost glad that I can't say anything at the moment.

"Think a few slaps with this will help you to forget the earlier indiscretions?" Cash asks. "Maybe I can make you scream for me tonight, that should give you something else to think about. Demanding boy — you want rough, I'll give it to you."

All I hear is threat. Is he angry with me? He let me off without so much as a warning for everything I did earlier. I thought we were coming in here to play and fuck, but maybe he had other ideas. I wonder if he's really going to beat me.

When he pulls the strap from my mouth and shifts on the bed, I lose my composure, twisting away to sit on my ass and reaching up to rip the blindfold off. The tears in my eyes make everything blurry, but they don't stop me from speaking.

"Please, Cash, I'm sorry, don't hurt me!" I cry out, skittering away from him on the bed. I don't trust myself enough to get up and run right now, so I don't bother trying.

Chapter 24

Resolution

"Sascha!" Cash snaps, his face conveying his shock. He drops the strap and grabs one of my ankles as I keep retreating further away, nearly falling off the bed. "I'm playing," he insists, shaking his head. "I was just fucking playing; I'm not going to hurt you!"

A part of me feels silly and rather relieved, but the prey animal part is still screaming at me to get away. It seems that part of me hasn't yet caught up with Cash's insistence of innocence. "Please," I whimper, and the image of an animal caught in a trap, gnawing off its own foot crosses my mind.

Cash sighs. "Don't fall off the bed when I let you go," he mutters, letting go of the grip he has on my ankle.

I pull away, slide off of the bed, and retreat to the far side of the bedroom, pressing my back against the wall. I watch, trembling, as Cash leans back against his pillows. He's relaxed and calm, but he reminds me of a snake about to strike.

I tell myself that he doesn't hurt me in bed, and he won't, and I have a little panic attack standing there against the wall as I try to convince myself of that.

"You like it when I hit you," Cash points out, calm as ever. "You asked me to do it. And you've got to know by now that I won't really punish you—fuck, Sascha, how long's it been? I've done everything I can to make up for those early months. And I'd never actually punish you when we're about to have sex! Even back when I first bought you, that was out of the question. You know that."

"I know," I say, because everything he's just said is true. I shiver, this time because of the cold. I curse the goddamned window.

Cash notices, and he rolls his eyes. "Do you want to get under the covers where it's warm, or should I go shut the window?"

I look at him, still nervous and confused, not sure what to say. Does he just want me close, or does he really care that I'm cold?"

"I'll shut it," he mutters, getting out of bed and doing so quickly before returning. "But you'll still be warmer over here," he reminds me.

"You're not gonna..." I start, unable to finish asking what I want to ask. I don't want to give him any ideas.

"I won't do anything to you right now," he says softly. "I'd like to hold you close and warm you up, but I won't if you don't want me to."

I go back to the bed, my head spinning, and I wrap myself up under the blankets. It's not warm enough. Within seconds, I start wriggling closer and closer to my master, pressing into his arms. Not long after, I feel those strong arms wrapping around me, pulling me closer, and I feel safe again.

"Is this all right?" Cash asks, stroking his hand gently over my back.

"Yes," I answer, snuggling closer. "I'm sorry."

He keeps up the gentle touch, calming me. "It's been a while since you've reacted like that."

He's right. It's been months, at least, since I've let the fear and panic take me over like that. Sometimes I just get confused; everything bad that ever happened to me seems to come back in a burst. I get scared and nothing seems to make sense.

"Can you tell me what it was?" he asks. "I didn't mean to scare you like that. I thought it was what you wanted."

I think about it for a minute. "I thought it was, too. And then it was too much."

Cash waits, holding me close and rubbing his hands over my skin. I wanted to run away from everything that happened today, but it caught me, anyway.

"You were acting weird," I admit. "Not that it's your fault, but it threw me off. And earlier... I should have asked for something different. I didn't know what I wanted, and then I thought that maybe you were really going to hurt me, and I didn't know how to make you stop. I know it was stupid, but I guess I thought you might want to hurt me for real. I thought I'd let you."

Cash kisses me, erasing every stupid thought from my brain. "I didn't really want to hurt you at all tonight, but I wanted to give you what you needed. It was my very poor attempt at meeting your needs. I picked the strap because you wanted something different, and we don't use it often. I know that you don't like it because it hurts too much, but I was just going to tease you. We both like to play with a little fear, and besides, it was sexy to see it in your mouth. You must know by now that I can hit you with anything I want and still make it gentle, don't you?"

It makes sense, but my heart is still racing. "Why did you blindfold me?"

"I didn't know if I could pull it off, tonight," Cash admits. For once, I think I see him blush. "I wasn't going to let you down by denying you, even if I wasn't feeling it. I think that was another mistake. I overacted, perhaps."

I manage a smile back at him, because, yes, it would have helped to be able to see his face.

"If I thought it would help to give you a safeword, I would, but you don't even manage to tell me to stop," Cash points out. "Sascha, you know I'll stop, right? Have I ever not stopped when you ask me to?"

"I pretty much never ask you to," I admit, because I don't. I panic, I run away, I beg him not to hurt me. But I don't ask him to stop. By the time I'm worried that he won't stop, I don't think he'd listen to a simple plea like that.

"Well, could you try to in the future?" Cash asks, still smiling. "I mean, panicking and jumping off the bed gets your point across, but I'd like it if you stopped me before you get to that point. You've gotten better at some things Sascha, and one of them is hiding how you're feeling. I had no idea you weren't enjoying that until you panicked. I know you pretty well, but I'm not a mind reader."

I didn't realize that controlling my reactions could backfire this badly. "I guess."

"And I'll try to check in with you more," Cash promises. "I suppose it might have been a little upsetting to not know what I was going to do."

I nod, feeling safe and comfortable again. My cock seems to have gotten the message, and simply being pressed against Cash is turning me on. "What do you want to do tonight? It doesn't have to be rough. We can do what you want."

Cash laughs a little, pulling me up and kissing me slowly, leaving me breathless. "I did like the way your ass warmed up for me. I don't want to scare you; I've done enough of that for today. I just want to make you feel good."

An idea crosses my mind, and I'm lusty enough to entertain it. "Can you show me what you were going to do? Now that I'm not panicking. Can we try again?"

Cash considers it for a while before he nods. "Promise you're not just looking to get hurt?"

I shake my head. "I'm curious, now."

"All right," Cash agrees. "Get back how you were. We won't use the blindfold, and I'll talk to you more. I know you like it when I hit you, and you like it when I order you around. I'm playing, but I'll be more careful."

"Okay," I agree, crawling slowly to my hands and knees and glancing back at him. With everything out in the open, my panic is calmed, and I'm left with only the slightest tinge of anxiety.

Cash comes up next to me, running his hands over my body until I relax completely. His hand rests on my ass, and as it does, he comes up to whisper in my ear. "Is it okay if I hit you?"

I nod, longing for the feeling of his hand on my skin. He doesn't disappoint, covering my ass and legs with light, sensual slaps that have me squirming and moaning. He rarely goes so lightly, but the slow burn that builds across my body makes me want to do it more often. His other hand traces over my body, scratching lightly with his nails, rubbing here and there, until I can tell that my breathing is as hard as my cock.

I feel something press at my mouth again, and I allow the strap between my lips, licking and sucking at it again. I'm turned on now that I'm not afraid. I look up at Cash, and his hungry look only turns me on more. After a few minutes of that, he pulls it from my mouth and I feel it resting lightly on my ass, waiting.

"I want to hit you with this," Cash says softly. "But I won't hit you hard, and if you don't like it, I want you to tell me immediately. Is that all right?"

I take a breath, steadying myself. "Yes."

He takes his time, lining the strap up, rubbing it across my ass, the slight wetness left from being in my mouth making it slide easily across my skin. When I've relaxed again, he draws back and strikes lightly, barely hard enough to make a sound. This lightly, it doesn't hurt; it actually feels pretty good. He lays a few more underneath, working down my legs, and I start to relax into it, feeling my cock jump with each one.

"That's nice," I hear myself saying, almost embarrassed to admit it. "You can go harder. I'd like you to—if you want to."

"So you like that, then," Cash teases, his hand coming underneath me to work my cock while he continues striking me, a little harder now, but still not hard enough to hurt. "I was far too harsh the first time we tried this. I didn't realize how heavy it was. I know better now."

The first time we tried it, I hated it; this time, he's barely touching me. Every smack is warm, solid, firm. It's a nice change from our usual frantic pace. "Thank you for doing this. This is definitely better than anything I planned."

"I never intended to hurt you, Sascha," he reminds me. "I just wanted to give you what you wanted. I need you, and I wanted to make up for earlier. I wanted to make sure you remembered tonight not because I was hurting you so badly, but because it felt good. It is still feeling good, isn't it?"

"Yes," I breathe, too interested in the feeling to say much else. It feels wonderful, actually, I'm keyed up from the panic earlier, and it's like it primed me to be turned on.

"Do you want it a little harder?" Cash asks, this time working down the backs of my legs. "I want your ass all warmed up by the time I drive my cock into you."

I moan at the thought of it, eager to feel him inside of me, knowing the burn on the backs of my legs and ass will put me over the top as soon as he starts fucking me. "Harder," I whimper, jutting my ass out in what I hope is a tempting manner.

"As you wish," Cash replies, and when I look over at him, he's smiling.

The next stroke lands with a sharp crack, and I arch my back, remembering why I didn't like the fucking thing the first time.

"Too hard?" Cash asks, stopping and setting the strap down to rub carefully at the spots where he just hit, allowing me to catch my breath. "I'm sorry. Tell me if you want me to continue with it a little lighter."

I think for a moment. "Yes," I manage, because I did like it a minute ago. "Just not so hard."

"All right," Cash agrees, and I feel him moving behind me, his tongue caressing the spots where I think the strap might have left welts. "But I want to do this, first."

I don't complain as he licks and nibbles my ass, making me shiver with excitement. Soon, he's working his tongue around my hole, dipping inside, rimming me with care. I moan and spread my legs further apart, giving him easier access, and he responds by slipping a finger inside of me, wet from his tongue. He works it around until I'm whimpering and struggling to hold onto the sheets.

"I assume this is good?"

He's teasing, but I tell he's checking with me, making sure I'm okay. In his own way, he's making up for all the things he missed earlier today. I nod, smiling at him and he smacks my ass with his hand as he goes to retrieve lube. He returns quickly. More fingers enter my ass, slippery and careful, and I feel myself opening to him.

"Fuck me," I beg, rolling my hips as he works his fingers in and out of me. "Please, Cash."

He doesn't reply, but he does remove his fingers after a few moments, and from the corner of my eye, I see him picking up the strap.

"Do you still want more of this?" he checks, dragging it lightly over my back, making me writhe desperately.

"Yes, please!" I answer immediately, because as much as I do want him to fuck me now, I want to feel that again, see if he can do it more softly.

"Five," he announces, shifting his position. "And then be ready, because I'm going to fuck you after that."

I barely have time to process before I feel the strap land across the middle of my ass, not hard enough to be unpleasant, but still hard enough to make me jump. I have a distant realization that it would probably hurt if I wasn't so turned on, but I am so turned on, and when the second one lands just below the first one, it's all I can do to keep myself from coming.

The third lands at the bottom of my ass, where it meets my legs, and I cry out in a blissful mix of pain and pleasure. The next one comes quickly and more lightly, still making my thighs burn. The last one is lighter still, lower on my thighs, and I've barely adjusted to the burn by the time I feel Cash gripping my ass and spreading me apart, driving his cock into me quickly and roughly, making me scream.

His flesh abrades my ass and legs, the heat spreading through the rest of my body as quickly as his cock pistons in and out of me. He grips my hips hard, jerking me back and forth on his cock, and it's all I can do to keep my head up.

That's not a concern for too much longer, because he pushes down on the middle of my back, pinning me to the mattress. I sigh as I let my head rest on the pillow, my arms relieved of the pressure of holding me up. He uses his forearm to pin my neck down, and takes his other hand and wraps it around my waist, grabbing at my cock. I'm his, now, his to position, his to fuck, his to make come. I love it. My ass burns for him, my cock burns for him, and the only thing I regret is how quickly I come, the warm spurts accompanied by whimpers.

A few seconds later, he takes his arm from the back of my neck, pulls me up, and leans me back against him. I don't even have to hold myself up with my legs anymore. I press my back against his chest and ride him; the muscles in his legs are holding me up and bouncing me on his cock. I cry out as he keeps going, fucking me deeper, and I reach back with my arms, desperate to feel his skin. I grip his legs as his arms wrap around me, and he pumps into me again and again. Finally I feel him coming inside of me, his cock seeming too big, the thrusts too hard. I wouldn't stop it for the world.

He leans back, still inside of me, and pulls me down on top of him, my back to his chest, his cock slowly softening inside of me. I'm glad he waits, because I am painfully sore; even when he does pull out, I let out a whimper, the act of having anything come in or out too much to bear.

Carefully, he helps me up, and I get off of him, crawling to the clean spot in the bed. Cash gives me a satisfied look before stripping the pillowcase off of one of the pillows and cleaning at least some of the mess off of us before coming up to lie next to me, wrapping his arms around me possessively.

"Was that as good for you as it was for me?" he asks, looking quite proud of himself.

"Maybe even better," I tease back. It's easy to play along now that I'm onto his game. I lean into his arms, perfectly content to fall asleep there, despite his general aversion to cuddling. "Thank you so much. Today was so hard, but you made the best of it. I couldn't have imagined a better ending to a day like this."

It's rare that I see him looking grateful, but the look on his face says it all. I relax as he places soft kisses all over my body, and I fall asleep feeling perfectly safe.

Chapter 25

Forgiveness

I wake up feeling stiff and sore all over. It's nothing worse than what I've felt in the past; some of my masters used to do worse for simple offenses, things like not looking threatening enough. In a way it makes me feel alive. I appreciate the fact that this is no longer a regular part of my life, but I pop another one of the painkillers that Cash pushed on me all day yesterday. It's nice to know he cares, and it's nice to feel the way all of my muscles seem to relax at once as they kick in. I can see why the drug trade does so well. Content, I start a video and marvel at my good fortune.

Sascha comes in not long after I wake up. He brings a tray of food with him, and I smile as he hesitates at my door, clothed in nothing but a pair of boxer shorts.

"Well, if getting beaten means I get to enjoy breakfast in bed and you half-naked, I'll have to ask Cash to beat me more often," I tease. From what I can see, he's put some effort into the food, preparing a full breakfast and coffee. It looks delicious, and so does he. The shorts he has on are entirely too tempting. "Care to join me?"

Sascha nods, getting into bed with me and placing the tray at the end.

I sit up, wincing at the effort and the unexpected pain. Lying down, I had almost forgotten.

"You can stay lying down!" Sascha protests.

"I can sit up and eat like a civilized person," I insist, gritting my teeth as I shift position, and then stay perfectly still. "I'm not disfigured or anything."

I'm also not used to being able to sit or lie around. My masters always had me back on my feet immediately; while it was exhausting, it did help me to avoid the problem of sitting on irritated skin. Sascha gives me a hopeful smile.

"Still not mad at me?" he checks, like he's expecting to hear the opposite.

"Not a bit, pretty boy," I tease, picking up some food and making quick work of it. "You can trust me when I say I'm not mad at you, just like you can trust Cash when he says he is mad at you. Now that I think about it, you're the only one around here who can't ever manage to say what you're really thinking."

Sascha grins. He never seems to mind hearing the truth when there's no threat attached. He's aware of most of his flaws, just like I am. It's necessary, given our status in life. We finish breakfast companionably, and when we finish, Sascha clears away the tray and returns to bed with me, moving close. He stretches out alongside me like a cat, pressing against my legs.

"Did you and Cash make up last night?" I ask, smiling at him as I feel him growing hard against my leg. A part of me had been nervous to leave them alone together, but they have so much history. They wouldn't still be together if they both couldn't handle themselves when they need to.

"Yeah," Sascha says, blushing a little. "We had an interesting night. Did you hear us?"

I can tell he's trying to be subtle. For all I know, the two of them had another loud and alarming night of fun together. It doesn't bother me like it used to, but there are still times when it sets off alarms in my head and I have to fight the urge to rush in and protect my client.

"Not a thing," I admit. "I took those painkillers once I left the two of you and I fell asleep the second I hit the pillow. Seems I was a little exhausted."

"Oh." He sounds relieved. "Well, I'm looking forward to making it up to you as well."

I frown at him. I doubt that Cash had him make up that way, and it bothers me that he thinks I would ever demand such a thing. "You don't have to have sex with me to apologize."

"I know! I didn't mean it like that. I just... I was just joking."

"You weren't," I point out.

Sascha flushes. I understand his need to clear the air, to offer me something, but it bothers me that he feels like he needs to do that. It bothers me more that he acts like his body is the only thing he has to offer me. I've been in his situation before with people who really did demand it, and it cheapened everything. I hope I've never given him the impression that I would be that petty or that cruel.

"It would make me feel better," he admits. "Not because I owe you or anything, just... it's like making breakfast. I like doing it anyway, but since it makes you happy, it makes me feel less bad, and so it would make me feel better."

I put my hand on his cheek, forcing him to look at me. I can see that this really isn't about me, it's about him. And it's not like I don't want to have sex with him. "Well, my prince, anything for you."

"Besides, you said that next time we have sex you'd smack my ass some more and I want you to do it," he demands, making his voice playfully haughty. I find his teasing reassuring. "So as soon as you aren't in too much pain, I'd like you to smack me and fuck me, please."

"Keep talking like that and I'll lean you over the bed and do both," I warn, meeting his challenge.

"I'll put the painkillers to shame," he continues, seemingly inspired by my willingness to play along. "I'll make all the blood just rush right to your cock, nothing else left for you to feel pain, and I'll make sure you're very distracted. You'll wish that I got you beaten all the time, because not only will you get breakfast in bed, you'll get me."

I shake my head, amused by his antics. "Put your money where your mouth is, pretty boy," I challenge. "Get up and lean over the edge of the bed."

"Really?" Sascha's eyes widening in excitement.

He doesn't move, though, and I realize he's almost too excited to comply. He probably doesn't think I'm up to it, but he's right, it will be a good distraction. I've been forced to do far more demanding things with far worse injuries. I don't mind the excuse to get out of bed, either. When I start moving off of the bed, Sascha rushes to do as I asked.

Sascha is leaning across the edge of the bed, resting on his elbows, and he shivers as I pull the shorts down over his ass and around his ankles, leaving him to kick them off and out of the way. I leave him like that, naked and waiting, as I strip off my own clothing. Cash has bandaged me up so well that I still feel clothed, but the rustle of fabric still stings over the raw skin. I'm naked very quickly, and I press my body against his, pressing my erection against his ass to make it clear what I'm doing.

"Fuck me," he whispers. He's not begging yet, it's more of an idle statement.

"I will," I remind him, pulling away after a moment and resting his hand against my ass. "But didn't you say you wanted a warm-up first?"

I hear Sascha draw a breath. I've scratched and bitten and pinched him before, I've fucked him hard enough to give him the pain he craves, and I've been there when Cash has hit him, but I've never really hit him during sex. I lean over him, feeling his heart racing.

He turns back and looks at my face, smiling at me. "Yes, please?"

I bring my hand down lightly on his ass, smiling in spite of myself when I hear him let out a soft sigh. I don't understand it, but I know he likes it, and I like being able to make him feel good like this.

"Harder?" Sascha suggests, wriggling his ass around a little bit more to entice me.

It works, and I comply with his demands. I hit him a few more times, hard enough that my hand cracks against his skin, making him rock forward on the mattress.

"God, yes," he mumbles, thrusting a little, clearly enjoying himself.

A few more slaps, and I see his skin starting to redden. "That feels so good," he whispers, relaxing as I continue.

I'm acutely aware of the size of my hands, it's like they're covering his entire ass. I hit him rhythmically, carefully, working all over his ass and a bit down to the tops of his thighs as well. When I break the pattern, I pause to press my body close against his again. My hands reach around to position him, one tight around his waist, pulling him up, the other around his cock, stroking it, making him feel good.

He lets out a little sound of appreciation and thrusts into my hand, his ass making contact with my body. I can feel the heat I generated, and I'm pleased that he's enjoying it so much. He lets his head fall back against my chest, and I reward him by dropping my lips to his neck, grazing my teeth against his skin.

He probably wouldn't mind if I bit down; he'd probably love it, but I'm just not into it. Cash might enjoy marking him up, but it just doesn't sit right with me. Besides, there are other things I can do with him.

I remove my arm from around his waist, and I work my fingers carefully into him. He grows more excited as I stretch him. The position is a little awkward, but it allows me to keep him close as I touch him while still not requiring me to bend or twist very much. He doesn't seem at all turned off. From his reaction earlier, he likes the thought of me bending him over the bed and taking him.

It's not long before I do exactly that, spreading his legs apart and rubbing between them. The friction against makes him whimper, and I can tell it's a good sound.

"Ready for me?" I tease him. It's not just teasing, though, I want to make sure he's ready, willing, agreeing. Unlike Cash, who likes to just shove it in whenever he's ready, I like to make sure. It's a courtesy too few people make good use of.

Sascha clearly doesn't need any time to adjust, and he arches his back up at me. "Yes! Sy, I can't wait to feel you fucking me!"

I laugh as I start to work my way into him. I take my time, drawing it out in agonizingly slow thrusts. I know he likes to be made to wait, and the way he squeezes around me confirms it. When he tries to push back against me, to take me at his usual pace, I grip him tightly by the hips and pin him in place, immobilizing him. He stills in my hands, submitting to my will. It's amazing what the slight show of force does to him.

I take my time, making my way slowly inside of him, letting him get used to the pace, watching as he relaxes and commits himself to going slowly. When I'm buried deep, I change course, starting to pound rapidly in and out of him. He gasps, breathing quickly and clutching at the sheets. The jarring thrusts remind me of the beating that I took earlier, but I don't slow down. It makes me feel alive, challenges me, and I thrust harder. It's good that I'm holding him up, because his feel must lose their grip on the floor. I hear him scramble for a minute, but

I hold him tightly by his hips.

That, and my cock seems pretty effective at holding him up.

Just like when I was hitting him, I fall quickly into a rhythm, moving fast and hard, and then slow and careful, and then faster again. When I have him gasping for breath and nearly unable to move, I reach my hand around him again and grab his cock, pulling him close and jerking it at the same time, bringing him to orgasm in seconds.

I last only a few seconds longer, holding Sascha's body tight to mine as I come, making him gasp. When I gently release my hold on him and pull out, he's left trembling, facedown on the bed. I leave and return with a towel, not surprised to find him exactly where I left him.

I pull him up on the bed with ease and hand him the towel before getting into bed myself, lying carefully on my stomach again. The lingering pain that the painkillers didn't erase seems to have given way to the pleasure I felt inside of Sascha. I feel great, sated and relaxed, and Sascha gives me a proud smile.

"I guess your little distraction worked," I comment, idly petting his hair as he cleans himself up. "I feel great."

Sascha slides up to rest next to me. He looks pleased, accomplished, and I have no doubt that he is relieved that I'm not angry at him, even though he should know I wasn't going to be, anyway.

"I'm glad." His tone conveys his utter sincerity. "Do you want company today?"

"Isn't that what I'm getting right now?" I point out, reaching an arm out to pull him close.

He grins. "Yeah, I meant later."

I like that he checks. I often prefer to be alone; I've been allowed the privilege of downtime so rarely, and I often feel out of place when Sascha and Cash are working. It's getting better, but they live in such a different world than I'm used to. Sascha always asks how I'm not bored, but I appreciate the ability to be bored. It means that I have no demands on me, no threats to watch out for.

"I'm probably going to take it easy today. You're welcome to join me, but I know Cash has left some work for you, so don't avoid that. Besides, you get bored watching videos pretty quickly, and I don't have nearly the sexual stamina as you do."

That makes him blush. I'm certain he really could go again, even though we just finished. I'm reminded that I'm considerably older than Sascha, and while I was being trained to kill and guard, he was being trained to give — and have — multiple orgasms.

"I might request your help in changing bandages later, though," I add. I realize that it could come out accusatory, make him feel guilty, but that's not my intention. I don't blame him; I just can't reach my own back to bandage it.

"Of course," he replies, a flicker of guilt crossing his face.

I don't hold it against him, but he clearly blames himself. I run my hand through his hair, like I used to at the detention facility, like I've seen Cash do. For as logical as Sascha is, it's not always logic that is most convincing to him. He leans into my touch and I hope he forgives himself.

Chapter 26

Sponsorship

Weeks of planning go into the sponsorship event that Edson advised. While Sascha researches the best possible attendees to invite, I handle the details. I busy myself finding an appropriate venue, arranging for food and entertainment, and preparing a brief presentation to inform my future business partners of the benefits they will receive as a result of sponsoring Michaud & Torenze in our new re-education center empire. It's strange to be doing all of this when I know I might be going to prison, but my lawyer keeps assuring me that this will not happen. I actually start to believe her.

By the time the event occurs, I am amazed by the sheer number of people who've actually agreed to attend. I'm certain that many are here just to see what this whole thing is about; a few more may have joined as a result of Oliver's connections. He's been somewhat removed from the process until now, but when it comes time to secure sponsors, he's suddenly interested.

"After all, who's going to continue after you and Kristine go to prison?" he teases.

I wonder just how serious that threat is.

Still, he's by my side as we take the stage at the event, calling the audience's attention and beginning our presentation. Sascha has helped me put together a video of what we're offering, the ways the re-education centers will change and the ways they'll stay the same. Most of the industry ties will remain, but there is no guarantee that anyone's contracts will be the same with Michaud & Torenze as they were with the Miller System. Many of the same players will be involved, and that's obvious from the mix of attendees we've gathered.

Oliver and I go through our speech, answer a few questions, and then break off to mingle with the crowd. Everyone, even those who seem to be there as a spectator sport, seems interested in meeting with me. I have a feeling it has more to do with my temporary celebrity status than anything else, but many guests surprise me with legitimate business questions.

The most surprising guest is Emile Argova. He was not invited; I assumed that Argova would have let me know if he wanted to attend a public event of mine. Perhaps this is his way of letting me know.

He waits until Oliver is busy with someone else, and he comes over, taking me by the arm like he's an old friend.

"Cashiel," he says, smiling. "It's nice to see you again. I must say, you look better in this context."

Last time I saw this man, we were in prison together.

"Likewise," I agree.

I must not hide my surprise very well, because Argova smiles at me. "Ms. Edson's high quality legal defense has benefitted us both," he explains. "My case was dismissed. Seems someone lost some of the evidence they were going to use. It's a pity, really. Our legal system is just so overworked."

I nod, not entirely sure of what to say.

"I was pleased to hear that you were interested in setting up a relationship," Argova continues. He glances at Sy, who's standing just a few feet away from me, one eye on me, the other on Sascha, who is unobtrusively spying on as many people as possible. "You reward loyalty. I like that. Your man will be safe."

"Thank you. I appreciate all your help."

Argova shakes his head. "It's nothing, I assure you. I like to see the best candidate succeed. The Miller System is becoming outdated faster than it can be fixed. In with the new, I say."

I nod, waiting for him to make a proposition, to ask about sponsorship, to tell me exactly what his business is, if he even has a legitimate business.

"Have you had luck today?" he asks, instead.

"Yes. We've had a few interested parties agree to join. Our corporate partnership options are particularly popular, and my partner has invited some strong investors. He has years of history in the industry."

"And years of history with the Miller System," Argova observes.

"Is that a problem?"

Argova just smiles. "You're the star of this project, Mr. Michaud. Mr. Torenze is a useful tool. I'm sure he's funded this event, and you're right, he'll help you with connections. I wish you and I had established a relationship years ago; you'll find my connections go a bit higher."

I give him a questioning look.

"Mr. Torenze has worked with my family for many years," Argova explains. "He's been very successful in arranging partnerships between the Miller System and my family's organization. However, we're moving in some different directions, and we'd like a new face to go with those associations. Yours, to be specific. We've established ties with some of the up-and-coming politicians in the region, and we'd like to extend those ties to you. That's why we were so interested in furthering this relationship. Some of those parties are in attendance—I hope you don't mind, but I brought along a few additional guests."

How he contacted these people, or how he got them through my guest list, is beyond me. Still, he's powerful enough that I don't question it.

Argova leads me over to a small crowd of people, capturing the attention of someone I am unfamiliar with. "You might recognize Mr. Lemoya," he introduces us. "He's a senator; not from here, but a few districts away. He's interested in one of the state leadership positions. Mr. Lemoya, I'd like you to meet Mr. Michaud. He and I share some business interests, but I think the two of you might have some shared political goals. After all, you're both interested in improving the resources of Nitorra."

The senator describes his political platform to me and I listen attentively. I've known that the Miller System was flawed, but I haven't kept up as closely with the politics of the Demoted System. At both the government and business levels, there is an interest in shifting toward something new. Even those who are satisfied with the Miller System are looking to shake it up, to give the public something new to attend to. A policymaker, recently involved with Miller System and looking for something better to replace it, joins our conversation.

Argova amazes me with his connections and his social finesse. For someone who essentially crashed my event, he conducts himself like he's the host. As the event continues, he introduces me to business contacts, smiles when I set up meetings, and quietly tells me inside information that I commit to memory. His contacts cover a wide range of personalities from business, policies, and government. Of course, they are so often one and the same. He even introduces me to the state head of media information, who I can't believe is attending my event.

Argova points them out to me like this is a common occurrence, like he facilitates political meetings every day. I wonder if perhaps he does, but I don't ask why that would be. Officially, the Argova family deals in pharmaceuticals and medical supplies. Oliver Torenze uses the same industry terms to categorize his role in the underground organ trade; I can only assume that the Argova family is just as involved, if not more. Given the scope of Emile Argova's connections, I would imagine that the family's unofficial business is involved in far more than the drug trade. They might let the disposable street gangs, like the 27s, take care of the risky business, but the Argova family is clearly in charge of more than just political socializing.

When he finishes, he gives me an encouraging smile.

"What do you get out of this?" I ask, unable to contain myself.

"Oh, I like to connect friends," Argova mentions, still casual. "But once Michaud & Torenze gets on its feet, you might consider making our company the exclusive partner for medical supplies and disposal."

I hesitate for a moment. "My business partner typically handles that end."

"Mr. Torenze will be adequately addressed. We would see that all his needs are met."

I nod. "You do seem like a good match."

Argova nods. "I'll let you be on your way, Mr. Michaud. It was a pleasure speaking with you again."

Amazed, and a little confused, I follow his advice and make my way around, visiting the people he's advised me to visit. They discuss plans freely, asking me about my project, what my plans for restructuring the re-education centers would include, invite me for future meetings. There is a surreal quality to it all, like everyone else knows something I don't. I wish Sascha was next to me, analyzing and remembering everything, but I know we can accomplish more if we're apart.

Cash has sent me to spy on his guests, an arrangement that we've perfected during our time together. It's strange, because in the past we've had to spend so much time being secretive. Today, the focus is on us, on our project, and nobody seems to mind that we're blatantly talking about overthrowing the Miller System.

In fact, most seem to support it.

"This new system will generate a number of new revenue systems," one person suggests.

"It's about damn time the Miller System went away," another mentions, a statement that would have been considered treasonous just months ago.

"I hear he's got some questionable connections, but who doesn't these days? Besides, Michaud is nice to look at. I wouldn't mind seeing him on billboards." It's hard not to laugh at these sorts of statements, but I suppose it's only fitting. Cash has come across as quite the personality.

While I our guests were mostly hand-picked, it surprises me that there is no mention of Cash's past. Nobody has made the connection, even though he's "nice to look at." I've seen pictures of him from his first venture into this world, though, and he did look different. He's aged over the years, and much of the official coverage has been destroyed. At least Kristine did some things right. The few criticisms I hear have more to do with regulations than anything; the amount of time and resources it might take to put a new system into place, the potential international fallout when the extent of the corruption within the Miller System really gets exposed. Our guests talk freely around me, but they know who I am. I hear them commenting on "Michaud's arm candy" and I smile like I have nothing better to do than gracefully accept compliments and wait for someone to need another drink.

I get alarmed when I see someone approaching Sy. There's little reason for any of our potential sponsors to speak directly to me, even less reason for them to interact with him.

I know he's supposed to be guarding me, and it's not like I have any means of defending him, but I make my way over, anyway. If anything, I can witness what is about to happen.

The man stands just a few inches from Sy, not looking at him, pretending not to engage. But he does.

"Syrus. Mr. Argova brought me here today. He's asked me to tell you personally that you're safe. Any dispute between us... it's over."

"Yes, sir," Sy replies, looking uncomfortable. He glances first at Cash, then at me, satisfying himself that we're safe. While Cash is busy chatting up some senator, I make eye contact with Sy. I'll cause a commotion if this man so much as looks at him wrong.

"It was business," the man says, shrugging.

Sy just nods.

"We would like to conduct more business with your master," the man begins. "Mr. Argova will facilitate any agreements of course."

I see Sy frown, but before I can hear his response, my arm is grabbed in a familiar way.

Torenze smiles as he pulls me along with him. I don't fight him, mostly because I know it will make my master, and therefore our project, look bad.

"How close are we to having the fully analyzed data?" he asks.

I can't help the curious look I give him. While he's fully aware of my role in this project, even Cash doesn't discuss it so blatantly in front of others.

"I've had a few potential sponsors ask me about it," he clarifies, dropping his voice a little. "They want to know how soon this data will be ready, whether it will be out before the trial or not."

I'm surprised, because I haven't heard anyone else mentioning that, but maybe they are discussing different things with Torenze than with my master.

"It will definitely be ready before the trial, sir. A few weeks at most. We've hired someone new, someone reliable, and they're almost finished with it."

I don't tell him that our new data analyst is someone Cash knew from his old position at Dean & Chanu, because I like knowing things that he doesn't. The analyst's skills aren't as strong as mine, but I've checked his work and his skills are adequate. Even better, he's loyal, and nobody but Cash and I know he's working with us. He's the perfect person to present our research in public, but until our results are ready for release, we're keeping any information about him to ourselves. The less Torenze knows, the safer I feel. I'm surprised that he's even interested. He's kept himself somewhat distanced from our project so far.

"Do you know who Cashiel is talking to?" Torenze asks, frowning. "I can't seem to keep up with him, these days."

I don't, and I'm glad, because it's easier for me to keep things from Torenze. "No, sir. I think he's just mingling."

Torenze makes a dissatisfied sound, but he turns his focus back to me rather quickly. He has a smile on his face, the kind that promises I will soon be miserable at his hand. "Will you be visiting me soon? I do miss spending time with you. And I'd hate to have to investigate that little story you told me about."

I try not to look as disturbed as I feel. I speak quietly, just in case anyone is listening. "You promised you'd give me a few weeks to recover. I'll hold up my end of the agreement. So will my master."

"And your big friend?" Torenze taunts, eyeing up Sy. From the looks of it, he's just finished whatever conversation he was having with the man who approached him earlier. I'm relieved that he is moving our way

"He'll be there, as requested."

"I do look forward to playing with you again," Torenze whispers in my ear, making my skin crawl.

Sy comes over, a blank expression on his face. "Excuse me, sir. My master has requested Sascha's presence."

Torenze frowns. "For what?"

"I wasn't given that information, sir," Sy replies. Nothing else; just that. With nothing to argue against, Torenze has no choice but to let me leave.

I try not to look like I'm running to Sy's side, but I am. Torenze scowls as we leave, but he's far too proper to follow two slaves around. He turns and makes his way to a small group of potential sponsors, hiding the fact that he just let Sy pull me away.

"What does Cash want?" I ask, once Sy and I are on our way to Cash.

Sy shrugs, the slightest smile crossing his face. "I assume he wants you away from his business partner."

We check in with Cash, who seems perfectly content with being used as my cover. He shows me off to a few of the people he's talking to, then sends me on my way again. We are making amazing connections, but I don't trust Argova the way the Cash does. It makes me uncomfortable that my master is so easily led along by someone else, someone who seems to have no reason to care about us or our project beyond the money it can bring to his organization. Torenze is enough of a threat; I'm not sure how we'll be able to handle a bigger one should it arise.

Chapter 27

Betrayal

Things seem to be going well after our sponsorship event. The first indication that anything is wrong comes when my lawyer coms me.

"Mr. Michaud," Edson addresses me, an irritated tone rousing me from my comfortable sleep with Sascha. "Have you seen the news?"

I glance first at Sascha's sleeping body, envious of him, and then check the time. It's well-past noon, a side-effect of being mostly unemployed and sexually satisfied on a regular basis.

"No," I admit, since I assume she's going to tell me anyway. "Has there been anything about the case?"

Edson sighs. "It's all about the case. Who have you been talking to? You're all over the news."

"The sponsorship event?" I ask, confused. I was under the impression that had gone well.

"The issue of your slave not only having access to your data and a tablet, but releasing that data without your knowledge. The fact that your research shows that your Demoted test subjects from this study and the one you did before scored better than non-Demoted test subjects."

I'm stunned. I've told her these details already, but last I heard, they weren't public knowledge, or even rumor. "How did that get out?"

"No idea," Edson admits. "But you need to find out. Who have you told about this?"

I consider it. "You, Oliver, my mother. Sascha knows, of course, but he wouldn't do a thing to harm the project. Or himself."

"I'd rather not see this case destroyed," Edson reminds me.

"We've put too much work into it and too many people are counting on it to succeed. You need to figure this out."

"It had to have been my mother. It's always my mother."

"Get a handle on it, Mr. Michaud. Your case is coming up. The last thing we need is a public scandal."

She hangs up, and I get out of bed. I don't need to wake Sascha, not just yet. I check my security systems; the alarms are set and ready to activate, my security team is visible from the window. I begin to scan the news, verifying what Edson just told me. As she described, my face is everywhere: there are speculations that my data has been tampered with, that my slave is "taking control" of my project, that my end goals are to sabotage the entire Demoted system. I read a few of the articles until they anger me too much, and then I curse and close the news screens. Everything inside of my house is in place, but the outside world is a different story.

I place a call to my mother.

"I saw you on the morning news today," she answers. She doesn't sound pleased.

"Don't act surprised," I mutter.

My mother laughs. "Cash, do you really think it was me? What purpose would that serve?"

"Undermining me. Making me look bad." I try to think of another reason, but I come up empty-handed. It doesn't make sense that she would reveal this, not now. But she's so often a step ahead of me.

"In case you haven't noticed, I've been forbidden to speak with the press," my mother reminds me. "My own board of directors put a gag order on me. You think the state officials are bad, wait until you have an angry board of investors breathing down your neck. The last speech I made was written for me, tele-prompted, and delayed before airing. I can't sneeze in public without approval."

"You know people," I remind her. "You could make this information come out if you really wanted to."

"I've told you before, Cash, I don't want to hurt you. Everything you've released about me is true. The more you release, the worse I look, the worse my company looks. My best bet is that you'll have pity on me."

I scoff. "Unfortunately, my mother never taught me about pity."

"I know this is hard to hear, especially from me, but I'm telling you this for your own good. Look somewhere else. I have bigger problems than your little pet."

My mother hangs up on me, surprising me again. It's rare to see her in such a damaged position, so vulnerable. I look through the news more closely, seeing what other rumors have cropped up.

An hour later, I come across something that makes me wonder if my mother's words were true. It's a tabloid article, so few people have given it much attention, but it's a piece of our data that hadn't been released. A piece that my mother's team had missed in their raid of the house, because it had been hidden on Oliver's servers. We've been using it since I was released from prison and it's helping to strengthen our case, especially since we are the only ones privy to the information. Whether Kristine was telling stories to the press or not, there is no way she could have had access to this information. I curse, loudly, and I read it again, making sure there is no way I could have misinterpreted it.

Sy comes out, his face held together and calm as usual. "Everything all right, sir?"

I look at him and it all makes sense.

"Go get the tablet I gave you," I order, not bothering to answer. When he obeys, I call in one of the security guards I've hired to guard my house. The idea of someone guarding me with a weapon sounds appealing.

To Sy's credit, he obeys, returning and handing the tablet to me without a word. He glances at the security guard with curiosity, but stays silent.

"Someone is releasing information without my approval," I tell him, trying not to lose my composure. There is always a chance that there was some sort of data breach, although it is so unlikely as to be impossible. "The major news that got released could only have been from a few people. Some other news could have been from ever fewer."

Sy nods. "I assume I'm one of those people, sir?"

"Yes."

Sy looks at me, and for a moment I think I see hurt on his face. It's gone before I have time to consider it.

"Are you working with anyone else?" I ask him. "Have you spoken to a reporter, answered a question—"

"No, sir," he cuts me off. "Not intentionally, nor accidentally."

I pause, considering how I want to handle this. The part of me that Kristine Miller raised wants to torture him, to cause him to suffer as much as possible until I'm convinced he's telling the truth. The part of me that's in love with Sascha knows that our relationship will be ended by those actions. The part of me that loves research and logic knows that a man like Sy won't give anything up, anyway.

"You will be confined to your bedroom until further notice," I inform him. "I'll arrange for locks to be placed on the windows and doors immediately. If you attempt to leave, you will be beaten and chained. I'll have someone look through your tablet to determine if there is anything on there that shouldn't be. If I find anything, even a hint that you have betrayed me, you will be disposed of."

I don't know what reaction I'm expecting from him, but it's not the one he gives.

"That's a good choice, sir," he replies. "I hope you find whoever did this before they do any more damage."

I just stare at him. If he's acting, he's good; if he's not, he's the most loyal servant I could ever ask for.

"Shall I go now, or would you like to accompany me?"

He asks it like it's not a problem, like I haven't just accused him of something horrible. I get up, motioning for the security guard to follow me. Sy returns to his room without a word and I order the guard to stay in front of his door. The ones outside will alert me if there is any action from the windows. I can't bring myself to look at Sy as he enters his room, closing the door behind him quietly.

I've spent my whole life being taught that the Demoted are untrustworthy, sneaky, easily manipulated. Sy has demonstrated none of these qualities, but I can't take the risk, not when we're so close. My mother was evil and abusive—she still is—but she was always good at security. She would never have allowed her house to be raided, never would have allowed a slave of hers to be taken in for questioning, and she never would have allowed a slave she suspected of betraying her to roam freely through her house.

I hire a locksmith to come and secure the doors and windows, and

I'm making these arrangements when Sascha comes out.

"Why is there a guard in the hallway?" he asks, taking a seat next to me, blissfully unaware.

I wish I could keep him that way.

"There has been a security issue," I inform him, handing over my tablet which still has a variety of new sites open. "I'm taking the necessary precautions."

He's quiet for a moment, reading through the articles, but as he does, I can see him growing angry. I wait for the fallout.

Sascha surprises me by typing something on my tablet and shoving it at me. I read the sentence he has typed.

Get the security guard out of here so we can talk freely.

I consider denying him, and then I think better of it. Syrus wasn't showing any signs of aggression or danger; if he's working with someone who wanted me dead, he could have killed me thousands of times already. To blackmail and discredit me, I need to be alive, and the longer there is a stranger in the house — another stranger, I remind myself — the more we risk exposure.

I tell the security guard I've changed my mind, but remind him to keep an eye out from outside. The moment he walks out the door, Sascha glares at me.

"You know it wasn't him," he says, furious.

"I don't, or I wouldn't have locked him up," I remind him.

"He's done nothing but protect us!" Sascha yells. "You, me, this project! He has no reason to give a shit, but he's always been there! This is how you repay him?"

"Exactly, Sascha!" I snap. "He has no reason to give a shit! Not about this project, not about me, not about you. He protected you in the first place because he thought you might be connected enough to keep him alive. What is his motivation for continuing now that he's safe? What, did he just fall in love with you from the second he set eyes on you? He has to be working with someone."

"Right, because I'm just that fucking undesirable," Sascha snarls back at me. "Are you that damaged that you can't imagine someone just doing something nice? Sy has done nothing but take care of me."

I feel myself losing grip. "Well, if that's all he wants, then he'll come out of this unscathed."

"Nobody comes out of dealing with you unscathed," Sascha reminds me. "What about your mother? Torenze? The lawyer? Don't they know the same information?"

"I thought it was my mother at first," I admit. "But some of the things that got leaked... she couldn't have known about them."

"She knows about everything. She always has. She bugged your house and raided it later. She's the obvious problem."

"Yes, and that's what doesn't make sense. She's never obvious. This is too transparent for her. If she was planning something, she'd wait and reveal it at the worst possible time—for example, during my trial. And Oliver wouldn't do this; he's part of the business. This would damage his career as well. Same with the lawyer. I'll keep an eye on them, though, if you think it would make you feel better."

"Maybe I did it," Sascha challenges. It's so obviously a bluff.

"I know you didn't. And so do you."

"I'll go through his tablet and prove it wasn't him," Sascha offers. "He's never out without you. You know he couldn't have met up with someone. He would have done it on his tablet."

"The sponsorship event," I recall. "I saw him speaking with someone."

"It was one of his old master's associates," Sascha counters. "The 27th Street Gang. They're associated with your new friends. Maybe the Argova family is involved in this."

"They've worked too hard to make things work out for me," I decide, shaking my head. I want to believe Sascha, but I'm worried that his feelings for Sy are clouding his judgment. I'm worried that Sy's old connections might outweigh his new interests. Outsiders are a threat. "Did you hear everything that transpired between them?"

Sascha looks at me nervously for a moment, torn. "No," he admits. "Torenze pulled me away before I heard the end of what they were talking about.

"I'll have someone else check out his tablet."

"Someone you trust?" Sascha accuses.

I sigh. "Sascha, you know I trust you. I just know Sy means a lot to you. I don't think you can be unbiased about this, nor do I think it would be fair to place that burden on you. I'll hire someone; maybe our new data analyst can handle it."

"Maybe our new data analyst is working with someone else," Sascha reminds me, his tone cold.

"I'll consider that," I concede. "If he finds anything on Sy's tablet, I'll let you review it first. I'm not out to place the blame on him, I just need everyone to be safe."

"You haven't trusted him from the beginning."

"No. I haven't." It's harsh, but true. I understand his attraction to Sascha, and I understand his need to protect himself. But his continued loyalty has always seemed too convenient. I like Syrus, but if he has any motives other than finding a kind master and fucking a pretty boy, I can't have him around.

"I trust him," Sascha reminds me. "I've saved your ass enough times. Why can't you trust me on this? I know he wouldn't hurt either of us."

I want to get angry, but I'd react the same way if someone accused Sascha of doing something like this. "I trust you, but I don't trust him. For the time being, he needs to be removed from the equation."

"What have you done with him? Did you hurt him?"

I shake my head. "No, Sascha, I didn't do a goddamned thing to him. I took his tablet, and I hired a locksmith to come secure his windows and doors. I'll make sure he has food, and he's not chained or anything. He'll be fine."

"I need to talk to him," Sascha decides.

Reluctantly, I shake my head. "It would be better if you didn't," I tell him, hoping to break the news gently. "I can't risk him knowing anything else, not this close to trial."

"You're not even going to let me talk to him?" he asks, his face showing his disbelief. "Not even with you in the room?"

"No," I tell him, more firmly this time.

Sascha looks upset, and I reach out to place a hand on his arm, hoping to comfort him. He pulls away, a look of utter disgust on his face.

"Don't touch me," he snaps.

I pull my hand back, trying not to show how deeply his words affect me. "I'm doing what's necessary, Sascha. I'm not doing this to hurt you."

Sascha stands up, a furious look still gracing his face, and he takes a few steps down the hall. "I lose him, you lose me."

I watch him walk out of the room. A few seconds later, I hear a door slam, and I know it's not the one to our bedroom. Perhaps more accurately, the one to my bedroom, because it's clear that Sascha wants nothing to do with me until this is all over.

Chapter 28

Unbalanced

Over the next few days, I attend publicity events on my own, as Sascha refuses to speak to me, and I'm still not sure whether I can trust Syrus.

It's a disaster.

I brought my slaves along to previous events in order to demonstrate my commitment to the Demoted system; now that I am alone, I am accused of switching sides, of joining the many abolitionist movements that have arisen as a result of my research. The movements have always existed; they just got stronger as a result of my work. Yet another thing I never intended.

Instead of focusing on my research, or the information I have exposed about my mother and the inadequacies of the Miller System, the questions focus on asking where my pretty little pet is and where the bodyguard is. Edson is calling me daily to criticize me for not "handling" my problem. She reminds me repeatedly that this sort of publicity can't be handled, and tells me that there's a possibility that I could be arrested on new charges — violating the gag order that was placed on me years ago as well as a new set of fraud and treason charges. The idea of Demoted subjects outperforming free counterparts is unthinkable; the only "logical" explanation, according to the officials, is that I falsified the results.

I'm exhausted and furious by the time I leave the publicity event. I don't trust myself to drive, so I put the hov-car on auto-drive and glare at the sky, resenting the good weather. As I do so, I am shocked to see my own face on a highway advertisement. It's an old picture, from one of the first events Sascha and I attended after I was released from prison. He's standing at my side, smiling, like the perfect slave. A tagline at the bottom of the advertisement reads: "Safe house? Penthouse? Where is Cashiel Michaud hiding his slaves?"

I am fed up, finished.

In the advertisement, Sascha looks like the perfect partner. That's where he belongs, and I know I'm the one ruining it with my paranoia. I need him, not just to look good on stage, but to help me with this project.

I storm into the house and make my way to Sascha's room, not even bothering to knock. He looks up at me with a mixture of surprise and irritation evident on his face. The nerve he has.

"I need you at publicity events," I inform him, not bothering with any sort of niceties. When this is all over, I can apologize to him, but until then, I have to make sure we stay safe.

Sascha shrugs. "I thought you wanted a bodyguard when I was out in public."

He returns to his tablet and I fight the urge to smack it out of his hands.

"Sascha, please," I say quietly. "I know you've kept up with the media, and you know I wouldn't ask if I didn't really need you. You need to do this for me."

He stays silent, although I can see from the way he tenses that he's getting nervous.

"You've put just as much into this project as I have. Don't fuck it up because you're angry at me."

He glares at me. "Why should I trust you? If I fuck something up, will you lock me up like you did Sy? Who knows what else you'll do."

I take a breath before responding. Forcing a slave to do something is easy, convincing one to do something is far more difficult. That is especially true for Sascha. "Don't act like I'm doing this maliciously, or like you don't know perfectly well that Sy is doing just fine."

"How would I know?" Sascha snaps. "You won't even let me talk to him."

I scowl. "Do you think I don't know that you try to talk to him through his door every single time I go out?"

This actually gets a reaction; Sascha turns bright red and looks away, nervous.

"There's a surveillance system," I remind him. "It wasn't supposed to be for spying on you, but it seems you've forgotten it. Sascha, I don't care about that. From the looks of it, you didn't get much of a response from Syrus, anyway."

Sascha nods, looking at me just as nervously. "He just told me that he was fine and to do as I was told."

"He's got a better sense of the situation than you do," I admit. It's nice to know that I can trust the man that much. It makes me wonder if I'm overreacting, if I'm channeling my mother too much, but I'd rather be safe. "Still, I'd appreciate it if you took his advice."

Sascha seems to consider it for a moment. "You're not angry that I talked to him?"

"I'm not pleased, but I have bigger problems to worry about. I need you by my side. For publicity and... Sascha, I miss you. I miss you so much. I know you're angry, and I'm trying to let you deal with that privately, but this project can't work without you."

He is quiet for a moment, considering it. I can almost see his mind working, comparing his options, weighing his trust of me. Finally, he nods. "What exactly do you need me to do?"

I explain the event we'll be attending tomorrow. It's supposed to be an educational event, sponsored by the state, and my visibility is supposed to strengthen my commitment to the Demoted system. I'm being allowed to participate in part to pacify the angry public, to demonstrate that even the man who is trying to "destroy" the Miller System supports the Demoted system as a whole. I'm supposed to discuss the "favorable" elements of my research, or so the lawyer explained it, so it is clear that any problems I found were not with the Demoted system itself, but with the Miller System. It's being held at a convention center near the local university, and the reserved seats disappeared within hours of my confirmation of attendance. Not only does it make the Demoted system look good, it improves my image: I am nothing more than a patriotic, Demoted-system-loving researcher who wants to improve the best peace solution the world has ever discovered.

And Sascha is my pretty arm candy, the good luck charm who will hopefully keep me out of jail. Or so I hope.

By the next afternoon, he looks the part—a professional yet appealing outfit, hair perfectly styled, a smile on his face. He's taken it upon himself to choose my clothes as well. Normally Sascha would help me dress, maybe surprise me with a revealing piece of underclothing that hints at the fun we will have later, but nothing of the sort occurs today. At least he hasn't purposely wrinkled them. He's all business, and I remind myself that it's an improvement. After all, business is where we started out.

The event features a few other players, including members of the Miller System board of directors, some of the state agencies, and a few local officials. Kristine Miller is noticeably absent. I recognize the politicians I spoke with at the sponsorship event. They're saving my speech for last, holding the audience captive. Regardless, there are countless pictures snapped of me and Sascha, to the point where I close my eyes to block out the blinding flash. I'm relieved when they finally welcome me to the stage.

Sascha and I walk up together, and as I take my place at the front of the stage, he kneels next to me, a look of utter contentment on his face. I begin to present my research, and as I explain some of the differences I found between the re-education centers I examined, he rises gracefully and takes my tablet from my hands, effortlessly taking over the technical aspects of the presentation. He smiles as he does it and the audience notices; he is the perfect complement to my professionalism. Without having to manage the display of the charts and graphs that our new data analyst has devised, I can focus on the audience, make small hand gestures, not have to worry about dropping the damn tablet. Sascha is communicating his own message, and it furthers our cause: the Demoted can be so much more useful when they're doing things they're good at.

I think I conclude the speech on a high note; surely I've convinced at least some of the audience. I have time left for questions, so I choose a young man standing eagerly in the front, waving a tablet at me.

"Mr. Michaud, what about the research that shows that the Demoted subjects scored better on tests than free people?" he asks, his face lighting up at the opportunity.

"An error in the data analysis," I respond, giving the stock answer that my Edson has prepped me with. "The official reports will not contain that data."

"But it's true!" the young man insists. "The raw data that got released, it proves it!"

I give him what I hope is a patronizing smile. Of course the data proves it, but I am no abolitionist, nor am I willing make myself look like one, even if the numbers speak for themselves. The numbers aren't at risk of being executed. "I'm sorry, but I support the Demoted system and so does my research. Don't believe everything the tabloids say."

The crowd becomes less friendly, with murmurs of disapproval. A group at the very back is holding signs protesting the Demoted system, and I can hear the faint echo of chants even from where I stand. I see things being thrown, and a team of armed guards enter through the back doors. I can smell a faint cloud of pepper spray making its way over the convention center.

"If that's true, look at my figures!" the same young man challenges me. "I looked at them myself. Put my tablet on the display screen and show me where I'm wrong!"

Edson prepped me for this as well, and I know the exact parts of my data to pick apart. I glance at the head of event security and he nods, clearly informed of the plans. Sascha is watching, and when he sees the plan confirmed, he goes to the edge of the stage to retrieve the tablet.

He's reaching down for it, unbalanced, when a sea of hands grabs him and pulls him into the crowd.

I stand there, frozen for a moment, before snapping at the security guards to do their fucking job and retrieve my property. But by then, it's too late.

Against his will, Sascha is dragged through the crowd, passed over their heads like a crowd surfer at a rock concert. Half the attendees look confused, holding him up only to avoid having him fall on them. The other half is cheering, chanting something about "save the slave!" and "no more Demoting" and all sorts of other things that shouldn't have anything to do with taking Sascha away from me. He's not fighting back, but he's not helping, either. There's nothing he can do but passively resist, and I am just as useless to him. He curls into a ball and tries to protect his face as they drag him further into the crowd.

As Sascha is pulled away from the stage, I struggle against the desperate urge to go to him. I curse, debating whether to take matters into my own hands when the security guards try and fail to follow him. I know it's not proper to be this upset about a slave, I want to preserve my image, but every muscle in my body tenses, ready to launch myself into the crowd after him. The crowd members who are not actively involved in pulling Sascha away from me are creating an effective blockade for the guards, standing in their way, grabbing their uniforms, and purposely spilling liquids onto the floor to create a slippery, dangerous mess. As I watch, the crowd members themselves start brawling, the pro- and anti-slavery sides fighting with one another, the guards struggling to prioritize the violence. They need to get Sascha out of there to even begin calming the crowd, but they can't be perceived as placing the safety of a mere slave over that of free people. If the issue of Demoted treatment wasn't already so inflammatory — and if I wasn't the wealthy and controversial target that I am — I'm certain they'd shoot him and end the conflict.

I make my way to the front of the stage and start to climb off. I don't care if the security guards can't make their way through; I am determined to get to Sascha. The crowd members who are still standing at the front are grabbing at me and throwing things at me, but I bat them away without concern. There is no way they will hurt me as much as they will hurt Sascha.

As I reach the floor below, I feel two sets of hands grabbing me by the arm and pulling me backward. I struggle against them, but they don't relent. They don't even bother speaking to me.

The entire room erupts in madness, and the security guards drag me back onto the stage and behind the curtains, blocking my view, but also protecting me from the projectiles being thrown at me. I try to struggle, to get back to Sascha, but the security guards have no plans of letting me go. Screaming, gunshots, and tasers can be heard even from my protected location, and I am terrified for Sascha's safety. I can't let on, so I pretend to be upset about my tablet. It's acceptable to worry about that being damaged.

"We're gonna have a full-scale riot," the security guard who's keeping me out of the way informs me, looking pleased. "Seems some abolitionist group planned to crash the event—even thought you might be on the same page, since you got rid of your slaves. They are pissed!"

"I didn't get rid of them," I mutter, but I'm anxiously waiting for Sascha.

They escort me rather forcibly to another room, one that has a lock on the door. I'm about to protest being locked up, but I realize that the room is where another security guard sits, overseeing the video feeds from the event itself. I sit quietly, not caring that I'm being locked in here against my will. I can't do anything out there, but at least I can watch Sascha from here.

The video feed is dim and grainy, but I still watch in horror as Sascha is pulled through the crowd, tossed from spectator to spectator, fought over like a bone between two dogs. To his credit, he's not fighting back, but I can only imagine the terror he must be feeling. His clothes are being used as handholds. I can see them ripping as the crowd pulls at him. I think I see blood, but I can't really tell due to the quality of the video feed. The guards retrieve my tablet first; I can see them waving the shattered pieces at the security camera, and the guard who's babysitting me gives me a thumbs-up. I don't even try to be happy.

"I want the rest of my property! How hard is it for a team of guards to retrieve one slave?"

The man just shrugs and goes back to watching as the rest of his team continues to pursue Sascha. The crowd is growing out-of-control, and I look at another security screen anxiously, wondering if they will really manage to steal my slave and take him out the back doors. There's a team of armed, uniformed guards at those very doors. The police force has arrived with reinforcements, and only moments later, the screens go dark.

"Smoke bombs," the security guard informs me. "Should get them calmed down quickly."

I don't reply, because becoming hysterical about the whereabouts of my slave will only cause problems. I hear a com device beeping in the hallway, and I overhear a voice announcing that they have secured the slave. I can only wait for them to bring him back up through the crowd and to where I am waiting for him.

The only time I've ever felt so helpless was when my mother took him away from me.

It seems like hours, but I know it's only a matter of minutes before a pair of security guards return him to me, his clothes torn and bruises visible everywhere skin is exposed, he's coughing, and his eyes bright red and puffy.

"You pepper sprayed him?" I snap, outraged.

The security guard rolls his eyes at me. "He was in the middle of it. Needed to get him out. Quickest way to get that done. He'll be fine in a few hours."

Sascha stumbles blindly toward me and I grab him, feeling my hands and throat burn as he gets too close.

"I know you have treatment for it," I remind the security guard, doing my best to act concerned about myself and not about Sascha. "Spray him or whatever you do so it doesn't spread to me."

The event coordinator rushes over with a spray bottle and some towels and starts spraying us both down, likely concerned about the liability. "Sorry, Mr. Michaud, this really should have been done before we brought him back to you. He assured us that you would want him immediately, though."

I nod, fully agreeing. "I didn't come here to have my property damaged," I remind him.

"We'll reimburse you for the full cost of the tablet and the medical expenses for the slave," he offers as he continues to spray. He even offers me a private room and a change of clothes for both me and Sascha, for when we deactivate the majority of the pepper spray.

I accept the offer, glad to have a moment alone with Sascha. "Are you all right?" I ask him, continuing to spray the soothing solution all over him. When he doesn't respond, I come in front of him, needing to see his reaction. He's barely able to open his eyes, but when he does, it's to glare at me.

"This was your fault."

Chapter 29

Damages

The ride home is tense and itchy. I'm sure Cash did his best to clean the pepper spray off of me, but it doesn't work all the way, and I'm too angry with him to tell him where he missed. Not only that, but the various parts of my body that were scraped or cut by signs or fingernails or who knows what else feel like they'll never stop burning.

I'm sore all over. Most of the crowd that was tossing me around wasn't particularly gentle, and many had tried to grab hold of me, to keep me in one place to prove some point. Maybe some were even trying to kidnap me. If that was their goal, perhaps they only needed little parts of me, because they were damn near tearing me apart. I haven't felt this much pain in my shoulders since Cash bought me, but my arms feel like they've nearly been wrenched from their sockets. My clothes are torn, and it bothers me that I was so quickly reduced to nothing more than a statement by members of both sides of the Demoted argument. Those in support of the Miller System saw me as nothing but a tool to be used in making their argument, those who supported the new system saw me as a valuable trading tool, those who opposed slavery all together were trying to "save" me—as much as one can be saved by being ripped apart.

If Sy had been there, none of this ever would have happened.

Cash tries to apologize to me, once, but I can't even listen to it. I'm silent until we arrive at home, and I go to clean off further, bringing oil and rubbing alcohol with me. I hear Cash offering to help, but I continue to ignore him. It takes well over an hour to clear my skin of the burning solution, but I manage. I hope he hasn't had as much luck.

He's waiting for me when I get out of the shower, lying on my bed with an unsettled look on his face. I know I've pushed my luck with him quite a bit already, so I just stare at him silently.

"You know I didn't mean for this to happen," he reminds me. "I've said I'm sorry... and I know that doesn't mean a thing. I'm doing the best I can and it's not enough. Would you like to go and talk to Syrus?"

I've almost tuned out; I figure this will just be another bullshit attempt to make me feel better. I'm surprised when he actually offers me something I want. But I still want to push back against him.

"Why? Still need me so much? More pepper spray you want to avoid?"

Cash shakes his head, looking defeated. I actually feel a little guilty for what I said.

"Sascha, I got so paranoid after our data was released," he confesses. "I know I can trust you, and I knew it then, but I was shaken. It was petty and wrong of me to forbid you to speak with him. If you think you're safe with him, you're welcome to see him."

I nod. It's a small consolation, but I value it.

"Don't tell him about what's going on," Cash requests, apologetic. "I still need to rule him out as the one who sold out our information. That will be easier if he knows less of what's happening."

"All right," I agree, because I want to prove Cash wrong as well. "Can I see him now?"

Cash nods at me, and I leave him without another word.

Of course, my dramatic exit is hindered by the fact that he's the only one with the key to unlock Sy's door, but he doesn't remind me of that fact.

I go in to find Sy lying back in his bed, fully dressed, staring at the ceiling. He glances at me as if nothing's wrong.

"Hey there," he says, sitting up and smiling at me. He frowns as he must notice the redness that still lingers around my eyes, or the bruises I've gotten today. "Are you okay?"

I nod, going to sit next to him. "There was some stuff at an event today," I explain, then remember Cash's request not to say much. "I can't really talk about it. But I got tossed around a little bit, and pepper sprayed... I'm fine."

Sy nods. "That's probably for the best. I'm sorry I wasn't there to protect you."

I lean into him. "Me too. I hate that he's doing this to you."

Sy puts an arm around me, pulls me close. "Cash is doing the right thing. There's been a leak; the sources of the leak need to be isolated."

I shake my head. "You're unbelievable. That bastard has locked you up in here for weeks with nothing to do but stare at the ceiling and you say he's doing the right thing? You know you don't have to lie to me."

"Sascha, it's been eight days," Sy reminds me. "Cash checks in on me multiple times a day, and you sneak and try to talk to me more than you should. And he's brought me some incredibly old tablet that does nothing but play videos or display books. I don't mind some down time. And he is doing the right thing. Security is my job, remember? If he asked for my advice, I would have told him to do exactly what he's doing."

"I hate him for doing this to you," I mutter, the statement bringing tears to my eyes and making them sting even more.

"You don't or you wouldn't be so upset by saying it," Sy reminds me. "He didn't do this to hurt you. He didn't do it to hurt me, either, but he really wanted to avoid hurting you. Again, if I didn't know either of you and he asked my advice, I would have told him to isolate you as well. It's just a precaution. Good security."

"You're always so logical," I mumble, even though his logic is comforting. "Who do you think it is?"

"Only a few options. The Argova family would never be so subtle, but they might be connected somewhere along the lines. If they haven't had him killed, it's because he serves their purpose. That leaves the lawyer, the mother, or the business partner."

"Torenze." The name makes me shudder. "I have my first debt payment with him in a few days. Do you really think he would have done it?"

Sy shrugs again. "Could have been any of them. None of them make sense, but that's just because we don't know why the information was released. I've seen plenty of backstabbing. My old master, the 27th Street Gang, the others they associated with... especially the ones higher up in the organization. They planned these sorts of things so carefully, making sure none of it ever tied back to them. It only ever makes sense after it's over. But my guess would be on Kristine Miller. She's the one who did it in the past, she's the one who would do it again."

"Yeah," I agree. I wish we just had an answer so Cash would stop accusing Sy. "Did Cash tell you about what Torenze did last time he borrowed me?"

Sy nods. "He's an awful man. You deserve far better than to be given to him."

The kind words make me smile. "I'm pretty sure Cash said the same thing."

"He cares about you, Sascha," Sy reminds me. "I'm surprised he's letting you go back there again, but I know you made a deal. You're brave. I wish I could be there with you."

"You probably don't want to see it anyway. The things he does... he hurts, he humiliates. He broke me down in ways I had forgotten were possible."

"If you can live through it, I can witness it," he says. "I know it just helps sometimes to know that someone in the room cares about you. And I do."

I can't respond, so I touch him instead, running my hands over his chest, feeling the strong muscles under his shirt. I've missed him, I've missed touching someone in general, and I want to feel connected to him. Before I go and let Torenze torture me, I want a reminder of how good it can be.

Sy kisses me when I rise to press my lips to his, but he holds back.

"Maybe we shouldn't," he says gently. "I'm not so sure how our master would feel about it at the moment."

"Fuck him," I decide, trying to pull Sy back down to kiss me again.

He pulls back, shaking his head.

"Come on, Sy, it will be fun!" I try to convince him. I slide my body against his, needing the contact, wanting to feel him touch me in return. "Let's just play a little?"

"All right," he relents, but I can see on his face that he doesn't really want to do it. The flash of reluctance is gone almost instantly, and

I think that anyone else but a slave would have missed it.

But I know that look.

"Hey, Sy, what the hell?" I ask, suddenly disinterested. "Look, if you really don't want to, you can tell me to go away. Jesus. You're acting like..." I don't say it, though, because saying out loud that he's acting like he has to please me is just too weird.

"Sascha, if you really want me to do it, I will," he says, shrugging. "It's not a problem."

But it is a problem, because I shouldn't be able to make demands of him like this. "If you said that to Cash, it might be true, but you're not talking to him, you're talking to me, and I thought... Sy, you don't have to pretend with me!"

Sy smiles down at me. His smile isn't placating, it's not even insincere. His face is calm and resigned, like it always is. "Cashiel may own us both, but don't act like you don't have some influence over him. Especially with the way things are now, if you give him any indication that you're displeased with me, he wouldn't hesitate to punish or more likely sell me. It's the way things are here, and I can accept that."

He's telling me that I have control over him, and it rips me apart. "Sy, no!" I protest, wanting to go to my knees and beg him to take it back. "I wouldn't do that to you!"

Too late, I realize that I've admitted that I know he's speaking the truth.

"I hope that stays true," Sy says smoothly. "At the detention facility, you tried to please me, I took care of you. Now that you're the one taking care of me, I'll do my best to please you as well. It's only fair. I don't blame you; it's just the way things are. I trust that you won't be petty about it."

The fact that he can choose to trust me or not make me realize that I am a threat to him. As much as Cash can hold things over me, and I usually trust him not to, this is how Sy feels about me. It devastates me. I don't know how Sy isn't devastated by all of this, but then, he just accepts everything that comes his way. I'm disturbed that I have this much power over someone else.

I can't handle it, and I drop against Sy's chest, trying not to cry. He reaches down to stroke my hair, letting me take time to think about it. I thought we were equals, but as he's so clearly pointed out, we are far from it. It hurts to have that taken away, but I can't deny that it's true.

"You really didn't realize it, did you?" Sy muses, his voice holding no tone of regret or anger. "It's easier to see the world from the bottom, I suppose."

We lie together for hours, not saying much. Cash has the decency not to disturb us, and I try to come to terms with what Sy has known since the day I made Cash bring him home.

Chapter 30
Paying Debts

Over the next few days, Cash lets me in to see Sy a few more times. The hard part is asking him. I don't want to speak to Cash, but I know I have to. To his credit, he doesn't make me beg, or even ask repeatedly. He drops whatever he's doing and lets me in. I start to trust him a little bit more.

He doesn't say much to me, either; he's cancelled the few public engagements he had arranged, on account of what happened the other day. He's angry, but not at me. I want to go to him, to feel his arms around me again, but I can't bring myself to do it. If anything happens to Sy, I won't be able to tolerate the sight of Cash. I don't know what I will do, but I can't think of that, not when I have the upcoming date with Torenze to feel sick about. I was already dreading it; the event the other day brought that dread closer to the forefront of my mind. I panicked in that crowd, clawing against the hands that held me down and threatened to pull me apart. What am I going to do when Torenze gets me alone? He'll detect that fear immediately and he'll use it to his best advantage.

As if it's not on my mind already, Cash asks me about it the day before.

"You're meeting with Oliver tomorrow," he says quietly. At least he waited until I had eaten to ruin my night.

I've thought about it for days, and there is only one thing that will make this even remotely tolerable. "I want Sy to come with me."

Cash frowns, shakes his head. "I can't let that happen."

I can tell he's trying to be gentle, but I don't care. I've been shaken ever since the event. "You and Torenze agreed that Sy would go with me," I remind him, hoping that his business sense will outweigh his paranoia. "I doubt he'll be happy to hear that you're going back on the agreement."

"He's not. But I've already told him that I need Sy for something else. He wasn't pleased, but I told him Sy would accompany you to the next few visits. Everything should be figured out soon enough."

I shake my head. "I want him there. He said he'd come, he'd be all right with it."

"Sascha, it just doesn't work," Cash insists. "I don't want to risk this project—risk your safety and mine—just for this."

"It won't risk anything. All Torenze will do is torture and fuck me. Remember? There won't be a thing about the project."

"If there is even a chance, which there is, I don't want to risk it."

I look away, fuming. After a moment, I look back at him, blinking back the tears that are threatening to fall. I don't want to admit that I'm afraid to go back to Torenze, but I'm terrified. I play the last card that I have left. "Cash, please. Don't make me do this alone again."

Cash drops his head, resting it on his hand as he considers it. I've just about given up, about to go back to my vow of silence, when he nods.

"All right. You've given me so much... I just hope I can trust you both. I'd feel better if he was with you, too."

I smile for the first time in days and I go to Cash, wrapping my arms around him. It goes against the active ignoring I've been sticking to, but it feels good, and I can tell he appreciates it as well. He doesn't make a move, probably aware that I would push him off, but he leans into me. It's nice to know he missed me as much as I missed him.

"Thank you," I whisper in his ear, and I try to hold on to this memory instead of worrying about what will happen to me.

Morning arrives all too soon, and if Sy is surprised to be taken to Torenze's with us, he doesn't show it. He's waiting by the door when I come out of my room, and he's impeccably dressed and groomed. I smile at him, and at Cash, and I try to feel safer as I join them in the car.

Torenze is waiting for us, and he has the slave with him that he had when he visited us at home. The boy is naked and he looks tired; I can only imagine what's been done to him over the past few months.

"Changed your mind about the bodyguard?" Torenze teases, eyeing up Sy like he's a piece of meat.

"Ended up not needing him," Cash replies coolly. "Decided I'd stay at home, instead."

If Torenze knows that Sy has been taken out of the public eye for weeks, he doesn't comment on it. He and my master quickly discuss the pickup time, Cash reminds him of the limits we've established, and Sy and I are left there.

The latch on the door has barely clicked before Torenze gives me a sharp slap on my ass. I recall that he's been instructed to leave my face alone, and I'm grateful for that arrangement.

"Haven't we had a discussion about slaves wearing clothing in my house?" Torenze challenges.

"Yes, sir," I mutter, stripping clothes off quickly before he finds reason to hit me again. I hand them to Sy, who folds them for me and places them on a small end table. He waits, looking bored, as I stand there naked and awkward.

Torenze glances at Sy. "And you?" he prompts.

"I'm here on business, sir," Sy reminds him. "I'll be staying fully clothed and non-participatory."

Torenze is startled, but he doesn't protest. He eyes me up, instead. "Your master put a lot of limits on me, boy. Tell your friend about the nickname you liked so much last time."

I cringe, remembering the hours of torture and humiliation I had been subject to just a few months ago. "He called me Trash-boy. And I loved it. I begged him to call me that again and again."

Sy just nods. I'm certain he can tell just how unenthused I am about the nickname, or about talking about it.

Torenze comes over and grabs my cock, hard, making me cry out. I look down at the floor, refusing to meet anyone's eyes. "Did your tight little ass miss being filled with my cock, Trash-boy?"

I know what he wants and I don't delay in giving it to him. "Yes, sir," I answer quickly. "I can't wait to feel it again. I fantasized for days about how hard you fucked me at the detention facility."

A slap across my face lets me know I've gone too far.

"A whore like you should know how to be believable!" Torenze snaps.

"Sir, his master has requested that you avoid his face," Sy reminds him without a trace of emotion in his voice. "I'm sure you wouldn't want this arrangement to come to an end."

Torenze glares at him with rage, but before he can say anything, Sy continues.

"I'd suggest the inner thighs in the future. They're very sensitive and still within Mr. Michaud's limits."

I'm not sure who's more stunned, me or Torenze, but there is a noticeable moment of silence as we both react to Sy's advice. Instead of following it, or perhaps, reserving it for later, Torenze grabs me by the hair and forces me to my knees. Once I'm there, he kicks me forward until I fall, my head barely held up from hitting the ground. I lie there pliant, waiting.

"Fluffy," Torenze calls, making his slave come running with a look of fear on his face. "I think the little whore would like to play doctor. Go get me the bag with the medical supplies."

I shudder to think of what that might entail. Cash made Torenze agree not to cause actual harm or to break skin, so at least knives and needles are out of the question. Torenze alternates between slapping and kicking me while he waits, pausing every now and again push a finger into my ass, making me squirm.

"Tell me how good that feels," he hisses.

"It's wonderful, sir," I reply, remembering to keep it believable. Old memories of the time I spent as a brothel whore come rushing back, and acting like a whore comes too naturally. "I love the way you touch me, sir. I can't wait to feel you inside. Will you make me beg, or will you just give it to me hard?"

I hear his slight intake of breath and I know I'm turning him on. He likes that I'm faking it, and he likes that I'm keeping it reasonable.

"Do you like being fisted, my pretty little whore?"

I try not to shudder, because it's not something I've ever enjoyed, and I'm definitely not looking forward to the first time in years being with Torenze. "I'm sure I'll like feeling you take control of me like that, sir."

Torenze laughs, then looks at Sy. "What about you, bodyguard? You ever just want to put your arm into this little whore?"

"Can't say I've had the opportunity, sir," Sy replies, friendly, like he's discussing foreign travel.

"This one will love it," Torenze decides, striking my ass hard enough to make me jerk. "Just wait until you hear him beg me to do it harder."

Sy doesn't reply. I hope that Torenze will settle for just fucking me and humiliating me today, leave the actual torture alone.

Of course, when "Fluffy" returns with the medical equipment, I doubt that I'll be that lucky. Torenze gives his slave a bottle of lube and orders him to get me ready. I'm surprised that he's not doing it himself, but it seems he's more interested in pulling out his tools. He tosses a few aside, the sharp ones that would violate his agreement with Cash, but the rest he pulls out slowly and deliberately. A speculum. A metal gag that holds a patient's mouth open. An electrical unit. An enema bag. A set of what I really hope aren't sounding wands. After pulling each out of the bag they're contained in, he glances at me, probably judging my reaction and making plans for later.

I remember that he was a professional torturer.

At the same time, Fluffy is working my ass quickly and efficiently. I'm sure part of it is to appease his master, but he probably wants to spare me some pain as well. I have no doubt that he is intimately familiar with everything Torenze wants to do to me.

Once Torenze decides I've been stretched enough by his slave, I see him pick up the speculum and I try not to wince. I know it won't hurt that bad, but it will be terribly uncomfortable.

"We need to get you nice and opened up," Torenze reminds me, slowly working the tool into my ass.

I bite down on my lips. The cold metal is unpleasant, and it's all I can do not to tense up, but I know that would only make it worse. It seems like hours before he slides it all the way in, and when he does, he slides it back out again, then in. He's fucking me with it as I wait for him to open it up.

"Ever seen the little whore get used like this, bodyguard?" Torenze teases, giving the speculum a sudden twist that makes me yelp.

I glance up at Sy, suddenly wondering if I should have had him come. I hadn't realized Torenze was going to use him as part of my humiliation.

"No, sir," he replies. "It's quite interesting, though. Thank you for letting me watch."

I'm as thrown as Torenze is, and a little disturbed. There is so much I don't know about Sy—is this really turning him on?

Before I have a chance to ponder it further, I feel the pressure as Torenze operates the tool, expanding it against the walls of my rectum. I force myself to relax, and as my body accommodates the intrusion, Torenze slowly starts working it in and out of me again. He manages to brush it against my prostate, distracting me from the pain. To my horror, I feel my cock getting hard. I try to will it away, but my struggles only make it worse. I hear Torenze snicker behind me.

"Has your loyal guard dog ever seen you rut like this?" Torenze asks, stopping his movements for a moment.

I feel a tremor going through my body. I remind myself that I don't really enjoy this, that it's just a sensation, but I still feel the shame of it. "No, sir," I mumble.

"Well, then, let's not block the view."

Torenze guides me to lie on my back, careful of the tool wedged into my ass, and he instructs his slave to come and hold my legs up in the air. Not only is my ass presented in full view, my cock is as well, and it's hard as a rock. When Torenze begins to slide the speculum in and out again, I barely manage not to cry out, but I'm not sure if it's from pleasure or sheer mortification. I manage to open my eyes, and I see Sy looking on with what could only be described as amusement.

"You liking this, boy?" Torenze asks, giving Sy an irritated look.

"Absolutely loving it, sir," Sy replies, a smile creeping onto his face. "I had no idea I was in for such a treat today. Such a pity my master forbids me from participating. You make him squirm so perfectly."

The rough slap that Torenze delivers to my thigh barely distracts me from the shock and betrayal I feel. Sy has never given me any indication that he would enjoy this sort of thing; I can barely get him to give me a little slap in bed. I feel strangely betrayed, knowing he's enjoying my torment.

Torenze must, too, because he yanks the speculum out of me and glares at Sy. "I didn't realize I'd have competition when I made this arrangement," he snaps, pouting like a child. "You stay out here. Sascha and I will be moving to the dungeon. I don't want to hear a word from you or see your face until your master picks you up, is that clear?"

"Yes, sir," Sy replies, looking sad still. "Is there a bathroom where I can... take care of something?"

My jaw drops, both at the implication and at the boldness. Torenze is on his feet in a second, striding over to Sy and smacking him hard across the face with the speculum, leaving a few spots of blood on his cheek and chin.

"You can take care of that," Torenze growls. "I said I wouldn't break skin on the whore, not on you. Bitch to Cash about it and I'll tell him what a disgusting pig you are."

Sy just nods, the blood welling up in one of the cuts. Before he can say anything, Torenze grabs me by the hair and drags me to my feet.

"Fluffy, bring the supplies!" he calls, dragging me to the dungeon.

Fluffy jumps to do as he's asked, and a part of me is certain that most, if not all, of the supplies are used on me. I block most of it out, trying to dissociate. It gets harder and harder the longer I go in between doing it, but Torenze is spectacular at drawing out those old fears and old habits. More than anything, I spend the next few hours playing Sy's words and actions over and over again in my head. They don't make sense. He's never been interested in seeing me hurt; even if this is something he's into, he knows who Torenze is, knows what he's done to me. I think that maybe he just couldn't take watching it, and while it hurts to think he enjoyed my pain, it almost hurts worse to think he abandoned me. The tears I cry for Torenze are real, but not because of the pain. I'm crying because, after this is over, I have no one left to turn to.

Chapter 31
Revelations

When I return to pick up my slaves, the first thing I notice is the cut on Sy's face. I give him a questioning look.

"What the hell happened to you?" I demand.

He shakes his head. "Nothing to be concerned about, master. An accident."

Torenze nods, like it's true, and I have no choice but to agree and go along with it. I don't like it, but if Sy got himself hurt, it was probably his own choice. Probably Sascha's fault, but Sy's choice to get involved. I won't stand in the way of that.

I give Oliver a friendly smile. "Everything go as planned?"

He shrugs. "Boy seemed a little less lively than last time. Still had fun with him, though. You should be happy, he's in a little bit of a better condition than he was last time."

I nod, glancing at Sascha. Physically, at least, he seems better, but mentally... I'm almost more worried about him than I was last time. When I first left him with Oliver, he was desperate, terrified, and clingy when I came to retrieve him, weak and sick. Today, he's just standing there, lifeless, like nothing matters. He glanced back and forth between me and Sy at first, but dropped his gaze, looking at the floor, instead. I need to get him home, where he's safe, where I can comfort him or at least allow Sy to.

"Well, I'd better get him home and cleaned up," I mutter, turning and heading out the door. "Are you ever going to agree to a public appearance with me? It would really help my case."

Oliver smiles. "When the right time comes," he assures me.

We leave, and I keep watching Sascha out of the corner of my eye as we drive home. He doesn't say anything, and when I ask how he is, he just shrugs.

"I'm fine," he mutters. "It doesn't matter."

Since Sascha has decided to act like a sullen child, I glance at Sy in the rearview mirror. "What the fuck did Torenze do to him?"

Syrus looks back at me, a puzzled expression on his face. "Some medical stuff, humiliation... maybe fisted him."

"Shut up," Sascha snaps. "I don't want to hear you talk about it."

I'm surprised, but Sy just continues filling me in, without the details. "He didn't do anything that violated your agreement, and—"

"How would you know?" Sascha cuts him off. "You weren't even fucking there! You're the one who said you could handle it, and you're the one who made sure he didn't want you there."

I'm stunned to see Sascha so angry, so hurt. It's rare that anyone but me provokes this sort of response, and when it's me, he's usually a little more reserved on account of our respective statuses.

"Sascha, I need to talk with you when we get home," Sy says, his voice quiet and calm despite the conflict. "I have something important I need to tell you."

"I don't want to talk to you," Sascha snaps back. "Go jerk off in your locked room for all I care."

I'm startled when something zooms past my head, more startled when I hear a thump, followed by a startled yelp from Sascha. I look over and see Sascha with a tablet in his lap, Sy pushing it back as Sascha tries to return it.

"Is that my tablet?" I ask, surprised. I haven't been able to find it all day; I thought maybe Sascha had borrowed it for something for the project.

"Yes," Sy confirms, seemingly unbothered by petty theft. "I would have taken Sascha's, but I figured yours would be easier to get into."

I frown as we turn down our street. "Why do you have my tablet?" I ask, trying not to jump to conclusions. The man knows full well that he's one of my suspects; this action should rightfully signal his death. Only the illogic of the activity prevents me from believing it.

"Oliver Torenze is the one who leaked the information about you," Sy explains. "I had hoped that Sascha would be able to piece together what I copied from his tablet today and explain it to you, but he's not cooperating."

I park the hov-car before turning around to stare at Sy. "You did what?"

"I arranged for Mr. Torenze to leave me alone in his home for a long period of time," Sy says. "I stole your tablet this morning after you asked me to wait by the front door. I used it to connect to Mr. Torenze's tablet after confirming my own suspicions that he was actually the one who betrayed you. Once I looked through his tablet and saw his correspondence with various reporters, as well as with investors, I made a copy of everything on it. It's encrypted, but I figured Sascha would get through it pretty easily."

The revelation stuns me. "How the hell do you know how to do that?" I ask him. I don't reveal that I probably don't have the skill to accomplish such a task.

"I was the slave of an organized crime boss for many years, sir," Sy explains, shrugging like it's nothing. "I learned a lot of useful skills."

Silently, we go inside, sitting around the dining room table. Sascha looks less broken now, and more confused, which I can understand. He doesn't say anything; he just takes my tablet and starts to search through the information. I recognize my own screen for only a few minutes, and then a series of numbers and symbols pop up and I'm lost. Sascha gets a little smile on his face, though, and I know he's onto something. He glances at me like he's suddenly aware that I can be useful.

"Get me my tablet?" he asks, engrossed in whatever he's tapping at.

I do as he's asked; it's strange, perhaps, to obey the requests of a slave, but I'm happy to indulge him. Even more, I want to see what he finds.

I no sooner hand it to him before he links the two; with the mess on my screen, I have no idea how, but he does it, and soon, another set of symbols appear on his. Seemingly satisfied, he sets them both aside, allowing the proximity technology to link them and do whatever it is he's doing with the data. I sit, waiting for his next move.

"We'll be able to prove it wasn't Sy," he tells me, a hopeful smile on his face. "Just give it a few hours. But I can see it there, the communication trails, the data that was released, everything. We can prove that Torenze was the one sabotaging this project."

"Good." I am genuinely pleased. The results might not be confirmed yet, but I assume Sascha knows what he's doing with the tablets, and I trust what he's saying. Not only that, but he was so angry at Syrus a few minutes ago that I can't imagine him lying for the man.

"It looks like it goes all the way back to right after your arrest," Sascha adds. "While you were in prison, he started working with some of his favorite investors. He released the data about your mother, although it looks like he had a lot of cooperation from some government officials in bribing our data analyst. After that, it's like he's on his own—a lot of contacts stopped responding to him, and the information that just got released? He sent that, just him, no help. That's why he started with tabloids. Nobody else would take it. I don't know if Kristine scared them off or if they just realized you had gained popular support, but it looks like Torenze found himself without powerful friends."

"As he should have." I sigh, realizing that Sascha's instincts have been right all along. I never should have trusted Oliver Torenze.

I'm glad that I could be of help. To see the relief on my master's face, to see the look of success on Sascha's, it makes me think that it's worth it. Still, I know how much I hurt Sascha in all of it. It was easy enough to plan; I've had years of experience working behind other people's backs. But actually hurting someone I care about was something different.

"I'm sorry for what I said back there," I tell him quietly. I can't get that hurt look out of my mind. "All those things, I didn't like them, and I didn't want to watch, or join, or... take care of myself in the bathroom after you left."

Sascha gives me a questioning look, like he doesn't quite want to believe it. I can't blame him. I had to act well enough to convince him and Torenze. I succeeded.

"I would never want to see you hurt or humiliated," I remind him. "It's hard enough to stop myself from protecting you when you like it; seeing you endure it when you don't like it made me want to be sick."

Sascha nods. "It wasn't that. I thought you did it on purpose, but I thought you did it so you didn't have to watch. I thought you just abandoned me. Were you planning this the whole time?"

I nod. Sascha's distrust of Torenze had warranted additional exploration from the moment that data got released. "I couldn't tell you because I knew you'd mess it up. You needed to be devastated by my absence, and I knew you'd be excited if you knew I was going to dig around for evidence."

"You're probably right. I would have been giddy at the thought of destroying him."

Sascha's been easy for me to read since I met him. I couldn't let that compromise our position. "And Cash, I couldn't tell you because you didn't trust me. It was too risky to trust you in return."

Cash nods. "That's fair. I'm certain the data will clear you completely."

It's business with Cash, which I appreciate. With Sascha, just telling him why I did what I did isn't enough. I know he understands it, probably even respects the decision, but I did more than betray his trust. I played on his biggest fears. I stand and make my way over to where Sascha is sitting, standing there for only a brief moment before dropping to my knees. I can't tower over him while I say this, and I'm not going to try to force him to stand. I need to meet him at his level.

"I am so sorry if I ever made you think I would leave you," I tell Sascha, taking his hand. "It had to be done this way, but I regret hurting you, even for a few hours. You mean so much more to me than that."

"I get it," Sascha says.

I can see how hard he's trying not to be angry, but only the logical part of him is letting this go. I abandoned him to someone who terrified him, just like Cash did. I'd rather he be angry, but I know he won't. This is his battle with himself as much as anything. He's quiet for a moment before speaking.

"Can I just go and take a shower?" he asks. "I feel disgusting. I can't sit here like this."

For a moment, I think he's asking permission from Cash. It makes sense; he owns us both. But Sascha's not looking at Cash, he's looking at me. He needs time to process this, to let his lingering anger cool. I rise to my feet, pulling Sascha up as well. He's weak, wobbly, and I steady him before placing a light kiss on his forehead. He tries to squirm away, but my grip is firm. It's not that he's unwilling, he's just dealing with the aftereffects of his day of torture. I know how it can twist your mind, make you feel unclean.

"Take your time," I tell him. "We'll both be here when you come back."

Sascha nods and flees, leaving me and Cash alone. I'm not sure what to say, but I've gotten to know Sascha quite well. Silently, I retrieve some cleaning products from the supply closet and wipe down the chair and the table where Sascha was sitting, putting them away and returning to sit when he finishes. Cash gives me a curious look.

"He'll want the smell of cleaning product," I explain. Sascha left no detectable odor, but senses can be deceiving. The citrus and soap smell of the cleaning products will be more convincing than any well-intentioned statement of truth.

Cash stares at me, a mixture of gratefulness and curiosity. I wonder if he wishes I had been involved in one of his studies.

"What you did today... it was dangerous, reckless. You could have gotten yourself killed for a stunt like that."

I nod. I was aware of that risk.

"Thank you. This doesn't just clear you—it helps us with this whole project. Now that we know what's really going on, we can move forward, secure our information. I don't know how we're going to deal with this, but now that we know, we have a chance."

I nod again. My choice had been simple. There was no other option as far as I was concerned. "It was important to Sascha."

"Do you love him?" Cash asks.

He's trying to understand my motivations. I consider it for a moment, consider what he's asking and why. "Not like you do, but yes."

Cash waits for the explanation.

"You and Sascha, you burn bright," I explain, smiling. "When you're not fucking, you're fighting, and sometimes you're doing both. Nothing is ever halfway with the two of you. For me... I've always wanted to protect, to take care of. I suppose guarding criminals is a form of protection, but it doesn't feel the same. I like that Sascha needs me, and I like that the two of you are taking on this project that could make things better. From what Sascha's told me, if your re-education system had been in place when I had been Demoted, I might have done something worthwhile with my life. I guess a part of me hopes I still can."

"You will. You have already. I know the information isn't ready yet, but I trust Sascha. If he says there's something in there to clear you, I believe him. I'm sorry I didn't believe you before."

I smile at him. I've never had a master apologize to me this much before. I've never had one mean it. "Would have been a lie if you said you did. You made the right choice. It threatened to tear you and Sascha apart, but you did it to keep your project safe, to keep him safe. I respect that. No hard feelings."

Cash laughs, a look of relief on his face. I know he wants to like me. He wasn't as devastated as Sascha was, but I could see that the thought hurt him. As furious as he had been when he accused me of betraying him, a part of him had been crushed. I'm pleased to rebuild that trust.

Sascha returns quickly, looking clean and a little more relaxed. I notice him sniffing the air a little bit as he returns, a satisfied smile on his face as he detects the cleaning products. I smile, knowing that I made the right decision.

Sascha checks the tablets to see their progress, looking pleased. "It will be ready soon," he informs me. "So what do we do now that we know?"

"What was the Argova family role in all this?" I ask, hoping I'm not too far off in my suspicions. "Like I said, a lot of what I found on Torenze was encrypted, but there were some contacts made toward the beginning. Can we trust them?"

"They've been my strongest supporters," Cash points out. "From prison, to the lawyer, to helping me make connections—"

"They pull a lot of strings in business and politics," I interrupt, startled that I am allowed such indiscretion. Cash doesn't seem bothered; he just waits for me to continue. "They're not just business, and they're not just criminals. They do both, flawlessly, and they have their hands in everything that benefits them. They have you exactly where they want you."

Cash goes silent, considering it. Sascha starts looking over the tablets, likely trying to prove or disprove my theory.

"They were in contact with Torenze," Sascha confirms. "They've been in business with him for years, since his split from Kristine Miller. They knew about this project before anything got released, before the raid. They've been following it for months."

"Anything in there about what they planned to do with me?" Cash asks, clearly annoyed by the turn of events.

Sascha shakes his head. "They dropped contact with Torenze not long after releasing the data about the Miller System."

"Right around the time you asked for their help in securing my safety," I remind Cash. "You agreed to work with them. To develop a relationship."

"So, what, they were just waiting to see who to place their bets on?" Cash replies, outraged.

"They have enough connections to make those sorts of gambles." I was never too closely involved, but I know they're major players. My master's associates did anything they asked; they still are, if the fact that I'm not dead indicates anything. They called off the hit on me and made it stick.

"Does that mean we don't trust them?" Sascha asks, a worried look on his face. "We need them — the lawyer, the sponsors...."

"And they need us," Cash says, a smile on his face. He glances at me. "I'm assuming they already would have arranged for me to be arrested or killed if they weren't interested in me, correct?"

I nod, confirming it.

"Then perhaps I need to get my lawyer over here to discuss all of this."

Chapter 32

Choosing Sides

I'm not sure what prompts me to be so confrontational with Edson; for all I know, she's as far into this as the Argova family, and I might end up murdered on the street or "eliminated" in prison, as Sy's last master was. But I'd rather know than worry about the safety of my life and my slaves.

"Care to explain why your associates and Oliver Torenze have been working behind my back?" I demand, the moment she answers my com call. "Or to tell me what happened with my data analyst and—"

"Mr. Michaud, stop speaking," Edson cuts me off. "You make the most rash decisions when your pretty little pet is in danger. Give me twenty minutes and I'll come over and meet with you in person. We can discuss whatever's gotten you so upset and review your case."

I pause. I should speak with her in person, it protects us from any number of surveillance mechanisms, but I'm not sure I want to agree to that. My bravado isn't as strong when I have a moment to think about the repercussions.

"Mr. Michaud, would the Argova family have invested this much into your success if they weren't interested in seeing it through? I have an important development to share about your case, anyway."

"All right," I agree. I hang up the phone. "She's coming over."

Sy looks like he's doing his best not to smile. He plays better in this world than I do.

I glance at Sascha, who's still engrossed with the tablets. "Did he hurt you, Sascha? Torenze? I know you don't want to talk about it, but I need to know."

He shakes his head. "Nothing out of the ordinary. I was more shaken by Sy than I was by him. Don't get me wrong, I didn't enjoy it by any means, but it wasn't as bad as it was last time. I knew what was coming. I'm just glad I didn't have to come home and deal with it alone."

I smile at him. "Never," I promise. I would never abandon him like that.

"What do we tell the lawyer? Or the public, for that matter?" Sascha asks. "That your slave bodyguard broke a few handfuls of laws and found some incriminating evidence? Sy is not getting caught in the middle of this."

I nod. "I hadn't thought it through. You're right. We can't put him or you at risk, and we won't. Make sure you have the data backed up somewhere safe; we won't let her release any of it until we have a plan."

Sascha nods, appeased by my idea. I hope it's good enough, but we are quickly running out of options.

Edson arrives soon, looking more inconvenienced than anything else. Sy lets her in and escorts her to where we're sitting, and she casts an expectant look at me.

"The Argova associates have been in business with Mr. Torenze for many years," she reminds me. "In both legitimate and grey market endeavors. But I suspect you already knew that."

"Yes," I agree. "What I didn't know was the extent of your involvement with him, particularly as it involved destroying my project."

Edson shakes her head. "Nobody ever intended to destroy it, Mr. Michaud. Well, Ms. Miller, perhaps, but nobody that the Argova family is associated with. You were overlooked. An error, as far as I'm concerned, and one that has been reconciled over the past few months. Wouldn't you agree?"

"Was conspiring behind my back an error?" I demand.

"Mr. Michaud, I've chosen my side," Edson reminds me. "My associates have chosen theirs as well. Aside from the industry arrangement, which will continue until a new one is established with the new Michaud & Torenze System, Torenze is out of the picture. Once you committed to working with the right people, there have been significant efforts taken to ensure that your project will be successful. My associates needed Torenze after he split from the Miller System. When he mentioned that he was working with someone new, you became of far more interest."

"I hope it was a lot of interest, because there won't be a Michaud & Torenze," I counter. "I'm going solo."

Edson smiles. "That's even better. But I'm curious, what prompted your change of heart?"

"Torenze was the one who released that data," Sascha informs her. He slides the tablet over, shows her a few of the communications. "He's the one trying to destroy this."

Edson frowns as she reviews it. "We need to remove him from this equation," she decides. "How did you come into possession of this information?"

I'm silent for a moment. I don't know if I can trust her with Sy's safety, and handing him over means destroying not only him, but Sascha. I'm not sure whether I can risk it.

I don't get to make that decision.

"I stole it while I visited his house today," Sy informs the lawyer.

Sascha gives him a worried glare, and I just wait for the response. To her credit, Edson waits a moment before responding, looking from Sy, to Sascha, then to me. She sighs.

"Well, it has to be someone else who finds the data," she decides. "Or someone who causes it to be found. It's hard to find loyal help. We can't place the crime on a slave."

"Could we send someone an anonymous tip?" I suggest. "He's interfering with a legal case, if nothing else. That could raise a few flags."

Sascha shakes his head. "He's too smart. He'll find out before the authorities do. If he knows anyone is coming, he'll destroy it all or turn it back on us. We have to do this right. We'll only have one chance."

"A raid on his house would provide a lovely cover," Edson suggests. "It worked well in the past. I could see if there are any connections at that level, although it might take a while. It's not guaranteed. This would require serious sway."

Sascha pauses, thinking deeply about that statement. I see a glow in his eyes and I wait for him to share his plan with us. "But we know someone who has that. She did it to us without a problem."

"My mother?" I shake my head. "We do not want to get involved with her. She's more interesting in ruining me, anyway."

Sascha shakes his head, leaning forward with a confident look on his face. "She was interested in stopping your research from getting out, but it's out. All she wants now is to save her own ass — how many times has she requested that from you? Torenze has plenty of information that could ruin her, just like we do. Why do you think he's been pushing us so hard to release it?"

I think about it for a moment, and everything starts to make sense. "Do you think he's trying to push both of us out of the industry?"

"He was certainly trying to push Ms. Miller out," Edson confirms. "I can't go into details, but I assure you, he had help with that."

The data analyst. The release of information about the Miller System. Edson had never seemed surprised by that. She had to have known all along that the Argova family facilitated it. She might even have been a part of it.

Sascha nods. "It makes perfect sense. He's been using us, Cash. He lets you take the fall, he destroys Kristine, and then he swoops in as the ignorant third party who just wants to pick up where his experience left off — he was her right hand man for years, then your business partner. He would be the perfect candidate."

Edson smiles. "He was the perfect candidate. But Cashiel Michaud is such a relatable public figure."

I try not to show my distaste. I hate being played, but in this case, it's working in my favor. This is what I wanted, after all. Success, ambition, wealth, a change to the system. I can have it; I just have to swallow a bit of my pride. I've done it with Oliver for years, and he's only been interested in helping himself.

There's a problem to this solution, though. "Do you really think my mother will help us?"

Sascha shrugs. "She'd be stupid not to. She's evil, but she's not stupid."

I nod, knowing it's true. Since her last attempt to destroy me failed, she's been oddly passive. She's asked for my help and I've been too busy turning her down to notice that she really did need it. For once, I can be the one in control.

"Get her to agree," Edson advises. "You know her better than most. Use that to your advantage."

"All right," I agree. "But what about the rest of the case? You said there had been a development?"

Edson smiles. "Right. In case you question my dedication, this should come as a pleasant surprise. I've engaged in discussion with some of the prosecutors at the state attorney's office. They aren't pressing charges for the data that was just released. They say it's old; it's irrelevant under some statute of limitations. They don't want to look like they ignored a threat all those years ago. They're burying this and accusing the tabloid editors of spreading libelous, inflammatory lies."

I give her a curious look. "Did that take some sort of threatening?"

Edson doesn't answer. "You're clear to proceed with your project, Mr. Michaud. Handle this Torenze issue and make sure nothing of the sort happens again. You've put on a show for the public for months. Convince your mother that you can be the son she always hoped for."

"I'll com and make my demands," I agree.

Sascha shakes his head, stopping me. "Ask for her help," he suggests. "It will go over better."

I frown. This woman has tortured Sascha on numerous occasions, caused me to hurt him, got me put in prison twice now... and yet, I can see Sascha's point. Edson nods her agreement.

"All right," I agree, placing the call.

"Cash?" my mother answers, surprised.

"Hi," I say, uncomfortable and wishing I wasn't doing this. "I... I need your help with something."

"Of course!" she replies.

I can hear the smile on her face; as usual, I'm glad I haven't I allowed the video feed. I don't think I've asked her for a favor since I was a teenager. After some of the things she did to me, I had promised myself I would never be at her mercy again.

I explain what happened with Torenze, the data we've found, the pieces that could be incriminating, both to her and to me. Sascha feeds me some information as I talk, sifting through what's been decrypted from the tablet. To my surprise, Kristine listens quietly, refraining from condescending or interrupting like she usually does. I explain how we need a more valid source to discover the data, and I ask her for my favor. She needs to do to Torenze what she did to me.

"I'll need to call in a few favors," she informs me. "You've really limited my ability to conduct these sorts of searches, Cashi. I wish you would have come to me sooner."

I sigh. "I wish you hadn't had my slave molested and beaten, or had me put in prison again," I remind her, sticking just to the most recent offenses. "I wasn't planning on trusting you again. I'm still not sure, but you're all that's left."

Kristine laughs, a sad, defeated sound that I don't even recognize as coming from my mother. "I spent years trying to win this fight, Cash, but I've been out of it since your little pet released your data. I thought I could save my place in the world, but all I want to do now is save myself. We will take Oliver Torenze down. He will suffer for what he did, for what you did, and for what I did. I always knew I couldn't trust that man."

"Thank you," I say, still unsettled.

"I know this doesn't change things between us, Cash," my mother admits. "But I hope it makes it a little better. Once this is over, you'll be rid of me. I'll retire, maybe focus on my garden — that sounds terrible — but I won't antagonize you any longer. You'll be rid of me, like you've always wanted."

A part of me wants to protest out of some moral dilemma, but the part of me who has suffered under my mother's hand for my entire life is nothing but relieved. "Thank you. I'll keep your name out of everything as much as possible."

"Good bye, Cashiel," my mother says, hanging up before I have a chance to do the same. It sounds strangely final.

Chapter 33
Touch

I watch my master's face as he sits, silent for a few moments after hanging up with his mother.

"What did she say?" I ask finally, unable to wait for him to decide to share the information.

"She's doing it," Cash tells us, sounding surprised. "I'm not sure if I can believe it, but she is."

"It's in her best interest," Edson reminds us. "She's been in this business for many years. She knows she's being pushed out of the industry. She's making the smart decision. I'll connect with a few contacts, see if anyone can help her make progress on this action."

"Thank you," Cash says, nodding. "I appreciate your help. I apologize if I was a little forward earlier."

Edson shakes her head, dismissing him. "I was warned that you could be volatile at times. But I do hope that you've realized how important it is to work collaboratively. I see a long future for you, Mr. Michaud. You'll be one of the biggest influences of the century. Make sure you remember who helped you to get there."

"I don't think I could possibly forget," Cash replies.

I smile, because I know he doesn't necessarily mean it in a good way. He must be aware, just as I am, of the risk we're taking working with the Argova family. Our research project has taken us to far greater lengths than we ever anticipated.

Edson leaves, and we're left alone. Cash is looking shocked, cautiously pleased. I feel the same way. We've both made so many sacrifices to get here. If it works, it will be worth it. If it doesn't, we may be the next targets of the Argova family.

"My mother said she'll stay out of our lives after this," Cash says, almost in disbelief. "I guess if we play it right, we get rid of her and Oliver."

I smile, pleased. Maybe I can settle down and be the pretty little pet I was always meant to be.

"My mother wants me to bring some of the data once it's ready, just so her team knows what to look for. She's going to say it was an anonymous tip, that her existing status with the Miller System authorizes her involvement. We'll be clear of this soon."

"Good," I reply. "I can't wait to be done with both of them. They've done too much to us, too many times. I just hope we're not worse off with the Argova family."

"We don't have much of a choice," Cash reminds us. "At least we had the option to pull away from Oliver. Even my mother could be ignored when things were going well. These people are everywhere. They got to me in prison, they have some sort of governmental ties... if things go badly, we're not just out of business or in prison, we're likely dead."

Sy smiles. "From what I recall, they focus on business. Stay on the right side of business, you stay on the right side of them."

It seems so easy for Sy. Then again, from what he's told me, he's always been the good soldier, following orders and shifting loyalties wherever he's assigned. I've never been so good at that, and neither has Cash. "At least they haven't resorted to threatening us, yet."

"We're playing by their rules," my master nods at me. "I think we're stuck with them. We'll make it work, for the project."

I never thought our little project would get this far. As much as Cash and I are committed to it, I know there's more to our cooperation with the Argova family than our research. With everything else at stake, it can very well be our lives as well.

Sy reaches across the table and takes my hand, gentle, like he's afraid he'll break me. "Besides, you're stuck with both of us," he teases.

I laugh. It's true; the two of them are committed to me, and I love it. I never thought I'd experience this from even one person, much less two. I never saw this coming, but I'm glad I did.

"Can I take both of you to bed, then?" I suggest, giving them both a hopeful look. "I'm tired, and I miss touching both of you. It didn't occur to me that if something happened between the two of you it would fuck things up with both of you."

Sy blushes, but he nods. I know he'll give me anything I want; I just need to figure out how not to take advantage of that. Cash gets up and comes over to me, reaching his hand around the back of my neck and putting pressure on me, not hurting me, but squeezing as he pulls me to my feet. I feel my heart race at the possessive move and I comply, standing up and staring into his eyes. He leans down and kisses me, rough and demanding, and I don't care that my lips are already sore from the hours of abuse my mouth was subject to earlier, I just want more of him.

"Have I ever turned down an opportunity to be with you?" he asks when he finally pulls away.

I smile, because I don't think he has. I also notice the way he phrases it; he never hesitates to tell me he's going to fuck me, but I'm guessing he knows that's unlikely tonight.

"I'm pretty sore. And while I would love to feel you both fucking me, I think it might end badly. But that doesn't mean I don't want to feel you doing other things. Maybe you can even entertain each other."

Cash gives Sy a playful smile, and Sy seems to consider it. He gets up, joining us as we walk to the bedroom. "Seems our master isn't the only voyeur in the house," he teases.

Cash huffs. "Haven't I told you not to call me that in bed?"

Sy just laughs. "You haven't gotten me in bed, yet."

"That can be fixed," Cash replies, rising to the challenge.

As we enter the bedroom, Cash pushes me down on the bed without a fight. I watch as he and Sy face each other. In the past, Sy has seemed nervous, reserved, but he's playful today, and he's the first one to strip off his clothes, keeping his eyes fixed on Cash as he does. Cash is quick to respond, pulling his own clothes off just as rapidly and tossing them aside. It's strange to be the only one clothed in the room.

Sy makes the next move, taking a step close to Cash, getting into his space but not touching him yet. "Think we should put on a show for the boy?"

Cash nods, reaching out a hand and placing it on Sy's chest. He pauses, waiting, and when Sy smiles at him, Cash touches him, bringing his other hand up to join. He traces his fingers along the outlines of Sy's body, trailing down his chest, his stomach, resting at his hips. Cash watches him closely, as I do, but Sy is enjoying this. Slowly, Cash brings one hand in front of Sy, barely grazing over his cock.

"Do you like this?" Cash asks, his tone serious.

Sy nods. "Yes." He brings his own hand down to cover Cash's, pressing it tighter.

I didn't realize how much it would turn me on to see them together.

Taking the cue, Cash speeds up his movements, taking Sy's cock in his hand and working it. Sy guides him at first, then backs off, letting Cash do what he wants. Apparently, what Cash wants is to make both me and Sy lose control, because he gives me a quick grin before proposing his next idea.

"If you go sit on the bed, Sascha can touch you while I suck you."

Sy seems quite interested in the idea. He makes his way to the bed quickly, sitting on the edge as Cash comes in front of him, pausing between his legs. I move behind Sy, running my hands over his shoulders and leaning in to kiss his neck. I have a perfect view of Cash going down to his knees, stroking his hands over Sy's legs as he does.

I stay clothed for the moment; I don't want either of them to see the colorful bruises I'm sporting. I'd rather enjoy the mood, because it is very, very enjoyable. Cash doesn't waste any time with words or games. He gets comfortable, spreads Sy's legs apart with his hands, and then takes Sy's cock into his mouth. I can feel Sy respond, he's tense for a moment, then he draws a sharp breath, releasing it after a few seconds. I continue to kiss his neck and run my hands over his skin; I've missed touching him so much. He relaxes as Cash develops a rhythm, and his breathing comes quicker.

"He's good, isn't he?" I tease. It's nice to turn the tables on these two.

I can hear Cash trying to stifle a laugh, and the vibrations must feel good, because Sy lets out a pleasured gasp.

"Very good," he agrees, and he leans back to kiss me.

The position is strange, but I like it, and I get up on my knees, leaning over so I can reach him better. Cash reaches up, groping for a part of me to touch, and he grabs my hand, holding it tightly in his. I've never been so close with two people before, not without the pressure to perform. Cash keeps working Sy's cock, and Sy leans back against the mattress, a smile on his face. I stretch out next to him, my legs dangling off the edge of the bed.

"Do I get to feel your soft skin?" Sy asks, giving me a hopeful look.

I pause. I do want to feel him touching me, I want to feel them both touching me. But I'm not sure how either will react to the condition I'm in. "I'm a little marked up," I admit. "Maybe it's better if we don't."

Sy reaches up to cup my face with his hand. "You do what you want," he assures me. "You can't scare me off."

Cash is silent, still focusing on Sy's cock, but I feel his hand creep up under my pant leg, taking hold of my calf, rubbing it gently. The touch says it all. I'm his; he'll touch me and he'll make me feel good. I want it.

I realize I'll have to wait, though, because Cash is speeding up his pace, bobbing his head up and down frantically, and I can see Sy getting closer and closer. He sits up, touching Cash's head gently, brushing his hair back and away from his face.

"I'm close," he announces. "I'm not sure...."

"We both want to see you come," I whisper in his ear. I wrap myself around him, feeling the way the muscles in his legs are tight, the way he seems to draw deeper and deeper breaths as he holds back. "No games. Cash just wants you to feel good."

Sy nods, glancing at me to confirm it, then looking back at Cash. Cash is staring up at him, looking into his eyes, and the intensity makes me shudder. I'm a part of it, and yet I'm not. This moment is just between them.

Sy comes quickly, the slightest of sounds escaping his lips. He has his hand on Cash's head, still, not holding him there, just touching him, staying connected. Cash keeps going until Sy has stopped moving, resting back against the mattress again. Cash comes up to join us, resting alongside Sy's left side, while I am to his right. Sy is distracted and worn out for the moment, but Cash looks at me with a predatory gaze and a smile.

"You know you don't like to sleep in clothes, anyway," he comments. I can see where he's coming from, and I can see the other point he's trying to make as well. He won't force me, but he's not going to let me think I'm turning him off, either.

Slowly, I take my shirt off, giving him and Sy a moment to process the bruises. Sy doesn't say anything, but he does run his hand over my skin, lightly, feeling good. I smile as I unzip my pants as well.

Cash just watches quietly, but a part of me can tell he's inventorying every injury on me. It's sweet in a strange way. And it doesn't seem to make him any less aroused. As I strip off my pants and toss them off the bed, I watch his face, waiting for his reaction.

"I don't know what you were so worried about," he comments. "You're perfect. Nothing will ever change that."

I let out a breath I hadn't realized I was holding. No matter how many times he says it, I still forget sometimes. Maybe a part of me just needs to be reminded.

Sy runs his hands over my legs, and the feeling of his skin touching mine makes me hot. He brushes his hand over my cock, and while it feels good, it's sore, and I wince. Sy pulls back, a confused look on his face, and I'm relieved when Cash interrupts.

"What are you up for tonight, Sascha?" he asks.

"I want to feel you both fucking me," I admit. "But... we should do that another night. I'm enjoying watching the two of you have fun."

Cash nods, and I can tell he understands. Sy does, too; he resumes touching me, but stays gentle, and he doesn't go for my cock again. Wanting them is its own form of torture, but I know I'll regret pushing myself too hard.

We reorient ourselves, sliding up to the head of the bed, me in the middle this time. Sy and Cash take turns touching me, making me feel good without turning me on too much. They are enjoying me as much as I'm enjoying them, and I let my hand creep down between Cash's legs.

Suddenly, Sy is there, leaning over me, his eyes locked on Cash's again. "I can help with this," he suggests.

Cash smiles. "I'd be honored."

He's playful, but he's still serious. The two of them rarely touch one another; I'm usually their buffer, but they both seem to be quite interested in exploring the other's body, especially while I'm a bit out of commission.

Sy slides over top of me and takes his place between Cash's legs, an eager expression on his face. As he dips down to take the tip of Cash's cock into his mouth, I marvel at how different they both look from a distance. So often, I'm on one end or the other of the fun, and while I enjoy it, I never really get the chance to study their reactions. I watch, amazed, as Sy brings Cash just to the point of coming, then backs off, leaving Cash surprised and pleasantly frustrated.

Cash beckons me over, and as Sy gets him worked up again, Cash kisses me deeply, making my cock hard again. He runs one hand through my hair; the other is resting comfortably on Sy's shoulder. They're both so different with one another than they are with me, but I can tell they enjoy it, and I love watching them. In no time, Sy has brought Cash to the edge again, and Cash grips his shoulder tightly. Sy is kind enough not to try to get him to beg, and Cash comes hard, pulling me close as he does and wrapping his legs around Sy. I end up pressed tight against Cash's chest, hearing the racing pulse of his heartbeat.

Sy joins us after a few minutes, coming up behind me and pressing close against my back, but not close enough to hurt. He puts his arms around me, and as he does, Cash reaches around me as well, touching us both.

"Did we put on a good enough show for you, pretty boy?" Sy teases as I relax into both of them.

I nod, perfectly thrilled to be where I am at the moment.

"You can join us next time," Cash decides. "I know how you hate to be left out of the fun."

Chapter 34

Agreements

Sascha sees the news about Oliver first; he's been watching his tablet eagerly to see if there are any developments with Oliver and the raid we've arranged. He seems to trust my mother more than I do, or maybe he just hates Oliver more. It's a tough distinction, but when we see the media coverage of the raid on his house, I feel a weight being lifted off of me. It's happening, and within hours, tidbits of news have leaked, many of them indicating that Oliver has been arrested, a few indicating that his property had been seized. My name is rarely mentioned, which I'm glad about. His insistence on keeping his distance from me ended up in my favor. From as far as anyone else can tell, he and I have been working on entirely different agendas. Or, more likely, some of the connections that we've made have helped to keep my name out of it.

I recognize some of the officials and political figures as those I made connections with at our sponsorship event. As much as it feels like I'm selling out, it pays to have strong connections. I always intended to further this project on my own—no slave, no partner, certainly no connections to organized crime or corrupt political figures. I was an idiot to think that would work. The Demoted industry is far more pervasive than I ever thought; the connections beyond the industry itself are frightening. But I made my choice to be a part of it. For now, at least, I'm on the right side of the people who matter. If I can stay here, I'll do well. If not? At least I'll have some time to prepare.

Sascha suggests we celebrate, even before we've really won any sort of victory, and I agree. As he starts to prepare something for dinner, I arrange for a nice bottle of wine to be delivered. I have plenty, but it's not every day we get to see someone we hate going down for his crimes and ours.

I hear the doorbell, and Sy answers it before I have a chance. I figure it's the wine, so I go to sign for it, surprised when I see uniformed officers waiting outside of my door.

"Cashiel Michaud?" one of them asks, giving me a stern look.

"Can I help you?"

"We need you to come with us. The state's attorney would like to meet with you and discuss your pending case."

I balk, immediately concerned not only for myself, but for Sascha and Syrus. "I'll need to make some arrangements. I'm not having my property seized again. I have someone on call, it will only be a moment."

One of the officers shakes her head. "No need, Mr. Michaud. You'll be home later tonight as long as you cooperate. The state attorney has asked that you leave your slaves at home. She wants a private meeting."

I hear her promise as clearly as I hear her threat. But the fact that I'm not being arrested outright gives me hope, and I nod to Sy as I'm putting on my shoes.

"I'll update Sascha and your security team, master," Sy informs me. I trust him to handle things; I've told my security team that they are to answer to him just as they would answer to me.

I follow the officers to their hov-car, trying not to be nervous when they place me in the locked section in back. I glance from the reinforced bars between the front and back to the unidentifiable sticky substance covering the seat, wishing I was riding in the front.

"Just policy," the officer explains. "If we were arresting you, we'd handcuff you."

I nod. I'm not being arrested; that would be a media-worthy event. I'm just being taken against my will. No paper trail, no attention. It's a demonstration of power.

I comply with the orders they give, wondering exactly why they want me here. They bring me to an office, and I'm stunned to walk in and see my mother sitting across from the state attorney.

"What did you do?" I hiss at my mother, taking my seat next to her. I can only imagine the sorts of things she's said about me. I was stupid to believe her.

"I was about to ask you the same," she replies, looking as confused as I feel.

I stare from her to the state attorney. Before we have time for another word, my lawyer joins us, a smile on her face that would put me at ease, except for the fact that she doesn't seem surprised that I've been effectively kidnapped from my home.

"I see paranoia runs in the family," the state attorney comments, shaking her head. At either my or my mother's startled look, she continues. "I know all about your history, your little family disputes. Your records might be sealed, but they still exist. It was my department that sealed them."

For once, my mother and I are both silent. We've been so busy fighting each other that we haven't considered the bigger threats that the state government can pose.

"Ms. Miller, the past few months have been very rough for you and the Miller System," the state attorney reminds her. "Unfortunately, that is a problem for the state as well. We simply cannot support a system that so blatantly disregards any sort of research opposing it. Your actions were reprehensible from a business standpoint. Personally, your actions were nearly criminal."

Kristine nods. As much as I want to see her pay, it's uncomfortable to see her so destroyed.

The state attorney turns on me next. "And Mr. Michaud, I'm sure you're aware of the charges you're facing."

"Hard to miss them when you sit in a jail cell for five weeks," I remind her. To my surprise, she actually smiles.

"Half the state is in love with you," she admits. "Either because they love your research, or they love your commitment to the Demoted system, or they love that you're paving the way to destroying the Demoted system—don't ask me how both of those things can be true—but I think they just like a new face. And you and the pretty slave of yours parading around like centerfold models is exactly the face they want. No matter how hard anyone has tried to discredit you, you've captured the hearts of the younger generation."

I'm not sure whether to feel pleased or just confused. I look to my lawyer for guidance, but she just sits there, calm and content, like she's not surprised by any of this. I wait as the state attorney addresses my mother once more.

"Ms. Miller, you are simply too big to fail. As much as my department would love to shove you out of the way, you are the face of the Miller System. Due to the close partnership of your system and many of our regulatory agencies and international development teams, we can't just dispose of you properly. And your ability to pull strings, even when clearly under surveillance and a stop order, remains impressive."

Kristine gives the state attorney a smile. "Whatever do you mean?" she asks, feigning innocence. "I just passed along some information about Oliver Torenze. It was your department that chose to act on it."

"It seems they had some motivation," the state attorney says, casting a suspicious look at Edson.

"The security of our state takes the commitment of every citizen," Edson comments. "That seems like adequate motivation to me."

The state attorney shakes her head. "I wouldn't be surprised if one of you planted the evidence in his home to frame him for this, but I don't care, either. We need a villain. Oliver Torenze fits that profile perfectly. He's wealthy, powerful, but doesn't pose a risk to the state if he falls. He's close enough to you and to Mr. Michaud to be a logical choice, and even his legitimate business is vile. Nobody wants to support a man whose major investments are in medical research on human beings."

Kristine smiles again. "That's why the Miller System specifically doesn't mention where our unplaceable slaves end up."

The state attorney nods. "Oliver Torenze will be charged with a number of crimes associated with inappropriate handling and releasing of data, dating all the way back to when he was a part of the Miller System. Our media team will confirm that it was him who arranged the raid on your home, Mr. Michaud, and that he was the one who released incriminating evidence about the Miller System. We've already contacted a number of the reporters he's spoken to recently and they've been very agreeable."

I sit there, shocked, but I nod. My mother looks pleased, and just as nervous as I feel.

"The world will welcome a new business partnership," the state attorney explains. "The Miller System has outstayed its welcome, but there is no denying that it will always be an important part of our history. We need to maintain that part, and to do that, we need you, Ms. Miller. You will join Mr. Michaud as a senior advisor. Mr. Michaud, you will bring your innovative research and pretty slave. You will be the head of the new company. The two of you will bridge the old and the new; you will welcome the next generation of Demoted research and re-education training with open arms."

I am both pleased and horrified. This is going well for me, except the part where I am saddled with my mother for the rest of the conceivable future. I try to think my way out of it, and I come up with nothing.

"I guess that would work," I say slowly.

The state attorney gives me a hard glare. "Mr. Michaud... we didn't offer you an option."

I shut my mouth, nodding. She doesn't even have to make a threat; I know all the things she could do. Being put in prison would be the least of my concerns. Edson gives me a warning look. I'm certain she played a role in arranging this deal; it would be in my interest not to destroy it.

My mother isn't taking the news very well, either. "You're expecting me to just hand my business over? I've put my whole life into making the Miller System the best it could be. How am I supposed to sit back and watch it be destroyed?"

"Ms. Miller, this was never your business in the first place. You, the Miller System, you were nothing more than a tool, employed in the interest of the state. You will step down, and you will do it with the Miller System smile that the nation has grown to know and love. You'll stay on, mostly for our public relations concerns, and you will provide everything that Mr. Michaud needs to be your successor. In return, you'll continue to enjoy the comfortable life you've worked so hard for."

My mother looks devastated, but she's not so stupid as to challenge the offer. She nods, quietly.

"Mr. Michaud, welcome to the business of Demoted resource

management," the state attorney says. "You'll have much to learn, and hopefully Ms. Miller can be an asset to you. You came highly recommended by many of the right people."

The state attorney hands us both paperwork to sign, indicating our agreement, our cooperation, and our pardons from the variety of legal charges we've accumulated. My mother signs hers quickly, but I pause, considering Sascha.

"Can I ask for a favor?" I try. I'm not going to back out either way; as I've been told, it's not an option. "My slave... he's told Torenze something personal, something about his family—"

The state attorney waves a hand, cutting me off. "The Assessment story?" she clarifies. "Believe me, Mr. Michaud, he's already tried it. The state has had enough riots this year. If anyone could even get that story out of Mr. Torenze, they wouldn't live to see it published. As far as this office is concerned, it's desperate lie from a desperate man. Our Assessment never fails, and it can't be outsmarted. We need this to be true just as much as you do."

"I'll have it put on record," Edson adds, looking pleased. "Documentation that it was a lie, perhaps another attempt to commit fraud on Mr. Torenze's part. If anyone tries to bring it up again, they can be subjected to the same charges. It should offer you some peace of mind."

I nod, slowly realizing how much sense it makes. Sascha is safe, and so am I, because they need us for now. We just have to make sure they keep needing us. I sign the agreement quickly.

"The press release will take place tomorrow afternoon," the state attorney advises us. "I'd suggest you both come prepared."

Without another word, we are escorted out of the office. While we wait for officers to escort us home, I look at my mother. She has a strange smile on her face, a little tear in her eye. If it was anyone else, I'd say she looked proud.

"I always hoped you'd succeed me in the family business one day, Cashi."

The press release is planned with cutting precision. Every member of the state's public relations team and the Miller System's public relations team have coordinated to make this event as spectacular and as controlled as possible. There are as many protesting audience members as there are excited supporters. Slavery has always been an emotionally charged topic.

I am next to Cash for all of it, because I am his loyal slave. Whether the audience views this as a positive endorsement of slavery or a sickening demonstration of the devaluation of human life, it doesn't matter. I am here, next to Cash, where I belong.

Sy is standing off to the side, looking professional. It's hard to tell him apart from the paid security team; they wear the same style clothes, stand in the same ready position, and have the same impassive expression on their faces. The only difference is, Sy's not carrying a gun.

Kristine Miller is to the other side of Cash; I'm glad to be a few feet away from her, but the fact that we're being forced to partner with her is troubling. I would like few things more than to be far, far away from her, not just physically, but professionally. She helped us with Torenze because it helped herself, but as Cash explained it, they were forced to partner. The state needed a replacement for a broken system, and our Argova associates needed an amenable source for future business. It's the best choice, but it doesn't mean I hate it any less.

The announcer finishes introducing everyone and thanking the sponsors, and Kristine Miller takes the microphone first.

"Hello everyone," she begins, the smile on her face reminding me eerily of the way the training materials at the re-education centers looked. "I'd like to start by saying that it has been a wonderful run for myself, and for the Miller System. For over thirty years, my company has led not only our great nation, but many others in the best training and preparation of the Demoted population."

She pauses, appropriately, as half the crowd cheers and other screams insults. Kristine smiles throughout it all. My master watches, his face masked as carefully as Sy's is. For all anyone watching knows, he and Kristine are nothing more than business associates.

"But the best and brightest cannot remain stagnant," Kristine continues. "Just like the criteria for passing the Assessment change every year to accommodate our ever-brighter youth, the way our re-education centers are run must also change with the times. And I believe that no one is more capable of making these changes than Cashiel Michaud."

She shoves the microphone into Cash's hand without another word. The state's public relations team looks annoyed, but Cash continues on as though nothing is wrong. Kristine was supposed to continue extolling the virtues of Michaud System for a few more minutes, but she's already receding to the back of the stage. For once, she looks defeated.

"Ms. Miller has been an inspiration to everyone in the Demoted industry," Cash acknowledges. "And she will continue to be. While she is stepping down from her position, she will be the head of the advisory board of the Michaud System. Many of you are familiar with me from the public engagements I've had over the past few weeks, and I hope you don't think that's all I can do. With the Miller System team backing the new system, we will bring the best of both worlds to the re-education center empire. I never intended to make this big of a change, but when I was offered the position, I was pleased to take it. Researching the re-education centers has been a passion of mine for many years, because I know we can make better use of this underutilized resource. My predecessor paved the way, and I can't imagine a re-education center without her influence. Personally and professionally, I commit to this nation. I commit to a stronger Demoted system."

The crowd goes wild; regardless of which side they are on, this is good news. I see my master's mother sneaking glances at him here and there, a pleased look on her face. A part of me wonders if this is really what she wanted all along.

The speech continues, and carefully selected reporters are invited to ask questions—pre-approved questions, of course, but they don't give that impression. Cash and Kristine take turns answering issues of what happened with Torenze, what fueled the animosity between them, and how they plan to move forward together. From an outsider's perspective, they make the perfect business partnership. From an insider's perspective, they are puppets, played by the state agencies. But there are worse things to be than a puppet.

One of the reporters asks "What inspired you to research the Demoted?"

It's a pre-approved question, but the smile on Cash's face says he's up to something. "A simple desire to see this resource be used to capacity."

From the script I saw earlier, he's supposed to move onto the next question, but he doesn't.

"Actually, that reminds me of something," Cash says. "A while ago, there were rumors that my slave, this one, right next to me, had been the one to prepare much of the data for the original release. Some even said that he was the one who released it!"

The crowd splits again, half cheering, half booing and cursing. I can hear the event staff making angry statements behind us.

"You could all have that level of skill and loyalty at your fingertips," Cash suggests. He places a hand on my shoulder. "Sascha has been instrumental in my work. He is a Demoted slave, but he is so much more valuable than most of you would believe. What's more — he's mine. All of his actions reflect on me, good and bad, and his accomplishments boost my own. This does not weaken the Demoted system. It strengthens it, and it strengthens the nation."

A quiet mood takes over the audience. To condemn the statement would be to speak poorly about the state, to agree with it would mean acknowledging that what Cash said about the Demoted is true. I feel my heart race in fear and excitement.

"This is what the new Demoted system can accomplish," Cash continues, as if nothing is wrong. "We will get the most out of our Demoted population, and everyone will reap the benefits."

The press release concludes quickly after this. The audience is stunned, and the event organizers seem worried that Cash will say something else inappropriate.

Edson greets us after the event, giving Cash a dirty look. "That was not an approved response."

"I didn't think the state could really afford to retire two systems on the same day," Cash replies, flippant. "And I don't want any more secrets held over my head. It's all out there, now. Let the public do what they want with it. It seems Sascha's taught me a few things about transparency."

I smile, trying not to be too obvious, and Sy comes to join us. Edson just sighs and walks off; we have trouble with any of the officials, so it seems that the information will be ignored. Over time, I even wonder if the idea of the Demoted being useful will come to be accepted.

We are escorted home by a team of state security agents. They have become a familiar figure in our lives, and I expect they will continue to be so, just as Kristine Miller is. Cash explained that we don't really have a choice. In this world, nobody does. You fail the Assessment, you get Demoted, your master rules the rest of your life. You pass it, the state rules you, but at least you have the illusion that you're free.

As future policymakers, I'm not sure where that leaves us.

Chapter 35

Intentions

When we come home, Sascha gives me a curious look.

"Are we safe?" he asks.

I can only shrug and take a guess. "From legal recourse, yes. For now, anyway. From the public... probably. It wouldn't do the state any good to see their new tool get broken. As far as the Argova family... we'll find out. They seem happy enough with us, now."

"We're as safe as we're probably going to be," Sy agrees.

We all know that safety is temporary and transient, but we've come down on the right side of the equation for once.

"We should celebrate," Sascha suggests, laughing a little. "Last time we tried, things went to hell. Maybe the Michaud System will provide us a little more safety."

I nod my agreement. I know we have considerable work ahead of us during the next few months, solidifying research, making partnerships, and using what we've found to redesign my mother's system—with her help, and likely the help of the Argova family, and the rest of the interested politicians who have put me at the head of this new system. Even in the best scenario, we'll end up working closely with my mother for years, testing out the new systems, making changes, making sure we keep pleasing those we need to please. But for now, all I want to concentrate on is relaxing, feeling good. We've earned it after all.

Sascha takes it upon himself to grab a few bottles of wine and some glasses. Sy announces that he's going to change into something more comfortable while Sascha and I make our way to my bedroom. He pours a glass for each of us and comes up to lie next to me.

"I couldn't have done this without you," I tell him. "I never thought that when I bought you, you'd play such a huge part in everything that's happened, but I can't imagine my life without you."

He blushes, resting his head against my shoulder. "Thank you." I know he means for more than the nice words.

"Sascha, I love you. I don't say it often enough, and half the time I don't act like it, but I do."

He looks up at me, his eyes wide with surprise, and I see a little smile creeping across his face. "I don't think you've ever actually said it out loud," he reminds me. "At least, not when I'm fully conscious."

I laugh, because he's probably right. "I don't think of you as something disposable, or even a favorite pet. I don't care if you're Demoted or free or something else entirely. I love you, and you're mine, no matter what happens. I'm sorry I've put you through so much, but now that things are calm, I want you to know that I still need you. I always will."

Sascha turns, kissing me. "I love you too, Cash."

I move our wine glasses to the nightstand so I can pull him on top of me, running my hands over his body as we kiss. He's healed up from his time with Oliver, at least enough that the damage is only superficially visible. He feels good, and I want nothing more than to touch him forever.

Sascha seems to share that goal, taking it a step further and stripping my shirt off, tossing it aside and pressing against my newly exposed skin.

Sy comes in, dressed casually, and he pauses in the doorway.

"Am I interrupting?" he asks. Just from looking at his face, I can't tell if he wants to join.

"Nope, just late," Sascha replies, answering for both of us. I trust him to judge Sy's moods and receptiveness better than I can. "Join us?"

Sy smiles and comes to sit on the edge of the bed, overly proper as usual. Sascha gets up off of me and hands him a glass of wine.

"Loosen up a bit," he teases. "I want to celebrate with you."

"Funny, I thought Cash and I might loosen you up tonight," Sy responds, sipping at his wine.

I laugh as Sascha blushes. It's rare for anyone else to outperform him in this department.

"I'd like that," Sascha agrees.

Without warning, I grab Sascha around the waist, unfastening his pants and sliding them off easily. He laughs, pulling off his shirt at the same time. I like to watch him get undressed sometimes, but tonight I just want to feel him. The sooner I get him naked, the sooner I can enjoy him.

Once he's naked, Sascha starts stripping Sy, pouncing on him eagerly. It's been a while since the three of us have all been able to enjoy this. Sascha is wasting no time. I finish undressing as well, having no desire to be left behind. In seconds, I'm watching as Sascha is leaning into Sy, pressing him backward, putting his drink aside as he leans our bodyguard back against the pillow and starts grinding against him.

Sy is wrapped up with Sascha, their lips pressed together tightly, his hands stroking over Sascha's back. Sascha is on his knees, straddling one of Sy's legs as Sy reclines below him. I like watching them; seeing Sascha come undone at someone else's hands is unusual, but the fact that he enjoys it so much gets me hard. It also allows me the creativity to do other things to him while he's distracted.

Moving quickly, I come up behind Sascha and grip his ass firmly, pleased when he jumps a little. I don't speak yet, I just lean down and bite at the soft flesh in front of me. Sascha whimpers a little as I leave marks, but he doesn't stop kissing Sy. I tease him for a while longer before trailing my tongue over the marks I've just left, pausing to circle around, dipping my tongue inside. I feel his muscles tense against my tongue and I push harder, demanding entrance. Sascha lets out another whimper as his body yields to me, welcoming me inside.

As I rim Sascha, he rocks his body over Sy's, grinding his leg against Sy's cock. They're both hard, and Sy works his hand between them, gripping Sascha as I continue to work his ass with my tongue. I flash Sy a smile; he seems to be enjoying this as much as I am.

After a few minutes, I can feel Sascha trembling, turned on so quickly by the two of us.

"Is this going to be a quick night?" Sascha asks, his breath coming short and shallow.

"Not for me," I remark, feeling Sascha shudder at the comment. "I plan on drawing it out as long as possible."

I return my attention to his ass, licking and biting and sucking. I can tell that Sascha is trying hard to hold back. Sy takes pity on him, removing his hand from Sascha's cock and stroking his hair instead. I try not to laugh as I uncap a bottle of lube and pour some out, replacing my tongue with my fingers and making Sascha squirm.

"I can't wait to feel you fuck me," he mumbles, pressing back against my fingers like he can't get enough. "Both of you. I want you both."

I do laugh a little at that, as does Sy. Sy kisses him gently.

"Who do you want first, pretty boy?" Sy asks.

Sascha just moans. I wouldn't want to make that decision either, if I were him, and I know Sy is too polite to state a preference. I slide another finger deep inside of Sascha.

"I think Sy should fuck you first," I suggest, glancing at Sy for approval. When he nods, I give Sascha a little slap on the ass with my free hand. "Want to know why?"

It takes Sascha a moment to reply, but he does. "Yes," he manages, the tremble in his voice making my cock hard.

As I keep working my fingers inside of Sascha, I lean forward to whisper in his ear. "Because Sy would be too kind to fuck you after what I'm going to do to you."

Sascha gasps, letting his upper body drop against Sy's chest. I take it as an invitation, because the position allows me to work my fingers deeper inside of him, stretching him. We've been careful with Sascha since Oliver returned him, but I want him good and ready for tonight.

Sy gives me a conspiratorial smile. "Slide him down a little," he suggests. "I've got something to keep him entertained while you get him ready."

With Sascha's full cooperation, I pull him down lower on the bed, positioning his head over Sy's cock, and I continue to finger him while he does his best to give Sy a blowjob. I can tell he's too worked up to do it as well as usual, but Sy enjoys it anyway. The simple fact that Sascha is trying despite his very worked up state is impressive. After a while, Sy reaches down, placing his hand on the back of Sascha's head and turning Sascha's face up.

"How do you want me, pretty boy?"

I can feel Sascha clenching around my fingers.

"Just like this," Sascha replies. "Let me ride you."

Sy smiles and nods, taking the lube when I hand it to him and coating his cock with it. I slide my fingers out of Sascha's ass slowly, pausing to land a few smacks before letting go of his hips. I see the faint red marks and I smile, knowing he'll enjoy them. I give him a playful shove, pushing him forward toward Sy, and I sit back on my heels for a moment, watching.

Sascha finds a position he likes and spreads his legs, using on hand to steady himself against Sy's chest while the other grabs Sy's cock and guides it inside. He comes down without hesitation, sighing when he has Sy fully inside of him. Slowly, he starts to move up and down.

I watch, entranced by the sight of my lover being fucked by another man. Maybe it shouldn't turn me on so much, but it does, and when Sy's eyes meet mine, I don't turn away. He has his hands resting lightly on Sascha's hips, but he lifts one off, beckoning me closer with his finger.

I'm not used to being directed in bed, but I go along. Sy looks pleased as I stretch out next to him, and Sascha runs his hand over my legs. As Sascha finds his rhythm and works himself up and down over Sy's cock, Sy reaches over and places his hand on my cheek. He doesn't pull me over like I'd pull Sascha, but his invitation is clear. I lean over, kissing him, feeling the warmth of his lips against mine. It's not the same passion that I share with Sascha; but it's sexy, friendly, fun. When we finally break apart, Sascha is staring at us with lustful eyes.

Sy reaches up to grab Sascha's cock in his hand, working it as Sascha struggles to keep his rhythm. I let my hand rest on Sy's body, content to watch them for a while. Sy starts thrusting up, bouncing Sascha and working his cock just as hard.

"Would you like to come for me now or later?" Sy asks, his hand going still on Sascha's cock as it becomes obvious that Sascha won't last much longer.

"Now, please," Sascha moans, thrusting desperately. "Please

don't make me wait."

Sy obliges, moving his hand over Sascha's cock again and pumping into him faster. I see the telltale signs as Sascha gets close, the way his hands curl into fists, the way all of his muscles seem to tense at once.

"Hit me," Sascha begs, working himself harder against Sy's cock with his eyes half-closed. "Make me hurt."

Sy isn't exactly in the position to accomplish that, so I help out. I sit up a little, run my hand down Sascha's back to give him a little warning, and then strike his ass, focusing on the small space available between his lower back and the part where Sy's cock is slamming in and out of him. Sascha lets out a delicious cry of pleasure, nearly drowning out the sound of the next slap I land on him. He comes quickly, his body shaking, and Sy keeps thrusting underneath of him, holding Sascha in place. Sascha puts up an effort for a few moments, then gasps as Sy holds him down hard on his cock, coming with a final thrust.

Sascha is panting, his body going limp as he rolls to the side, sliding off of Sy's cock and lying next to him. I run my fingers up Sascha's leg, stroking the inside of his thigh, and he whimpers, looking at me with a pleading expression.

"See why I wanted him to fuck you first?" I tease.

"Can I have a minute?" Sascha asks, and the look on his face tells me he needs it.

As much as I want to drive into him right now, I want to make sure he enjoys it.

"Only if you'll kiss me," I pretend to bargain, sliding up next to him and rubbing my cock against his body.

Sascha is happy to comply, especially since he doesn't have to move. I kiss him deep, hard, holding tightly to his hair as rake my teeth over his lips and bite at his tongue. He makes a few deep sounds of satisfaction, but I can tell how overwhelmed he is. Sy moves around Sascha, coming to the other side of me and leaving me in the middle.

"Care for a little something else while Sascha recovers?" Sy suggests, giving my cock a pointed glance.

I smile. Knowing Sy, he's doing it because he wants to make sure Sascha gets his recovery time, but I won't argue. I like the idea of letting Sascha rest for a moment as well, and the last time Sy's mouth was around my cock, he demonstrated a very nice skill set. I nod, turning my body to give him better access. Sascha cuddles up against my chest, his breathing slowing as he calms a little.

Sy wastes no time taking my cock into his mouth. He wraps his lips around it tightly and swallows deep, catching me off-guard. Sascha usually teases and plays; Sy takes me immediately to the brink of pleasure, only to back off a moment later.

"It is so hot to watch the two of you," Sascha mumbles, pressing himself against me and resting in the crook of one of my arms.

I agree, and the feeling is even better. I let Sy work me up, enjoying the way he moves his tongue around the head of my cock, the way his hands stroke up and down every now and again, the way he takes me deep into his throat, swallowing and contracting the muscles around my cock until I have to hold myself back from coming. What gets me the hottest is the way he looks up at me, a perfectly content expression on his face as he's the one who almost puts me over the edge.

Finally, I know I can't take much more, and Sascha seems to have relaxed enough for me to fulfill my promise to him. As Sy keeps sucking me, I run my hand through Sascha's hair.

"I'm gonna fuck you hard," I tell him in a low voice.

He gives me a nervous, excited smile as he nods. I reach around until I find the lube, and Sy takes it as his cue to work himself down on my cock one last time, swallowing deep, almost pushing me to come before pulling off. I gasp, keeping myself under control, and he shoots me a satisfied smile.

I waste no time disentangling Sascha from my arms and placing him on his back, spreading his legs apart with my hand and dripping some more lube onto him and onto my cock. He smiles as I position myself between his legs, and he yelps as I enter him in a single thrust.

I slam into him roughly, again and again, and his hands fly up to grab at me.

"Cash," he whimpers.

I'm not sure he if he's begging me to stop or to speed up, but I speed up anyway. I can tell he's struggling to adjust, but his cock is getting hard again. I know it will only be a matter of time before he's as hard as I am.

I glance at Sy. "Lend a hand?" I offer, knowing it will turn Sascha on even more to have us both touching him at the same time.

Sy nods, taking Sascha's cock in his hand and stroking it gently, bringing him to full hardness as I pound Sascha's ass without mercy. Sascha is alternating between moaning in pleasure and yelping in pain.

"Sore?" I ask, keeping up the rhythm.

"Yes, but don't stop," Sascha begs. "Whatever you do, don't stop. Either of you."

I continue, grabbing Sascha's hips and using them to pull him down harder as I fuck him. I'm fortunate enough to be worked up already, and I can see Sascha is getting ready to come as well, the combined stimulation bringing him to the tipping point far more quickly than usual.

"Come for us," I demand, making my thrusts deeper and slower, knowing exactly how to hit the spots that Sascha likes the most. "Show us how much you like us fucking you."

"I love it," Sascha agrees, throwing his head back as he comes for a second time.

I feel the tightening of his muscles around my cock and I don't hold back. I come as he does, thrusting in and out of him just a few more times before I, too, am lost in my own ecstasy. I realize I'm gripping his hips tightly enough to bruise and I loosen my grip somewhat, feeling the lasting pulse of muscles around my cock. We stay, locked together for a few moments as we both catch our breath, and then I slowly ease out of him, pleased when I hear a slight whine escape Sascha's lips. I come up next to him and kiss him lightly before stretching out next to him.

We lie there, sated and tired. Sy gets up to leave, like he always tends to, and Sascha gives me a hopeful look. I reach out and place my hand on Sy's leg.

"You're welcome to stay," I invite him. He smiles, and I know he's considering it. The sex is easy; it's the intimacy that threatens him.

"Please?" Sascha asks, still playful despite his exhaustion. "There might be a round two in the morning."

"All right," Sy agrees, slipping under the covers to the other side of Sascha.

Somehow, Sascha manages to wrap himself around both of us, looking quite pleased with himself.

"I'm glad I brought you home," I tell Sy. "You're as much a part of this as either of us."

"Worked out well for me, too," Sy reminds me.

He puts his arm around Sascha, his hand brushing against me for a moment. I don't feel the passion for him that I do for Sascha, but a familiarity, camaraderie perhaps. He and Sascha are the only two people I trust, the only ones who have earned it.

"We should get some sleep," Sascha teases. "We start our new lives as state employees tomorrow."

It's quiet. I can hear the breathing of the two people sharing my bed, and I'm amazed by how quickly it has all happened. I never meant to become so involved in the Demoted system, never meant to own slaves, certainly never meant to fall in love with one. But as I drift off, contemplating the idea of working with my mother and making my life work with Sascha, I have a feeling we are just getting started.

If you enjoyed this story, you can sign up for a free membership at ForbiddenFiction and discuss it with other readers and the author at the *Succession* story page at http://forbiddenfiction.com/story/AC2-1.000250.

We do our best to proof all our work, but if you spot a text error we missed, please let us know via our website Contact Form at http://forbiddenfiction.com/contact.

Author's Notes

When I was writing one of the earliest drafts of Succession, I remember asking some friends if "because he's sexy" was a good enough reason to include a third main character into my story. While the answers varied from "of course" to "does he have anything to do with the plot?" the character Syrus was just too good to pass up. Fortunately, he worked himself into the plot as well as he worked himself into Cash and Sascha's lives.

Writing threesomes was far more difficult and exciting than I originally anticipated. On one hand, there are three people who get to tease, torment, and enjoy each other... on the other hand, there is so much more to keep track of! From body parts to emotions, it's a lot more work, but I think Sy balances out the other two quite nicely. I spent many weeks writing, rewriting, and rewriting Succession some more, but the finished product wraps up this section of their lives completely.

For the third book in a trilogy, Succession introduces quite a few new variables. Sy is probably the biggest addition, but we also meet the mysterious Argova family — where their interests really lie remains to be seen. The stories in the Demoted world are finished, but only for now. I've grown to love these characters more than is probably reasonable, and I'm as curious as you probably are about what happens next for them. Currently, there is at least one short story in the works, exploring Sy's life before *Succession*. While you wait, I'd encourage you to check out the *Inherent Gifts* series for another story about a master and slave fighting for each other in a dystopian future.

About the Author

Alicia Cameron has been making up stories since before she can remember. After discovering erotica during a high school banned books project, she never really turned back. She lives in Denver, Colorado with two tiny dogs and a rabbit who conspire regularly to distract her from doing anything productive. By day she works in the mental health field and is passionate about youth rights and welfare. In her spare time, she enjoys traveling, glitter, and punk rock concerts.

ForbiddenFiction works by Alicia Cameron

Inherent Gifts Series
Inherent Gifts
Inherent Risk
Inherent Cost

Short Stories
Cuts so Deep
Dangerous Steps
In Other Hands
Jingle Boy
Twisted Gifts
Party Favors
Hot Rain
Lessons Learned

Demoted Series
Subjection
Sedition
Succession

Demoted Short Stories
Bethel's Brothel
Call It Even
For Science

DEMOTED

The superior lead. The inferior are DEMOTED.

Cashiel and Sascha aren't revolutionaries. Cashiel just wants to use his privilege to make the world a better place. Sacha just wants to save his brother from being Demoted. Unfortunately, they're both trapped within the system.

In the past, lesser people rose above their natural station, and greater persons found themselves stifled under the incompetent leadership of their inferiors. Today, the Miller System conditions the Demoted to serve; persons otherwise lost are given purpose, and placed under the ownership and guidance of responsible citizens.

Cashiel's mother invented the Miller System, and trying to prove that the Demoted should be treated humanely sets him against his mother and all her political power. Sascha succeeded in saving his brother from the system, but only by taking his place and being made into a brothel slave.

It isn't exactly love at first sight when Cashiel buys Sascha. If they can work together, though, they might be able to bring down a system of institutionalized abuse, and find some happiness for themselves.

About the Publisher

 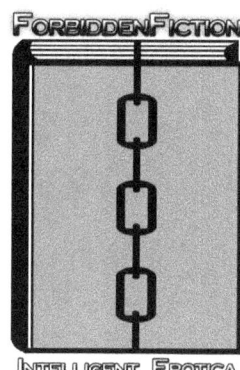

ForbiddenFiction.com is a publisher devoted to writing that breaks the boundaries of original erotic fiction. Our stories combine intense sexuality with quality writing. Stories at Forbidden Fiction.com not only arouse readers through sensations, but also engage them emotionally and mentally through storytelling as well-crafted as the sex is hot.

ForbiddenFiction.com is also designed to be a social reading environment. You'll have fun even if just reading the latest post each day, yet you will have the chance for so much more. Readers and authors can be part of ongoing discussions of specific works and individual authors as well as more general topics.

Sign up for a FREE Membership today at ForbiddenFiction.com